River of Dreams

by Robert E. Ferguson

First Edition – December 2012

ISBN
978-1-77097-898-0 (Hardcover)
978-1-77097-899-7 (Paperback)
978-1-77097-900-0 (eBook)

Contact Information: Three Trees Publishing Inc.
Email: info@threetreespublishing.com
Website: www.threetreespublishing.com

Produced by:

FriesenPress
Suite 300 – 852 Fort Street
Victoria, BC, Canada V8W 1H8

www.friesenpress.com

Distributed to the trade by The Ingram Book Company

To: Khan,

Dedication

As I begin to write this dedication to Bobby Ferguson, it brings to mind the last conversation I was honored to have with him before he passed away, and his request to me that I would see his writings all brought to life in print and on the screen. Little did I understand what I had promised to do, and the amount of time, energy, and dedication to fulfill this promise which lay ahead of me. When I took on this challenge, I truly realized just what an incredible writing talent he owned, as I committed to fulfill my obligation – a long and exciting journey – I made to him, and the publication of his first book "Fool's Paradise" came into print. Now, with his second manuscript "River of Dreams" appropriately named Book two of the McAllister trilogy, I learned so much about Bobby's character, his dedication to fulfill his goals, his incredible writing skill that literally places you in every scene, so clearly, as if you are directly a part of the action, adventure and fulfillment of the story's goal. So much can be learned from his writings and it is such a loss to us all that Bobby is not here to share this with us, but we must always keep our hopes alive and never give up on our goals and dreams.

Let the journey continue.....Joe Ganzenhuber

Dear friend, enjoy this book,

Joe Ganzenhuber

17 Sept. 2019

RIVER OF DREAMS

Book Two (McAllister Trilogy)
(SUMMARY/OUTLINE)
By: Bobby Ferguson

In 1917, in Czarist Russia, revolution is brewing and the country is about to undergo radical change. With the help of the British, Carl Faberge', the Imperial Jeweler, flees to exile in Switzerland, leaving behind a fortune in art and raw materials in his Saint Petersburg salon. In the face of an unruly mob, one of the many Faberge' apprentices makes a bold decision. Young Arkady Deniken will loot the fabulous shop himself before rioting citizens can destroy the store or the provisional government can nationalize the business. The normally honest Arkady hastily loads two boxes of items that, under normal circumstances, would have found their way to the homes of the nobility, as well as a fortune in loose gems and precious stones waiting to become priceless ornaments for those same clients. Arkady seeks to enlist the help of a one of his old friends to spirit the crates to a secure location, but before he can return to pick them up, both boxes mysteriously disappear.

In modern day Monaco, an obnoxious drunk appears at a formal auction and bids outrageously on a Faberge' egg. When he leaves the sight of the quasi-charity event, he is accosted by professional thugs. Offering resistance at being robbed, he is severely beaten before being relieved of his recently acquired work of art.

On the other side of the world, five professional burglars close in on the estate of a wealthy South American cattle rancher with more than simple larceny on their minds. Unknown to them, a sophisticated security system thwarts their plan with drastic consequences for the raiding party.

This is the third such attempt in recent months and the owner of the estate believes he must turn to the offensive to prevent further incursions.

In the present day, part time author and full time gin mill proprietor, Granger Lawton is lured from his low mountain Arizona home by a summons from his old friend, renowned treasure hunter, Bobby McAllister.

After six years of living in Venezuela, McAllister wishes to return to his hometown of Savannah, Georgia where he plans to enroll his kindergarten-aged twins in an American school. His ulterior motive for returning to the States is to build a base of operations for pursuing matters concerning his latest interest and obsession, Faberge' eggs. McAllister is convinced there is a sinister plot to flood the art market with counterfeit eggs and specifically blames the Russian government as the origin of this conspiracy. He is also of the opinion that his good friend, Granger Lawton, will assist him in an endeavor to expose this scheme.

Citing the mission as potentially dangerous and possibly foolish, Lawton returns to Arizona and a temporary rift develops between the two men. McAllister's wife, on her way to a Beverly Hills shopping spree, detours to Lawton's Payson home to try to convince him to mend the estrangement. Her persuasiveness and charm is successful and the two men meet over the Christmas Holiday to reach a compromise that will please the brash and impulsive McAllister as well as the cautious and conservative Lawton.

A few months later, McAllister and his wife entertain Lawton and his lady-friend aboard McAllister's luxury yacht as they set sail for Europe. The first stop is France where the ladies spend a few carefree days sightseeing while McAllister and Lawton conduct their business with a Faberge' art expert through whose writings McAllister became convinced of his conspiracy theory. McAllister is informed that, amongst his small Faberge' collection, he has two fakes and that information strengthens his resolve to gain the reputation of a serious collector by exposing the seditious cabal that is perpetrating the fraud.

Tragedy interrupts the still innocent investigation and after the small group temporarily returns to their respective homes to bury their dead and recover from their wounds, it is normally moderate Granger Lawton who, surprisingly, takes up the cause, not for the honor or integrity of his friend's collection, but solely for revenge. They return to Europe where McAllister's seemingly plodding methods produce little information, prompting Lawton to call in an old favor to be put in touch with someone better qualified to produce results.

Their travels take them from Paris to London to Switzerland to The Netherlands before bringing them to Saint Petersburg, Russia, home of the original Faberge' salon. While McAllister explores the city as a tourist, Lawton uses his surreptitious connections to ferret out the instigator of the Paris catastrophe. In his usually reckless and brazen manner, McAllister finds out about his friend's clandestine activities and they combine efforts and resources to probe the significant facts of their, now, two-pronged objectives.

From a surprising source, a startling third element is added to their inquiries; the possible existence of a Faberge' treasure missing since 1917.

McAllister and Lawton must contend with dealing with a group of master forgers, a black-marketer, imposters everywhere, agents of the KGB, an attractive and suspicious In-tourist guide, secret meetings, assorted spies, traitors within their own ranks, electronic eavesdropping, and the ever present threat of physical danger, as they try to sort out their priorities while assimilating information that comes their way with incredible speed.

The McAllister contingent is forced to flee Saint Petersburg when a man meets with a violent death and one of their party is implicated in the cause. Two refugees join them in their flight back to America, both for reasons other than purported, and Lawton is seriously injured during the trip. Recovering from the grievous harm he has suffered, Lawton believes he finally has all the answers to their questions except for the exact location of the treasure, a fact that McAllister is convinced he knows. They spend a couple of weeks testing McAllister's theory when the two men discover that the troubles that spawned in Russia may not be over. As equally as startling is the fact that the treasure they have been seeking may have been under their noses from the very beginning of their quest.

On an island off the East Coast of the United States, the unlikely group of mixed nationalities has a revealing and violent confrontation with the same circle of undesirables that plagued them in Soviet Russia and Europe. Their decimated party is saved from total extermination by a dubious source and an amazing recovery is made.

The story is far from over as a cloud of uncertainty hangs over the survivors. One of the conspiracy masterminds may still be unidentified and Lawton begins an exhaustive paper search to help McAllister terminate the threats that very well might face them on two distinctive fronts.

A quick trip to Caracas, Venezuela all but neutralizes the danger from one of the areas of concern, so Lawton redoubles his efforts to eliminate the other. His research not only uncovers the figure who is partially responsible for the entanglements and perils he and his friends have suffered, but also reveals new information about the final days of Czar Nicholas II and his ill-fated family.

The claims of a traumatized young woman who once maintained that she was the Grand Duchess Anastasia and the only surviving member of the Romanov dynasty play an important role in Lawton's inquiry and the true identity of an unexpected conspirator is revealed.

A final return trip to Europe exposes the complicity and the treachery of the scheme that has endangered the group from the beginning of their involvement and a final confrontation restores to McAllister property he had thought lost forever.

Throughout their exciting and often risky undertaking, McAllister and Lawton receive an education in art, history, and greed, the three principal pillars of their venture. Amid authentic locations and situations, the two men, often at odds with each other over both philosophy and method, once again combine to face peril and reward while wading through a period of history steeped in mystery, intrigue, and controversy.

RIVER OF DREAMS

A Novel By
Robert Edward Ferguson

Another Day in Fool's Paradise

Arkady Deniken Georgievick nervously watched the furious activity that was taking place throughout the dimly lighted shop. The huge outside wooden shutters were closed, but the noise from the streets filtered into the cramped back-room quarters of his workplace. He watched with uneasy apprehension as his fellow apprentices quickly gathered their tools and other belongings in preparation for a hasty abandonment of the store.

"What's keeping you, Arkady Georgievick?" Feodor Bukov asked as he passed the young man's workbench. "We must act quickly or risk being overrun by the unruly mob."

"This demonstration is not against us." He answered with far more bravado than he felt. "And that unruly mob, as you call it, are our fellow citizens."

"Those that march against the Tsar are no comrades of mine." Feodor stated flatly, making a spitting gesture at the floor.

"These are sad times, my friend, and when this treacherous gang is turned away from the Winter Palace by the Cossacks, they will undoubtedly turn on the merchants."

Arkady didn't answer his friend. He knew his countrymen were divided over everything from staggering war losses to the starving people. Dissent ran rapid, notably by the newly industrializing class who lived in wretched poverty. Strikes plagued the very industries that were finally helping Russia develop economically while Tsar Nicholas II and the German-born Tsarina, Alexandria, lived aloof of the needs of the peasants. In the middle of this heterodoxy was the slowly growing merchant-class of which Arkady worked hard to obtain membership. The intelligentsia, or professional sphere, was sharply divided over allegiance to the Tsar or the emancipation by the elected Dumas who had elevated these men out of the normally inflexible system that had held them in little more than free serfdom.

Outwardly, the upper classes continued to enjoy their luxurious life-styles while anarchists and terrorist assassins vied for the approval of the working-class. Only last year, over two-thousand strikes had over one million men participating as the Bolshevik Party began to show an increase in popularity. Although Arkady knew that nothing compared to the savagery and tragedy of that Bloody Sunday in 1905, the seeds of revolution were in the air and the Tsar was losing the loyalty of subjects, soldiers and even his ministers.

With the murder of Rasputin, political lines were drawn among those who were previously denied the right to an opinion. As quickly as members of the Tsar's retinue resigned or went into self-imposed exile, they were replaced by unpopular and often psychotic officials such as Protopopov, the Mad Minister of The Interior. As quickly as Nicholas dissolved the Duma, a new popular assembly was convoked as the only weapon the Russian nation had against the destructive rule of the Tsar.

Arkady had not yet formed a concrete opinion about his beliefs. Although he longed to experience the opulence and lavish lifestyles of the elite members of Nicholas' and Alexandria's Court, he could not envision how this new Bolshevik Party could provide for the millions of dispossessed. In his capacity as an apprentice in the employ of the great Carl Faberge, the Imperial Jeweler since 1884, Arkady was assured the coveted position of merchant as long as the Romanovs remained in power. Without the noble minority to purchase the imaginative and ingenious designs, the studio that employed Arkady and over one hundred of his fellow craftsmen would have no reason to remain open.

Arkady's father, a moujik – one of the many little men in bright colored shirts who swept carpets, carried firewood, cleaned windows, and washed dishes for the Youssoupovs in their palatial residence on the Moika Canal – was forever faithful to the Tsar. Unlike Feodor, however, most of Arkady's friends were disdainful of the upper class as well as the contemptuous and spineless servants who came running to the call of "Tchelovyek!"

Arkady had seen firsthand the apartments of Prince Felix's father, crowded with paintings by old masters, and showcases sagging with miniatures, porcelains, and jewel encrusted snuff boxes. Furniture that had once been owned by Marie Antoinette and crystal chandeliers that had come from Madame de Pompadour's boudoir competed with gold, amethyst, topaz, and jade statuettes and other valuables. Surely, some of these priceless heirlooms could be used to relieve the suffering of the poor. Today, the striking workers, unable to stay at home because there was no light, no gas, no water and provisions, and wood was scarce, thronged the streets for yet another funeral procession for some poor soul shot during the disturbances. A hundred thousand men, women and children walked with the scarlet covered coffin, carrying great red banners as they sang the "Marseillaise" in a low, somewhat careless, chant. The people were passing quietly and orderly, but the underlying tension was as thick as borscht. Only a week ago, the German owned piano works had been vandalized and burned while thousands of students, doctors, workmen, and people in various kinds of uniform stood at a distance and watched.

Carl Faberge had fled to Lausanne, fearing the constant violence, mutinies, and resistance, leaving his spineless and inept assistant, Yuri Sadokov, to run the firm. It was Yuri who had panicked in the face of the huge, but still peaceful mob outside and ordered the workers to gather their tools and flee. His insipid cowardice proved both contagious and provoking as Arkady's fellow workers raced around the shop, anticipating riotous and savage destruction while hoping to escape with the utensils needed to craft the adornments and finery that only the disappearing well-born and nobles of Imperial Russia could afford.

"Hurry, Arkady!" Feodor brought Arkady back to the present with his reminder of their perceived predicament. "It's time we found a place far away from the banks of the Neva. Perhaps the art of our master is still appreciated in cities like Moscow or Kiev."

"What makes you think things will be better in Moscow?" Arkady asked, not willing to believe his friend would consider trading one hotbed of unrest for another.

"St. Petersburg is the home of the Tsar." Feodor answered simplistically. "In Moscow, this Bolshevik scum have none of the Imperial Family to spit on. Without the Tsar to blame for their troubles, there is no strife."

"I have heard that the strikes are worse in Moscow." Arkady replied. "Grand Duke Serge was murdered in the shadow of the Kremlin."

"Ten years ago." Feodor replied. "By a madman who followed the uncle of the Tsar from St. Petersburg. The assassin Kalayev promised mountains of corpses. Hanging was too good for him."

"You would be better off in Kiev or Odessa." Arkady remarked. "Or perhaps you should join our illustrious tutor in Switzerland."

"Maybe I will." Feodor said defiantly. "We should not have these barriers that have divided our citizens." He said, quoting the patriotic line "We should all be joined in one common effort."

"And what effort is that?" Arkady asked, challenging the rhetoric.

"Why, our responsibility and loyalty to the Royal Family." Feodor answered incredulously. "And all they stand for."

"Like war?" Arkady snapped, surprising himself. "The Tsar appoints that hooligan protégé of Rasputin, Sturmer to replace Goremykin as Chairman of the Council of Ministers while the army is suffering from poor administration, a shortage of ammunition, and malnutrition. While at home, the Tsarina and her daughters try to earn our respect by nursing wounded soldiers and the Tsar thinks he should lead his armies in the field. Dimitri killed Rasputin to save Russia, but his actions have had the reverse effect. No one in Petrograd can. . ."

"St. Petersburg!" Feodor gasped, correcting Arkady's apparent blasphemy. "You sound as if you are one of the intelligentsia, against God and the existing order. You use the name the insurgents have given to holy St. Petersburg!"

"Maybe it's time to end the rule of an autocrat." Arkady argued, shocking his inflexible friend. "Vladimir Ilich speaks to us from exile of a communist state. Maybe we should begin to listen to the likes of Lenin and Trotsky."

"Sacrilege!" Shouted Feodor. "Was it not Tsar Alexander who emancipated the serfs? Was it not Nicholas and Stolpypin who reformed that position even further? The people of Russia have never had it better in their lives!"

Arkady shook his head sadly. "The peasants cannot afford to buy the lands they work." He said. "The market place is crowded with many people and more empty stalls and carts. Gypsie thieves roam the alleys and the countryside. Transportation is at a standstill while the Putilov factory turns out thousands of cannons for a war we are losing.

"To be a merchant, we must pay the state a fee plus enroll in the business guild. We apprentice for twenty years. We are merely peasants with a permanent job. The only way we could ever rise above our humble backgrounds is to become Jews."

Feodor reacted as if he had been slapped, but recovered quickly. "And what of Morozov?" He asked. "He was the son of a serf."

"Morozov who supported Gorki and contributed to the war chests of the revolution?" Arkady asked sarcastically. "He was so confused he shot himself. Even his son was torn between the working man and the government.

That he maintained Moscow's leading textile mill and continued to make millions is just another of the contradictions that has plagued the Russian mentality since the days of the first Romanov over three hundred years ago."

"I feel sorry for you, Arkady." Feodor was tiring of arguing with his young friend. "If the Tsar ever knew how you felt, you would be lucky to have the job of your father." His ears picked up the sound of the growing unrest through the shuttered windows. "I will pray to St. Alexander for your deliverance from such foolish notions."

In spite of his own confusion, Arkady smiled. "And I will pray that you might one day take the beautiful Grand Duchess, Tatiana for your wife."

Feodor blushed. "Da svedahnya, my confused friend. May your dreams for Mother Russia fall under the skis of a fast moving troika." Feodor gathered his belongings in a cloth sack and left the shop by a rear door.

Without the normal lighting that streamed through the windows, the interior of the shop was gloomy with long shadows that stretched the length of the wooden workbenches. With a sense of loss and prematurely approaching nostalgia, he looked around the deserted warehouse that had been his workplace for the last six years. He had never been so isolated in the usually active and crowded room. Slowly he packed the implements that had virtually been extensions of his own hands since the great Faberge had agreed to take him on as a marginally talented apprentice shortly after his sixteenth birthday. Under the great master's tutelage, Arkady had displayed an astonishing aptitude for the business. With a keen eye, he was uniquely qualified to the finely detailed work of miniaturization, a trademark of the exclusive salon. The fragile and elaborate diminutive pieces were a favorite of the Tsar and thus, the assignment of working on such a production was a coveted appointment. Only last week, Arkady had completed a scaled version of the Dowager Empress" coach, fashioned with perfect accuracy. Fine crystal was used for the windows and the coachlights were miniscule diamonds. The carriage was faultless in every aspect including the convertible top and the step where the Tsar's mother, Marie Feodorovna would have her black bearded Cossack bodyguard stand.Just thinking about the magnificent piece caused Arkady to look toward the enormous safe where his priceless treasure, along with dozens of others, were stored. The free standing iron behemoth had stood so long in the same place, the six inch wheels had sunk to their hubs in the soft but solid wood floor. Every night for four years now, Arkady had watched Berlov, the shop foreman and comptroller, inventory the various ongoing projects and place them in the huge vault. But something was wrong tonight.

Perhaps the nightly ritual was such a permanent part of his subconscious that any abnormality would have been evident. But whatever it was,

Arkady's attention had zeroed in on the fact that the locking handle was not in the correct position. Normally the hand grip was in the three o'clock position, but tonight it was definitely pointing in the opposite direction. He was certain that, in order for the safe to be locked, the handle had to be pointed to the right.

He approached the safe slowly, almost reverently.

In a hurry to abandon the store that was a symbol of the Tsar's autocratic oppression, Berlov must have neglected to secure the safe. Arkady hesitated before placing his hand on the knob. While part of his brain told him to twist the locking mechanism and spin the combination dial, the other part told him to open the heavy door for one final look at the riches inside.

He braced his feet and used both hands to swing the weighty door. Although Berlov's departure had been hasty, he had exhibited his usual fastidious manner in stocking the secure storage safe for precious metals and gems. On the top shelves were the most valuable stones; diamonds, rubies, emeralds, and sapphires. Immediately below them were the less valuable, but equally impressive amethyst, opal, and topaz. The loose stones, hundreds of each variety, lay loose in trays lined with black velvet. Both cut and uncut stones manifested their brilliance in spite of the constantly fading light. Arkady knew that each individual stone had been examined by experts for the three most important factors in determining the worth of a gem; color, cut, and carat. Those stones not measuring up to the high standards of Faberge, were sold off at wholesale prices.

On the third shelf were the unfinished projects; cigarette cases, picture frames, parasol handles, and miniature flowers and animals. Each item, in its own stage of incompletion, was nestled in its own compartment and covered with a soft buffing cloth. Directly beneath, the finished products stood proudly, each protected by its own glass dome, each made separately and exclusively to protect its own irreplaceable treasure. Most of the pieces were the beautifully crafted Easter Eggs that had helped make Carl Faberge famous. Each egg was brilliantly colored with the enamel that was also characteristic of his work. There must have been thirty or forty eggs on the shelf, all waiting to be delivered to various members of Nicholas II's family for the Easter celebration, now less than six weeks away.

The bottom shelf held the ore, bars of silver and gold, stacked neatly in piles of fifteen or twenty ingots each.

With the contents of this safe, Arkady could live in an opulent style that would rival that of even Prince Felix and the Tsar's niece, Princess Irina.

That was the thought that froze Arkady to the spot in front of the open safe.

As he gazed at the accumulated wealth in front of him, he pictured himself in the traditional Russian costume, much like the Tsar himself had worn during the tercentenary celebrations. The vision of Arkady, son of peasant stock, standing erect in the city's Kazan Cathedral in a tunic of crimson silk, patent leather top-boots, a bejeweled floor length vest, and a sable hat stitched with gold thread and decorated with pearls and rubies was a heady experience for the young man. It was probably that very thought, however, that also turned a loyal, mild mannered apprentice into an uncommon thief.

Without stopping to consider the consequences, Arkady rushed to a storeroom at the rear of the poorly lighted workroom. Two large wooden boxes with rope handles, each about the size of a small steamer trunk, lay on the floor. Pulling both together, he dragged them to the center of the room and set the flat lids next to each of the crates. With his hands on his hips, he reviewed the contents of the safe. The blocks of raw gold and silver were far too heavy to support, so he would leave them where they were. He began with the eggs, carefully packing them in the coarse straw that lined the boxes. Next came the unfinished projects which he wrapped in their soft protective dust cloths before positioning them carefully in the second box. Finally, he removed the loose gems, covering the trays with thick leather coverlets which he secured with thin twine. He stacked the trays along the sides of the second box and, pleased with his work, slid the lids into place.

Rummaging in one of the workbench drawers, he found two dozen narrow spikes which he used to nail the lids into place, using his gem cutting mallet as a hammer. The boxes were considerably lighter than he had expected and he briefly thought about including a few of the precious bars of gold and silver. Just as quickly, he resolved to leave the ingots and he quickly closed the safe and spun the combination dial to keep him from changing his mind again.

Belatedly, he realized that he was now committed to a course of action that would forever change his life. As a fugitive, he had no idea how he was going to transport his newly acquired wealth, let alone disburse the treasure, converting the objects D'art into rubles, the only thing he could spend without getting caught. He needed help.

His friend, Leonid, always bragging about his connections with black marketers, was the perfect choice. He would find Leonid, tell him what he had done, and give the quasi gangster a cut for his troubles. Then he would go. . .where?

Rubles were no good anywhere but Russia and the exchange rate with other countries was notoriously one sided. Besides, with new and different forms of government vying for control of the country, who knew what form of currency would be good tomorrow. Still, Leonid would know what to do. In the meantime, he would have to find a place to hide his new found wealth.

Arkady rushed to the window and peered through the slats in the shutters. The streets of the Nevski were still teeming with people, peasants in varied costumes, some in national dress, members of the clergy, and even white coated doctors aboard their ambulances, a precaution that was, so far, unnecessary.

Nevertheless, it would be foolhardy and dangerous to carry two large crates worth billions of rubles through the streets during such an unstable time.

Arkady opened the rear door of the shop. The alley was deserted and silent, other than the sounds of hundreds of shuffling feet, the low discordant chanting, and the mumbled prayers drifted between the concrete brick of the buildings. In the dead-end of the passageway was the wrapped garbage of the restaurant next door to the store. Normally crowded with the elite from the arts theatres, business meetings and conferences often lasted until four o'clock in the morning. Today, the rear door to the kitchens, as well as the doors that fronted the busy street, were shut and boarded.

Arkady quickly hauled the boxes into the darkest corner of the alley. With deliberate but casual efficiency, he threw the bundled trash into a heap over the crates. He finished the concealment with a sheet of old canvass sail he had found in the storeroom and stepped back to survey his work. It passed his personal inspection since it would have to suffice only for the short time he intended to leave the hoard. He closed the back door of the shop, gathered his tools in a small leather bag, and stepped through the front door of Carl Faberge's famous showroom into the thronged streets. As inconspicuous as possible he moved against the flow of the still peaceful mob until he broke free of the masses. Leaving the demonstration behind him, he began to run.

Leonid lived in a dark, one room apartment furnished simply with a bed, a table, and two chairs. The entire building smelled of black bread and cabbage, and crying babies could be heard through the thin walls of crumbling plaster. Arkady had dragged Leonid from the traktir, the equivalent of an English pub, where a blind musician had been playing traditional Russian tunes on a battered violin.

"What is so important that we cannot discuss this among the scholars and philosophers of the finest traktir in all of St. Petersburg?" Leonid asked, weaving slightly from the effects of too much vodka.

"I need your help." Arkady pleaded, helping his friend down the narrow corridor. "You no longer have your tenant, do you?"

Leonid stopped in his tracks and tried to stand erect. "No." He stated indignantly. "The peasant returned to his squalid little village. The worthless shit left me to pay a full five rubles a month for this dump all by myself. He must think that spring is in the air."

Arkady guided his friend to one of his mismatched chairs and lowered his voice conspiratorially. "With what I have to tell you, you may never complain about the price of this place, or any other, again. With what I can do for you now, you could even open your own traktir."

At the mention of opening his own public house, Leonid's eyes opened wide and he sobered immediately. "What have you done, Arkady?" He asked with real concern. "Have you finally taken over that extravagant house of moneyed whores where you slave?"

Arkady blanched at his friend's insight. He hushed him quickly and began to tell him of the events of the day. When he finished, Leonid had been shocked into total sobriety.

"And you left a fortune in the rat infested alley of St. Petersburg's biggest meeting place for the rich?" He asked incredulously.

"That's why I need your help." Arkady answered pleadingly.

Leonid bolted for the door. "Meet me at the University in one hour." He shouted over his shoulder. "You and I are going to be rich!"

Fifty minutes later, Leonid breathlessly met his friend in front of the red fronted buildings on Vasili Ostrov. In his hands, he held the reins of a horse who pulled a small, closed-sided sleigh whose wooden runners clacked noisily on the snow cleared pavement.

"Let's go, my friend." He whispered over the noise of the nervous horse and the clamor of the sled. "It is time that these two citizens joined the ranks of the elite!"

Arkady led the way along the now deserted streets. When they turned off the Morskaya and approached the shop, Leonid held up a hand.

"You go ahead." He instructed. "When I see you bring out the second box, I will make my move and we will be on our way to Moscow."

"Moscow?" Arkady was startled by his friend's announcement.

"Why Moscow?"

"I have connections in Moscow." Leonid answered ambiguously. "But never mind for now. I'll explain on the way. Just get those crates and make sure no one sees you."

Arkady, now almost overcome with fear and paranoia, tried to take on a casual appearance as he walked down the Nevski. When he reached the intersection of the alley next to his former employer's shop, he glanced around furtively and quickly. Seeing no one or nothing suspicious, he took two hasty steps and disappeared into the narrow passage.

Before he reached the end of the alley, he knew that something was wrong. He sensed, more than saw, that something had changed. Things were not as he had left them. Furiously, he ran the final steps to the dead end. He tore away the canvass tarp and began throwing aside the bags of garbage. He dug all the way to the cobblestone pavement and brick wall before he finally confirmed his worst fears.

The boxes were gone.

* * * * *

The five men crept slowly and silently through the tall plains grass. There was no moon and the heavily camouflaged men could barely discern one another as they crawled forward, each bent on the successful completion of their well – rehearsed mission. So professional and experienced that they had no need for verbal communication, they converged on their objective carefully, knowing that one false move could jeopardize their entire operation and possibly cost them their lives. Their leader, a Viet Nam veteran who had recently escaped prosecution for the murder of two Tallahassee coeds because the police illegally searched his van, held up his hand in silent command. The other four members of the group, equally repugnant for their various degenerative and nefarious deeds, took their cues to fan out in an offensive line as they made their final approach to the handsome main house of the estate.

Their orders were simple and specific. Kill everyone in sight but make certain that the owner, his wife, and two children were among the dead. After that, they were free to sack the mansion of the valuable articles that adorned the walls, pedestals, or the jewelry boxes of the wealthy owners. If they found any of the tons of gold that was rumored to be hidden on the property, they were free to help themselves, splitting the take with their boss, a shadowy and bitter man who was also the brains of the job at hand.

Normally Web "Tank", Coolidge would not have accepted such a commission for a mere twenty-thousand dollar retainer, but after researching his potential victims, he decided that the opportunity for bigger and better profit far outweighed the meager down payment.

Now, seeing his objective only yards away, he was pleased with his decision. For a man worth as much as this guy was reputed to have, his security was woefully lax. No guards walked the perimeter and he was beginning to believe that he could have motored up the river to the manor's private dock instead of creeping ten miles overland to his target. At the edge of the clearing, Coolidge knelt, waiting for his small contingent to take their assigned positions. As soon as he saw that the men were in place, he moved his arm forward, signaling the final approach to the house.

The five men raced across the fifty yards of open ground and flattened themselves against the walls of the house. Coolidge confidently looked up at the balcony above him, smiling at the ease at which he had gotten this far. He held up his heavy assault rifle and the other four men immediately began checking their weapons. When the last man finished inspecting his heavy armament, Coolidge uncoiled a length of rope he had been carrying over his shoulder. With a practiced swing, he threw the grappling hook, covered with heavy rubber to muffle the noise, onto the second floor landing. It held firm on the first try and Coolidge was the first to climb the knotted rope.

When all five men had reassembled on the second floor, Coolidge quietly tried the terrace door. It was unlocked. He stepped back thoughtfully.

This was almost too easy. No guards, no alarms, and unlocked doors. Either this was a set-up or the guy he was after was an idiot. He decided to take extra precautions which, to a man like Tank Coolidge, meant sacrificing his men before exposing himself to danger. With a few more gestures, he communicated his orders and stood away from the door.

Two men flanked the door while the other two faced the portal, their guns at the ready. When Tank dropped his arm, the two men on either side of the door, pushed the entry panels open and lobbed two grenades into the room. The concussion explosive, designed to stun, and the flash shell, aimed at temporarily blinding, detonated within a milli – second of each other. Lowering arms that had been raised to shield themselves from the twin blasts, the four men charged into the room, guns set on full automatic and firing lethal lead at an incredible rate. They were in the room for only seconds when a third blast ripped through the suite. Far more powerful than the initial two shocks, the explosion threw skin shredding and bone shattering shrapnel into every corner of the room. The devastation within the enclosed space was so sudden and violent, only one of the invading force of four had the opportunity to scream before he joined his companions in a bloody and brutal death.

Tank Coolidge, shocked and astonished, but otherwise unhurt, vaulted over the balcony railing and hit the ground running. His sixth sense had saved him again and now it was a matter of retreat and escape, something not unfamiliar to the veteran mercenary. Un-panicked and unsympathetic over the loss of his small paramilitary support, he dashed toward the tall grass.

Two levels below ground, another man watched Tank Coolidge's unceremonious withdrawal on a bank of closed circuit monitors. The sophisticated and expensive security apparatus, activated by the motion of its object, tracked Tank on four separate screens. The cameras themselves were so well concealed, their fiber optics disguised as everything from decorative wall frescoes to stalks of tall plains grass, Tank could have no way of knowing that his every move had been monitored and recorded for the last hour.

Running his fingers through his shoulder length, gray flecked, black hair, the man turned to his chief of security.

"Pick him up, Jose." He ordered. "Bring him to me at the dock. Alive if possible."

"Si, Senor." Jose turned to the three men behind him and relayed his orders in rapid Spanish. The men saluted informally and left the high tech security control room.

Jose's employer took another look at the bank of over fifty screens and shook his head sadly. He patted the shoulder of the man seated at the counsel. "Have that mess cleaned up right away." He directed, pointing to the screen that was still transmitting the carnage in the mock master bedroom. "I want everything sanitized and re-set before my wife wakes up. Dispose what is left of those men in the usual way."

Without waiting for a response, he left the control room and walked up one flight of stairs to the underground living quarters. Using a computer coded key card, he opened the door to the nursery. The night shift nanny stood up and put a finger to her lips. The twins were sleeping peacefully, each cuddled in their beds with their favorite stuffed animals at their sides. It was less than a week from their fifth birthday and time to start thinking about separate bedrooms. Although different sexes, the twins had been playmates and soul mates since birth and the idea of separating the pair was going to be painful for parents and siblings alike. Their proud father had other, more pressing matters to attend to at present, so he gave a thumbs up sign to the babysitter and backed out the door.

A little further down the hall, he used the same key card to open another door. In the king sized bed in the real master bedroom, his wife slept tranquilly, unruffled and untroubled while totally oblivious to the earlier intrusion. Without disturbing her, he went to his dresser and opened the third drawer from the top. Behind a false back, covered by socks and underwear, he withdrew a heavy revolver. It was one of three weapons that were placed strategically about the bedroom, all loaded and kept secret from his loving wife. He left the bedroom by another of the perpetually locked doors and ascended to the outside ground level.

Standing on the dock, he looked out over the dark, sluggish waters. This was the third attempt in the last five years and he wondered when it would stop. The night, however, had no answer for him, so he just stood motionless as he waited for his men to return. In the distance, he heard the sounds of the search, probably thirty of his men, closing in on their prey.

In constant communication with security central, the men would be circling, drawing the net on their quarry. There was some shouting, a couple of gunshots, then quiet. Fifteen minutes later, he saw his men approaching, some in four wheel drive pick-ups, some on horseback.

"Any trouble?" He asked when he saw Jose descend from the cab of one of the pick-ups.

Jose shrugged. "He shot Ricardo." He said, unemotionally, "He will live. It took two shots with the Taser to bring him down. He is a big man."

Three of Jose's men dragged their cargo from the bed of the lead pick-up. Their captive didn't struggle, but he wasn't cooperating either. Handcuffed and hobbled, Tank Coolidge was half dragged, half pushed onto the well-constructed pier and forced to kneel in front of the man who had ordered his capture.

"What's your name?"

"Fuck you."

One of Jose's men struck a vicious blow to Tank Coolidge's kidney with the butt of his rifle.

"What's your name?" The man asked again patiently.

Tank hesitated before looking into the coal black eyes that held absolutely no emotion. "Coolidge." He answered, recognizing that compliance was better than pain. "Web Coolidge. People call me Tank."

"Well, Tank." The eyes had not changed. "We seem to have a situation here. Someone sent you down here to bother my family and me and I don't like that. I would like to know the details of your unfortunate employment, but since I already probably know more than you, my only problem now is how to guarantee you won't be back."

Tank saw a glimmer of hope. "I'll tell you everything I know, mister. You can be sure I won't be coming back."

"Oh, I know that, Tank." His captor told him calmly. "If you were to have succeeded in your mission, my wife, my children and I as well, would have been slaughtered and you wouldn't be in this embarrassing position, kneeling as a captive prize before your intended prey. Would you, Tank?"

Tank knew that it would do him absolutely no good to lie. "That is unfortunately correct."

"Were you in Nam, Tank?"

Tank nodded his head and looked down at the ground. "The Corps."

"Then you realize as well as I do that it is time to meet the Grim Reaper. Is that not correct, Tank?"

Tank did not reply. He continued to stare motionlessly at the ground.

"And you do realize, don't you, Tank, that if you were to leave here, you might be able to tell someone else about my elaborate and very expensive security system and how it works, thereby placing my family in further jeopardy?"

Tank was still silent.

"Of course you do, Tank. I was in Nam myself and, like you, Tank, I know the rules of combat aggression. You lost your intended deadly assault. . . Now you must suffer the consequences that your fellow comrades-in-arms have suffered. I don't have a hell of a lot of choices, you know."

The spark of hope had long faded from Tank's eyes as the man dropped to his haunches in front of him.

"Let me tell you how things are." He said. "You are in a foreign country. You don't have the rights down here that you might have enjoyed in the good old U. S. of A. You are in a country where the justice system has a limited understanding of words like civil rights, speedy trials,

Miranda warnings and juries. Around here, you are guilty until proven innocent. The prisons are hellholes, and those that go in have only a half chance of coming out. That, of course, is assuming you escape a hanging, which you probably will not. By the way, the last public hanging they had in these parts was about a year ago and it didn't go very well. I guess the executioner didn't know his job very well because the drop didn't break the guy's neck. It took him almost fifteen minutes to die. Poor devil twisted and turned every which way. I don't know whether he was trying to break free or trying to finish the job."

Tank swallowed. . . Hard.

"The last two times something like this happened, nobody managed to survive my little reception for unwanted visitors." The black eyes never left Tank's. "So you, my misguided friend, are somewhat of an embarrassment to me, as well as to yourself." As he talked, he withdrew the revolver from his waistband and began unloading the ugly pistol. "I hope you understand that I'm giving you a chance which, I'm sure, you would not have afforded my family, Tank." When only one shell remained in the cylinder, he snapped it shut and turned it around, holding it by the barrel. "I hope, for your sake you make the right choice."

Tank Coolidge lowered his eyes. When he lifted his head again, a single tear was sliding down his cheek. He nodded his understanding.

"Un-cuff him."

Jose stepped up and hooked a hand under Tank's arm and lifted him to his feet. The cuffs came off and Tank massaged his wrists.

"Take him to the end of the dock."

"Can I have a cigarette?" Tank asked in a voice he didn't recognize.

"No." The black eyes turned even darker. "Cigarettes can kill you."

He handed the gun to Tank and walked away. By the time he had reached solid ground, he had almost changed his mind. The crack of the pistol sounded before he had a chance to turn around. The single shot was followed two seconds later by a splash. Instead of turning around, Bobby McAllister looked at the ground.

"This shit," He said aloud, "has got to stop."

* * * * *

The auction floor was crowded with men in tuxedos and women in brightly colored evening gowns. At the first ever charity auction sponsored by Christie's and held in the tiny principality of Monaco, it was understood by all those in attendance that all bids would include a twenty-five percent surcharge which would be donated to the two Baltimore clinics engaged in AIDS research. Everyone was engaged in the looping red ribbon that signified AIDS Awareness and, in spite of the somber and sad reason that prompted the event, the atmosphere was festive. Antonio Tumbas had made the trip from Seville for two reasons; First, he had several items on the program which were being offered to the highest bidder and he hoped that the occasion would generate higher prices for his merchandise. Not that he needed the money. Far from it. If he began spending his personal fortune on half of what his eyes fell upon in the morning, he would probably not run out of money before he ran out of time. He was greedy and the charity event was just another outlet for him. The second reason was the real attraction that had drawn Antonio from his family holdings in suburban Spain. The Christie's catalog contained, as item number sixty-three, a beautifully crafted Easter egg from the studios of the famous Russian jeweler, Peter Carl Faberge.

The egg, sitting on a delicate pedestal of gold with four perfect pearls mounted on the base, was enameled in a royal shade of purple with an intricate weaving of gold and diamonds that circled the entire exterior. At the top, a clear, deep blue sapphire clip gave access to the interior as a hinge at the bottom split the egg in half like a blossoming flower. Inside, a miniature castle, complete with operating drawbridge, was crafted in splendid detail from solid gold. The grounds of the tiny fortress was a field of diamonds and the torchlights at regular intervals along the castle walls were made to appear lighted, an effect created by diminutive rubies. Antonio didn't know the worth of the magnificent treasure or why it and others like it were so popular with the Tsars of Russia. All he knew was the tiny castle bore a remarkable resemblance to the estate built by his great-great-great uncle and his present home. He wanted it and, in recent years, he got what he wanted. He even had a place picked out for the unusual piece once he got it home. It would rest on the mantle in his newly furnished library, right under the spot where the hundred odd year old painting of the woman who looked strikingly like his sister used to hang.

With the lovely Emma, or Lena, or Lana, or whatever-the-hell her name was, Antonio strode confidently down the center aisle toward his seat. He nodded polite greetings to the dignitaries and members of the National Council, saving a deep bow for the Prince who acknowledged the respects with a curt tilt of his head. Antonio had met the Chief of State of one of the smallest states in the world several times in the past, but neither man had taken a liking to the other. Antonio considered the reigning monarch a dinosaur who ruled a politically insignificant spit of land. Rainer thought, quite accurately, Antonio as an overbearing, overdrinking candidate for the very disease this auction was attempting to combat.

Antonio contemptuously snapped his fingers at one of the white coated waiters indicating his need for another drink. The man looked at Antonio distastefully, but nodded his acceptance of the order and walked off in a leisurely manner of feigned indifference and annoyance.

The Regal Salle Empire dining room of the Hotel de Paris had been converted into a gallery to accommodate the event and the walls were lined with those unfortunate enough to receive an invitation, but allowed to attend by virtue of the fact that the publicity was welcome. Directly across the street from the Grand Casino, the affair was attracting glamorous patrons from all over Europe who were arriving in limousines, sports cars, and antique classics, their checkbooks and their pens ready.

Antonio would have rather been in the European gaming rooms of the world famous landmark across the street, but he could not afford to relinquish his reserved seat in favor of one of the poorer cousins standing against the wall. After all, an auction was a psychological battle as well as a public sale. Someone with enough influence to be seated on the gallery floor equated the same as having a private audience with the Pope. Antonio knew the bidding would be spirited, even playful, and he fully intended to take full advantage of any leverage, perceived or real, to obtain his objective.

The affair was begun with several impassioned and sincere speeches by local dignitaries and celebrities and the bidding finally began with an early Rembrandt of an old peasant woman. It was going to be a long evening and Antonio told the snobbish waiter to keep the liquor flowing. With his female du jour watching his every move with undying devotion, he leaned back and waited for item number sixty-three.

"Ladies and gentlemen." The Auctioneer, a bald, bland, and boring man intoned, bringing Antonio out of a self-induced stupor. "Item number sixty-three, an Easter egg from the salon of Carl Faberge, dated and initialed by the Imperial Jeweler in 1898 and believed to have been owned by the Dowager Empress and Tsar Nicholas II's mother, Marie Feodorovna. The bidding is in dollars and will begin at one hundred thousand."

Through an alcoholic fog, Antonio raised the paddle that indicated him as a serious bidder. The auctioneer nodded acknowledgement, and immediately pointed to another bidder who had upped the bid to one hundred fifty thousand. Antonio decided to refrain from any more bidding until the bargain hunters dropped out. He looked at his companion and desperately tried to remember her name.

"Six hundred thousand." The auctioneer called for the second time, pulling Antonio from his lethargy. He immediately raised his paddle.

"Thank you, sir." The Auctioneer replied, and almost as quickly, "Six hundred fifty thousand. Thank you, sir."

Antonio looked around, trying to establish the identity of his competition. He could not tell who had raised his offer.

"Six-seventy-five." He said, adopting the custom of leaving the zeros to the right of the first comma off of the price. Turning in his seat, he watched for any sign of the silent opposition.

"Seven hundred." The Auctioneer called. Antonio had not seen any indication that anyone was bidding against him.

"Seven-oh-one!" He shouted indignantly.

The auctioneer cleared his throat nervously. "Pardon, Senor." He said, addressing Antonio and using the Spanish title rather than French as a sign of respect. "Bids must be in increments of ten." He said. "That's ten thousand." He added as a precaution.

"Yeah, fine." Antonio replied without turning. "Seven-ten, then."

Almost immediately, the auctioneer countered. "Seven-twenty-five."

"Seven-thirty-five!" Antonio was becoming angry and frustrated.

"Seven-fifty." Was the response.

"Seven-sixty!" Antonio shouted defiantly.

The onlookers began to murmur among themselves.

"Seven-seventy-five."

Antonio threw his paddle on the floor, eliciting a renewed round of low whispers. "Seven-eighty-five!"

"Eight hundred."

Antonio glared at everyone and no one. "Eight-ten." The cutie seated next to him clapped her hands in delight.

"Eight-twenty-five..."

The auctioneer coughed into his hand and paused. "At this time," he began, placing both hands on the sides of the lectern. "It is my duty to inform you that, although Christie's will stand behind the authencity and provenance of each and every one of its offerings, your generous bidding has far exceeded all appraisals on this item. I am bound by the honored reputation of my company..."

"Eight-thirty-five." Antonio interrupted as if he had not heard a word of the courteous disclaimer.

The auctioneer drew himself to his full height and looked out over the assemblage. "The bid is now eight-hundred-fifty-thousand dollars." He said, acknowledging the secretive bidder.

Antonio slapped the back of his chair and lurched into the aisle causing another round of low muttering. "Goddammit!" He shouted. "Eight-sixty!"

The auctioneer blanched at the language. "Gentlemen." He gently rebuked as he avoided looking at anyone in particular. "I must remind you that those of us who are gathered here tonight are above vulgarities and. . ."

"Fuck it!" Antonio smashed his empty glass on the thick carpet. "Nine hundred thousand dollars." He said, enhancing his own bid. He glared at the room in general, waiting, practically daring the flustered master of ceremonies to respond. When a full ten seconds had elapsed, he spun to face the stunned auctioneer.

"I have a bid of nine hundred thousand." He said, shaking his head as he recovered. "If I hear nothing further?" He paused. "Item number sixty-three is sold for nine hundred thousand dollars." He sighed, visibly relieved. The applause was scattered and weak.

With a self-satisfied and triumphant smile, Antonio squared his shoulders and marched to the accounting desk as the sweating auctioneer breathed easier and announced the next item on the program.

The clerk, anticipating and fearing trouble from the argumentative man in front of him, bowed his head over his prerogative, Antonio scribbled a check for one million one hundred twenty-five thousand dollars and dropped the check on the table as if it were a five dollar tip.

"How would you care to arrange delivery, Senor?" The clerk asked, filing the check in an accordion folder.

"I'll take it with me." Antonio answered brusquely.

The astonished clerk's head jerked up. "But, sir," He objected, "that just isn't done."

"Why not?" Antonio stopped looking at his latest paramour and glared at the clerk.

Fearing another outburst, the timid clerk scooted his chair closer to the desk and lowered his voice. "There are certain formalities, certain procedures, that must. . ."

"You mean you want me to wait until my check clears?" Antonio asked, raising his voice in anger and annoyance. He leaned forward, placing his face less than two inches from the terrified auditor. "Just who the fuck do you think you are, you little bean counter? Or better yet, do you have any idea who the hell you're talking to?"

The stuttering clerk was rescued by a tall, elegant looking middle aged man in the best fitting tuxedo Antonio had ever seen. "Accommodate the gentleman, Mister Weatherby." He instructed the agitated clerk. "I will accept full responsibility for this transaction."

"Oh, thank you, sir." The fretful clerk responded. He hurried off to complete the sale while his superior stood at ease next to the desk. He didn't speak again until the clerk returned with Antonio's purchase, wrapped carefully in a soft jeweler's cloth and nestled in a foam lined attaché case.

"A lovely acquisition." He said, gently taking Antonio's elbow and guiding him toward the door. "I'm certain you will enjoy it for many years to come."

Antonio was so flattered by the man's attentions; he failed to realize he was being thrown out of the swank hotel. When the stout, carved wooden door at the side exit of the exclusive dining room slammed shut behind him, he finally became cognizant of the fact that the handsome and well – mannered man had insulted him even further by not even bothering to introduce, himself.

Antonio looked up at the Plaza du Casino, further realizing that his latest girlfriend had been left behind. He nonchalantly shrugged his shoulders and began walking toward the Leous Monte Carlo Hotel on Avenue des Spe'lugues. Since the entire country was about three times the size of the Washington, D.C. Mall, there was no need for a cab. Besides, the walk would give him a chance to clear his head so he could pick up some new bimbo in the Casino of the hotel where he was staying. What's-her-name was still sitting at that stupid auction and would probably leave with the first monkey suited jerk who bought her a drink.

Turning his back on the Hotel de Paris and the Grand Casino across the street, he began walking past the lush gardens and into the dimly lighted old city. The adrenalin rush of his victory at the auction was beginning to wear off and, even as he was congratulating himself for his triumph, he was starting to wonder why he had paid such a price for a trinket he didn't fully understand. Other than its intrinsic worth, he could not understand why anyone would value the replica of something that fell out of the ass of a chicken. He laughed at his own humorous analogy and hefted the million dollar case in his left hand. Given another hundred years or so, it might be worth as much as he had paid for the damned thing. Until then, it would stand on his mantel as a curiosity item, along with how he had obtained the relic, a story that he would undoubtedly embellish with each telling.

Within sight of La Condamine, the port and parking lot place for the finest collection of yachts in the world, Antonio passed the closed shops that normally attracted the rich and famous with vintage wines, rare jade and ivory, costly jewels, and stylish clothing and furs. He had just entered the final block of the rows of fashionable shops when, halfway up the street, two men stepped out of a darkened doorway.

It never occurred to Antonio to have cause for alarm. Crime in the tiny principality was practically unheard of and the only disturbances were usually when the occasional drunk was discreetly expelled from the presence of the other affluent and mannered gentry. He failed to recognize the irony of that thought as he confidently continued on his way.

The men were apparently engaged in deep conversation and Antonio was even prepared to offer a polite greeting until he was within ten feet of the duo. As one, they both discarded their cigarettes and turned to stand shoulder to shoulder, blocking Antonio's path. Antonio stopped and weighed his options, but before he could decide on a course of action, the man on the left pointed to his case.

"What?" Antonio said belligerently, quickly deciding that the best defense was an aggressive offense. "You guys got some kind of a problem?"

Instead of answering, the man who had pointed repeated the gesture, this time snapping his fingers.

"Fuck off, boys." Antonio started around the pair. "This isn't charity days at the gorilla farm."

Neither man reacted other than separating slightly to reduce Antonio's opportunity for escape. Realizing he was in for a confrontation, Antonio first considered running, but quickly changed his mind. His antagonists were wearing loose cotton slacks and sports shirts and he was in tight fitting formal wear. They would be able to overtake him in seconds.

Taking a half step backwards, he tried to draw one of the men closer but they responded by stepping further apart. The one on the right, the one closer to the buildings, reached behind his back and produced a leather covered blackjack. His casual handling of the old fashioned truncheon made Antonio believe that he had long and expert experience with the weapon. Thinking that the path of least resistance was the best chance for evasion, he swung the aluminum case, hoping to connect with an adversary's knee or groin. Unfortunately, choosing a target in mid-swing is not the best of tactical maneuvers and Antonio's attacker knew that. With agility that was almost reminiscent of ballet, the man avoided the arcing case by taking a quick sidestep. The momentum brought Antonio in an almost full circle and the big man stepped inside the sphere of his swing and delivered a crushing blow to Antonio's solar plexus. As he doubled over in tear wrenching pain, the second man sunk his fist into Antonio's kidney in three, rapid fire blows. Antonio lost his footing, but not his grip on the case. On all fours between the two men, he tasted bile in his throat and blood in his mouth. He must have bitten his tongue.

Hatred and indignant fury gave Antonio a burst of energy he should not have used. Still holding the case, he lurched forward while using his right hand to cradle the improvised weapon to give the force of the intended blow some added muscle. Driving upward with all his remaining strength, he hit the man he had originally missed squarely between the legs. The man howled with pain and rage. It was a useless act of bravado on Antonio's part. Off balance and still kneeling, the second man was again offered an open target. He swung the blackjack with more force than technique, connecting solidly with the back of Antonio's head. Bone cracked, blood spurted, and Antonio saw bright lights explode in the back of his brain. His attacker was not satisfied with his single skull crushing blow, seething and seeking further retribution for his partner's disabling injury; he raised his arm to render the final and deadly blow, but somehow returned to his senses when he realized that his partner required his assistance. Antonio lay on the pavement in a state of unconsciousness. But, with a look that could have melted ice, he delivered one final kick to Antonio's head. This sparked a renewed frenzy but his gasping partner held out his hand, pointing to the aluminum attaché case. The first man bent reluctantly and painfully to pick up the case, pausing only to spit contemptuously on Antonio's back. Both men checked each other for appearance, took a final look up and down the deserted street, and calmly disappeared into the shadows.

It was two hours before anyone discovered Antonio. By then he had lost a great deal of blood and his untreated trauma had caused him to slip into a protective coma. The emergency room doctor refused to give the Monacan police any odds on his recovery.

* * * * *

CHAPTER ONE

In the six years since I had last been to Savannah, nothing much had changed, most notably among any of the factors, the weather. In spite of the gentle breeze that drifted softly among the outdoor tables of the Port Royal pub it was considerably more humid than I was accustomed to back in Arizona. The glass of iced tea on the table in front of me had sweated a sizable puddle, the ice itself completely melted, and even the straw sticking out of the glass looked wilted. The excessive humidity didn't seem to bother the other people who were browsing in the shops, waiting in line for tickets to any number of the river boat rides, or having a snack at the countless stands, stalls, and windows of the various vendors selling everything from popcorn to five course meals. Of course, my idea of high humidity was double digits and I was in a geographical part of the country where perspiration flowed in the same way as the southern accent; slow and continuous.

Knowing McAllister as I did, I strongly suspected that his reason for wanting to meet at the riverside of his City of Dreams was more than a friendly reunion and another chance to show off his beloved hometown to me, or to his newly acquired family for the first time as his telegram suggested. It was entirely possible that McAllister's presence within the borders and jurisdiction of the contiguous forty-eight would attract more than a pargraph in the Savannah Morning News. Given his track record in dealing with numerous law enforcement agencies across the southeast, even as far west as Arizona, there was probably more than one or two thwarted and rejected badge-toting individuals who would like to have some meaningful dialogue with the billionaire rancher from Venezuela. On the other side of the coin were less savory persona that had some sort of score, both real or imagined, to settle with the transported Georgian. My participation in this unexpected summons was reminiscent of the time a half dozen years ago when I first met McAllister in this same city. His security measures at that time included running me to and through hell and half of Georgia, beginning at the various landmarks in the city to make sure I wasn't being followed while he waited for me at some pre-arranged location, usually in air-conditioned comfort. The riverfront was not an area that had escaped McAllister's attention in the past, which is probably why I was instructed to be in this particular place, on this date, at this time.

I was about to order another glass of tea when a young man, barely out of his teens, walked up to my table and looked at me as if he were considering a purchase while showing some apprehension.

"Are you Mr. Lawton?" He knew exactly who I was; he was just opening the conversation with the first thing that came into his head.

"You have me at a disadvantage." I said. I had been expecting one of McAllister's beefy bodyguards instead of this skinny little reject from an acne commercial.

"I'm Denny. . .Dennis Feathers." He answered.

My eyebrows went up. "I know that name." I said. "At least the second half. Care to tell me why?"

The kid smiled, a combination of embarrassment and self-consciousness. "Mister McAllister said my name would send up a balloon. My grandfather sort of works for you. He maintains your boat down in Florida."

"And what do you do for Mr. McAllister?" I asked.

"Same thing." He answered, bouncing from foot to foot as if he had to go to the bathroom. "I work for Bobby in the summer months. The rest of the year I go to school at the University of Miami. On weekends, I help my grandfather when he has charters with Excalibur. I guess that means I work for you too."

A technicality. Since there wasn't much call to have a boat in the low mountain town of Payson, about seventy-five miles north of Phoenix. I had left my boat, Excalibur, in the care and custody of Jim Feathers, crusty old salt and experienced ocean going captain who had worked with and for McAllister for many years. It was a symbiotic relationship that fulfilled both our needs. I got an excellent caretaker for a boat that was twenty-five hundred miles away from my driveway and Jim Feathers got a comfortable place to live and an opportunity to make an excellent living while doing what he loved the most; being a crusty old sea captain and taking on charters.

"It's a pleasure to meet you, Dennis." I said, eliciting a broad grin from the youngster. "What's on the agenda for today?"

"I'm supposed to take you to Bobby." He said as if I should have known that from the moment he walked up to the table. "You ready?"

I pointed to my suitcase.

“Is that it?” He asked. It was my first indication that this trip was going to be more than just a weekend in the country.

“I travel light.”

Dennis picked up my bag, slinging the strap over his shoulder and headed toward the public piers. The boat of his choosing was tied up at the end of the dock, an eighteen footer that was more of a recreation craft than a launch. At first I thought we might be taking a short cruise to someplace like Pirate’s Cove until I noticed there were no numbers stenciled on the bow of the craft. That could only mean that the little outboard belonged to a much bigger boat.

Dennis wedged my bag into a space between two seats and jumped out to untie the bow line. The current of the Savannah River nudged the bow away from the floating dock and Dennis had to hustle to loosen the rear tie down and jump into the stern. With a practiced move, young Dennis started the engine, popped the throttle open halfway, and joined the river traffic headed for the Atlantic. It didn’t take long to cover the eighteen miles and reach open water.

“Better be prepared for things to get a little rough.” Dennis said apologetically. “This baby wasn’t exactly made for choppy waters.”

I looked through the spray splattered windshield at the empty ocean. When I glanced over at Dennis, he was dividing his attention equally between a dash mounted compass and the horizon. After a bone jarring fifteen minutes, we reached deeper and calmer waters and Dennis opened the throttle all the way. In the distance, a ship began to take shape, growing on the watery edge of the world as we approached.

“That’s her!” Dennis shouted over the noise of the whining outboard. “The Second Prize.”

She was magnificent. Since taking over ownership of the Excalibur, I had considered myself the proud owner of one of the finest ships to have ever been constructed. Next to the Second Prize, however, my barge was nothing more than an insignificant little tug. Her sleek lines and modern design boasted of power and comfort and her upkeep and appearance would have shamed the maintenance crews of the British Royal Family Yacht. Probably not more than twenty or thirty feet longer than Excalibur, she was easily less than two years old and I wondered what interesting innovations McAllister might have added to the mini liner.

We sided up to the flat stern of the commanding yacht and, single handedly, Dennis hooked up two sets of ropes and pulleys to bow and stern cleats, honked the little boat’s horn twice, and we began to rise. The mechanical lift brought us even with the spacious rear deck where McAllister stood grinning like a kid at the gates of Disney World. Next to him stood his wife Larkin, whom I am still absolutely convinced is by far, the most beautiful woman in the world. And that's no exaggeration. Larkin was holding the hands of her mirror image twins who were alternately hiding behind their mother's legs and darting out to give me cursory, giggling glances.

When I stepped onto the deck, Bobby took two steps forward and grabbed me in a powerful bear hug. We slapped each other on the backs for a full ten seconds before he allowed me to breathe again, backing off to give his wife a chance to say hello. Larkin dropped the children's hands, placed her hands on my shoulders, and gently brushed her lips against my cheek. I might have blushed.

"You haven't changed a bit." McAllister made a show of looking me over after his wife stepped back.

"Neither have you." I responded, "You're still a hopeless liar."

Actually, to the best of my knowledge, McAllister had never lied to me. His idea of the truth, however, often bordered on less than scientific or objective facts.

"You look well." He countered anyway. He stood aside, proudly waving an arm in the direction of the twins. "May I present the newest in the continuing line of the clan of McAllister; Janelle and John."

"Who gave Janelle her name?" I asked suspiciously?

My daughter, Jennean, of course." He then placed his hand on his son's shoulders and added: "Pirate John, remember?"

I just smiled and shook my head. Aside from the fact that they were incredibly good looking children, having the luck or sense to inherit their mother's good looks and their old man's smile, they were typical five year olds. Since I wasn't Santa Claus, the Easter Bunny, or an interesting looking domesticated animal, they could not have cared less about me. They gave me a haphazard inspection, looked at their mother, and scampered after Dennis, thinking my bag contained presents for them. I had never once forgotten their common birth date, but I imagined they were far too young to be able to connect me with the packages that arrived on their doorsteps every June the sixth. Larkin used her eyes to offer an unspoken apology for the unintentional slight, but I waved it off. I knew they were not used to strangers and I was probably as strange as they came.

McAllister steered me towards the bar. "Is it too early for an adult beverage?"

"You know better than that."

He indicated an upholstered bar stool for me as he stepped behind the counter to make the drinks himself. Larkin had a bloody Mary while McAllister and I had our usual rum and coke.

"To friendship and fools." He toasted. "May we forever find ourselves in paradise."

"Here, here." I took a drink. "Right now, paradise seems to be a long way from land. Does this thing have so many basements that you can't get closer to shore?"

McAllister smiled, recognizing my reference to the extravagant security measures he had taken at his home in South America. "We are well outside the territorial limit, no matter who is doing the measuring." He explained. "In addition to that, we are well away from shipping lanes and recreational areas, which means that any radar sightings heading our way will have a proper and well prepared reception."

Larkin reached across the bar to take her husband's hand. "Bobby still insists we need all these silly precautions." She smiled in his direction. "We spend our nights in the bowels of the Earth even though nothing has happened since that day at the church. If I didn't love him so much, I would think he had some kind of Howard Hughes syndrome."

My eyebrows went up as I looked at McAllister. I knew that the threats and attempts on his life were real and I wondered why Larkin was being left in the dark about anything as serious as premeditated attempted murder. McAllister warned me off the subject with a quick look that Larkin either missed or ignored and I changed the subject, but only slightly.

"How do you expect to show your family around your beloved Savannah without compromising your security?" I asked, "That is why you decided to make the trip up here, isn't it?" I was fishing for a clue as to why I was invited.

"That's not a problem." McAllister was cautioning me with his tone. "We have the situation under control."

I took the hint and dropped the entire matter.

"Tonight is a party!" McAllister continued, lightening his mood. "For the first time, my other friends and family get to meet my lovely wife and our twin joys."

"I thought your kids would have been down to see you by now." I said, referring to the grown children from his first marriage.

"Just Jolie. She brought my grandson down to see his 'Poppy.'" He replied. "Jennean and Jason are also parents themselves now and they've been kind of busy.

"Let me show you around, Grange." McAllister came around the bar and took me by the arm. "As you can probably tell, I've created quite a little bathtub toy here."

I have no idea why he changed the subject and thought he had given me a proper answer or that his explanation was an appropriate excuse for his children not seeing their father for the better part of a decade. It was obviously a sensitive subject with McAllister, so I did not pursue it.

Indeed, Unlike Excalibur, which was designed to be a work boat and crewed by a minimum of personnel, the Second Prize was a floating castle, complete with the world's largest moat. The oceangoing palace required not only a half dozen full time sailors to attend to her marine adeptness; a regular household staff of at least four were in constant service to the family. I counted at least eight more men on board, invisible because of their constant attention to their surroundings. Bulges beneath their casual, almost uniform shirts, further attested to their true function, and McAllister's indifference to their presence led me to believe that he preferred pretending that they didn't exist or weren't necessary.

Instead, he spent a great deal of time pointing out the function, capabilities, and luxury, options featured on the Second Prize. Four impeccably clean diesel engines, fourteen staterooms designed for the optimum in comfort, a master suite the size of most three bedroom homes, a dining room equipped to seat and serve fifty for a sit down meal, and a lounge rivaling that of my own humble. Pub-In-The-Pines of Payson. The walls were paneled wood, the carpets were thick, the furniture in vogue and comfortable, and the trappings tasteful. Knowing McAllister, I would not have expected less.

"You look tired, Grange." We had toured five decks and the engine room, walking the length of the two hundred six foot ship several times. Prior to that, I had traveled three time zones on a variety of conveyances and I knew I was expected to be bright and witty at a party that was going to begin in four hours.

"Old, tired. What's the difference?"

"Six years of good life is making you soft." McAllister noted, poking a finger in my mid-section. "You ought to think about getting in shape."

"I have thought about that." I replied. "I just haven't decided which shape to choose."

McAllister grunted his appreciation at my humorous remark.

"Yours is number five." He said, pointing to the corridor that led to the staterooms. "The festivities begin at nine." He paused as if he were thinking of adding something but he turned away to leave. Changing his mind at the last second, he stopped, turned around and said: "It's good to see you again, Grange." He said in a serious tone. "It really is."

I laid down on the king sized bed fully dressed. I was touched by McAllister's last remarks. I would shower and change when I woke. All I needed was a one hour nap.

For some reason, I began to think about Savannah. I don't know why. I was aware of the town's magical history; a town that was built on dreams. The dreams of General James Edward Oglethorpe, who built Savannah on the banks of a magical river bearing the same name in 1733.

A dreamer was born there on a Christmas Day who followed his dreams of finding treasure and a beautiful mythical but real golden haired girl, guided by ghosts of pirates past who sailed down the River of dreams…

His name was Bobby McAllister.

I fell asleep.

I dreamt about a newspaper headline:

ADVENTURER BOBBY MCALLISTER AND
AUTHOR GRANGER LAWTON MISSING!

The article was short. I supposed it was because the average attention span was much shorter in dreams.

Famed treasure hunter Bobby McAllister, former Georgia resident and native, and his close friend and biographer, author Granger Lawton, have been reported missing while on their latest adventure, searching for the Lost City of Golden Dreams. Authorities fear they may be the victims of foul play at the hands of unfriendly natives.

The scene changed and McAllister and I were furiously paddling a canoe down a jungle river. We were both dressed in 1950's safari outfits and arrows and spears flew dangerously close to us as we raced downstream. Painted natives with feathered headdresses and bones stuck through their nostrils were chasing us, their sweating bodies straining as they pulled with their paddles, their hollowed out tree trunk canoes gaining on us with every stroke.

"Throw out the gold!" I shouted over my shoulder.

"Never!" McAllister shouted back.

"It's our only chance!" I hollered.

"Never!" He repeated, digging his paddle into the water even harder. "We can make it!"

But it was painfully obviously that he was wrong. The bronze skinned Indians gained on us by the second and it was only a matter of time before we would be overtaken. The jungle drums echoed around us, growing in volume and intensity. It felt as if we were rowing in tar as the angry natives were so close, we could see their facial expressions and hear them grunting as they slashed at the water drawing ever closer. Above all, however, was the rhythmic beat of the drums growing louder, more intense, louder, and louder, and l-o-u-d-e-r-!

A Rolls Royce pulled up alongside the river bank. The Savannah River?! The chauffer opened the door and the beautiful Voodoo priestess,

Desiree Sousan stepped out with her arms outstretched beckoning us to come. . .

I sat up, soaked with perspiration and fighting for the return of reality.

I knew where I was, I knew I had been dreaming, I didn't know why I could still hear the drums.

It took me an uncomfortable moment to realize that the drums were real and coming from above decks. I looked at my watch. It was nine-thirty and McAllister's party had already begun. A half hour later, I walked onto the stern deck and into the middle of a party I had no business attending.

With the exception of Larkin and the twins, I was the only person on board who didn't know and wasn't known by everyone else.

The twins were taken to bed shortly after ten and Larkin was never more than an arm's length from her husband. That left me with little to do except drink. Always the perfect host, McAllister introduced me to several of his friends and relatives, most notably his three other grown children, Jennean, Jolie and Jason, but conversations that included me were short, almost embarrassingly perfunctory so I spent the night in a quiet corner reflecting on the various friends and relatives that McAllister had introduce me to.

Lois, and Ruth Kicklighter, his 'double-second-cousins', his favorite uncle Johnny McAllister who looked like a real pirate, McAllister's brother, Johnny, his cousins, Tinker, Debbie, his aunts, Josephine and Frankie, his friend and Lawyer, Ned Hoffman and so on and so forth...

There was one point when a well-dressed, middle aged man appeared with a forefinger extended and a puzzled look on his face.

"Don't I know you from someplace?" He asked, wagging the finger.

"Aren't you famous or something?"

I smiled politely. "I don't know if I'm famous," I answered, "Maybe semi-famous, or something. My name is Granger Lawton."

"Oh, right." Recognition flashed from somewhere behind his eyes. "I know you now. I've seen your picture on the back of one of your books. You must have written that book a long time ago."

I had to work hard at keeping the smile in place. "It's an old photo." I said, my teeth just short of being clenched. "I'm trying to make an old girlfriend think I look even better than when she dumped me."

"I read about two books a week." He bragged. "I liked the one about the Lost Dutchman Gold Mine. What else have you written?"

"You mean besides the one I wrote about Bobby?" I asked, pointing towards McAllister.

The guy followed the direction of my indication. "Wow!" He said, looking back at me. "You wrote a book about that guy right there? What's it about?"

I was about to ask him who the hell he was when the bartender and head of the catering crew called out. "Hey, Bill!" My latest admirer turned around. "Your drink order is ready."

He went for his tray and I looked for a hole to crawl into. And that was the high point of the party for me.

I went down the companionway to the lounge. I would have retired for the evening but the four hour nap I had earlier was bound to have me staring at the bulkhead of my cabin. I looked over the selection of books on the shelves, found nothing of interest other than a gold bound copy of the bestseller book I had written about Bobby McAllister's exploits. Fool's Paradise. Since I had already read that book, I leafed through a collection of old Playboy magazines I found in a bottom desk drawer.

Shortly after two in the morning, I heard the sounds of the party breaking up, mingled with noise of departing boats and the service people packing their equipment. When the fairly good, but mostly ignored band had played their last tune, I stuffed the magazine back in the drawer and started – back toward the upper deck. McAllister met me at the door.

"How long have you been down here?" He asked.

"If you don't know, you don't want to know." I answered. "This was not a party to which I should have been invited. You want to tell me why the hell you invited me to this shindig?" You and Larkin are the only people I knew at this thing. I felt like a priest in a synagogue."

McAllister walked around me to push' a wall switch that turned an entire bookcase around to reveal a fully stocked bar. If I had known it was there, it would have saved me a dozen trips upstairs. He mixed a couple of rum and cokes and handed me one, at the same time directing me to a plush chair.

"Now you know everybody." He scratched his head and took a swallow of his drink, then jerked a thumb toward the deck where the party had taken place. "I'm sorry I bored you with all of that."

"I wasn't looking for an apology." I said, embarrassed with myself for my ungracious attitude. "This was just a party where I didn't fit in with the group. I'm not a relative, an old school chum, a native of Savannah, or even a Braves fan. I simply had nothing in common with anyone else here tonight. I would have been more comfortable if this had been a book signing session."

"Don't be silly." He said, and then added: "You're Uncle Grange, to the twins." He said, flashing his trademark Georgia McAllister smile. "You're right. I guess I made a mistake."

"That's all right." I said, trying to dismiss the situation as lightly as possible. "At least it's good to be able to see you again."

"I mean I made a mistake." He elaborated. "When we planned this trip, it was rather on the spur of the moment. Our arrangements were not the most carefully or thoughtfully designed. Actually, we didn't expect you until tomorrow." He looked at his watch. "Today, really. Larkin's secretary thought Larkin had made an error and took it upon herself to include you in tonight's get-together. I'm glad you had the opportunity to meet some of my family and friends, but that's not the reason I invited you."

Aha.

"Actually, I need your help."

There were a number of reasons why I would not have refused a summons from McAllister regardless of motive but I was, and forever would be, very suspicious. He had a habit of deciding what he wanted and, once his mind was made up, very little could dissuade him from his planned course of action, even if there was a better or easier way to proceed. I also knew he was secretive and protective of his reasons and methods, so I hid my impatience and apprehension by going to the bar and constructing another drink. A very strong one.

"So, I can safely assume you would like to discuss this in greater detail tomorrow," I corrected myself, "later on tonight."

He smiled gratefully. "If you don't mind." He added deferentially, even though he knew I wouldn't object. I shook my head.

"Make yourself at home." He said instead of saying good night.

"Thanks. I'll see you in the morning."

Twenty minutes later I went to bed, wondering how McAllister was going to change my life. Again.

I found Larkin eating breakfast with one of the security looking types in the morning. I nodded to him, not expecting an introduction, and helped myself to some bacon and scrambled eggs. Larkin smiled in a conniving manner and I wished her good morning, she graciously poured me a glass of fresh orange juice.

"Where's Bobby?" I asked, making idle conversation.

"He's on the phone making arrangements for our visit to Savannah." She said, trying to sound like a Southern Belle, before changing the subject. "Did you enjoy the party?"

"It was nice to finally meet some of Bobby's relatives." I answered evasively. "Have you been to Savannah yet?"

"Today will be the first time and I am looking forward to seeing Bobby's 'City Of Dreams', as it is known to him."

"Do you feel like you've ever been here before, Larkin?"

She stared past me, focusing on a point somewhere out on the deep blue Atlantic. For a second, I felt a light breeze blow through my body toward Larkin as her emerald eyes seemed to glow. "Yes".

I often wondered if Larkin felt a part of the magic that surrounded the gateway to the River of Dreams. After all, it was near here that some sort of apparition resembling Larkin lured McAllister on his previous journey to find her and the lost treasure of the PRIZE.

I changed the subject.

"You'll enjoy the beauty of Savannah."

"We can't wait. It's good to get away from the ranch for a while.

We went to Europe on our honeymoon and a three month Mediterranean cruise when Bobby bought the Second Prize a couple of years ago, but other than that, we hardly ever even leave the estate.

"Since you were last in Ciudad Bolivar, we have done much at El Empleado." She continued. "We have more than quadrupled our stock since Bobby began working with daddy and we reclaimed most of the land grandpa had given up years ago. We have our own slaughterhouse now and, in addition to sending livestock to every port in South America, we send butchered stock to Ciudad Bolivar, Caracas, Maracaibo, and Valencia."

"How is your father?"

"Very well, thank you. He gets around well since Bobby had wheelchair ramps installed everywhere. He goes on vacation twice a year and the twins are the light of his life. He plans, on running for public office next year and we strongly suspect that he has a lady friend in Caracas, since he makes the trip there every time the opportunity arises."

"Why didn't he come with you on this trip?" I asked. "I would have enjoyed seeing him again."

"He will be happy to hear that." She answered. "He enjoyed your company and always looks forward to the cigars you send to him. He says they are better than the ones he gets from Cuba. I think he enjoys the variety.

"He would have come, but he insists that one of the family is always on the estate. He doesn't trust anyone to make a decision in his absence and only grudgingly allows Bobby to act on his behalf although Bobby has never been called on any of his decisions. He is very active in the rights of the physically impaired persons but bristles if anyone calls him handicapped. He even rides horses when the mood suits him."

"He can do that?" I asked, genuinely surprised.

"He can do anything except walk." She answered. "If I didn't know better, I would think he had been in a wheelchair all of his life."

"I'm happy for him." I said, and then realizing I might be misunderstood, I tried to cover myself. "I mean. . . I just. . ."

Larkin reached over and patted my hand. "I know." She said. "It's all right."

"So what are you going to see today?" I asked, changing the subject and retrieving my hand. The last thing I wanted was Bobby coming on deck and finding me holding hands with his wife.

Larkin smiled again, that funny look that said she was holding in some kind of a secret. "I don't know." She said, transferring her eyes to her bodyguard. "Why don't you ask my personal bodyguard?

Her bodyguard looked Italian. He had bushy eyebrows and slick, comb marked hair. He was about my height, but built" like a golf tee. Extra wide shoulders and a torso that tapered off into a narrow waist and skinny, almost feminine legs. He was wearing a dark sports coat and a stiffly starched white shirt. I didn't like his looks and wondered why Larkin seemed so taken with him.

"I'm sorry. Where are my manners?" She said genuinely embarrassed. "Please meet Gary Caldwell. He grew up with Bobby. . That is, if you want to call them grown up."

"Pleased to meet you, Grange." He held out his hand and when I accepted his handshake, I barely got it back in one piece. "Bobby's told me so much about ya'll's exploits and I've read Fool's Paradise several times." He said in a southern accent as thick as his biceps.

Before we could say anything further, McAllister walked up to our table. He was wearing a 'safari-looking-outfit.'

Just like in my previous night's dream. . .

He kissed Larkin and sat beside her. "I see you've met Gary."

He said, ignoring the confused look on my face.

"Yeah," I recovered. "The name sounds familiar."

"Gary and I joined the Marine Corps together and he wound up becoming my Flight Commander. I used to have to salute this guy! Can you imagine that?" McAllister said jokingly.

"Yeah, well I still can't understand why Bobby's given up airplanes for boats." Gary said, then: "I never thought I'd live to see the day when Bobby's idea of 'living in the fast lane' is having twelve items or less."

Everyone joined in laughter.

"So where do you intend taking Larkin, Gary?" I asked, but McAllister answered.

"We'll be giving her the Grand tour."

"We?"

"Yes. We, meaning, I'm taking my family to see Savannah." He said, as if he shouldn't even be questioned about his attentions. "

"Yeah, but. . ."

"We've got everything under control, Grange." He said, cutting me short.

But I continued. “Bobby, your picture is probably part of the police academy training course in over half the confederacy, are you willing to risk confrontation?”

“Grange,” He admonished. “I have everything. . .”

“I know, I know, under control.”

“Exactly.” McAllister concluded.

Larkin was amused. “I think all three of you guys are being silly.”

“Bobby’s being silly.” I said.

“I keep telling you folks that there’s absolutely no reason for the police to be bothering me here. Or anywhere.” McAllister said.

“Well you don’t know the same police that I know, besides, the police shouldn’t be your only concern.” I said.

McAllister gave me one of those ice cold stares.

“That means I have as much to fear as you.” Larkin countered, looking directly at McAllister.

I knew I had said too much.

“You don’t have to worry about a thing. Not with Gary watching your every move. When he was Jimmy Carter’s Secret Service body-guard, no harm came to him.”

I couldn’t resist. “Yeah, but who in the world would want to harm Jimmy Carter?”

“The Ayatollah Khomeini harmed him.” McAllister said.

I recognized that no amount of logic was going to keep McAllister from following through with his plan to visit Savannah. No matter how hard he tried, he could never maintain a low profile. It just wasn’t in his nature. I tried to put myself in his shoes. For six years he had lived in what amounted to, was his wife’s home, living her culture, even working her land. Granted, McAllister had enough of his own money to support the national debt of several small countries, he still had his pride and his own heritage. He not only wanted to share his upbringing and background with his family, he needed this opportunity, this catharsis to preserve his dignity and poise. This was not my argument, so I dropped out.

With no one willing to argue with McAllister, especially me, I said, “Have a nice trip.”

Larkin thanked me and asked me to join them. I respectfully declined. She patted my hand as she rose to get the children. Bobby stood up and Gary began issuing orders into the intercom mounted on a pole next to the informal dining area. He exhibited a sense of professionalism that was in contradiction with his laid-back southern demeanor. Within minutes, a landing party was assembled on the stern and Gary accompanied the McAllisters as they boarded a forty-foot speed boat. . . McAllister shouted: “You sure you don’t want to come along. Grange?”

"Not this time." I answered. "I got my fill the last time I was here.

I don't imagine a few years change much of anything that's already over a couple of hundred years old."

McAllister wasn't pleased with my attitude, but we had had worse arguments. I waved as they headed for the river and their tour of Savannah.

It was approaching noon when a flurry of activity attracted my attention. Several of the non-descript security men were assembling on the starboard side of the ship and I peered through a decorative porthole in time to see one of the men lift a bullhorn to his mouth.

"Attention, please." The metallic voice boomed toward something I couldn't see from my angle. "This is a private vessel in International waters. We are not expecting visitors and if you persist in your approach to this ship, we will take certain action to repel your advance."

There was a pause and I heard the sound of a marine engine throttling back. Another disembodied voice, this one from a distance, replied to the warning.

"This is the police."

The security man didn't hesitate. "You have no jurisdiction out here, officer. This is a ship of Venezuela registry and any attempt by you to board will be met with force. We are a far superior squad and this encounter and both warnings we have already delivered are being videotaped."

I headed for the deck. McAllister had a way of attracting confrontations like chum draws sharks and I wanted to see how his private army handled potentially ticklish situations.

"This is not an official visit." The voice boomed back. "This is more of a courtesy call."

"Then it would have been far more courteous to have made an appointment. We monitor all maritime frequencies and respond to any hailings addressed to this ship or any of its passengers."

When I reached the rail, three of McAllister's men, each wearing flak jackets or bullet proof vests, stood pointing automatic rifles at the Boston Whaler rigger with blue flashing lights and official markings, I couldn't make out, that was idling fifty yards away. When I was certain that there was no danger to the Second Prize or myself, I turned my attention to the intruders. Standing next to the helmsman, a microphone for an electronic speaker in his hand stood Frank Kipper.

"Let him on board." I told the head security agent.

He lowered his bullhorn and stared at me.

"I can't allow that, Mister Lawton. We don't know who this guy is or what his intentions might be. Just because he came in a police boat doesn't mean he really is a cop."

"Oh, he's a cop all right." I said. "Bobby knows this guy better than he knows you or me."

Security man waited for me to continue.

"Let him on board. I'll talk to him."

"I don't believe I should do that."

"I think Mister McAllister would like to know what he has to say."

He hesitated.

"I'll take full responsibility."

That's what he wanted to hear. He raised the bullhorn to his lips.

"Officer." He hailed. "You have been granted permission to board on the condition you leave any and all firearms behind and agree to submit to a search. Please signal your acceptance to these conditions."

Even from a distance, I could tell Kipper was seething. He turned to his partner who listened to what he had to say and shrugged. Kipper reached behind his back and, with exaggerated movements, produced his service revolver and handed it to his associate. He held up both hands as if to ask what next. McAllister's defense force had not lowered their weapons.

"You may approach at idle speed."

From somewhere below decks, a hydraulic sigh indicated the lowering of the boarding ladder. Kipper stepped onto the small platform and two men rushed down the stairs. While one of the men trained his rifle on the back of Kipper's head, the other conducted a thorough and professional body search. When he finished, he held up an arm and his boss addressed Kipper's driver.

"Back off to a distance of fifty yards." He ordered. "You will be advised when you may return to pick up your passenger."

Reluctantly, the police boat shifted gears and backed off.

Kipper took his time ascending the stairs, the only psychological battle he was capable of winning at the time. I waited for him at the top of the stairs, allowing him his non-existent triumph, I had all day.

"Where's McAllister?" He demanded when he reached deck level. He either didn't recognize or remember me. I didn't know whether to be relieved or disappointed.

"Who wants to know?" I felt like baiting him. It worked.

"Listen, buddy," Kipper hadn't changed a bit. "I don't know who the hell you think you are, but if you know what's good for you, you'll run off and find your boss before I lose my patience."

Typical. Frank Kipper was a self-serving, crooked cop who thought that a badge had dictatorial powers and that laws governing the decorum of officers were far beneath him. He was a stereotype red neck, a bigoted bully, and, worst of all, so far, relatively unchecked except for the efforts of Bobby McAllister and a few of his friends. Kipper blamed McAllister for everything negative that had ever happened to him from bunions to the death of his niece, none of which was true. Kipper's problems were created by himself and circumstances had offered Bobby up as the perfect scapegoat.

"You're not in a position to throw your considerable weight around." I pointed to the guns that, although at rest, were still very much in evidence. "As for McAllister, I've been delegated to find out what your unwanted visit is all about. So, state your business or be prepared to have your fat ass thrown overboard." I could be as unreasonable as him, especially with a small but heavily armed paramilitary force backing me.

"I'm here to find out his intentions." He answered, barely controlling his temper. "I want to know why he's here."

"That sounds to me like George Custer asking the Indians if they were planning to attack. I also think that information of that type comes under the heading of none of your business, Officer Kipper." I deliberately diminished his rank while letting him know that I knew who he was.

"That's Lieutenant Kipper to you. . ." He paused, squinting at me. "Hey! I know you, don't I?"

"We've met." I conceded. "Tell me, Frank, why do you persist in hounding Bobby McAllister? You have constantly overstepped your jurisdiction and authority to pit yourself against a man who has enough money and clout to have you squashed like a bug, both professionally and physically. When are you going to learn that you can't win against this man?"

The squint turned to recognition, a realization that, for some reason, unsettled me. "You're that writer guy." He said. "The one I had trouble with before."

"The only trouble you had from me was of your own making." I answered. "Now why don't you tell me why you came out here this morning? All the time remembering, of course, that I probably won't tell you anything that appears to me to be a response to one of your stupid questions."

"I'm here to tell McAllister that I haven't forgotten."

"Forgotten what?" I asked.

"Forgotten that he is a wanted man."

"Wanted for what?" I challenged.

"Fraud." Kipper answered vehemently. "He cheated the United States Government out of millions of dollars when he took his treasure to South America. He stole that gold from a friend of mine's legal claim and refuses to return it to the rightful owner. He is also the prime suspect in the murder of several men, including a group of men of a deputized delegation sent to South America to arrest him and return him to the United States.

"Let me tell you what I think." I said, leaning on the rail with what I hoped to be a superior and unconcerned pose. "I don't think there is one single arrest warrant for Bobby McAllister issued by any responsible law enforcement agency in the entire United States. I have no doubt that there are certain individuals who, however misguided, feel that they can prove some idiotic claim against him, but I sincerely believe that they have about the same chance as Elmer Fudd has of having Bugs Bunny for rabbit stew. There are no criminal charges pending against McAllister and you are in danger of facing civil rights charges.

"As for your so called deputies, I think they were a mercenary force sent to kidnap or kill him and his family and they had no government backing or sanctions.

"McAllister hasn't defrauded anyone. Why he hasn't dealt with you in the same way he handled others who have tried to hurt him or his family is a mystery to me. When are you going to learn that what goes around comes around? You're long overdue, Kipper. If I were you, I'd be very careful. And while you're at it, you might seek some professional therapy."

"Are you threatening a police officer?" His tone was menacing.

I shook my head in exasperation. "You haven't heard a word of what I've said." I replied. "You are not a police officer out here. You're not even a cop on the nearest point of land. You're miles from your office in Florida and how you persist in finding sane local enforcement agencies to go along with your stupid forms of harassment is beyond me. You are a paranoid clown without circus make-up. You're to be pitied, Frank. If I wanted to be understood any better, I'd tell you to go fuck yourself."

"You talk mighty big for a guy with a half dozen guns backing you up." Already, he was exaggerating his disadvantage. By the time he got back to Florida and his own department, he would be bragging how he stood up, unarmed, in front of fifty guns.

"Don't bring more grief on yourself, Frank." I advised. "Think about it."

Kipper had already started down the stairs. "The day I start taking advice from some piss-ant book writer is the day they shovel dirt on top of my coffin." He said acidly. "Tell McAllister I'll be watching him. He can't do anything in the States without me knowing exactly what, why, and where he's doing it."

"Frank, if you knew how stupid you sound, you wouldn't be so stupid. Would you?"

"We'll see who's stupid!" He spat.

"So now I see what happens when your parents are related." I summarized.

Shortly after dark, I heard boats approaching again, but this time the security force wasn't scrambled so I correctly assumed the family was returning to the relative safety of International waters. The crowded speed boat was winched up and the twins were lifted over the gunwale by Gary, followed by their parents. The children were anxious to tell anyone about their day's adventure and I was the first person they laid eyes on.

"Uncle Grange, Uncle Grange!" They cried in perfect unison. I was a bit surprised that they knew my name. They had met so many "Aunts and Uncles" in the past twenty-four hours, I was certain they had to be reminded as to who I was. "We saw ghosts!" My eyebrows went up as I looked at McAllister, still wearing his ridiculous Georgia smile.

"Now children." Larkin gently chided the youngsters. "We didn't actually see any ghosts. We just saw where they supposedly live."

"Do you believe in ghosts, Uncle Grange?" John was gently tugging at my hand. "My daddy says if it wasn't for ghosts, he never would have met my mommy."

"I believe your dad believes." I answered.

"We saw the waving lady too!" Janelle said excitedly.

"The 'Waving Girl.'" Larkin said.

"Florence Martus." McAllister said. "She was known as the 'Waving Girl' by sailors who were greeted by her from around the world. She actually waved at every ship that sailed up the Savannah River into Savannah from the turn of the century until she died back in the thirties."

I knew the story.

"Legend has it that she waited for the return of her newly wed husband who was a sailor. She greeted every ship, waiting for his return. I guess she died after thirty years or so waiting." He continued.

"How touching." I said.

"We saw where Pirate John lives!" Exclaimed John.

I rolled my eyes toward the heavens.

"See, we did see ghosts!" Said Janelle.

"Okay, that's enough about ghosts." Larkin interrupted. "You two need a bath. Why don't you go down and get in the tub. Daddy and Uncle Grange want to talk."

"Let's go John." Janelle said. "Daddy and Uncle Grange want to talk about ghosts.

We all smiled.

"We had a visitor." I told McAllister as he took off his sweat soaked Safari shirt.

"I know." He said. "Have you had dinner?"

I nodded.

"So have we. Why don't you make us a couple of drinks in the lounge and I'll meet you there after I take a shower."

Ten minutes later he came into the lounge, still toweling his long and unruly hair.

"Ghosts?" I asked, handing him a drink.

"Why not? Savannah is rife with things that go bump in the night."

"And I suppose you're on a first name basis with all of them." I replied.

"Well, not all of them, but some." He replied. "You're still a non-believer, aren't you Grange?" He remarked feigning disappointment.

"Let's just say I'm spectrally agnostic." I replied.

"You of all people should have more of an open mind." He was getting in the mood for one of his lectures and I knew I had unwittingly invited the speech.

"Even John Wesley, the founder of Methodism, knew a ghost. The rectory where he grew up had 'Old Jeffery' a groaning, chain rattling, bottle breaking spook."

"I would be willing to bet the bottle breaking was half empty bottles of communion wine." I observed.

McAllister was well aware of my sense of humor that border lined on facetiousness, so he didn't take offense. "It's a matter of ancestry. The number of people who live here, generation after generation, in houses as old as two hundred years, are bound to come face to face with apparitions of those not quite departed.

"Over on St. Julian Street is an old, three story New England style house that was built in 1796 and moved to its present location in 1963. The new lot contained a grave site and people always see light and dancing figures in the house when no one is home.

"The Owens-Thomas house, an elegant mansion built in 1819 is the home to a phantom named Margaret Thomas, a spinster who was noted for the lavish parties she threw. The small slender ghost of the old lady is seen on the back stairs used by servants as if she were looking for slaves to give orders regarding the latest party. The lights in that house go on without anyone turning the switch all the time.

"Davenport House, a Federal-style house built in 1820 and used as a boardinghouse had a big yellow cat that was always seen dashing through the front door but then never found in the house.

"Telfair Academy of Arts and Sciences is over one hundred seventy-five years old and now a museum. It used to be a mansion owned by Mary Telfair, of a prominent local family and her portrait is in one of the drawing rooms. Whenever someone moves that oil painting of her, strange things happen. Once, a large part of a rotunda caved in five minutes after Mary was removed.

"Even Juliette Gordon Lowe's birthplace and the founding home of Girl Scouts has the ghost of Willie Gordon looking for his wife, Nellie."

He paused, but when I didn't have a smart remark, he relaunched himself into more spooky stories. His dissertation included apparitions in St. John's Episcopal Church, River House Restaurant, the Shrimp Factory, the 17Hundred90 Inn, the Harbour Inn, a converted nineteenth century warehouse, and then, quite naturally. . .

"Then, of course, there was Pirate's House on East Broad Street."

I had wondered when we were going to get around to something like that.

"Pirate's House was a sailor's tavern built in the 1700's; it's probably most famous as the place where Captain Flint died after leaving his treasure map to Long John Silver in Robert Louis Stevenson's Treasure Island. The shutters on Pirate's House are painted 'hain't blue' because it 'hain't quite blue and it hain't quite gray. The paint was made with indigo powder and buttermilk and was believed to be good for warding off evil spirits."

I knew the oration was just about over so I steered the talk to more pressing matters.

"Maybe you should be painting the Second Prize 'hain't blue.'" I said.

"You mean because of Kipper." He wasn't asking but I nodded anyway.

"You handled him very well."

"Huh?"

He leaned over the desk and opened the top drawer. "Everything was recorded." He said, holding up a video cassette tape. "Security precautions."

"Remind me to take my lady friends ashore." I said. "I wouldn't want to see myself in your home movies."

"They were doing their jobs." McAllister explained away the actions of his security force. "Remember, they have only known you for one day. I pay them very well to be overly cautious."

"No harm." I meant it. I wasn't insulted. "He practically took credit for one of the attacks on your compound." I continued. "If he wasn't responsible for the other two intrusions, who was?"

"I don't know." McAllister's brow furrowed. "I came to exactly the same conclusion. I would have bet he was responsible for all three attempts, but I guess I was wrong.

"I admit that I came up here intending to put a stop to Frank Kipper's shenanigans, but something else came up in the meantime that I have to talk to you about."

"Why me?" I asked, genuinely wanting to know.

"You have a good analytical mind." He answered. "Larkin and I talked it over and agreed that you would be the best person to talk to about this."

Here it comes, I thought.

"You heard about Antonio?"

"Only what you wrote." I answered. "The Arizona Republic doesn't have a European crime bureau, so we don't get much news about street crime in Monaco."

"It was more than a mugging, Grange." McAllister's voice was growing somber, a signal that the time for levity was over. "What do you know about Faberge eggs?"

"Not much." I searched my memory. "Faberge was a jeweler in Imperial Russia. He was famous for making decorative Easter eggs for a couple of Tsars, Nicholas the number something and Alexandria, the one who was murdered with his entire family, the last one of the Tsars and the end of the Romanovs. The Russian Revolution allowed the Soviet Government to, for lack of a better word, 'nationalize' the Faberge holdings and Faberge died in Switzerland sometime in the 20's.

"The eggs are collector's items, most of them smuggled out of the country after the Revolution. They aren't as valuable as they should be because provenance is hard to track down and because serious collectors suspect that the Faberge branch in London, I think – anyway, the only branch outside of Russia, might have flooded the market with 'unofficial' pieces after the Bolsheviks took over. How'm I doing?"

"Go on."

"The only really valuable eggs, other than the gold, silver and gems tones involved in the making, are ones that can be matched to turn-of-the-century photographs that showed them in the homes of the high society of pre-communist Russia. The two biggest collections are in the Hermitage in St. Petersburg, or Leningrad, or whatever they're calling it this week, and the Forbes Collection in the States." I paused, but that was all I could come up with. "That's it." I said, raising my hands.

"Very good." McAllister's compliment sounded professorial.

"Now, what do you know about the Hermitage?"

"Even less." I was really digging now. I would have studied if I had known there was going to be a test. "It's the former Winter Palace, home to the Tsars, and now one of the most spectacular museums in the world. Some say even more impressive than our own Smithsonian."

McAllister dismissed my answer with a wave of his hand. "Good enough for now." He said. "Now what do you know about the KGB?"

"Exactly what half a dozen fiction writers want me to know." This one was easy. "Which is twice as much as the KGB itself wants me to know, but that doesn't make a bit of difference. Two times zero is still zero."

That revelation seemed to take McAllister by surprise.

"Surely you know something." He insisted. "It's one of the most written about organizations in the world."

I could tell that we were going to have another discussion about the differences between fact and fiction. As best as I could tell, McAllister thought that the terms were interchangeable. While I agreed with him that most legends had some basis in fact, he felt that the Brothers Grimm, Hans Christian Anderson, Arthur Conan Doyle, and Steven Spielberg were all investigative reporters for the New York Times. If it was in print, it must be real. Instead of being called gullible, he was a dreamer.

"I know a lot of things, Bobby." I explained. "I know the earth is round, the sun shines during the days even if clouds are in the way, and the world's tallest building is the Sears Tower. I know the laws of gravity, the basics of thermodynamics, the capitals of most states, and I know the odds in Vegas. I know my zip code, area code, social security number, and IRS identification number." I took a breath. "Hell, I know I'll probably never break eighty on the golf course, I know Elvis and Hitler are dead, and I know Roseanne and Tom Arnold will never have real talent. But what is arguably the most secret organization in the world, I know zip, squat, zilch, nada, in short, nothing."

"And I know you are a complete smartass." He said, flashing one of his world famous smiles. "So, let me tell you what else I know." He caught my expression.

"At least, what is generally accepted as fact." I had to wonder about his source.

"The KGB." He began in his usual dramatic fashion. "Komitet Gosudarstvennoy Bezopasnosti, or the Committee for State Security.

"It was founded in 1953 as one of the Soviet Union's two secret police organizations. Definitely the more powerful of the two agencies, the KGB is responsible for both internal and external order and, as the name implies, security. They do not only spy on every country outside of Russia, they maintain regular surveillance on key members of the Communist Party, the administration, the military, and, of course, dissidents."

"I'll accept that as relatively common and acceptable knowledge." I said indulgently. "What's your point?"

"They have many departments within their rather large collective; espionage, subversion, disinformation, and another dozen or so I don't know anything about. The one department that concerns me right now is Antiquities."

"Antiquities?" I had no idea where this was going. "Old furniture police?"

"Antiquities as in the arts." He answered reprovingly.

"Painting police." I corrected myself. "Are they critics too?"

"No." He was tiring of my humor. "They are responsible for the protection and preservation of valuable art of all types as well as," He paused for theatrical effect, "the recovery of Russia's lost treasures."

"Recovery?" It must have been my night for short sentence responses.

"During World War II, the Nazis raped and looted the art communities of most of Europe. Paintings, sculptures, jewels, all kinds of creations meant to appeal to the senses went into hiding in Germany, never to be seen by the general public again."

"I've heard stories like that." I was happy to be talking about something that was accepted as reality again. "Most people believe that all that stuff went into some cave in Germany or with the escaped Nazi war criminals to South America." A sudden thought entered my mind. "Wait a second. Don't tell me you think you know where that cave is or what reputable South American businessman is really a former Nazi with a fortune in stolen art in his basement."

"That art is in Russia." McAllister smiled, happy to have me interested in what he was saying. "When Berlin was sacked, the Russians found all that treasure and moved it to Moscow."

"Now how the hell would you know something like that?"

"Okay, I don't." He conceded. "But it's the only logical explanation for what follows."

"Why not." I assumed the role of devil's advocate, a part that McAllister expected me to play. "Russia has the Pushkin Fine Arts Museum and the Central Exhibition Hall in Moscow as well as the Hermitage in St. Petersburg, all three of which display the works of some of the finest masters in the world, and after the war, our former allies took the first cousins of those pieces and put them in Joe Stalin's garage behind a bunch of bags of peat moss. Shortly after old Joe dies in 1953, a special branch of the world's most feared secret police is formed to guard these items that nobody else in the world can see."

"It's not as strange as it sounds." McAllister replied. "Consider for a moment that it's true that Catherine the Great's jewels would pay off the national debt of over half the countries in the world, yet there are lines three blocks long in downtown Moscow with people trying to buy a loaf of bread."

"So, you're suggesting the Communists sell the Empress' jewels so half the population of Eastern Europe can have bologna sandwiches for a week?"

"I don't know why the government holds on to income generating treasure when families of eight live in one room apartments with the toilet down the hall. The point is, Russia is not only one of the largest art collectors in the world, they are constantly adding to that collection."

"First of all," I said, trying to explain, "You're comparing apples with oranges. The United States has thousands of homeless people but we're not going to open the Metropolitan Museum of Art to auction off the galleries to put bag ladies up in subsidized condos. Secondly, the CIA doesn't guard those very same museums and the OSS didn't split the Nazi treasure trove with the Russians after the war. I don't see what you're trying to tell me with all this stuff about the Hermitage, the KGB, and a bunch of eggs that ties in with anything you have said."

Uncharacteristically, McAllister laid all his cards on the table.

"Antonio bought a Faberge egg at a charity auction in Monte Carlo. He got involved in a bidding war with a Russian national by the name of Kopov, but finally won when he paid over a million dollars for something that was appraised at a little over four hundred thousand.

"A half hour later, he was mugged on the waterfront and the egg was stolen."

"Small surprise." I commented.

"Antonio wasn't carrying the egg. Apparently he was drunk and being obnoxious so the auction house shunted him out with a replica, intending to replace it with the real thing when his check cleared. I understand it's a fairly common practice used to avoid scandalous behavior.

"When Antonio was taken to the hospital in Paris, the auction people sent the real egg to me. Well, to Larkin. Anyway, we put the egg in one of our vaults for safekeeping. The story might have ended there, but shortly after that, we had another incident at the estate.

"Two days before we left to come up here, one of my security foremen saw a car hanging around the perimeter of the ranch. That night, we had a bunch of alarms go off, but no one was spotted lurking around. The next night, the same thing happened and, if Jose hadn't reported seeing that car, I would have thought the equipment was malfunctioning.

"The first night after we left, two men made a run at the house. One of the pair met with predictable results, but the other one got away. Jose and his men managed to catch up with him in town and, since it would have been impractical to do anything else, had him arrested.

"The guy didn't spend four hours in jail. He gave his name as Alexander Malik, a Cultural Attaché from the Soviet Embassy in Caracas with full diplomatic immunity. He was picked up by private jet, returned to the capital, and hasn't been seen since."

I thought I knew what was coming, but I wanted to hear it from him. "Then you've drawn some conclusions from these incidents?" I asked.

"I think this 'Cultural Attaché' is really a KGB agent and the KGB is trying to buy or steal Russian antiquities to return them to the Motherland."

I sighed. "The KGB?! Well, I guess that's the only agency in the world that hasn't investigated you yet." I said incredulously. "Even you would have to have some kind of reason for thinking something like that. You didn't pull this out of thin air or have another one of your dreams, did you?"

"Of course not." He said as if something like that had never happened before. "You remember me talking about Sir Godfrey Stewart?"

I did. Godfrey Stewart was an archivist and archaeologist who had assisted Bobby and Leo Troutman with the recovery of the Hacha del Oro, the sunken treasure ship that made Leo famous.

"Sir Godfrey has a friend who is an art expert." This was coming as no surprise. "This guy, Anthony Wilson is his name, has been working for the French Government since the war. His job is officially listed as curator at Le Centre National d'Art et de Culture Georges Pompidou. It's a contemporary museum, but Wilson's specialty is the old masters.

"Anyway, this Wilson fellow insists that the Hermitage is the repository for all the stolen art of World War II. He is an authority on two very interesting topics; forgery and provenance."

I faked a yawn to show him how interesting I thought that was.

"Please, Grange," McAllister entreated, "give this a chance."

I apologized halfheartedly and told him to continue.

"Wilson says there have been three dozen documented cases of stolen art that have resurfaced since the war in private collections. With one, and only one exception, Wilson says every single piece is a forgery." He held out his hands, palms up, as if he were revealing the whereabouts of the Lost Continent of Atlantis.

"Did I miss something?"

"Picture this." McAllister said patiently. "The Russians steal some of the greatest art in the world. Instead of returning the originals to their rightful owners, they manufacture incredible forgeries and sell them to private collectors on the black market. This way, they not only retain the original, they get paid incredible sums of money for the fakes."

"But they never get to show them." I argued. "What good does it do the Russians to have something they can't do anything with except take up storage space in the basement of one of the most respected museums in the world?"

"Who cares?" McAllister asked rhetorically. "The Hermitage already has one of the greatest art collections in the world. That we agree on. If the time ever comes when they want to liquidate any of their masterpieces, they have the provenance, having 'discovered' them in some former Nazi hideout, or even some forgotten corner of the basement. The owners of the fakes, rich people who have bought what they know had to have been stolen, are left with clever reproductions.

"So let's assume this Wilson fellow, a funny name for a Frenchman by the way, has seen only a small percentage of whatever exists, a very reasonable conjecture, considering the nature of persons who possess stolen property. Suppose the Russians sold copies of everything they ever found, and loved the way their little scheme worked. They loved it so much; they decided to keep it going long after they ran out of the loot from World War II."

I was beginning to see his point.

"So they start buying or stealing pieces from all over the world, duplicating them. That way they get to have their, cake and eat it too." I concluded. "So why all the interest in something as specialized as Easter eggs?"

"I think there's a fairly good explanation for that." McAllister said confidently. "The original eggs were crafted by Russian artisans who very probably passed their skills on to following generations. Who better to copy the works of art than the students of masters?"

"Good Point." I observed. "But one thing still bothers me. If the Russians are buying real art and selling fakes, it seems as though they have to wait a long time to realize any real profit. If they buy something like an Easter egg for a half a million and re-sell the phony for the same amount, they are still at the break-even point until they decide to release the original."

"For years, the Russians have been in world courts trying to recover what they say are the property of the Russian people.

They have instituted lawsuits against any known .possession of an egg, but, so far, haven't gotten very many favorable decisions. What they can't get back for nothing, or the price of a lawsuit, they steal."

"What about the one piece that this Wilson guy says is real?" I asked.

McAllister shrugged. "Two simple explanations come to mind. First, it was a mistake. Somebody goofed and the original was delivered to the buyer. Knowing the KGB's reputation, somebody had to have gone to the land of the frozen dissidents for that one. The second explanation was that some defecting Russian took it with him when he made the move."

"Okay," I said, holding up a hand. "But I'm still confused on one point. If they are stealing instead of buying, why did some pseudo Russian KGB officer bid against your brother-in-law to the point of being well above the margin as far as value goes?"

"Two reasons again." McAllister smiled, knowing his answer was logical. "First, they never intended to win the auction. Second, just by bringing the bidding into the million dollar range, they effectively raised the value of the item.

"Look at it this way. The KGB guy sees Antonio, drunk and belligerent, and he sees that Antonio really wants this particular piece. The Russian bids it up, all the time intending to let Antonio have the final bid. True, a touchy psychological game, but the Russian is quite sober and Antonio does have a bit of a reputation as an antagonistic son of a bitch as well as being a lush.

"The next time that particular piece comes on the market, the Russians cite the last selling price as a beginning point for negotiating a price for the copy. When was the last time you heard of a piece of art selling for less than the last sale price?"

I hadn't.

"So, in Antonio's case, the Russians wound up with the copy. That's rather ironic."

"It was ceramic." McAllister responded. "It wasn't meant to be a forgery, just a placebo."

"This still sounds like Antonio's problem." I observed. "Why are you so interested?"

"Do you know Liugi Paretti?" McAllister asked, seemingly changing the subject.

"The Italian Billionaire who was killed in the auto accident in Switzerland last week?" I asked. "Of course. We had dinner together last Groundhog Day." I added sarcastically.

"Well, you're wrong on two counts and lying about the third." McAllister was unoffended by my smart remark.

"Paretti was known as a billionaire, but he had lost most of his fortune. He went to Switzerland to withdraw some of his art treasures from his safe deposit box which he intended to sell.

Also, the accident was not an accident. He was murdered for the art he wanted to sell. Unfortunately for both him and his assassins, he had already concluded his business without even leaving the bank. He had nothing in his possession except a checking account deposit slip when his car went off that cliff."

I was beginning to see the light.

"How many? I asked suspiciously.

McAllister's Georgia smile practically split his face in half.

"Five." He answered.

"So now you have five Faberge Easter eggs, six, if you count Antonio's, and you are wondering how you are going to prevent a theft in your backyard. I'd love to know, myself."

McAllister straightened up, almost bringing himself to attention. "Easy." He said. "I'm going to do what every military minded man in his right mind would do."

"What?"
"I'm going to fire my own pre-emptive strike."

* * * * *

CHAPTER TWO

That's it. I'm outta here." I stood up and firmly placed my glass next to the sink on the bar.

McAllister stepped sideways, blocking my retreat from the lounge. "You're over reacting again, Grange."

One thing McAllister was not short of was brazen audacity.

"I'm over reacting?" I was astonished. "Let me tell you something, Bobby. Just because you have balls doesn't, for one second, mean you have brains. Did you even hear what you just told me? You plan to take on an entire country, one that, in the last few years, hasn't been exactly on the best of terms with any government that I am personally enamored with. By your own admission, this very same country employs a secret police force the size of the State of New Hampshire and regularly practices oppression, coercion, demoralization, intimidation, manipulation, and even sanctioned murder.

"This is not a confrontation between you and a crooked cop, a Mafia Don, or even a vindictive and sadistic hit man. This is like trying to fight a nuclear war with spit balls. What makes you think that you, one person, one insignificant collection of cells and organs, can end a conspiracy that has been going on since before either of us was even born?"

"That's exactly the type of defeatist attitude I might expect from someone who was afraid to follow a dream."

"Bobby," I implored, "this has nothing to do with dreams. You have everything you could ever want or need. You already have everything anyone could ever dream of. Why are you insisting on rocking the boat when it's as stable as this one?" I pointed to the deck.

McAllister almost replied with an answer he had rehearsed. When I saw his expression change and the air go out of him, I was glad he didn't try it out on me. It would have been contrived and I probably would have seen right through him. When he drew oxygen back into his lungs again, he walked over to the bar and mixed us another drink. Using the time to decide what he was going to say. He was so mentally knotted up, I forgot I had been on my way out the door.

"Don't get me wrong, Grange." He began. "I know I have been blessed beyond comparison. I have a beautiful wife, a total of five lovely children, a home and a boat with every imaginable luxury, and enough money to buy Euro Disney, as if anyone would want to.

"What I don't have is a life." He handed me my drink. "I'm worth more than I can calculate and I live on my father-in-law's ranch with my head buried two stories beneath the ground. I've spent the last six years in the same place, hiding in a cellar in Venezuela with nothing to do but count cattle. I love my wife, adore my children and grandchildren, respect Larkin's father, but I cannot resign myself to living on that oversized beef buffet for one more day. I need something to avoid mental meltdown and this business with these eggs might be just the thing to give me a reason to be on this Earth other than to sire children or punch cattle."

"Take a vacation." I suggested. "You can take this floating palace into any port in the world. Your personal army can protect you on land and sea. You can have the time of your life traveling all over the globe."

"It's not about walking around the ruins with a Minolta." McAllister protested. "You're right. I can do that anytime I want. This is about me doing something that makes me feel alive. If I wanted to be a simple minded tourist, I'd buy a Hawaiian shirt, some Blue Blockers, and one of those helmets that holds two cans of Budweiser. I want a "fix", something that gets my juices flowing. Something that turns me on."

"Then pick something that doesn't piss somebody off." I took a drink.

"Look for another sunken ship. Find some pharaoh's lost tomb. Find out why Goofy can talk and Pluto can't. You already have some law enforcement people pretty annoyed with you. If you keep it up, you'll find yourself persona non grata everywhere you drop anchor and that subterranean country home you call a prison will be the only place you can show your famous face."

"You might be able to live like that, but I can't." He started pacing as if to emphasize his feeling of entrapment. "I'm not looking for any more treasure, Grange. I'm looking for answers. Secrets. I have so many unanswered questions. Things that I need to know. Things that the ordinary man wouldn't give a shit about."

"Like what?"

Bobby wasn't prepared for that question. He scratched his head and answered: "Well, what about the 'Waving Girl', Florence Martus for example."

"What about Florence Martus?"

"Where did her husband go? Why didn't he return to his loving wife? Why did she have the fortitude to greet every ship that entered Savannah for over forty years? What makes someone so obsessed? What. . .?

"Exactly!" I caught him. "What does make someone so obsessed?"

"I don't know that either, Grange. But I have to find out."

"What the hell does Florence Martus have to do with your silly Easter eggs, Bobby?"

"I don't know. Maybe nothing. But. . ."

"Give me a break, Bobby. You're not making very much sense."

He brushed my last remark away. "Besides, I spent two million dollars on those Russian Easter Bunny huevos. I now have a financial stake in this Communist plot."

I shook my head. McAllister's logic was always seemingly linked to some entirely different cosmic orbital parity. "I wonder if I have my chronological perspective in order. Which came first in this little plan of yours. The chicken plan or the egg?"

"What does that mean, are you trying to be cute?"

"I mean," I said, enunciating very clearly, "did you buy those eggs before or after you heard about this so-called KGB scenario to destroy the market for collectible art?"

"Actually, I never heard that scenario. I sort of dreamt it." McAllister smiled. "Anyway, what difference does it make?" He asked evasively. "I still have an interest to protect."

"Give me a break." I said, rolling my eyes. "Two million dollars is chump change to someone like you. You would write a check for twice that much on any Labor Day weekend just to be seen on the same stage with Jerry Lewis and Ed McMahon."

"Jerry Lewis?" He scratched his head. "No way. Maybe somebody else."

"That's not the point!" The man could exasperate an inanimate object.

"Grange," this time his tone was a combination of pleading and conciliation. "Help me with this. What have you got to lose?"

"How about my ability to breathe?" This conversation was sounding familiar.

"Then just get me on the right track." He said, holding up his glass. "You can leave anytime you want, but I need your input. This is something I have to do."

"Now that's a familiar tune." I shook my head. "No you don't have to do anything." I insisted. "You need to be a good husband and father. Where is it written that life has to be one great and exciting challenge after another just to keep you from being bored? You have more experience in your lifetime than most families have had in generations. You can't fight at the Alamo one day and land on the moon the next."

"Why not?" He asked facetiously.

"Be serious, Bobby! You can't have it all." I admonished.

"You act like you're entitled to one continuous roller coaster ride. It doesn't happen that way, Bobby. One of these days you're going to go looking for trouble and it's going to find you. You're going to go calling on your old friend 'Luck' and he's not going to be there. If you want something to better your life, try resolving your problems here in the States so you don't have to employ a damned army to use as a buffer between you and the real world, or have to sneak around in your own home town."

"That's already in the works." He said, dismissing my suggestion as if it were a minor dilemma. "You don't think I came all the way up here on a little clandestine pleasure cruise, do you?"

"Why not?" I stood up to make another drink. This was shaping up to be a long and frustrating evening. "The way you make decisions, nothing would surprise me."

"I want my kids educated in the States." He continued with his new subject, hoping I would approve of at least one thing he was saying. "Do you remember the plantation where we met for one of our interviews years ago?" I nodded. "Well, that's going to be my new home. I bought my friend's remaining interest last year. It's all mine now."

As I recalled, the place either didn't have a name or, if it did, I wasn't told what it was. McAllister and I had sat on the front porch of the antebellum mansion sipping mint juleps while he told me about the recovery of the Hacha's cannons and Bret and Naomi Troutman's fatal accident. I was writing about his search for sunken treasure and the house, a relic of pre-Civil War days was one of many out of the way places where we met for the interviews necessary to assemble enough material for the story he wanted to tell.

About twelve or fifteen miles south of the city limits of Savannah, the perfectly restored picture of the old south was a step back in time for me. The acreage, seemingly unlimited from the vantage point of the main gate, was surrounded by a white painted fence of flat boards and square posts and thoroughbred horses romped in the wide pastures. Azaleas and camellias bloomed on both sides of the main drive, and massive moss draped oaks, their branches shadowed the honeysuckle in bloom and hid the buildings of the manor from the sleepy two lane road that wound its way past the picturesque countryside.

"So, you're moving into a house that would be impractical to live in." I said. "That makes me happy that we don't share the same financial advisor."

"The house is undergoing extensive renovations." He said, once again ignoring my spurious comments. "I had to add a central heat and air conditioning, structural changes, security precautions, and extra quarters."

He shook his head as if he had done all the work himself. "It's been a hell of a job and I'm proud that I haven't compromised the historic value of the property.

"Anyway, I enrolled Janelle and John in the Savannah Country Day School, which is one of the finest schools of its kind in the world. These two kids are going to get the best education that money can buy."

"That's very admirable." I replied insincerely. I was mentally divided about extensive parochial education. After all, it didn't help Amy Carter. "Tell me, does Larkin know about all these plans?"

McAllister looked down his nose as if I had suggested something distasteful. "Of course." He said, somewhat disgustedly. "They're her children too."

"I'm talking about your other plans." I said, leaving the subject of scholarship behind. "I'm talking about your plans to go head-to-head with the KGB."

He hesitated, so I knew that I knew more about his latest scheme than his own wife. "Tell me something, Bobby." I made a show of studying my drink. "Do you lay awake at night dreaming up stuff like this?"

"Yes, I do." He answered, banging his glass on the desk. "That's what I've been trying to tell you. I have to get back in the main-stream of life. If I didn't have this thing, it would just be something else."

"For one thing, I don't see this as 'main-stream', and I knew it was the quest, not the moral issues that you're interested in. On the surface, I think I would prefer something else."

"Then you'll help?" He asked hopefully.

"Hell no, I won't help." I said, amazed that he still expected consideration from me. "If you don't even tell your wife what the hell you're doing, how can I expect you to be telling me the truth about what's going on?"

"Are you questioning my credibility, Grange?"

"No." In fact, McAllister had never consciously lied to me that I know of. "I'm questioning your sanity."

"I'm protecting Larkin." McAllister answered. "The less she knows the better."

"Did you learn that while sitting on some dinosaur? That is one of the stupidest, most archaic, male chauvinist pig things I have ever heard anyone utter. Do you think that with-holding the fact that you are intending to throw down the gauntlet at the feet of the KGB is protecting your wife and kids? For that matter, how the hell did you blow up that fake bedroom of yours on three separate occasions without her finding out?"

He waved me off again. "What she doesn't know can't hurt her."

"Forewarned is forearmed." I countered.

"I don't want Larkin armed."

"No." I observed. "You want to be lord and master, a pre-war southern colonel with a wife in hoop skirts and children with finishing school manners while you run around the globe like some twentieth century Rhett Butler, chasing your fantasies. Stop being selfish! Stop feeling sorry for yourself! You grabbed the brass ring several times, Bobby. Most people never even get a shot at it. Settle down and enjoy yourself."

McAllister's expression hardened again. "I'm not like most people, Grange. So stop trying to compare me with others, damn it!" He glared at me. "I put the fucking brass ring in your hand, Grange. You probably don't even have dreams of your own. It's real easy to shoot someone else's dreams down. I don't know why I expected you to change."

"Bobby, do you realize what you're asking me to do?" I ignored his last remarks and continued to try to make sense of an irrational situation. "In violation of Federal Law, you are seeking to engage in espionage against a foreign country."

"I'm protecting my investment." He interrupted again.

"There are other remedies for that kind of assurance." I took a deep breath. "What in the name of God do you expect to accomplish that is not considered dangerous and illegal by both countries? How do you intend to eliminate your problems around here if you turn around and embark on some new personal crusade that, in spite of its merits, is still irresponsible and, quite possibly, deadly? You can't continue to replace one problem by creating new ones."

"One has nothing to do with the other." He scoffed.

"That's not my point!" When McAllister got an idea fixed in his mind, it was nearly impossible to change his opinions. He was, singularly, the most determined person I knew, or will probably ever know, and something he had just said made me grow even more suspicious.

"Are there any warrants for your arrest in the States, or anywhere else?"

"Not that I know of." He answered, suddenly wary at my abrupt change of the subject.

"You intend to fix your so-called problems while outside of the law." I accused, knowing he had something up his sleeve. "What are you planning, Bobby?"

"It's been a lot of years since I've been able to walk down the streets of my own home town." He said. "There would be no interest in me by anyone if it wasn't for Frank Kipper who keeps fanning the coals of a long dead fire, hoping it will burst into flames. I almost succeeded in neutralizing him once; I should have finished the job when I had a chance."

Frank Kipper unreasonably and erroneously blamed McAllister for the death of someone close to him. Prior to that, Bobby and one of his investors had caught Kipper participating in an interesting but flawed con game that cost Kipper his job as a local Key West law enforcement officer and gave further fuel to the flames that burned Kipper's ass. Since those two incidents, Kipper spent all his free time as well as some official duties, and every bit of his energy, trying to harass McAllister in any way possible. Nothing was beneath his efforts, legal or otherwise, and I suspected that the man was certifiably mentally disturbed.

"Then I can safely assume that Ned Hoffman is not involved."

Ned Hoffman was a lawyer who was more comfortable living with sand crabs than he was in the courtroom. Less than professional looking in grooming and wardrobe, he had endeared himself to Bobby on more than one occasion with his ability to understand the intricacies of marine salvage laws as well as criminal law. He was clever to the point of being devious, but he would never risk operating outside the law. Not even for Bobby.

"If you're not interested in helping me, I think I should keep that information on a need-to-know basis." He said, rather icily.

I stared at him for a full thirty seconds. He blinked first.

"You're making this very difficult." He said.

"No, I'm not." I insisted. "If you are asking me to join in your insanity, or be a crew member on your ship of fools, the answer is no."

"You didn't say no when we went looking for gold." It was a closer attempt to reminding me that I was enjoying a comfortable lifestyle because of his generosity. "That wasn't exactly a safe and secure set of circumstances."

"I was told that it was supposed to be." I could idly toss reminders around myself.

"Let me ask you one more thing." I continued. "Where would you start? What would you do first?"

It took him a moment to consider. I couldn't believe that he had no idea where he was going to begin this fantastic plan. "I suppose I'd have a little talk with that Kopov guy, the one at the auction. Lacking that, I guess I'd track down the guy that's hiding in the Embassy; Malik."

"And how do you expect to find these guys?" I asked. "Look up their names in the KGB directory?"

"That's why I need you."

"No."

"Oh."

I went to the bar and fixed myself what I silently promised would be my last drink of the evening. I certainly didn't want to be impaired enough to start agreeing with McAllister.

"So I guess we have reached a stalemate." He said to my back.

I turned and shrugged using my body language to answer him.

"I'm very disappointed in you, Grange." He sighed heavily and walked out of the lounge.

I broke the promise I had made to myself by taking the bottle to my stateroom.

* * * * *

"You two have some kind of an argument last night?"

I had joined Larkin at the breakfast table earlier than I would have thought I was capable of rising after staying up in my room half the night trying to figure out how to pacify McAllister while I finished off the bottle of rum.

"You can tell that just because I haven't combed my hair?" I asked.

"I can tell that because Bobby came to bed grumbling last night and woke up still in a bad mood."

I looked around. "He's already up?"

"Up and gone." She pointed to the vacant spot where the little outboard should have been. "He took the twins for an interview at their new school."

"When will he be back?"

This time she didn't smile. "He's very upset." She said, hoping I would understand. I did.

"Perhaps I should give him a chance to cool down." I said with less feeling than I felt. "Is there another way off of this battleship?"

"The skiff will be back in less than an hour." She said solemnly. Then she reached for my arm. "Is it really so serious that you two can't work this out?" She asked. "I know Bobby has his stubborn streaks, but surely two mature adults, who have been friends as long as you two, should be able to straighten out your differences."

I toyed with a fork.

"Darn, I hate this." Larkin was so unoffending that language like that was tantamount to using the **F** word. "Sometimes you men and your male egos are as silly as you are insufferable. I've seen it in my father. I'm living it because of my brother, and now I have to go through it all over again with my husband and his best friend."

I had no idea that McAllister considered me his best friend.

"Would you care to tell me about it?" She asked, hoping there was something she could do.

I looked at my watch and patted the back of her hand. "It would take far too much time." I said. She gave me a look, so I felt obligated to elaborate. "It's Bobby's option to tell you about this. It's not my place to say."

She shook her head sadly. "So you're just going to leave?"

I hesitated, trying to think of a different solution. "How about inviting me to the plantation for Christmas?" I suggested. "That will give us both a chance to reconsider our positions." I was hoping that McAllister would fall into some sort of routine by then and forget about his desire to play secret agent.

"I certainly hope so." She said, straightening up. "I think you're both being very silly."

"I think so too." I said, trying to lighten the mood. "In the meantime, I had better get packed. There's a noon plane connecting in Atlanta for Phoenix, and I have a business to run back home."

With a heavy heart, I went below to pack my bag.

* * * * *

A gentle but unusually heavy dusting of snow covered the streets of Payson, halting the city works crew in the middle of putting up the annual lamp post decorations for Christmas. If it had not been Saturday, I would have stayed at home, but I knew the icy roads and unsuitable outdoors working conditions would triple the patronage of the Stage Stop, my little watering hole a block off the main street in the downtown area, so I donned a parka and goggles and drove my snowmobile down the hill into town. I was right. By eleven o'clock the small but popular little bar was packed with those intrepid souls unable to get to work, but perfectly capable of making it to the neighborhood tavern.

Arizona State was playing Michigan, both teams guaranteed second place in their respective conferences, but the winner would go to the Fiesta Bowl for a chance to knock off the number one team in the country, Florida State. It was a seesaw game with ASU ahead by three in the fourth quarter when an unusual hush fell over the normally rowdy but mannered crowd and I looked up from what I was doing to see what had caused the abnormal lull in the spirited cheering for the closest thing Payson had to a home team.

Larkin McAllister, looking every bit as if she had just stepped out of the pages of a high fashion magazine, stood just inside the door, drawing appreciative stares from the men and envious gazes of appraisal from the women who, to a person, had abandoned the televised game to take stock of the beautiful stranger.

Believe it or not, it was the first time I had seen Larkin in public. It was gratifying to learn that she had the same impact on others as she had on me and I was secretly pleased that she was there to see me in front of forty or fifty of my friends and customers. Although I would never allow my feelings and attraction to Larkin to interfere with her relationship with her husband, I intended, through silence, to let the imaginations of my acquaintances and patrons to elevate my social status a few steps. Standing near the door in her sable parka, the melting snowflakes glistening like tiny diamonds, she was so captivating that over half of the room failed to see the ASU Trophy candidate on the eleven yard line, let alone notice her wedding ring that was the size of most stick shift knobs. I took the time she used getting out of her expensive outerwear to self-consciously check my appearance in the back bar mirror.

"What'11 it be ma'am?" I asked, nonchalantly placing a bar napkin in front of her.

"You don't seem to be surprised to see me." She said as she draped her coat over the back of the bars tool.

"I'm not." I lied. "I knew that, sooner or later, you would come to your senses and leave that no good bum you call a husband. My only surprise is that it took this long." I showed as many teeth as possible to let her know I was kidding.

"Brandy." She said, placing her gloves on the bar. I could see every bachelor in the room, as well as a few of the married men, mentally reaching for their wallets, gauging their chances of having the privilege of buying her a drink.

In the meantime, I was making a show of looking over her shoulder. "Are you alone?" I asked. "It ain't seemly for an unescorted lady to be comin' into no bar in these here parts."

She smiled. "My escorts are outside. I told them to wait."

I placed a snifter of my finest brandy on the napkin in front of her. "Why are you here?" I asked. Getting right to the point. "Is everything all right?"

She looked around at the crowded room. Although most of the room had become a full level quieter, as if everyone was hoping to overhear some snippet of conversation that was none of their business. Larkin noticed it too because she dipped her head and lowered her voice. "Is there someplace we can talk?"

I tilted my head toward the door in the corner. "There's my office." I suggested.

Larkin picked up her glass and started for the door. "Bring the bottle." She said over her shoulder.

I turned the function of running the bar over to my full time bartender and part time companion, Sally Barnes, who glared at me as if following Larkin to my storage room office meant she had been dumped. I wrinkled my brow and arched an eyebrow to show my disapproval at her attitude, but several cat calls and verbal expressions of wonder showed her suspicions were not exclusive. I ignored them all as I shut the door behind us.

My office was actually a windowless catch all closet that had a desk and a few chairs. I motioned Larkin to one of the mis-matched seats and squeezed between a couple of empty kegs to take my place behind the desk. "When I asked for an invitation to your Christmas party, I thought a simple engraved card would be enough." I said. "Did you buy that coat just to come to visit an old friend?"

"It gets cold in Savannah too, Grange." She chided gently. "Are you one of those activists who strongly disapprove of wearing animal pelts?"

"Not me." I dismissed her concern with a wave. "I just envy the fur." The remark was out of my mouth before I could stop it. Fortunately, Larkin was the type of woman who was used to compliments and her only response to my flippant comment was another of her disarming smiles.

"You have a charming establishment here." She said, eying the disarray of my storeroom. "Is this the place that really keeps you from helping Bobby?"

The question caught me completely off guard but I thought I hid my true emotions effectively. "What possible help could I be to Bobby in doing anything?" I asked. "Your husband is one of the most independent and capable persons I know."

"He is also one of the most over-protective, single-minded, stubborn, and impatient persons that have been placed on this Earth." She said, not without a trace of disapproval. "But I'm not here to talk about some of his better points." She took a deep breath.

"You, however, are also a model of stubbornness and tenacity which makes me wonder why I came here to plead with you on his behalf just the same."

I was treading a fine line and I resented being placed between husband and wife, especially when I had no idea what the man was telling, or not telling, his primary soul mate. I was trapped between the proverbial rock and hard spot and I didn't see any easy way out.

"You don't know what you're asking me to do." I said, a little lamely.

Her eyes grew hard, an expression I had never seen on her face before.

"I know exactly what I'm asking." She said levelly. "I'm asking you to help me get my husband back."

"I think you're exaggerating, Larkin." I said, breaking eye contact. "You put too much importance on something that happened a long time ago."

"And you have no idea how much influence you have over Bobby." She countered. "If it had not been for you, he would have gone off to Europe with some half-baked idea about toppling the entire government's infrastructure. You're Bobby's conscience. Whether you know it or not, Bobby listens to everything you say, whether he agrees or not.

"As little as six months ago, Bobby had plans to eliminate Frank Kipper. Instead, because of something you said, he hired Ned Hoffman to insure that his legal issues were handled, all warrants and law enforcement agencies were neutralized, and Frank Kipper has been warned to drop his harassment of Bobby by a Federal Judge, or suffer Contempt of Court, civil and criminal prosecution.

"I agreed to move to Savannah because I thought that Bobby would be happier and because I thought that living in America would cause those stupid attempts on our lives to end."

I looked up sharply.

"Oh, don't look so surprised." She scoffed. "You can't hide something like blowing up half a house no matter how quickly or efficiently a security force works. Although Bobby has acted in a manner he excuses as protecting me, he still hasn't bothered to learn the language of my Country or remember that over half the employees of El Empleado were around long before you guys ever showed up in your Excalibur." Some of those people think their allegiance is still to me regardless of who signs their paycheck."

"So how much do you know?"

"I know everything." She answered positively. "I know how many times our home has been invaded. I know that Bobby throws the bodies to the piranha and those who aren't torn to bits by our high tech security measures are handed a gun with one bullet. I know that the Russians want the eggs that my husband bought from Senor Paretti, and the one that my brother bought at the auction in Monte Carlo. But most of all, I know that Bobby isn't happy.

"When someone coined the phrase that money can't buy happiness, they must have had Bobby McAllister in mind. He makes a show of doing the most menial of tasks with the greatest amount of attention. He drinks entirely too much. He has driven the weaker minded employees away, he badgers the remaining staff who accompanied us from El Empleado, he constantly bothers the children's teacher and tutors by insisting that his children be taught his own prescribed curriculum, he bullies the construction crews that are working on the projects around the plantation, he has alienated himself from his younger brother, and he hates even the tiniest suggestion made by anyone, including me. Just to name a few points.

"Bobby may not be able to live like he's living now, but neither can I. If I didn't value our life together, I might suggest going to a marriage counselor but it would be just another idea for him to shoot down. We... I need your help, Grange. I can't stand alone and watch my husband deteriorate into a household tyrant."

The woman I considered to be the most beautiful creature on the face of the Earth was sitting in my office, asking me to save her marriage to a certifiable nut case when I would have preferred her dumping him like a bad habit. I don't really believe that I was ever in love with Larkin McAllister, but I did hold her in near exalted regard and being married to Bobby was like living with a ticking bomb. I was certainly envious of Bobby's boldness, unafraid of not only attempting the impossible, but achieving it, who had known at the very age of ten that he would someday share a marital bed with this seemingly mythical beauty and his wife of six years. But, I would never act on feelings that were superficial. At least I hoped not.

"I don't think you understand what Bobby wants to do." I said, now trying to reason with yet another dreamer. Being fairly wealthy all of her life had placed her at a disadvantage when dealing with the realities of everyday life. Rich people were used to getting what they wanted by virtue of their station in life. All too many people in the world would be willing to give up body parts to be able to accommodate the affluent in hopes of ingratiating themselves to what they considered greatness. I hoped I was different. I knew that McAllister was.

"He wants you to end some silly KGB plan to double dip into the investment art world." She said it like she was reading from T. V. Guide.

I looked at her in mild astonishment. "And you see nothing wrong with that?"

"You're a reasonably well informed writer. . ."

"Thanks for remembering."

". . . and as such, you should be able to know where to draw the line. Bobby doesn't. Do the same thing you did the last time you worked with Bobby. Tag along. Watch over his shoulder. Trip him when he wants to do something stupid. Watch his back. Nothing Bobby could do is going to make a country like Russia back down from a single person acting without the endorsement or sanctions of someone or something much more powerful than a mere southern plantation owner. All you have to do is make sure he doesn't hurt himself or anyone else." She paused and stared directly into my soul. "After all, Grange. You did do your part in leading Bobby to me. Didn't you?"

"Well, I guess. . ."

"Please."

"You're making it very difficult for me, Larkin."

She continued her stare.

"Besides, you make it sound so easy."

"There is no reason why it shouldn't be." She said. "Make it a vacation. Have some fun. From what I understand, you had a great time in Spain while Bobby was tied up in some musty old library. Just let Bobby have enough rope to get tangled up, but not enough to hang himself. You can use the time to satisfy the scholar in yourself.

"If Bobby spends one more day bitching at the help, heckling school faculty, irritating his friends, plaguing art historians and academics, only to retire to the gallery he had excavated behind the house to stare at those stupid eggs every night, I swear I'm going to make an omelet out of every one of those surrogate chicken droppings.

"You know Bobby is capable of not only jumping, but taking a flying leap at conclusions. What do I do when he goes off the deep end? I can't stop him anymore than I could stop a runaway freight train. When he gets to moving, he has a habit of building up some pretty impressive momentum."

Even with one of the most incredible women in the world asking me for a personal favor, I wasn't convinced that I should become involved. Other men – normal men – would have instantly fallen under Larkin's genuine spell and it wasn't that I was unaffected by her beauty and charm, it was a matter of caution and experience that caused me to hesitate. My personal safety had been positively guaranteed before and more than once I wound up staring into the business end of a lethal weapon.

"If I'm still invited to Savannah for the Holidays, I'll talk with Bobby again." She brightened as if someone had thrown a switch causing me to hold up a warning hand. "Just talk."

I qualified. "I can't promise to be anything but reasonable with your often unreasonable husband and I'm now risking my favorite time of the year and a solid friendship to do that."

"A solid friendship that my 'unreasonable husband' considers very shaky at this time."

"That's funny." I commented, almost to myself. "I didn't get that impression from any of his letters."

Larkin suddenly found something interesting about my magnetic paper clip. "I wrote those letters." She confessed. "Bobby hasn't written you since before you came to Savannah last summer."

I took the information stoically, but inwardly troubled. McAllister's regular letters had never been archive material and were usually limited to one page, but in spite of our many differences, he had always been open to communication.

"Does he even know you're here?"

"I'm on my way to Rodeo Drive to do some Christmas shopping." She answered. "I told him I might stop off to see you."

"And his response to that?" I persisted.

"He told me that I was wasting my time. He said you had grown complacent in your old age."

The 'old age' remark was said at least partly out of context. McAllister was seven months older than me. Still, I was hurt by Bobby's attitude and none too pleased with Larkin's admission of subterfuge. Only my desire to salvage an important relationship kept me from changing my mind about going to Georgia for what now promised to be a delicate yuletide. "You better be on your way to Beverly Hills." I suggested. "I'll see you on the twenty-fifth." I stood up in the cramped space indicating I felt that our conversation was over. "Unless I can buy you one more drink for the road?"

"I'd like that." She said. "I'm beginning to enjoy the atmosphere of the wild west."

When the door of my office re-opened, every head in the bar turned and every eye carefully scrutinized us for a moment before returning their attention to the game, now an assured victory for Arizona State, ahead by thirteen with less than a minute to play. When Larkin resumed her seat at the Bar, I noticed two men sitting at one of the tables that definitely were not locals. Larkin gave a reassuring nod to one of the strangers to let her bodyguards know everything was alright, when Sally grudgingly poured another brandy and I got busy at the job I was best suited for; washing glasses.

Larkin stayed for another hour during which time she struck up a friendly exchange with my head bartender. I overheard a couple of feminist remarks in the vein of men being impossible and by the time she tugged on her sable, the two women were acting as if they were long lost sorority sisters. She blew a kiss in my direction and smiled again at Sally in that maddening conspiratorial manner women save solely for the purpose of annoying men. A collective sigh went up among those who had stayed on after the game and there was a sudden renewed interest in the video games when the door finally closed behind Larkin. The real conversations would start up again after I left the room.

Sally smiled smugly as I retook my position behind the bar. "She invited me to Savannah for Christmas." She said snobbishly.

"Impossible." I responded. "Who would watch the bar?"

* * * * *

Sally squirmed in the seat beside me. "Is that Savannah?" She asked for the third time. She had never been on a plane before, a fact I considered amazing.

Since I had felt the slight jar of the gear going down and heard the electric whine of the flaps lowering, it was easy to answer without looking up from my copy of the latest Clive Custler novel. "Yes, Sally." I replied patiently. "That is McAllister's 'City Of Dreams.'"

Against the onslaught of a combination of cajoling, pleading, and veiled threats, I had caved in like a house of cards in a Texas tornado and agreed to close the Stage Stop until New Year's Eve so Sally could escort me to the McAllister's gala Christmas party. Had the truth been known, I actually welcomed her company, as well as her favors, but at the same time, was hard pressed to identify with the child-like anticipation and importance Sally was placing on the trip. I had been subjected to fashion shows, diet tips, etiquette advice, and a million questions about our hosts that apparently were not covered in my best-selling novel, a missive I strongly suspected Sally had yet to read.

Flying on Christmas Eve had one distinct advantage; we had missed all the pre-holiday activities that centered around the historic district and the riverfront. The only notable activity of the season still taking place was the traditional ice skating at the civic center but even that was enough to make Sally's eyes glitter like the tiny lights that sparked on every tree in the downtown area.

We stayed at the 17Hundred90 Inn on President Street and managed to get a table in the quaint dining room five minutes before the Kitchen closed.

"Larkin invited us to stay at the plantation." Sally reminded me as the appetizers arrived.

"This way makes it easier to leave if we overstay our welcome." I answered.

"For two people who are supposed to be best of friends, you seem to pussyfoot around each other quite a bit." She observed.

I dipped a cheese stick in the dressing. "Let me tell you something about Bobby McAllister." I said, taking a small bite. "Whenever you find yourself bored, distracted, melancholy, or just plain uncertain about your future, that is the time to hitch your wagon to the human dream machine. However, when that same contraption starts running out of control, you might find out that there is no way to pull the pin on that connection and you're along for the ride of your life.

"The reason there are two sides to every story is so a third person can determine the middle ground. Bobby doesn't recognize the fact that there might be an alternative to any idea that might pop into that fertile and dangerous mind of his.

"I've watched people become physical and mental cripples because of one of McAllister's schemes. I saw people die when they trusted, or crossed Bobby and I personally witnessed a side of him, however provoked, that was remorseless and borderline cruel. He may be one of the greatest philanthropists, or have a heart of gold, but he is so determined that nothing can stand in his way of achieving his objectives. Not even me, my dear.

"He sincerely believes that anything he conjures up has the potential to benefit all of mankind, especially himself, and that the means justify the end. And finally, he is very convincing. In another time, he would have been a carpetbagger, a snake oil salesman, or" I hesitated meaning – fully, "a pirate."

"Then why do you continue to associate with him?"

"Because, despite all of his faults, he does have a heart of gold. . ." I paused. "And I owe him." I answered honestly. "And because, he is redeemable. He has a talent for attracting money and excitement, and sometimes he is the only one who knows how all the pieces of a puzzle fit together, even when he doesn't know it. His enthusiasm is highly contagious. I know it sounds pompous, but I would give up almost everything I have just to know that he and his family are safe. The only thing that really threatens them is Bobby's own ticking bomb mind.

"Larkin told me that I was the one calming influence in his life. If that is true, it's worth a couple of plane tickets and a few days out of my life to use that prerogative to keep him alive and his family intact."

"How noble." Sally said, slightly sarcastically. "But you're making one big mistake."

"What's that?"

"You're giving yourself the option to leave." She replied. "You just stated some very magnanimous reasons for being here while at the same time leaving yourself with a back door for an easy and quick exit. You can't have things both ways. Friendship is not a conditional proposition. I think you need to reexamine your motives."

I looked thoughtfully at the filet the waitress had placed in front of me. I told McAllister exactly the same thing.

* * * * *

At least the weather was more tolerable at this time of year; cool enough for a coat but not cold and air that wasn't measured by the pound. The car I had rented was in the hotel parking area with typed instructions to sign the rental agreement and leave it with the front desk clerk, a concession I attributed to the fact that the Hertz agent wanted to spend the day with his family.

We loaded the trunk with the presents and headed south on Highway Seventeen on a beautiful, but far too green, Christmas morning. The entrance to McAllister's plantation was decorated lavishly with holly wreaths and bright red bows on every fence post and thin green lines and tiny bulbs that attested to the thousands of lights that would frame the drive at night. A half a dozen cars were parked in front of the house and, except for the season's decorations and the hidden changes I knew were in effect, the house looked no different than it had the last time I was there, what seemed like a lifetime ago. The twins rushed out the front door as we were unloading the trunk and Larkin watched from the door as the children enthusiastically tried to guess which gaily wrapped packages were for them. Sally made a show of checking the tags before giving the kids the two largest boxes and they whopped with delight as they struggled back up the stairs under their newly acquired burdens. Our hostess greeted us with her usual warmth and charm and, before we got much further than the threshold, we were relieved of our remaining load of packages and our coats and, in exchange, handed punch glasses of a nog-like drink. We were ushered into the luxurious living room, dominated by the largest tree I had ever seen indoors. Amid a sweeping pile of crumpled wrapping paper and boxes of all shapes and sizes, McAllister smiled tentatively as his two youngest children tore at the covering of their newest attainments. Being Bobby, he rose immediately to focus his attention and charisma on my date.

"You must be Sally." He said, gathering her hand in both of his. "Grange has told me so much about you." It was a diplomatic lie. I had no occasion to ever update him on my personal life, even in letters.

"I've heard a great deal about you too." She replied.

"And Grange," He turned to me, extending a hand speculatively, almost timidly. "It's always good to see you." It sounded like another lie.

"Merry Christmas." I said, trying to sound more sincere than him. "And Happy Birthday."

"You remembered" His eyes lit up unexpectedly.

"I not only remembered," I said, proudly pointing to the stack of presents his staff was placing under the tree, "I even brought separate presents." I grabbed at the package that was wrapped in distinctively non-holiday gift wrap. It was because McAllister had off-handedly mentioned that he felt he was always cheated out of a personal holiday because his birthday fell on Christmas that I felt the necessity to buy a separate gift.

He accepted the offer with his usual verve. "I hope it's not a Thigh Master."

I had to suppress the urge to tell him what needed squeezing between the fiberglass arms of the well-advertised exercise device. While I was smiling benignly, he was already introducing Sally to the other guests.

Aside from the twins, none of "McAllister's other three children were present. Jolie and her husband Dan, and McAllister's grandson, Wesley, lived in Northern California. Jennean, and McAllister's two granddaughters lived in Phoenix, Arizona as well as His son, Jason, and his wife Jennifer and McAllister's other two grandsons, Erick and Corey. That gave McAllister a total of five children and five grandchildren while he wasn't even grown-up himself. I did not ask McAllister why they were not there.

An impressive and costly buffet of southern cuisine was set up against one wall, a sure sign that the house was expecting more visitors and I wondered how the security personnel were screening the guests and, for that matter, from what hidden vantage point they were conducting their duties.

While the ladies pretended they were hustling back and forth from the kitchen, McAllister played Lord of the Manor for the constant flow of well-wishers. Shortly after two o'clock, during my shameful fifth trip to the goodie table, McAllister appeared at my elbow.

"Come with me." He said, glancing around as if he didn't want to be overheard. "It's time for Santa Bobby to give you your Christmas present."

My eyebrows went up involuntarily. While, reciprocally, McAllister had never forgotten to remember my birthday or Christmas, the gifts were usually extravagantly frivolous. One time he had every square inch of available space in my cabin filled with balloons while another time, the Stage Stop had, overnight, been converted into a 1890's Barbary Coast saloon, complete with dancing girls in period costume. I automatically wondered what he had up his sleeve.

We walked through a series of corridors, proof that the house had been remodeled several times over the years, and out a side entrance. An old fashioned breezeway led to the carriage house with several diversions that led to various unmarked buildings, all modern with the plantation composition. Almost next to the former stable, now a four car garage, the path divided again and this time we veered to the right and came to a halt in front of a formidable looking door. McAllister smiled conspiratorially as he extracted a code key from his shirt pocket and slid it through the slot next to the door. We descended a short, narrow staircase into a room about the size of the average mall boutique. A rheostat controlled the lighting and McAllister turned the dial slowly, bringing up the illumination in a theatrical fashion that was typical of McAllister's style. I turned full circle, slowly admiring my surroundings.

It was as if I were in a private room at the Metropolitan Museum of Art. Under the perfectly placed illumination, the art treasures in this private gallery shone from the walls, alcoves, pedestals, and display cases. The center of the room was devoted to artifacts and historical riches from McAllister's days as a salvor of sunken ships, gold and silver coins, emeralds and rubies, and even archaeological remnants of eighteenth and nineteenth century life on the oceans. The spectacle was laid out professionally and skillfully and the glass was so cleanly polished as to appear non-existent.

Three of the walls were covered with paintings and, although I am not an art critic, I recognized more than a few names signed in the corners of the canvasses and I even remembered a few of the titles and subjects.

I knew, however, why McAllister had brought me to this underground studio for the fourth wall was made up of custom recessed compartments that housed the subject of his latest obsession: Faberge eggs.

The collection had grown to nine since I had last seen him and one glance was ample explanation of his fascination. Each finely crafted masterpiece had its own special personality and distinctive features and each piece varied in theme from the original intention, a celebration of Easter, through the historic, and on to the frivolous. Next to each niche was a framed certificate of authenticity as well as the individual item's provenance, signed by people I assumed to be experts in the field.

They were grouped together in rows of three; the religious themes occupied the top row, historic subject matter the middle, and the whimsical topics on the bottom.

From left to right, the eggs on the top row were, by far, the most awe inspiring. On the left, the open egg showed a manger scene, complete with barn animals, wise men, and of course, a baby Jesus. There was nothing humble about this miniature diorama, however. The figures were finely detailed and each was carved from solid gold or silver. The wise men held gem encrusted boxes and even the eyes of the sheep and cattle were made from precious stones. On the right, John the Baptist lovingly lowered his cousin into a jade Jordan River, surrounded by fields of golden grass. Diamond chips floated on the river, giving the sensation of the sun glittering off a moving current. Both figures were wearing robes of opal, making the figures appear wet from nature's baptismal font. The egg in the middle was the most unique of the collection. It was a transparent opal depicting the resurrection with the Son of God standing on a huge nugget of gold, benevolently holding his hands toward two winged angels kneeling on either side of the Savior's feet. His crown of thorns was a golden wreath and small rubies marked the nail wounds in his hands, feet, and gash in his side.

I easily identified all three of the historic representations. On the left was a miniature of Prince Youssoupov's oldest estate at Spaskie Selo near Moscow. Once a large castle on the edge of a forest, the real estate was, at last report, a decaying ruin. The tiny castle bore a startling resemblance to El Cemetario, Larkin's late uncle's manor in suburban Seville. On the right was a replica of the St. George's Salon, the magnificent throne room of the Winter Palace. This particular egg opened sideways rather than from the top and each half shell held a suspended chandelier of incredible detail. An almost microscopic train was the subject of the center of the egg, a lavish reproduction of the Tsar's private locomotive and eight coaches. With a magnifying glass, it was possible to look through the leaded glass windows into the cars where features were depicted faithfully, right down to the piano, green leather armchairs, and the Tsarina's sitting room, upholstered in gray and lilac. The outside of the egg was engraved with the route of the Russian rail system, a scale that must have been very difficult to establish on the surface of the unusual shape.

Just because the remaining three eggs were of a more trivial personality did not defer from their individual refinement. On the left was an enamel and gold shell enclosing a basket of wood anemones made of gold, diamonds, garnets, and chalcedony. On the right was an egg that held a finely crafted bridge that spanned a miniature garden of callow lilies, iris, and daisies, all created from precious metals and gemstones. The final masterpiece stood on four legs of finely carved silver and was adorned with jade leaves and pearls to resemble lilies of the valley. On the top were three picture frames, each ringed with diamond frames and pyramided under a replica of the Imperial Crown. The pictures were of Nicholas and two small children I assumed to be his eldest daughters, Olga and Tatiana.

Far more tangible than a mere painting and historically more significant than a coin or some ancient artifact, the small collection was the most impressive part of the private gallery.

In front of the wall dedicated to the Imperial Jeweler was a free standing marble pillar, carved to resemble a Greek column, with a box the size of a football, wrapped in silver paper and tied with a red bow, resting on top. It didn't take a sheepskin from Harvard to guess what the box held.

"Merry Christmas, Grange." In his own little shrine, even McAllister's voice sounded hushed, almost reverent. "Go ahead," He said, pointing toward the gift, "open it."

Holding it as if it were as fragile as the thin shelled product it was certain to represent, I removed the bow and wrapping and set it back on the pillar to remove the lid. The egg was perched on a pedestal of carved gold with a ring of diamond chips halfway up the base. The egg itself was bright blue enamel with intricate ornamental work of fine gold wire. Inside, three tiny dogs, possibly carved from ivory, romped around a fountain that spurted fine silver wire made to simulate water. The puppies, probably terriers, had playful expressions and they danced among flowers whose blossoms were diminutive stones of ruby, amethyst, jade, and topaz. Along with the egg was a certificate that attested to its validity. I scanned the provenance, which claimed the egg belonged to the Grand Duchess Marie, a gift from her grandfather, Alexander III. It was last owned by a Swiss banking consortium who sold it for an undisclosed client to McAllister who had added my name to the bottom of the page in neat stylish calligraphy. I was overwhelmed.

"I don't know what to say." I knew it was useless to protest the gift as inappropriate or too expensive. McAllister was generous to a fault and truly enjoyed giving. "Other than thank you."

He smiled, almost blushing. "I know the concept is somewhat abstract," he said, "but you are now part of Russian history. As long as that little knick knack survives, you will be listed as the proud owner of something that was part of the decor in a bedroom of the famous Winter Palace."

Behind the generosity of the gift, however, was the nagging sensation that there might be an ulterior motive for his magnanimity. Having never learned the definition of the word subtle, McAllister was not beyond using the traditions of the season to remind me that he still had a mission to perform.

"I guess we have my clever, but slightly deceitful, wife to thank for you being here today." He said, abruptly changing the subject. "Sometimes I don't give her credit for having brains as well as beauty."

It wasn't the time to reply, so I didn't.

"I know you think I'm crazy for wanting to get involved in this thing about the eggs and what they represent." He said, switching subjects again. "But I can't help the way I am when it comes to something like this. It's what I do. It's who I am."

I couldn't help showing my disappointment with his self-gratifying rationale. If there was ever a worse excuse for doing something lunatic and possibly illegal, I had not heard it yet.

"People are not born to do or accomplish specific things." I said. "You just can't stand the thought of anyone doing something before you or better than you. I'm honestly amazed that you weren't the first person to do a multitude of things." I started counting off points on my fingers. "The first man to eat a raw oyster, travel in outer space, the biosphere, jumping over Snake River on a motorcycle, making the Statute of Liberty disappear." I shook my head. "Where does it stop, Bobby? What lightning bolt has to hit you to make you tuck in your horns and learn to enjoy what you already have?"

"I have proven to you, Grange that a man can be born with a predestined mission haven't I?"

"Well. . ."

"Look, are we going to start this argument again?" He asked, showing his displeasure and impatience by the way he held himself.

"One of the reasons I'm here is to tell you that I am going to help you with your little game." His expression changed but I held up a hand. "But this time there are definitely going to be conditions that I must insist upon and you're going to have to abide by them if you expect me to stick around. I mean it, Bobby." I said with a note of finality.

Flashing his trade-mark Georgia smile like he had just won first prize, he said a little too quickly: "No problem, Grange.

"I mean it, damn it!" I repeated, pointing a finger to emphasize my stance. "I don't want any more surprises this time. You may think that your survival depends on adventure, but not me, that kind of stuff is poison. I don't want or expect to see one single person even annoyed, or even sprain a pinkie finger, let alone die, because of your exploits."

"Don't worry, Grange." McAllister answered, making a gesture indicating that it was time to leave the underground showplace and return to the party. "Nothing like that is ever going to happen again." McAllister patted me on the back. "Besides, Grange, you now seem to have a vested interest to protect in this matter." He laughed heartily but I did not enjoy his humor. It's a good thing McAllister didn't make a living by telling fortunes.

Having gotten past the unpleasant undercurrent that was putting a damper on the festivities, we returned to the main house where Larkin watched us carefully during our re-entry to the living room of the mansion. Seeing the expression on her husband's face, her inner tension diminished noticeably and the party seemed to move to a higher, more enjoyable level.

Although I don't particularly like surprises, I expected them from McAllister, lessening the surprise effect. And, even though McAllister was always full of surprises, I had never seen him more surprised than when we returned to the large living room of his manor. I'll never forget the look on McAllister's face when he was greeted by the entire McAllister clan, Jennean, Jolie, Jason, their spouses and all five of his grandchildren. It promised to be a perfect Christmas and Birthday for the Georgia Dreamer. The jovial mood increased and we seemed to be magically transported to another time and place, there was an entirely different, more pleasant, atmosphere that everyone seemed to notice. Around midnight, however, the celebration began to show signs of losing its personality, so Sally and I made a discreet exit, promising to telephone our host and hostess in the morning. We had a night cap in the hotel lounge before we went up to the room with the mirrored convertible ceiling, where Sally gave me the Christmas present she had been saving for me. I hope it didn't hurt when I removed the stick-on bow.

The bedside clock radio said eight in the morning when the phone rang and I managed to get the receiver to my ear after only the fourteenth or fifteenth ring.

"Where do we start?" I think I have already mentioned that McAllister was not very subtle.

"With more patience than you're showing right now." I said as I fumbled with my watch to check the accuracy of the hotel clock." Do you know what time it is?"

"Of course." He never understood that I was seldom out of bed before eleven o'clock and ignored my protests when he called me earlier than my usual reveille.

"What have you got in mind?"

"Lunch." I answered. "At about two this afternoon. You pick the place."

He paused, probably because he wasn't happy at being put off for another six hours. "The Pirate's House." He suggested. "On East Broad Street."

"I can't eat sea food." I reminded him.

"Then the Boar's Head on River Street." He said. "You know where it is, right?"

I nodded into the phone. "Two o'clock." I reiterated.

"You're buying."

Lunch lasted through dinner into Happy Hour and post-holiday diners came and went as we went through two meals, appetizers, and half the Boar's Head's supply of rum. It took me that long to convince McAllister that we had to wait for more favorable weather before we made a trip to Europe which I was hoping would result in a wild goose chase. While the discussion took over six hours, it never neared the boiling point as it had in the past and, in spite of the length of the deliberations, I felt that McAllister was making concessions that he was certain to remind me about in the future.

We finally agreed on the seventeenth of May as a departure date, time enough for him to outfit the Second Prize for an ocean crossing, and time enough for me to assimilate background information and renew my expired passport. Since Larkin and Sally would be joining us, I also needed to arrange for Sally's passport, as well as hire and train someone to cover her hours at the Stage Stop. When I finally got back to the hotel, a handwritten note from Sally informed me that she had gone shopping with Larkin. I didn't even wake up when she came in.

The McAllisters continued to play the perfect hosts for the next three days, guiding us around Savannah as if it were the eighth wonder of the world. Most of it I had seen before, but I was pleased with the continuing efforts of the Historical Society in their aspiration to restore the downtown area to the splendor of the nineteenth century. Almost daily, new homes, businesses, and other landmarks were being added to the National Historical Register, all making the port of Georgia into one of the most authentic and commemorated cities in the south.

Sally was disappointed when she found out how much of the pre-holiday local festivities she had missed. Bobby was a fountain of information as he guided Sally by the elbow, monopolizing the conversation with lectures of traditions from the late 1700s.

Every December fifteenth, Bobby's church celebrated an old English custom, the Yule Log Ceremony. Members of the church would gather at one house, this year, quite naturally, McAllister's, and giant bonfires were set up all over the yard to keep the guests warm as well as light the area. McAllister told us of his memories as a kid when the locals would build bonfires in the plentiful city parks throughout the town instead of their small backyards. But, fortunately, that wasn't the case with McAllister now. The custom was that a log decorated with magnolias and greenery was taken by an adult and hidden while the singing of Christmas carols signaled the beginning of the ceremony. The children would search for the log and the lucky child who found it would return it to the gathering on a wooden sled and present it to the presiding minister. A formal observance followed including the sprinkling of oil over the log while the pastor gave three wishes for the New Year and a light was taken from the log and passed among the congregation, a symbol of Christ's light in the world.

Thankfully, we also missed the contest of two separate hunting parties going in armed search of squirrel or possum. The party returning with the least game would have to pay the expenses of a pre-Christmas feast of possum, squirrel, sop, tater, pone corn bread, collards, smoked bacon, ginger cake, apple cider, and persimmon beer.

We also missed the "Fantastics", a Christmas group of merrymakers, who held several different parades on the streets that included raucous singing, dancing, and political caricatures. Old Fort Jackson and Fort Pulaski had several dramatic presentations about Christmas during the Civil War and River Street was the scene of several pageants and events.

When it came time to leave, McAllister cornered me in a remote area of the departure lounge. "You know," He said, glancing over his shoulder at Sally and lowering his voice unnecessarily, "you could do a lot worse than that little lady over there."

Now that was a strong selling point.

We said our good-byes and for the next four hours, I divided my time between finishing the latest Dirk Pitt adventure and watching the back of Sally's head as she sat with her nose pressed to the window, watching the landscape of most of the country passing below us.

* * * * *

Why I didn't take my part of the bargain I had made with McAllister more seriously, I'll never know. All of a sudden it was my birthday and less than a week before Sally and I were due to leave for Europe and the sum total of research and background information I had gathered would not have filled the backside of a postage stamp. When I was in grammar school, my mother once accused me of being a procrastinator. By the time I finally got around to looking the word up in my Webster's Dictionary, it was far too late to be mad at her.

It wasn't entirely my fault. The library in Payson was the size of a bookmobile and the promotions I was always planning at the Stage Stop kept me from running into Phoenix to the better equipped book bins. I know that's not the best of excuses, but I haven't had the time to think of a better one.

The end result was that I was as unprepared to embark on a trip to Europe, for which exact purpose I was still uncertain, as I had been at time I went along with McAllister's crazy, but successful quest for the Prize. Sally, still unaware of our true mission, had been packed since St. Patrick's Day and when her passport finally arrived in the mail, she carried it around, showing it to friends and strangers alike as if it were a treasured trophy.

When we stepped off the plane in Savannah, Bobby and Larkin greeted us warmly and we engaged in typical small talk until we had claimed our baggage and were being whisked toward some river port in a chauffeur driven limousine.

"Is that the stuff?" McAllister pointed to the briefcase on the floor next to me.

"It's a beginning." I answered evasively.

"Let's see what you've got so far."

The only thing pertaining to McAllister's latest quest in that big and otherwise empty suitcase for important papers was a telegram from Anthony Wilson, confirming our appointment with him at his office at Le Centre National d'Art et de Culture Georges Pompidou on the twenty-second. I had sent a request for a meeting five days ago and that flimsy piece of yellow paper from the office of Western Union shamefully represented the only real accomplishment of my months of supposed research.

"I think it's important that one of us keep an open mind." I hedged. "If I brief you on all the things I've learned, you would be bored and possibly influenced to my way of thinking. Since you're so good at it, I want you to play the devil's advocate and the best way for you to do that is to work from the position of having a clean slate."

McAllister flashed one of his famous Georgia smiles and said: "Sorry, Grange, try again. You know I don't even do the devil's advocate thing." He stared at me suspiciously, "but, I will keep an open mind." He slapped his knee and looked at Larkin. "I told you this man was a genius." He said. "He's got the right answer for everything, if only he could learn to lie better."

I felt guilty; I tried not to show it.

We took Interstate 16 into town from the airport where it emptied at Liberty Street and from there; we took Wheaton until we got to Bonaventure Road. After that, I was lost until we pulled into the Savannah Bend Marina on the Wilmington River in Thunderbolt. It wasn't hard to spot the Second Prize tied up next to one of the floating docks. McAllister's security forces must have been going nuts because the pier was crowded with people trying to get a better look at the most beautiful and luxurious yacht they had probably ever seen. When the limo stopped at the entrance to the docks, everyone who had been admiring the boat turned their attention to the car, hoping to get a glimpse of their favorite celebrity. Their expressions went from expectation to disappointment as no one was recognizable, although Larkin must have caused more than a little speculation. Finally the looks changed to envy as the four of us went up the short gangplank and the security personnel closed the gap in the railing after we boarded. The crew began scurrying about as we made our way to our staterooms, taking positions and preparing to cast off lines as an almost unnoticeable vibration at our feet announced the starting of the powerful engines. I had barely finished unpacking when the tempo of the engines picked up and, through the porthole, I saw the marina slowly slide past.

By the time Sally and I made it up to the fantail bar, McAllister was already busy stirring up some concoction in a twenty gallon Coleman cooler while the Second Prize broke free from the river delta and headed for the open sea.

"This is Chatham County Artillery Punch." He said, popping a champagne cork over the side and pouring the contents of the bottle into the keg. Before the bottle was empty, he was opening another from the open case at his side.

"Happy hour by the barrel?" I asked.

"This recipe is over two hundred years old." He said, ignoring my question. "It was originally made by the gentle ladies of the south and somewhat augmented by the officers of the company so as to supply a little kick.

"The Chatham County Artillery is the oldest military organization in Georgia. It was originally commissioned on the first of May in 1786 and their first official duty was to pay tribute at General Nathaniel Green's funeral.

"Five years later, when the Regiment honored George Washington with a twenty-six gun salute, Washington was so pleased, he presented the Company with a gift of the guns captured at Yorktown in 1781.

"President Monroe was saluted by those same guns in 1819 at the launching of the S.S. Savannah, the first steamship to cross the Atlantic. As a commercial enterprise, the S.S. Savannah was a bust, but the formula for this stuff, along with the Regiment, survived very nicely."

He emptied the last bottle of bubbly into the plastic cask and stirred the contents with a huge wooden spoon. When he tapped some of the contents into four tall glasses, it came out of the spigot with the same consistency and color as maple syrup. He handed the glasses around.

"What is in this stuff?" I asked.

"Orange juice, lemon juice, tea, brown sugar, maraschino cherries."

"I mean, in the way of booze."

"Catawba wine, rum, gin, brandy, Benedictine, rye whiskey," He held up his glass in an unspoken toast, "and, of course, some fine champagne."

I wrinkled my nose as I prepared to take a sip. To my surprise, it was delicious. "Drink up." McAllister prompted. "We have to finish that in the five days it will take us to get to France or it will go bad." As it was, McAllister had to make another batch after the second night.

Although the comforts of the Second Prize exceed those of my boat as to make Excalibur's amenities seem almost non-existent, I missed the fellowship and familiarity that passengers and crew shared aboard McAllister's old ship, which was the Excalibur. While McAllister had introduced me to the captain, a serious looking Swede with a no nonsense attitude and a penchant for smartly pressed and tailored uniforms, I had yet to learn anyone else's name by any means other than overhearing random exchanges between the remaining six crew members, two security agents, the cook, and the combination serving girl/maid. I wondered if McAllister had lost some of his personable traits when he came into all of his money. It was hard to picture him as a snob, but the gulf between employer and the hired hand was obviously wide and seldom breeched.

When I commented about the security force being no more than two beefy guys who spent all their time on the bow lifting weights and working out, McAllister told me that the remainder of his personal legion was flying over after escorting the twins along with his oldest daughter, Jennean and two granddaughters, Ashley and Savanna to the twin's grandfather's ranch in Venezuela, where they would be spending the summer.

Shortly after noon on the fourth day, the ship's horn brought us all to the bridge for our first glimpse of land since leaving the Georgia coast. During dinner, the Second Prize dropped anchor among a dozen other ships at the mouth of the Seine River and Captain Olson approached our table in the lounge formally and apologetically.

"We must anchor here for the night." He said, standing at attention with his cap under his arm. "It is difficult and dangerous to attempt to navigate the river by night. Additionally, because of a variety of restrictions within the city limits of Paris, I believe we will only be allowed as far as the commercial port on the north west side of the City."

McAllister didn't even look at the captain. "Fine." He said, finishing his glass of punch that packed a punch. "Have Mark see me first thing in the morning." From my strictly professional habit of eavesdropping, I knew that Mark was one of the linebackers who used the bow area as a personal training gym.

Long after everyone had retired for the night, I sat next to the fantail bar, staring at the west coast of France, wondering how I was going to orchestrate a scenario that would keep our little group from harm while satisfying McAllister's need to throw a wrench into the Russian Police's plot to bring the art world to its knees. The more I thought about it, the more convinced I became I would pull this off while, at the same time, enjoying a long overdue vacation. Should we actually come across anything that might be considered evidence, we could always be on the next Concorde back to the States to show our findings to anyone who would listen, although I was certain that McAllister would not go along with that idea. Even if he did, I thought about the amount of collective credibility a former treasure hunter and a, primarily, writer of fiction novels would have on the listening ear of a six-dollar-an-hour receptionist at the State Department or someone trained to be patient with crackpots at the C.I.A. I felt we could probably start a letter writ-campaign that would bring minimal attention to us while sending collectors scurrying to the experts to have their works re-authenticated. I didn't think even McAllister would enjoy settling his beef with the K.G.B in some kind of World Court, so I felt it essential to use whatever means short of what McAllister would consider subterfuge or the under-minding of his plans, to keep our little vigilante investigation low key and relatively ineffective. After all, even if we stumbled into something concrete, it would probably have little impact on world affairs. While there was no doubt that McAllister enjoyed being a recognized and often controversial leader in any of his undertakings, I didn't expect our seemingly innocent foray into France to cause any escalation of diplomatic tensions or threaten the peace between Superpowers.

"Is this a private party?"

I practically jumped out of my skin.

"Sally!" I took a deep breath, trying to get my heartbeat back to normal. "Are you trying to get me to jump overboard?"

She ran a gentle hand across my shoulders. "I just wanted to thank you again for inviting me along for the most exciting time I've ever had in my life."

She had said the same thing when we had returned to Payson from Savannah.

"You haven't seen anything yet." After I said that, I realized how clichéd and mundane it sounded.

"Oh, I know." She said, clasping her hands together and looking to the stars. "I just can't get over the fact that this time tomorrow, I'll be in Paris. I thought this kind of thing only happened in the movies. Or in your books."

I smiled. It made me feel ten feet tall to be able to be responsible for giving such great pleasure to someone who had never expected anything from me other than a weekly paycheck. Sally certainly wasn't in the same class as Larkin, in fact, I couldn't think of anyone that was. But where she lacked Larkin's looks, charm, education, or sophistication, she was still attractive, lively, and very good company. I was glad she had come along.

She poured the last of the Artillery Punch into a couple of mugs and we sat on the stern of McAllister's luxurious yacht, enjoying the night air and the stars.

* * * * *

McAllister allowed us to sleep in until after ten, a concession both rare and appreciated. When he finally could contain himself no longer, he banged on the door and announced: "A strategy meeting in the lounge in ten minutes." Dutifully, I made the assignment in just under nine, and without preamble or an offer of coffee, he began telling me the reasons for my summons.

"Captain Olsen was right." He said. "We can't go any further than the public docks at some place I can't pronounce." He looked at a piece of paper and immediately dismissed it as unimportant. "We hired a car to meet us at the marina and we have reservations at the Meurice on the Rue de Rivoli. It's close to the Le Centre Pompidou thing where we're supposed to meet with this Wilson guy this afternoon, but I don't think we are going to have much time for lunch. We'll have to find a McDonalds. They do have them over here, don't they?" He smiled.

Great. I was in the culinary capital of the world and for the last week I had been experiencing epicurean fantasies and gastronomic dreams and my first meal in the home of such names as Lasserre, Maxim's, and La Bourogne was going to be in a fast food restaurant whose roots were in Des Plaines, Illinois.

The location of the Meurice couldn't have been more convenient. Although we were across the river and some distance from Paris' most famous landmark, we were within walking distance of the Palasis Grand and Petit, the Place de la Concorde, the Louvre, and the beautiful gardens of Jardin des Tuileries. The hotel was of refined Louis XV and XVI with especially nice suites and was the home to the world renowned Pompadour tearoom and Le Meurice restaurant, two amenities that would have to wait for my personal scrutiny.

The door had barely closed behind the bellhop when McAllister had us out of the room and back in the car. Forgetting his promise of a Happy Meal, he ordered the driver to Le Centre Pompidou in French that sounded like sandpaper against a rock.

Le Centre National d'Art et de Culture Georges Pompidou is known locally as the Beaubourg, after the plateau on which it is built. It is six stories of glass and steel with exterior escalators and pipes painted in bright blue, white, and red. It is a tremendously popular museum that brings together all the contemporary art forms; paintings, sculpture, plastic arts, industrial design, music, literature, and even cinema and theatre. Not only are the exhibits inside interesting and absorbing, the courtyard is a gathering place for jugglers, acrobats, mimes, and magicians, their impromptu shows garnering as much attention as the museum itself.

We entered through the Rue Rambuteau and Rue St. Martin entrance and asked for directions to Anthony Wilson's office. Instead, the girl pushed a button on the console in front of her and asked us to wait. In less than two minutes a short man, but the perfect weight for his height, approached us with his hand extended. In perfect, unaccented English, he introduced himself as the man we were scheduled to meet. Young looking for a World War II veteran, Wilson dressed for comfort and had a spring in his step that matched the twinkle in his eye. After introductions were made, the ladies politely excused themselves and Wilson led us toward an elevator.

"You know," McAllister began conversationally, "Thomas Jefferson once said that every man has two countries; his own and France."

Wilson had heard the quote before. "That would leave me with only one." He replied.

Much to Wilson's delight and my surprise, McAllister actually blushed.

Wilson led us to a fifth floor office that overlooked the courtyard and I used the time it took to get there to question his unusual surname for a Frenchman.

"My father was an Englishman." He explained. "A correspondent during World War I who settled in Paris after the conflict and married a local girl. I was educated in England and did a five year internship at the

Field Museum in Chicago. When I returned to Paris, I worked as both apprentice and journeyman at the Archaeological Crypt of Notre Dame and moved to the Musee Marmottan in the late 70's. After the great robbery in 1985 when several superb Monets were stolen and never recovered, I came to Le Centre and have been here ever since."

"From natural history to archaeology to Monet to contemporary art." I observed. "When did you have time to get interested in Faberge?" "Like most people, I found that hobbies and work don't mix." He said. "Do you play golf?" I nodded. "And how many books have you written about golf?"

"None." I admitted. "You make a good point."

"My father's uncle was a salesman for Faberge before the revolution. He was even a pall bearer at the master's funeral when he died in Switzerland less than four months after the British Embassy helped him escape from Russia. My great uncle says he died of a broken heart however he was seventy-four and in poor health for many years. Faberge had two sons, Alexander and Eugene, who opened Faberge and Cie, in Paris shortly after their father's death and my relative worked for them until they sold the business in 1932."

"And today they sell perfume instead of jewelry." McAllister observed.

"Actually, no." Wilson corrected. "Faberge and Cie still exist as a jeweler, but no longer have any connection with the family. An American, Sam Rubin, was responsible for the toiletries and perfumes and the Paris firm spent six years, between 1945 and 1951, in litigation against Rubin for using the name. It was finally settled when Rubin paid twenty-five thousand dollars for the rights to use the name as long as he restricted the use of the name to cosmetics."

We had reached his office, done in Danish Modern, and made ourselves comfortable while Wilson graciously ordered soft drinks for us. When his secretary left after serving us, he continued.

"Carl Faberge has two grandsons. Igor designed pieces for the Franklin Mint in the United States until his death in 1982 and Theodore still designs and produces objects for a private concern in London."

"So your great uncle worked at the shops in three different countries?" I thought I was making a clarification but it came out as a question.

"Far more than that." He replied, knowing he was going to impress us with his answer. "My great uncle Lucas was not just a clerk in a retail store. He traveled to the Courts of the Royal Families of Denmark, Britain, Greece, and even Bangkok. Some of his customers were Queen Alexandra of Great Britain, Consuelo Vanderbilt, who became the Duchess of Marlborough, Leopold de Rothschild, Napoleon 111's wife Empress Eugenie, King Manuel of Portugal, Prince Aga Khan, King Ferdinand of Bulgaria, and King Chulalongkorn of Siam.

"'Plain old, Lucas Wilson' was welcomed in those palaces and royal residences as an equal, with almost dignitary status. The rich and titled from around the world looked forward to the day when the Faberge salesman knocked on the door."

"So why are we here?" I asked, testing his credentials. "Why don't we look up Theodore Faberge and get his views on the questions we have?"

Wilson leaned back and folded his hands over his mid-section the way a much heavier man might do. He wasn't insulted by the question, but he was bored with having to answer it yet again.

"Although I sincerely believe Theodore Faberge is an honest and hard-working man, I also believe I have forgotten far more about his grandfather's art than he will ever have the opportunity to learn. I have devoted a lifetime to the study of Carl Faberge and it is me that the other experts and collectors call when they want an opinion."

"Then you can evaluate my collection." McAllister suggested. Wilson smiled patiently. "And just what do you consider 'a collection', Mister McAllister?"

"I have a total of nine eggs."

The little curator's expression changed appreciatively. "Nine, you say." He said, showing new respect for his visitor. "How many Imperials?"

"Imperials?"

The patient look returned. "Easter eggs have been a long established tradition in Eastern Europe. Long before Faberge's time, eggs of precious materials had been made for Tsars and Tsarinas including Alexander II and Catherine The Great.

"Faberge didn't invent the art, he refined it. Tsarina Marie Feodorovna was the first to receive one of the newly defined eggs in 1885. In all, fifty-four eggs were presented to the last of two Tsarinas and their families. The whereabouts of forty-five are known, two others survive in original photographs, and the remaining seven are a mystery.

"I would love to view your collection," he continued with new respect, "but to travel to America at this time would be terribly inconvenient."

"No problem." McAllister said casually. "I brought them with me."

I shouldn't have been surprised, but I was.

So was Anthony Wilson.

"Here?" He asked, unable to believe his ears. "In Paris?"

"Sure." McAllister answered as if carrying around art treasures were an everyday occurrence. "They're on my boat." He tried again to pronounce the name of the marina.

"I would welcome the opportunity to see this accumulation of prized possessions." Had the truth be known, Wilson probably would have traded the Eiffel Tower to see the collection, but he hid his enthusiasm well.

"How about tonight?" McAllister suggested.

"Would nine o'clock be acceptable?" Wilson asked.

"Sure."

Wilson reached for a pad on his desk. "What was the name of that marina?"

When McAllister attempted to pronounce it, Wilson winced.

The ladies had enjoyed the museum, but I could tell that Larkin would have preferred to tour the more traditional sights. Sally was happy to be anywhere other than behind the bar in rural Arizona and sat in the rented car's jump seat, trying to see everything at once, not unlike a kid at Disneyland.

"We haven't eaten." McAllister remembered. "Do you guys want to pick up some take out on the way back to the hotel?"

We groaned in unison and Larkin hit her husband on the arm with her museum guidebook.

Since we were not dressed for Maxim's or Le Grand Vefour, we stopped on Av. F. D. Roosevelt at Lasserre, which is probably just as sumptuous, but certainly less stuffy. It was too early to watch the ceiling which opens periodically to reveal the nighttime sky, but we ordered from the popular classic menu and dined from plates that were rimmed in gold on meals that were garnished extravagantly and prepared to absolute perfection.

The only thing that marred the otherwise flawless meal was a slight undercurrent of tension between the McAllisters. It must have come from some unspoken understanding that I was not privileged to know because, when Larkin caught the puzzled expression I was wearing, she attempted to lighten the mood with some trivial remark.

Sally interrupted my thoughts by asking if we could stop on the way back to the boat for a view of the city of lights from the Eiffel Tower. We unanimously agreed that it was the perfect evening to satisfy such a simple request.

It is difficult to imagine Paris without the "temporary" symbol of the Universal Exposition of 1889 coming to mind. Often described as Gustav Eiffel's Folly, the tower was scheduled to be torn down in 1909, but again became useful with the advent of the first transatlantic wireless telephones.

We were all glad we had made the slight detour. From a platform high above the noise of the city, we were treated to a bird's eye view of one of the most material minded capitals of Europe. To the north was the Arc de Triomphe, with its twelve thoroughfares radiating away like the spokes of a wheel. To the southwest was the golden dome of Les Invalides, the Louis XIV refuge for disabled soldiers. Over ten miles of corridors laced through the complex which included the impressive tomb of Napoleon as well as one of the richest museums in the world that, quite naturally, specialized in arms, armor, and French military history. Eastward, past the palaces and the Louvre, the 225 foot towers of the Cathedral of Notre Dame, stood next to the Palasis de Justice and Sainte-Chapelle on the tiny island of Lie de la Cite in the middle of the Seine.

When it was time to return to the Second Prize for our meeting with Wilson, Sally was reluctant to leave and those of us who were better traveled knew the emotions she was feeling. From high upon the tower, it was impossible to imagine the sins of Les Halles, the erotic and almost pornographic theaters in the Rue Saint-Denis, the increasing crime in the streets, and the haughtiest of the citizens. Only the polished jewelry sparkled from our vantage point high above the city and it was difficult to tear oneself away from such a grand illusion. When we arrived back at the marina, Sally was still breathless with the excitement of the day.

"If I didn't live to see another day, I would die happy tonight." She said as we walked along the luxury yachts of the boat hotel. We smiled at her simple and honest naiveté, never recognizing the prophetic quality of such an innocent statement.

* * * * *

CHAPTER THREE

After McAllister instructed his security force to expect our art expert's arrival, we retired to the ship's lounge where Larkin began to fix us drinks. McAllister busied himself with a complicated looking task of removing a floorboard in a corner of the lounge and when he finally lifted the three by three section of decking, he revealed a safe tucked neatly into the space beneath the floor.

"It's not Fort Knox," He said as he twisted the combination dial, "but it's waterproof and fireproof. If this tub ever went down like the Hacha did, I don't want to have to spend a couple of days trying to free this safe. If any would-be crook made it this far, past me and my security, it would probably mean I was in no position to care about this stuff anyway." He shrugged fatalistically. "Give me a hand with these, will you, Grange?"

He began passing aluminum attaché cases of the type used by photographers to protect fragile equipment, except that they all had combination locks. There were eight cases in all, but he removed only six.

"The combination is my son's I.Q." He said, handing me one of the cases.

I took a chance and dialed one-six-three and hit the latches. The clamps popped up. When I looked back at McAllister, he was grinning like a Cheshire.

Although I had seen the objects before, they were even more impressive nestled in their thick foam packing, only inches from my fingers. The two in the cases I had opened where the St. George's salon and the basket of flowers. I ran a hand lightly over the fine craftsmanship and admired the pieces as if I were seeing them for the first time.

"Set them on the bar." McAllister ordered. "It's not as fancy as the gallery back home, but it will have to do."

In a matter of minutes, we had all nine eggs on the counter, mounted on their pedestals and ready for inspection.

"The replica of Spaskoie Solo belongs to Antonio." McAllister turned the little castle so it faced me and out of the corner of my eye, I caught Larkin's expression as I turned. It was the same look of concern I had noticed in the restaurant a few hours earlier.

"If there's one piece in this collection I want to be genuine, I hope it's this one." McAllister continued. "I would hate to think Antonio took a beating for some cheap imitation."

I wondered why a previous owner made so much difference in the price of an object when the materials used for a duplicate were very probably the same. I tried to imagine what could possibly entice a collector to pay thousands of dollars for a notable object, not for its material value or who created it, but it's one time owner. Then I recalled McAllister's long ago lesson he gave me concerning "intrinsic" value versus "provenance" value, when Anthony Wilson's arrival interrupted my thoughts. McAllister brought him into the salon and stood aside, giving the curator an unobstructed view of the collection. To his credit, he didn't screw a jeweler's glass into his eye socked and rush to the bar. He greeted the ladies again and shook hands with McAllister and me before he approached the counter.

He took a full thirty seconds with each piece, examining them carefully without touching them. Halfway through his inspection, he accepted a drink from Larkin but placed it on the bar untouched until he had completed what seemed to me to be a less than cursory study. After five full minutes of silence, he took a seat at the end of the bar and turned to McAllister.

"I have good news and bad news." He announced, sipping his drink for the first time. "Which do you want first?"

Uncharacteristically, McAllister was undecided. He waved a frustrated arm in the direction of his guest, indicating he was entrusting the decision to the expert.

"The good news first, then." Wilson continued. "Maybe that way you won't be tempted to shoot the messenger."

He looked back at the collection. "You appear to have seven eggs that are authentic; including one that I had no idea existed before today." He pointed to the John the Baptist egg. "Even though Easter was the reason for the manufacture of the eggs, direct reference to religion was rare. This is truly a unique find.

"The bad news is that two are counterfeit, and one of those is a very poor imitation." He picked up the Resurrection Egg. "The gold, diamonds, and pearls on this one appear to be real and this was a carefully constructed facsimile but nevertheless, it's still a mere copy.

"This," he replaced the egg he was holding and casually hefted the egg that depicted the miniature garden of lilies, "is trash. I doubt if any part of this abomination is anywhere near what could be considered authentic."

McAllister looked dumbstruck.

I took over since McAllister seemed suddenly unable to speak. "How can you tell?"

"The Resurrection Egg was presented by Tsar Alexander the Third to his wife, Tsarina Marie Feodorovna in 1889. Its present home is in the Forbes Gallery in New York City. It is one of the premier items of their collection."

"How do you know that it's still there?" I thought I was asking the obvious question.

Wilson looked at me over the rims of his half glasses he had donned for a closer look at the John the Baptist egg. His expression was tolerant but his tone was condescending. "Nothing in the Forbes Collection is for sale, Mister Lawton." He said as if I suggested melting down the Holy Grail for scrap. "Nor do I imagine anything ever will be offered to the public."

"I didn't bother to suggest that the collection might have been robbed. He would have been one of the first to know. While I was trying to think of something intelligent to say, McAllister bounced back.

"You didn't even look at them." He accused. "How could you make a judgment on such a superficial inspection?" We're not talking about produce here."

"Indeed." Wilson turned to face McAllister. "But you are forgetting why you asked me here tonight. Mister McAllister. It is because I am an expert and in such a capacity, I can tell you two things. One; you have been incredibly blessed to become the owner of seven magnificent pieces of Faberge art and two; you have been very lucky to have been burned only twice. Most amateur collectors suffer far greater losses before they think to contact an expert."

McAllister bristled at being called an amateur, but he would have taken offense at being called a rookie at anything he decided to try for the very first time. "You still haven't convinced me of anything." He argued. "How can you call something as beautiful as that, trash?" He pointed to the Garden Egg that Wilson was holding.

"The House of Faberge developed the art of enameling to the highest level ever recorded. Do you understand the process of enameling?"

McAllister hesitated and Wilson continued without waiting for an answer.

"Good. I'll review the process for everyone.

"Enameling is the fusion by heat of finely pulverized glass onto metal. The most brilliant of all techniques perfected by Faberge is its en plein, a translucent enameling over a guilloche ground. It's a smooth covering of gold or silver surfaces engraved in a variety of patterns with near transparent layers of color. As often as not, decorative embellishments are brushed on prior to final firing.

"Another example of enameling is a stained glass effect achieved by applying the powdered glass to a mica surface that is burned away when the piece is fired. This is the plique-a-jour style.

"Finally, the cloisonné method are raised metal enclosures into which are fired opaque enamels. This was a process that was more often than not, sub-contracted to Saltykov or Ruckert, and then sold in Faberge salons.

"This piece," He held up the lilied egg, "was fired in a kiln in Miss Neidermeyer's third grade art class."

I couldn't tell if McAllister's scornful look was directed at Wilson or the bogus egg.

"I see."

"But you must consider yourself fortunate, Mister McAllister." Wilson continued. It was easy for him to say. McAllister would grouse about someone having taken advantage of his kind trusting nature until his dying day.

Wilson spent another half hour extolling the authentic eggs, but McAllister wasn't listening. Even when the kindly art expert left a little before ten, it was Larking who thanked him for coming, while her husband sat at the bar, staring dejectedly at the two offending forgeries.

It was a good night to be away from McAllister, so Sally and I took advantage of Wilson's departure to make our own, preferring to stay at the hotel and be alone. We promised to meet them in the morning, a message we depended on Larking to deliver since McAllister wasn't listening.

He was even late the following morning, and when the car finally pulled up, we were already on the outside steps as Sally couldn't bear sitting in the lobby when all of France was at the door. We piled into the rear of the French equivalent of a lime, and it was impossible not to notice the aluminum case resting between McAllister's legs.

"Taking out the garbage?" I asked, pointing to the case.

McAllister prefaced his answer with a scowl. "Hardly." He said, tapping the case with his heel. "This belongs to Antonio."

I raised a questioning eyebrow.

"We're on our way to see him." I recognized the look of uneasiness between Larkin and her husband, the same look I had seen twice last night. Sally saw it too and started to say something, but a sharp glance from me stopped her before she got a word out.

Traveling southwest, it wasn't long before we passed the most magnificent and famous of all chateaux, Versailles. Louis XIV took a small chateaux formerly used by Louis III, and converted it into his personal tribute to excessiveness. With vast and intricate formal gardens designed by Le Notre and over six hundred fountains for which an entire river had to be diverted, the grounds covered well over two hundred fifty acres. At one time, the palace housed over six thousand people with a court that numbered over twenty thousand. Also on the grounds are Louis XIV's smaller palace, Grand Trianon, and the Petit Trianon, a particular favorite of Marie-Antoinette who also liked Le Hameau, a model farm where she and her friends played at being peasants. With the Hall Of Mirrors, the Royal Apartments, and the Chapel, the complex is so large; it even has its own tourist office. I could see the longing in Sally's eyes and admit to a desire to tour the grounds myself, so I patted her knee and mouthed the word 'tomorrow' as the perfectly manicured grounds slipped past the windows of the speeding car.

Thirty minutes later, we came to the outskirts of Chartres, where the medieval cathedrals reflected the midday sun off stained glass that the town is famous for. In the center of the city that looked as though nothing had been built since the time of the Bourbon Kings, we turned east into the countryside of Napoleon's Renaissance palace, however. With so much to see and without so much as slowing down, I might have joined Sally in demanding we stop to see the sights.

Less than five minutes out of Chartres, we turned onto a gravel drive and approached a centuries old farmhouse, meticulously kept up and modernized since its original construction, probably sometime in the seventeenth century. I was glad the drive was finally over. The constantly mounting tension in the car was something that was making a beautiful drive in the country, a labor of patience that would have tested the saints that came from this very area.

No one greeted us, so, after a slight hesitation during which McAllister and Larkin exchanged one more look between them, McAllister banged on the heavy oak door. It was just as he was about to try again when he heard the lock turning from inside. The weighty door swung inward and Antonio Tumbas blinked in the bright light.

"I might have known." He said his tone unfriendly and disgusted. "Not only my sister and her loving husband, but the world famous 'fictitious' fiction writer who glorified all of my dear brother-in-law's heroic efforts. Who's the dame?"

It was barely eleven o'clock and Antonio was already drunk. Nevertheless, I attempted a diplomatic approach.

"Sally, I stepped back to give Antonio a better look, "meet Antonio Tumbas, Larkin's brother and Bobby's brother-in-law. Antonio, Sally is a friend of mine from Payson.

"Payson? Where the hell is Payson?"

"Arizona, USA."

"Oh." Antonio said, stopping short of saying something else, but changed his mind. Instead, he nudged the door open all the way and turned to lead us down a corridor. In a dimly lit living room, he motioned us to be seated as he took a chair next to a small occasional table that held a half empty bottle of scotch and a glass. He grabbed the bottle and waved it, silently asking if anyone cared for a drink. We all declined, but McAllister made the first mistake of the visit.

"Don't you think it's a little early for that drink, Antonio?"

Antonio stopped midway in raising his glass to drink.

"Oh, great." He said sarcastically. "Not only are you the savior of my family and my sister's knight in shining armor, now you're the Bourbon police."

I wondered if he knew he had just made a pun or if he really didn't know what he was drinking.

"Back home," He continued, consulting his watch, "it's only five o'clock in the morning. "This," He held up his glass, "is still last night's party." He downed the contents in a single swallow.

I knew that relations between Antonio and his family were strained, but as yet I was not privy to the reason. With the exception of a few gray hairs at the temples, he had changed outwardly very little. When I first met him, he was the son of a gentleman cattle rancher, heir to a sizable estate, and an amiable young man who used his good looks and winning personality to his best advantage. The love and cherish he felt toward his sister had turned to a one-sided rivalry, and his bitterness and rancor reached into eyes that couldn't have been more than thirty-five years old, and looked on the world around him with scorn and distaste.

"I didn't mean anything." McAllister backtracked. "I'm sorry."

Antonio snorted.

"It's good to see you, Antonio." Larkin spoke for the first time. "It's been a long time. How are you?"

Antonio had not lost the sharp edge of his tone. "Oh, is it?" He asked. "Well, I'm just peachy." He struggled to lean forward and for the first, I noticed that his left arm hung at an awkward angle. "By rights I should be enjoying my life in my own home in South America, but instead, I'm living in exile four thousand miles away nursing this." He slapped his left shoulder with his right hand.

"Oh, knock it off." Larkin stood up and took a half step toward her brother. "Just how the hell do you expect to get any sympathy from us when you have no one to blame for your self-pitying problems but yourself.

"Nobody told you that you had to leave El Empleado. You made that decision yourself and when you left, you slithered out like some thief in the night, not telling a soul where you were going or why. As far as your present condition goes, you can't blame that on any of us. You were the victim of a crime. If you had just given your attackers what they wanted without putting up a fight, you might have use of that arm today."

"How could I stay in Ciudad Bolivar after that bastard's book came out?"

He shouted as he pointed to me. I was taken aback. I had no idea that Antonio considered me as part of his problem.

"Everyone was snickering behind my back. How two gringos saved my father and my sister while I sat in an abandoned church and sniveled, begging for my life. Everywhere I went, people were laughing at me, wondering why I hadn't acted like a man.

"You don't have to worry about anything like that." He continued as he poured himself another drink. "You have your Sir Galahad to protect you. He did a nice job of moving himself right in to take over as soon as I was gone, didn't he?"

I looked at McAllister who was carefully studying a painting on the far side of the room. It was clear that he had heard all of this before and was doing his best to avoid joining the fray.

"Don't you dare blame Bobby or Granger for your troubles." Larkin snapped. "What they did almost seven years ago was instinctive, not necessarily heroic. Your priority was keeping daddy alive and you did exactly that."

"Larkin is right." Since McAllister obviously considered the argument a hopeless cause, I decided to add my opinion. "We were six unarmed people against a paramilitary force with automatic weapons. Nobody expected you to charge into the barrel of a loaded gun."

"Shut up, ass hole!" Antonio pointed at me. "You were the one who made me look like a coward in front of everyone."

"That's not true, Antonio!" Larkin was building up some steam. "You left home a good two months before the Paradise novel even came out. And it's a good thing Bobby was there to help with Daddy in the hospital and me spending all that time with him. Why do you insist on trying to blame others for something that is the product of a self-pitying and drunken mind? Shame on you, Antonio."

With three quick steps, she covered the distance between them and knocked the bottle from the table. With surprising quickness, Antonio grabbed his sister's wrist, but with an atrophied left arm, he was able to do little more than wrench her arm. That was enough for McAllister, however. He was on his feet and in Antonio's face before much else could happen.

"Knock it off, Antonio!" He said, grabbing Antonio's wrist just below the point where he was holding Larkin. "You're way out of line now. If you ever do that again, I'll flatten you like a bug. Do you understand?"

"Sure," Antonio snarled. "Now you pick fights with someone who can't fight back."

"Well, listen to who's talking! I'll beat down any man who thinks he's tough enough to push women or children around."

"She's my sister." Antonio argued.

"Does that give you the right to hurt her? Bobby glared darts. "She's my wife!"

The three of them stood there, frozen in some bizarre pose of daring, for a full thirty seconds. Finally, Antonio lowered his eyes and his body, surrendering to McAllister's iron grip. I took a quick look at Sally who seemed somewhat surprised to have crossed the ocean and a continent only to wind up the sole unaffected witness of a rather petty, but steamy family fight. I didn't expect what happened next.

"That's it?" Sally asked, scooting to the edge of her chair. "This whole thing is about something that happened over seven years ago when you were attacked by a bunch of murderous gangsters?"

When nobody answered, she must have thought she had license to continue.

"What's the matter with you people? I've seen some real family feuds in my life, but they were over something important, not over who would be the hero or villain of a book. All of you ought to grow up. I wish I had a family I could relate to on something as petty as this. "I'd have it straightened out in a matter of minutes."

None of us answered. We were all rendered speechless at her little outburst of enlightenment. When she saw she had become the center of attention, she suddenly became very self-conscious.

"I, . . . better wait in the car." She was up and out the door before anyone recovered from her little tirade. When I heard the front door close, I broke out of my lethargic state.

"Me too." I said, rather lamely. "I mean maybe I should wait in the car too."

"No." McAllister insisted as he stepped away from Antonio. "We came here to conduct some business and you're going to sit right there until I've had my say."

Reluctantly, I sat in the indicated chair.

McAllister retrieved the case that held Antonio's egg and set it at his feet. "That's your Faberge Egg." From the look on Antonio's face, he had never been told that the real product had been sent to his family for safekeeping.

"When the auction people sent it to us, I got interested in your little acquisition and did some checking on my own. In the meantime, I got interested in the eggs myself and started my own collection."

He spent the next twenty minutes bringing Antonio up to speed on his thoughts and theories. Instead of appreciating McAllister's objectives, however, Antonio seemed to sink further into his depression. When McAllister finished his monologue, Antonio was sitting dejectedly in his chair, holding his damaged left arm with his right hand, staring at his lap.

"So, my big-brother-in-law is, once again, trying to bail his poor helpless relations out of trouble." He summarized.

"Wrong." McAllister answered. "We came here to ask you for help."

We did?

Antonio was shaking his head. "Thank you for returning my egg." He said, pointing to the case with his chin. "But I think you had better leave now."

"Yes." Larkin interjected, surprising her husband. "That might be a good idea. Why don't you two gentlemen wait for me out at the car."

McAllister started to object, but a determined look from his wife stopped him before he could say anything. We bid an unanswered goodbye to Antonio and made our way back up the corridor, glancing over our shoulders at the two siblings who were seated three feet apart, silently assessing one another.

"The arm," I asked when we were back in the car, "that was a result of the beating?"

McAllister nodded. "Don't feel sorry for him though. He's had these paranoid delusions long before someone did the nerve damage that froze up that arm. You probably noticed that he has trouble focusing his left eye too."

I had attributed the slightly off-balance look to alcohol.

"Larkin came over twice while he was in the hospital, but he refused to see her. Before that, it was literally hundreds of letters, phone calls, and invitations. We did everything to try to convince him that nothing he did that day in the chapel was wrong and anything he might have done could have gotten us all killed.

"We were lucky, you know that, Grange?" He continued, looking back at the forlorn house. "Any number of things that happened that day could have turned out a lot different for all of us. I mean, who in the world would expect Jeff Camper and Dumpster to show up when they did? Hell, I'd almost completely forgotten about my old prison pals!" McAllister shook his head in disbelief. "But you know what? Antonio doesn't buy it. All he can see is himself laying over his father, begging for a doctor. He thinks his present physical condition is God's punishment because his father will have to spend the rest of his life in a wheelchair."

"That's ridiculous."

"Not to Antonio." We joined Sally in the back seat.

"Everything work out all right?" She asked. Our expressions answered her innocent question.

McAllister continued the conversation as if Sally had been in from the beginning. It was one of his bad habits but both Sally and he knew I would bring her up to speed later. "When he got out of the hospital, he rented this place. We know that a physical therapist comes to see him three times a week but, other than that, we know very little about what he does now."

"It looks as though he sits in dark rooms trying to preserve his liver for some thirtieth century archaeologist."

Instead of taking exception, McAllister nodded sadly.

"I like Antonio." He continued. "I mean, what little I know about him, I liked a long time ago. I wish I knew what I could do to set things right."

"You can start by not beating yourself up about his situation." I said. "If he wants to turn himself in to a drunken version of Howard Hughes, there's not much you can do about it. You didn't cause any pain or injury to the Roberto Tumbas clan. You brought grandchildren to Roberto Tumbas and turned a few struggling South American ranchers into some of the richest and most influential people on the continent. That Antonio elected to take a different route is neither your fault nor your responsibility."

"But he's family." McAllister argued.

"He's your wife's family." I reminded him. "He lives the life he wants to live and when he realizes that he is acting irresponsibly, he will either change or. . ." I couldn't think of an appropriate alternative. Fortunately, Larkin picked that moment to return to the car. The regrettable part was that she was trying very hard not to cry.

We made the trip back to Paris in almost total silence.

By dinnertime everyone was in a much better mood which was a good thing because the highly recommended L'Ami Louis restaurant turned out to be one of the most aesthetically unattractive dining establishments I had ever seen, an unusual contradiction, since it was supposedly a favorite among Americans. I was glad I didn't judge this particular book by its cover, however. The selections of roast chicken, spring lamb, ham, and Burgundy wines came in huge portions and we all ate ravenously.

McAllister's after dinner concession to me was a trip to Harry's Bar where the son of the original Harry greeted us warmly, the same way his father might have greeted Ernest Hemingway, Gertrude Stein, and George Gershwin. Among the university flags and banners that decorated the paneled walls, we faced each other across a table and two glasses of some local overpriced wine while the ladies made a trip to the powder room.

"Now what?" I asked.

McAllister looked confused.

"We didn't spend four days crossing an ocean to get your goodies appraised and visit your brother-in-law." I elaborated. "As far as I can tell, we have pretty much wasted the last couple of days. At least we haven't accomplished anything that could remotely be considered a crushing blow against Communistic tyranny. We should be gathering information and documentation, not trotting all over the globe with no real purpose."

"Everything I do has purpose, Grange."

Here we go again, I thought.

"I thought it might serve a purpose to talk to this Wilson guy to see what we can learn. I take it you don't think we are headed in the right direction."

"We could have authenticated your eggs without leaving your fancy gallery in Savannah." I told him. "You told me that Wilson was one of the believers in your theory, but you didn't say a word to him when he told you that you had two forgeries. I thought our job was to assemble evidence of a conspiracy. So far, all we've done is take a cruise and do some sightseeing."

"Well, Grange." McAllister smiled. "There are a lotta' sights to see here," 'wouldn't' you say?"

"Yeah, but. . ."

McAllister cut me off. "What do you suggest, Grange?"

I wasn't prepared for his question.

"Wilson said the Resurrection Egg was a good copy."

"Yeah, so?"

"He very well might have an idea who made it. Like anything else, the art community is a pretty specialized and close knit community. These people know, or at least have their suspicions, about who is capable of creating a facsimile or, for that matter, may have an idea who some inept forger might be."

"I don't think the forger is all that inept."

"Maybe not. But that's beside the point. I think you should lay your cards on Wilson's table and establish an ally."

"The last time I followed that advice, Grange, Larkin's father laughed me out of his home."

"That may be true, Bobby, but you do come up with some wild cards." McAllister half smiled, half laughed at that remark. I continued. "If Wilson doesn't want to be a part of your expose' or whatever your mission is, he can at least point you in the right direction. As of now, you know nothing more than you did six months ago. I know you hate having been sold a wooden nickel, but without knowledgeable assistance, you aren't going to get further than you are now. When you said you were looking for some phantom treasure ship, you went to the maritime archives in Spain. In this case, Wilson is your first available archive, only in human form. You can't walk down the Champs-Elysees expecting information to fall in your lap."

"Involving Wilson might place him in danger." McAllister answered. "After all, look what happened to Antonio."

"Antonio got mugged because his attackers thought he was carrying a priceless art treasure in the dock area of Monaco. His attackers have yet to be apprehended and therefore, could have been anyone from street punks to professional career criminals."

"Or the KGB."

"What am I going to do with you, Bobby?" I said on the edge of exasperation. "Give me a break. We don't know that!" I insisted. I know that there is an element of the crime world that specializes in reading obituaries for the sole purpose of burglarizing homes while the bereaved family is at the funeral. There well could be an underworld facet that doesn't know that standard procedures at art auctions is to arrange for secured delivery rather than allow a patron to walk out of the door with a small fortune under his arm.

"According to you, Anthony Wilson has made a study of Faberge art forgery since World War II. Since no overt action has been taken against him in over fifty years, it's highly unlikely that he would be in any additional danger because he expresses opinions he has been formulating for over half a century.

"The bottom line is, we can't continue to walk around in circles. The entire art world is not going to hold its collective breath while we stumble around in the dark. The Maltese Falcon didn't build a nest in Sidney Greenstreet's shorts."

McAllister tapped his fingertips on the table. I knew what he was thinking.

"You can't have this one entirely to yourself." Seeing his own name in print was like an aphrodisiac to McAllister. Having to share the limelight with someone, however remotely, was something that grated on his nerves like coarse sandpaper on his tongue. In fact, it was unheard of. "Look at it this way. Even Don Quixote had his sidekick, Sancho Panza."

"That was a job I had earmarked for you, Grange."

He was also good at laying on the humbug. I started to reply, but the ladies took that moment to return.

"Can we really tour the palace at Versailles tomorrow?" Sally reminded me of my earlier promise.

I had my mouth open to reply when McAllister interrupted, apparently coming to a decision at the same time.

"Grange and I have another appointment with Anthony Wilson tomorrow afternoon." I'll arrange for you girls to go out on the train tomorrow morning as soon as I can arrange for an escort for the two of you."

"We don't need an es . . ." Sally began, but I placed a hand on her arm to quieten her. Picking up my message quickly, she continued, "An escort will be fine, Bobby. Thank you so much."

Larkin smiled but made no comment.

That was enough good news for Sally anyway, and she showed her appreciation to me that night back at the hotel. McAllister had to collect his own reward which I'm sure he did. When in France . . .

In spite of being up, – – – well, awake – – – late the night before, Sally had been ready for an hour when the phone summoned her to the lobby at seven thirty. I slept in for another three hours until McAllister called to inform me that he had arranged for further discussion with Anthony Wilson at one thirty. He graciously informed me that I was free to tour the sights alone until then. I went back to sleep.

Since we already knew the way to his office, we didn't stop at the information kiosk but straight to the elevator. Wilson was waiting for us with a patient but quizzical expression on his face.

Once in the office, McAllister wasted no time in coming to the point, succinctly stating our mission in what sounded like a prepared speech that took less than five minutes. Wilson listened intently and when McAllister had finished, went to open a wall safe behind a picture behind his desk. He returned with a file the same thickness as a phone book and pushed it across the surface, but didn't remove his hand from the stack of papers.

"That file represents thirty-five years of my attempts to document Faberge forgeries." He said. "It also contains copies of correspondence I've had with the governments of six countries, including the former Soviet Union, as well as their replies, all of which call my theories unfounded."

He leaned forward and tapped the file. "You're welcome to everything in that file, Mister McAllister, if you answer one rather delicate question."

McAllister raised his eyebrows.

"One of the eggs in your collection, one of the authentic pieces, does not legitimately belong to you. Its ownership has been documented by someone who, to the best of my knowledge, has a vested interest in the work. Would you care to explain how it came to be in your possession?"

McAllister had an aversion to being accused of improprieties, which was odd for one that has been accused of many. He suppressed a natural tendency to become indignant and defensive, but though I thought I already knew the answer to Wilson's frank reasonable inquiry .

"The Spaskoie Egg was being held in trust." I said, sensing an outburst from McAllister. "In fact, it was returned to its rightful owner just yesterday."

Realization dawned on McAllister. "He's right." He said. Antonio Tumbas is my brother-in-law."

Wilson let that revelation sink in slowly; digesting the new input like a teacher who had just been told that homework had been eaten by the dog.

"Thank you, Mister McAllister. That is very satisfactory." He pronounced, still looking for a hint of a lie. "The man who was probably responsible for your resurrection Egg is Dorn Kublec. He did most of his work in the late sixties and claims today to be 'reformed.'" His expression said that wasn't a tune Wilson intended to dance to. He lives in Westerham, Great Britain where he lives comfortably in spite of the fact that he hasn't worked an honest day's labor since his parole."

"You think he will help us?" McAllister asked.

"Undoubtedly." Wilson answered. "However, the real question is whether he can. He's a very old man now and I believe he tends to embellish stories of his past with a thick sprinkling of fiction."

"What's wrong with that?" McAllister muttered.

"Any hints on how we can effectively deal with him?" I asked, ignoring McAllister's question.

"Appeal to him as an artist." Wilson's sardonic expression indicated his distaste. "Like anyone who believes he is creative, his ego is his most vulnerable spot. If you go there expecting to confront a criminal or ex-con, you won't get the correct time of day."

"What about the other egg?" McAllister asked.

Wilson stared at him smugly, "Go to Taiwan," he suggested, "or any other place that makes those gift shop models of the Eiffel Tower or the Statue of Liberty. In my opinion, it is a lead that is not worth following."

McAllister grumbled, "That bad?"

"I'm afraid so."

It was a six block walk from the Centre Georges Pompidou to the Louvre, a trip I didn't realize we were making until we stood before the new and highly controversial glass pyramid entranceway. The Louvre became a museum in 1793 and since then has become one of the most recognizable art repositories in the world. In addition to its more famous residents like Venus de Milo, Winged Victory, and the Mona Lisa, are the French Crown jewels and two hundred thousand significant pieces in six different collections. Quite naturally, McAllister was interested in Faberge items and he thumbed through a thick guide book, all the while complaining that there was no index to make his task easier. While he stood in the middle of the Cour Carree, the old courtyard of the Louvre that dated from 1550 and the oldest part of the palace, I found a uniformed tour guide and asked directions to any display that might have interested McAllister. She kindly directed us to one of the newer wings near the Arc de Triomphe du Carrousel and I had to urge McAllister by tugging on a shirt sleeve forcing him to follow me rather uncertainly.

Up a short flight of stairs we found in a small room off a gallery, a display of Faberge art. Regrettably, the collection contained no eggs and McAllister's interest waned almost as soon as he entered the room. Still, there was an interesting collection of cigarette cases, picture frames, feathered fans, cuff-links, cane and parasol handles, and two beautiful mantle clocks.

My visit to the home of French kings pre-dating Louis XIV was short lived as McAllister's patience wore thin and he insisted on leaving. He was clearly depressed but very thoughtful, telling me we would make our future plans at dinner as we separated in the hotel lobby. I had just fallen into a comfortable chair next to the window overlooking the Rue de Revoli when a knock at the door startled me.

My last little adventure with McAllister left me very wary of opening doors without knowing who was on the other side and the Meurice had no peepholes, so I called through the door, excusing my rudeness as on balance with my unknown visitor's lack of foresight to call from the lobby. I was answered by Antonio Tumbas.

"Bobby and Larkin are in the other room." I told him when I had swung open the door. McAllister had rented both rooms in his name, but anything else than a suite would have been unacceptable to him. I actually preferred the smaller, more traditional sized room.

"I came to talk with you." He answered. He was slightly sullen but sober so I stood aside to allow him into the room.

"What's Bobby got you writing about this time, Mister Lawton?" He asked without preamble and rather stiffly. We had never established a close relationship but we had certainly been on a less formal basis than he was affecting now. I decided to answer him honestly and openly.

"Nothing, really." I answered truthfully, smiling to show my sincerity. "I'm just along for the ride on this one."

"You had a hell of a ride on the last one, as I remember. In fact, that little ride was taken at my expense. He paused to study me skeptically. "You're telling me that you haven't already depicted me as some self-effacing drunken cripple, hiding out in a remote farmhouse, friendless and afraid to face my family?" I sighed theatrically. "What do you want from me, Antonio?" I matched his tone and rigid demeanor. "I'm not going to take any position in a one-sided misunderstanding between you and your family."

"You wrote that damned book!" It was an accusation.

"Tell me one thing in that entire novel that wasn't fact." I challenged, trying to raise my voice. "Just because you didn't ride off into the sunset with a beautiful woman and an orchestra playing in the background is no reason to turn your back on your family. You've managed to convince yourself that you're a martyr, but the set of circumstances surrounding that unfortunate time in our life still made you a very wealthy man."

"I suppose it put you in a state of penury?! You didn't even have to write that damned book, Mister Lawton!"

"Why is it Mister Lawton all of a sudden, Antonio?"

He didn't answer.

"It's what I was hired to do, dammit!" I was getting a little agitated. "You can't expect me to apologize for a book that sold over a million copies in hard back alone. Besides, nobody even believes that story anyway. Even though it's an accurate depiction, most retailers have it on their fiction shelves."

"It's made my life hell." He said still feeling sorry for himself but at least he was no longer yelling or combative. "You have to make things right."

"You want me to re-write an already published novel?" I asked incredulously.

"No, no." He shook his head. "Of course not. I just want to be treated more fairly in whatever project you're working on now."

I groaned. "Antonio," I pleaded to be understood. "Nothing is going on here. The most writing I'm going to do on this project is on the back of a couple of postcards. There is nothing we are doing here that would make good reading."

"You don't think this is worth mentioning?" He pointed to his limp limb.

"Unfortunate, yes." I answered. "Interesting enough to write a book about, no. I can't re-write the past, nor can I predict the future. I am truly sorry about your regrettable incident, but it's nothing to write home about, much less, write a book about."

"One incident?" It was Antonio's turn to act surprised. "This story is just as real as McAllister's story."

I thought about what Antonio was telling me. I was reasonably sure that any story involving McAllister's errant exploits would eventually involve mystery, suspense, danger, and Antonio was probably more correct than he realized, especially under the circumstances that brought us here, but still. . .

"I think you should talk to Bobby." I said, hoping McAllister would be able to snuff Antonio's fuse. "He can set you straight."

"I'm sure he thinks he can." Antonio replied sarcastically.

"Antonio." I stared at him shaking my head. "Why are you so down on Bobby? He's done nothing but help you, dammit!"

"Oh, nothing. Mister . . ., excuse me, Grange, nothing at all."

"Then talk to him. He's not your damned enemy. He's your brother-in-law and your friend."

"Oh, I intend to talk to him." He responded confidently. "After all, he did come to France to enlist my help, didn't he?"

I held my breath. I guessed it was about time for honesty to take a flying leap off of the tallest landmark in Paris. Since I didn't want to run this particular play as a naked end around, I was happy to pitch the ball to McAllister.

"Good idea." I said, leading him to the door. "You talk to Bobby and we can re-hash this again after dinner."

"All I ask is a chance to prove I'm more of a man that you or Bobby thinks." Antonio pleaded like an adolescent.

After he departed, I needed a drink or an aspirin. The aspirin was closer. I didn't want to argue with Antonio about who was depicted to be a good guy or bad guy, or competent or incompetent in the book. I wrote the truth. I didn't make myself the hero because I simply wasn't. I told the truth according to my notes and memory regardless of how much of a doubting, blundering, less than brave character I depicted myself to be. It was the truth, and there was no doubt as to whose dream we were in pursuit of, and whose dream was realized. It was McAllister's tenacity that placed him in the arms of his dreams, both in flesh, and tangible treasure. I went along for the ride of my life. It was as simple as that. I think.

That Antonio did, in fact, go to see McAllister was confirmed by the fact that he met the four of us in the lobby of the Meurice to join us for dinner at Le Traillevent. McAllister must have greased a few palms to get us in to a dining establishment that normally required at least sixty-days advance reservations, but I considered it well worth his effort. Sally ordered the seafood sausage while I preferred the duck in cider and we traded bites of Alsatian pear and cinnamon chocolate soufflé for desert. The only thing that marred the cuisine classique was the table conversation. Sally wanted to talk about her tour of Versailles while Larkin was divided between the expedition to the Sun King's home and her good spirits and optimism at having her prodigal brother returned. Although McAllister was also thankful for his brother-in-law's change of heart, he was clearly agitated with Antonio's monopolization of talk of how we should proceed in our egg investigation. Hampered by the use of only one arm and trying to control the dialogue, we were well into our second hour at the table when Antonio finally wound down – He had used all of the charm and diplomacy I had remembered from our first meeting years ago, trying to convince McAllister that the obvious starting point in our quest was to find the men who attacked him in Monte Carlo and force them to confess their involvement. To my horror, McAllister appeared to agree with everything Antonio suggested.

Back at the Meurice's dimly lighted and intimate lounge, Antonio hesitated before ordering bottled water while the rest of us excluding McAllister, who shared Antonio's water, enjoyed an after dinner drink. Antonio acknowledged McAllister's gesture of abstinence by offering a two word toast. "Salud, Bobby." We all joined Antonio's toast.

"Salud, Antonio." McAllister replied in kind. After downing his glass of expensive bottled water, he addressed Antonio. "Grange was right, Antonio." He began. "He's not here to write a book, he's here as a friend. I've got to be honest with you, whether you like it or not. He's here to help me find the assholes that attacked you in Monte Carlo." That caught our attention. "Although, I promised that at the first sign of trouble or danger to any one of us, I'd abandon this project like a snagged eel from the Orinoco River. But, if we go looking for the guys that did the job on you, we go looking for trouble. And, if by some miracle, we find them, I'm afraid that all we find is hired help. It will give us some perverted sense of satisfaction, but I'm sure it will be the same as cutting the tail off the lizard. It just grows a new one. We have to establish a definitive line of which we will not cross over. I'm afraid, Antonio, that that will be very difficult to do."

Antonio looked distastefully at his water.

"You said you wanted my help, Bobby."

"We . . . I do." McAllister was choosing his words carefully. "But I have no way to turn you into a hero, and I'll be damned if I'll let you be a martyr. You've suffered enough already."

Antonio slammed his hand on the table, upsetting a couple of the drinks and drawing the attention of the other late night drinkers.

"I'm not a helpless kid, Bobby. Let me be the judge of how much I can suffer. You come to France with a bag full of good intentions and a search that will make you even more celebrated and illustrious." He was angry, but he was regaining his composure. "But you refuse to allow me any dignity. You continue to treat me as if you expect me to behave like a coward. Now you want to use me as your personal lackey."

"Antonio!" Larkin was tired of listening to her brother riding his emotional roller coaster, and cast baseless aspersions at her husband. "You know we have all the hired help we need. If we wanted an errand boy, all we would have to do is place an ad."

"You can't possibly think I would believe such rubbish." Antonio addressed his sister. "I know that husband of yours and I know how he likes the lime light. If there's profit to be had or a front page headline to be written, he demands full billing. That's what rings his bell. One minute he tells me he wants my help and the next; he wants me safely tucked away in the shadows."

"And you and Bobby think that by finding the two thugs that beat me up, you can win back the respect you think you lost in Ciudad Bolivar, and Bobby can satisfy his perceived macho image?" Larkin was now looking at her brother and her husband as if she had just scolded two children. All she knew for sure was that none of this made any sense to her delicate balance of things. Larkin was speaking her mind but seemed somewhat astonished by what she was saying.

"Wait a second." I should not have interfered, but I felt justified since Antonio did consider me to be part of his problem. "Maybe we do have a story here, Antonio." As long as I had thrown honesty off the top of the Eiffel Tower, integrity might as well take the leap too. McAllister looked at me as if I had just walked on water.

"I don't know why I didn't seriously consider this before." I lied.

"Yeah, well, we don't have time to write another book." McAllister stared at me. "We might not want to document this adventure."

We? I thought.

"A writer must write." Sally said, smiling.

"Maybe so, but that may not be the right thing to do now." Said McAllister, also smiling as he continued the word play.

"You just don't want to give me an opportunity to redeem myself from the last slanderous book Grange wrote, making me look like a coward idiot!" Exclaimed Antonio.

"You're talking about righting a wrong?" McAllister asked Antonio sarcastically.

"Bobby." Said Larkin, placing her hand on her husband's arm. "You people are sounding like a bad skit from Saturday Night Live."

McAllister looked a little embarrassed. "You're right, Larkin." Then to Grange, "Write a book if you like."

"Great! Bobby." Antonio's mood took an instant upward turn. He turned to me and said enthusiastically, "Now you're on the right track. After all, you never thought you had a book before with Bobby's story until you were totally involved."

He was right, but he was a little off his mark.

"In that case, we can start right away." Antonio continued, suddenly not caring that he was drinking soda water. "I can spend the next couple of days giving Grange the background information he needs and we can go from there. Who knows? Maybe we'll go out like Butch Cassidy and the Sundance Kid!"

My mother always told me my big mouth was going to get me into trouble.

McAllister was so relieved that Antonio's despondent mood took a positive turn that he just smiled and remained silent.

We finished our drinks and left Antonio in the lobby, happily arranging for a room for him. McAllister, Larkin, and Sally took the elevator up but, out of cigarettes, I excused myself and detoured to the lobby gift shop, happy to find a pack of American cigarettes. I was emerging from the small emporium when I looked up to see Antonio headed back into the bar. I was betting he wasn't ordering more sparkling water.

As usual it was the incessant ringing of the phone that woke me from a fitful sleep early the next morning. McAllister wanted an early start and that meant we had less than a half hour to pack and meet him in the lobby.

Perhaps if I had slept better or if I was not preoccupied with the thought of having to listen to Antonio relate his life story, or if I had not sampled several of the country's famous wines the night before, events that transpired that sunny Paris morning might have been different.

If.

Blinking in the bright sunshine, I failed to notice that McAllister's security man did not spring from the driver's seat to open the door for his passengers. Nor did it seem odd to me that the man standing next to the driver's door was reading a magazine in a busy hotel driveway. I was concerned with making sure that our entire luggage made its way to the trunk and how I was going to react to spending the day listening to how Antonio was fully potty trained at an early age. McAllister and Larkin were thanking the manager of the Meurice for a pleasant stay, assuring him that our early departure was not the result of any deficiency by his staff and Antonio, true to the prediction I had made to myself, was nursing a hangover. Nevertheless, it was Antonio who attracted everyone's attention by snatching off his sunglasses and pointing at the man reading the magazine.

"That's him!" He shouted.

The man reacted to Antonio's outburst by dropping the periodical and backing away from the car.

"That's the son-of-a-bitch!" Antonio again shouted, starting down the steps. "The asshole from Monte Carlo!"

Already next to the car, Sally turned to look at Antonio as he rushed toward the limo. The man who had attracted Antonio's attention, a big brute in an ill-fitting suit, continued to backpedal as he reached for something beneath his coat. I started to move, but McAllister's shout of alarm caused me a millisecond of hesitation. Still unaware of any possible danger, Sally was distractedly reaching for the door handle as she watched with innocent curiosity as Antonio continued his rush toward the front of the car.

Timing his move carefully, Antonio's antagonist waited until he was certain of Antonio's intention to vault the hood of the limo. From beneath his jacket, he pulled a remote control device, extended a foot long antenna, and pushed a button, all in one lightning quick motion.

His timing was perfect. The explosion emanated from inside the car, catching Antonio as he was sliding across the hood. The blast blew out the windshield and dramatically altered Antonio's intended path, heaving him at a ninety degree angle in a flailing of limbs. Simultaneously, the rear door of the limo, partially opened by Sally, blew outward by incredible force, breaking the hinges and slamming her with tremendous impact. Her expression was a combination of surprise and pain as a fountain of blood erupted from her mouth and she went down hard.

There was very little fire, but a white cloud billowed out of the shattered windows and a secondary explosion again rocked the ill-fated vehicle. A black cloud of burning gasoline mingled with the white plume of the initial detonation and pedestrians and hotel employees screamed as they dove for cover. The primary blast had knocked me off my feet and I landed painfully against the steps, cracking a couple of ribs. Instinctively turning my face to avoid the flying glass, I saw McAllister fling himself on top of Larkin, taking her down with a body blocking tackle.

I rolled to face the car again and focused on Sally who had slumped to a sitting position, her back against the crumpled remains of the car. That she was dead was unquestionable. She had vomited a massive amount of blood which was soaking the front of her clothing and the pavement around her and her saddened expression told that before her awareness faded into final oblivion, she had known her ultimate fate. Against the pain in my side, I struggled to my feet, only to be knocked back down by the shock and fear generated by the post traumatic blowing of a tire. When I realized that someone was pressing against my shoulder to keep me from trying to stand, I looked up to see McAllister cautioning me not to attempt mobility.

"I'm alright, Bobby." I said, pushing his hand away. "It's just my ribs."

Larkin was running down the steps toward where her brother had disappeared over the car and McAllister made an ineffectual grab at her arm as she passed. He was momentarily torn between helping an injured friend and protecting his wife from emotional pain so I waved him off and attempted to rise again as he followed her down the stairs.

Getting over the initial shock and fear, dozens of people began reacting in a variety of ways. Several rushed to Sally's side while others sought to assist Antonio. In a daze, I watched people running around aimlessly, shouting at each other or curiously seeking a glimpse at the carnage. One of those two-toned European sirens sounded in the distance.

I knew that physical and mental shock were blocking out the real pain I would feel later but I also knew the true meaning of a heavy heart. As I approached the once vibrant and, more importantly, innocent and adoring woman who had been my friend and lover, I silently cursed the misery and torment that would cause the sickness that made one human being perpetrate such a horrid travesty upon another.

As I felt the sting of tears come to my eyes, I looked up to see a flurry of activity at the front of the limo. The fluent French was a bit hard to follow, but a smattering of understanding told me that Antonio was still alive.

At first, I wondered how such a lack of fire could have caused such severe burns, but then I realized that his upper body had been flayed by flying glass. His entire body was shaking violently and his eyes were wide as he focused on something in the sky while he gulped oxygen through his shredded lips. Larkin was kneeling over him, her hands making ineffective gestures as she prevented herself from touching the injured man and possibly aggravating his mutilation. McAllister was forcing people, both the would be Samaritans and the intrusive onlookers away from the maimed man when I heard Antonio whisper McAllister's name.

Larkin stopped sobbing long enough to clutch at her husband's leg, forcing him to kneel next to her and lean in to hear what Antonio was trying to say. I couldn't hear the words, but it was clear that Antonio was fighting intense pain as he stuttered words at his brother-in-law. McAllister nodded several times and, as the police and medics finally arrived, immediately demanding that everyone back away, he whispered something into Antonio's ear. In a matter of seconds, the authorities had us separated and the emergency crew had Antonio whisked away in an ambulance. I watched over the shoulder of the uniformed policeman who was talking far too fast for me to understand as the ambulance disappeared down the wide boulevard.

* * * * *

On an unusually gray Friday afternoon, Sally Davis was buried in the small hillside cemetery northeast of Payson. The ritual was attended by about a hundred and fifty friends and former customers, as well as her parents and younger sister. Although no one actually accused me of anything, it was clear that her mother and father were holding me responsible for the circumstances that had suddenly and violently taken their daughter from them. As the casket was lowered into the concrete burial vault, they stared at me over the descending coffin with looks that could have withered the flowers that surrounded the open grave. While every Christian belief teaches us that a funeral should be a celebration of the beginning of eternal life, the mood was hardly festive as the mourners were probably split down the middle with those who considered me a victim and those who thought I was a contributing factor in Sally's premature demise.

As the minister intoned a final amen and the funeral director began ushering the family toward the waiting cars, I stood rooted next to the final resting place of a young lady whose greatest lifetime adventure had ended in tragedy. Long after the last shovel of dirt was replaced and the brown scar of freshly turned earth covered with a mound of useless flowers, I stood without moving, an impotent rage burning at an empty spot deep within my soul. When I finally convinced myself that the rest of my earthly existence would be spent without the company of this remarkable woman, I made my way slowly down the hill.

Throughout the entire service, aside from the occasional nod of recognition, no one had spoken to me or offered their condolence. Solace, sympathy, and comfort were reserved exclusively for the immediate family, and I was left to deal with my feelings without the compassion or understanding of others. I felt as if I had been accused, tried, and subsequently acquitted of murdering Sally and those who felt I was truly innocent of any wrongdoing were afraid to talk to me for fear of offending those who felt my guilt to be questionable.

I was practically a stranger in my own home town and was experiencing what it felt like to be left totally alone in the world. I could no longer suppress the tears. That's when I felt the gentle hand placed on my shoulder.

"I wish there was something I could say or do to bring Sally back, Grange. I'm truly sorry."

"Bobby! You're supposed to be in Ciudad Bolivar. What are you...?"

He put a finger to his lips to cut me off. "We're in this together, my friend."

"But. . ."

He cut me off again. "She was a great lady." He looked down at the ground. "Do you want me to talk to the family?"

"I don't think that will help."

"Okay. Whatever you like." He lightly gripped my arm. "Let's get the hell out of here, old buddy. Arizona makes me nervous."

* * * * *

We caught the red eye special flight in Phoenix on a flight to Dallas, connecting with another flight to Atlanta, then on to Caracas, Venezuela. In spite of the reason for my trip, and McAllister's comforting presence, I was happy to be heading to South America. Other than the first class flight and a steady diet of rum shared with McAllister, I can't remember any details of that long and uneventful journey.

We arrived in Caracas and chartered a flight to Ciudad Bolivar. We were met at the small airfield by one of Roberto Tumbas's employees. It was at that time that I met the third member of our traveling party, one of McAllister's bodyguards who had apparently been with us throughout our long journey. The unidentified man loaded our luggage that he transported from the small aircraft into the Land Rover and rode next to the driver. McAllister and I sat in the back seat as we rode back to the estate.

Larkin was waiting for us in the wide driveway that fronted the newest mansion at El Empleado. She threw her arms around McAllister and held him for a long time, as if she hadn't seen him in a million years. I guess she finally realized that I was there too as she released her hold on McAllister long enough to give me a sisterly hug. "I'm so sorry, Grange. Sally was a very special person." She smiled soothingly. "We all miss her."

While still holding her husband's hand, she held my arm and led us to the combination living room and den where McAllister went to the bar to pour drinks.

"How did it go?" Asked Larkin to no one in particular.

McAllister recognized the discomfort in my eyes and replied. "It was sad, Larkin. I'll tell you about it later, honey." He smiled and Larkin gave an understanding nod.

"The most precious commodity one can have is a family. It is very difficult when one does not have one." Roberto Tumbas had glided silently into the room in his custom electric wheelchair, causing me to start at the sound of his voice. "Friends sometimes fear that their expressions of sympathy are hollow and unwelcome." He rolled to a stop in front of me and extended his hand. "I hope that we can become your family, Senor Lawton. You are always most welcome in our home."

I smiled for the first time in days. "How do you do, Senor Tumbas? It's been a long time."

"Pardon me for not rising," He said, dismissing his disability, "but I fear that my advanced years have greatly affected my physical ability."

As a matter of fact, other than the obvious, Tumbas had changed very little. He was still the sensitive, perfect gentleman and, amiable host, always concerned with the comfort and cares of his guests, ever mindful of proper manners fitting a man of his upbringing and refinement. He was dressed impeccably in a loose fitting white shirt and military creased trousers.

"I also regret that the only times we seem to meet are periods of stress and sorrow." He continued. "You have my deepest sympathy over your recent and tragic loss. We would have understood if you had not returned with Robert for yet another regrettable commemoration." He then turned to McAllister. "Welcome home, Robert."

"Thank you, Senor Tumbas." McAllister replied rather formally.

"Under different circumstances, I would counter by saying it is always a pleasure to renew old and treasured friendships." I responded. "Let me just say that your misfortune is also a loss that I share equally."

Tumbas raised his eyebrow. "That is a very charitable attitude considering that, however wrongfully, my son considered you to be a major factor in his estrangement from this family."

"I cannot hold a man's mistaken conclusions against him." I answered. "Antonio had nothing to prove to me. I never questioned his honor or bravery."

Tumbas nodded sadly. "Thank you, Senor Lawton. You are most kind."

With the formalities out of the way, McAllister interrupted by asking his father-in-law to excuse us so we could get unpacked. Gaining his permission, McAllister guided me down the hallway to an elevator, leaving Larkin and her father behind. Instead of buttons, the car had key holes and McAllister inserted a key he had retrieved from Larkin, in the bottom slot and we descended. Our destination was an underground office where McAllister signaled me to a comfortable chair in front of him as he took position behind a heavy desk of carved oak.

He just stared at me.

"Well, don't you think it's about time for you to fill me in? I mean, you weren't exactly a fountain of information on our long flight down here . . . I don't think." I still couldn't remember much of the flight.

He looked as if he was considering my request. "I didn't feel it appropriate to discuss much on our flight. We certainly kept the stewardess busy with the drinks though."

"Well. . .

"Well. . . Antonio died less than two hours after you boarded the Concorde back to the States." He began, matter-of-factly. "He never regained consciousness after surgery."

"But you talked to him before he went into a coma." I reminded him.

McAllister cocked an eyebrow. "I didn't know you saw that."

"Was I not supposed to take note of that little exchange?" I asked cynically.

McAllister dismissed my question and my attitude with a careless wave of his hand. "It really doesn't matter." He said. "What he told me wouldn't help those idiot French police if they had the guy who did this already locked up in the Bastille."

It was my turn to pull the trick with the eyebrow.

"The Paris Police Department is as outdated as the Napoleonic Code they follow." He continued. "They're calling the attack a terrorist act, aimed at wealthy Americans because it is easier to assault United States citizens when they don't enjoy the protection of their own government."

"You didn't tell them that Antonio recognized the bastard that set off the explosion?" I asked incredulously.

"Of course I did." McAllister reached for my glass and took it to a small wet bar in the corner of the room. "Since the police in Monaco attribute Antonio's original beating as a street crime, the Paris cops figure he was mistaken." He said over his shoulder as he refilled our drinks. "They consider it highly unlikely that common muggers would wait almost a year and follow Antonio to Paris simply because they wound up with a worthless imitation during their first attack."

"So you didn't try to convince them differently by telling them what we were actually doing?" I asked, suspicious that McAllister might be withholding information from me too.

"The hell I didn't." McAllister said indignantly but not angrily. "The police told me that France was 'enjoying an excellent liaison with the government of the Soviet Union' and to accuse a foreign nation of 'common hooliganism' at a time when diplomatic relations were going so well had the potential of causing International repercussions."

"So, instead of blaming a quasi-friendly administration, they shifted the culpability onto a political body that is supposedly abhorrent to all four nations. That makes France a victim too. I don't suppose the police received any information from any group claiming responsibility?"

"Not that I know of."

"A curious fact, considering these so-called radical groups will phone a newspaper when a pigeon shits on a statue claiming the 'People's-Liberation-Revolutionary-Front-For-Oppressed-The-World-Over-As-Long-As-They-Believe-In-Extremist-Fundamentalism' arranged the desecration as an example to the misguided masses.

"I think it's safe to assume that the file in this case is either sitting on some inactive shelf or the authorities have assigned the matter to the most ineffectual anti-terrorist squad on the face of the Earth. Therefore, it follows that we can expect no results from their investigation and justice will not be served. At least not at the hands of France."

McAllister placed my drink in front of me and eyed me carefully. "That's a very cynical attitude." He said. "You sound as if you're angry enough to do something irrational."

I took a deep breath. "You couldn't be further from the truth." I corrected. "The very last thing I want to do is act in a manner that could be considered injudicious."

"However?" McAllister sat down again and leaned back, studying me deliberately.

"Between your generosity and my talent, I have more money than I ever thought one person could ever have." I said. "I'll spend every dime I have to be able to see the man who pushed the button that killed Sally and Antonio kneeling in front of me, begging for his life.

"I won't listen to him, Bobby. I'll let him whine and plead, but it will make no difference. I don't want him to die in the electric chair or the gas chamber and certainly not by a process as benign as lethal injection; I want him to suffer for a very long time. I want him to know real pain and I want to be the one who administers every agonizing and tormented turn of the screw." Without realizing, I was squeezing the glass that held my drink. With a firecracker pop, the glass exploded and ice cubes flew in all directions. Miraculously, I was merely shocked and not cut by the shattered glass. McAllister almost seemed not to notice as a wry smile crept at the corners of his mouth as he watched me intently over the tips of his fingers.

"I don't believe it." He said quietly. "The man who, for almost seven years now, has preached patience and pacifism, now wants to exact his own measure of vengeance." He leaned forward. "How does it feel, Grange? Is it something that eats away at your insides? Something that causes you to lose sleep? Affects your appetite? Tell me about it, Grange. Help me understand."

I lowered my eyes. "You're mocking me, Bobby." I said. "I don't deserve that."

"Apparently you do deserve it. Some people learn with easy lessons, some people it takes a drive by shooting, some people . . . never learn." He smiled reassuringly. "Unfortunately, you've learned a hard lesson, my friend."

"Forget it." I said, I'll leave right after the funeral tomorrow." McAllister prevented my rising by sitting on the edge of the desk directly in front of me. "There are a couple of things you should know." He said, handing me the drink. I took it without thinking.

"Antonio gave me a name." He said, "Apparently the shock of the explosion or some other unknown factor psychologists would argue about forever triggered some subconscious memory about a guy with the button. "Anyway, Antonio had some kind of flashback to his beating in Monte Carlo. He said the guys spoke Russian, but he thought he understood the mention of a name. He said it sounded like a Russian gun. . . Kalisnikov."

"How did he know they weren't talking about the gun?"

McAllister shrugged. "I don't know that he didn't. However, Antonio spoke several languages and, even though Russian wasn't one of them, he had a good ear for languages and knew the difference in the way things spoken had meaning."

"A noun and a name are the same thing." I reminded him. "You were listening to a mortally wounded man who was remembering a beating that did severe brain damage ."

"It's more than we had a week ago."

"All right." I conceded. "What else?"

"Our driver was shot once in the head at very close range with a silenced pistol."

"Now how the hell would the cops know whether or not a pistol had a silencer attached?" I challenged.

"Apparently the bullet, essentially traveling through what amounts to be two separate barrels, picks up markings from each cylinder. Ballistics is a reasonably exact science, you know."

"Okay." I waved away my objection. "Other than the fact that one of your employees was murdered, how does that affect us?"

"The bullet was a thirty-three caliber." He answered. "A Russian gun."

I was getting exasperated. "A Russian with a name like a Russian gun shoots someone with a Russian gun and the police refuse to believe that he might be a Russian? What other contradictions of basic logic are we dealing with here?"

McAllister held up a hand. Let me just say this, Grange. I got the impression that our shooter/bomber was not the name, nor did he call his partner by the name in Monte Carlo, but simply the name as if he were referring to a third party."

"As far as the gun, a thirty-three caliber Russian gun is a very common gun in Europe. They were also a familiar weapon for North Vietnamese officers during the conflict in Southeast Asia, and since France was the major occupying force before the Americans arrived, many wound up back in Western Europe as souvenirs."

"So there are three people dead and the only thing we have is the name of a Russian who may not even be involved." I observed. "With that kind of luck, the name we have will probably turn out to be the Soviet equivalent of Smith." I leaned forward and looked directly at my host, doing my best imitation of a hardened anti-hero.

"Do you have any more surprises that I should know about now, that I would be very pissed about if I found out later?"

McAllister seemed to deflate under my steady gaze. I wondered if I should employ the tactic more often. It was proving to be very effective. . . I thought.

"Grange, let me tell you something." He regained his composure. "There is a proper time for everything. It's called timing. I did not delve into any details of the past during our flight down here because you needed a mental escape. I escaped right along with you, in fact." He crossed his arms over his chest, a defensive gesture that I rarely saw McAllister display. "I know, uh, feel that I am on the right track here."

"Would you please be more specific?"

"Alright. Sometime after the attack, Antonio's house was burglarized. There was only one thing taken."

Great.

I didn't bother to ask.

* * * * *

I had expected Antonio to be buried somewhere on his father's vast estate, so it came as somewhat of a surprise when the services took place in the large church in the center of town and the burial in the small cemetery behind the Cathedral. I had forgotten that Catholics were sensitive about consecrated ground. About four hundred people attended the mass and not once did I hear anyone mention the incident when Antonio's father was wounded. Since Antonio's absence from his home had covered a number of years, most of those in attendance were there not because they were mourning, but to give support and understanding to the area's most influential citizen. I never realized that attending a funeral could be a politically correct move.

Back at the estate, Senor Tumbas excused himself from the small gathering of close friends and employees who had returned after the service. Always in control while in front of contemporaries and guests, I knew he needed time by himself and wished that there were words or actions to remove the pain and sorrow he was experiencing. I wished that someone had known the things to say to me that would cure the anguish and bitterness gnawing at my soul.

Shortly after I had returned to my guest room in McAllister's mansion beneath a mockery, a light knock at the door interrupted my wandering thoughts. Robert Tumbas, looking smaller and older than I had ever seen him, quietly asked permission to take up some of my time.

"Of course." I said, standing aside to allow the wheelchair to convey him into the room. I offered him a drink. He declined.

"What next, Senor Lawton?" He asked. "What do you do now?"

I knew what he was getting at; I just didn't know how to answer.

"You have always been the voice of reason to my son-in-law." He continued. "Is there something you can do to stop him from participating in anything that will only cause this family more grief?"

I sat down on the edge of the bed and looked at my hands. "In all honesty," I said, choosing my words carefully, "I sincerely believe that to abandon our pursuit at this time would be a grave mistake."

Tumbas sighed as he rested his elbows on the arms of his chair and laced his fingers together. "You too seek revenge." He said dismally. "And you are wrong, Senor Lawton. Robert does not know that I am aware of his plans. But when he sent our precious twins away with his young daughter Jennean and her beautiful little Ashley to California, I was heart-broken. I knew he was up to something mischievous by his actions. You are my last hope, my dear friend."

What plans?

Senor Tumbas," I began, "You just lost your only son. Several years ago, you lost the use of your legs. Doesn't that make you angry? Don't you want to lash out and make someone pay for the atrocities that you have had to endure?"

Tumbas looked at the ceiling as if an answer was written in the roofing plaster. "If we lived in a perfect world, we would not be having this conversation." He said. "The truth of the matter is that I would love to have the man who took my son from me at my mercy. The reality is, I have no desire to risk another member of my family in order to achieve that purpose. The men who robbed me of the use of my legs paid dearly for their greed and brutality. We must weigh the returns against the investment.

"It is true that I am a wealthy and influential man. I know it sounds condescending, but I would trade everything to know that no one in my family would ever be at risk again.

"Remember, my friend, we have twice been reminded that we are capable of losing things that can never be restored. All I have left is my daughter and two beautiful grandchildren. Would you be willing to wager the health and security of those two adorable children in order to satisfy a vendetta that will do nothing to regain that which we have already lost?

"If you cannot think in those terms, please listen to the pleadings of an old man who has only a short time left to enjoy his blessings. I have attended far too many funerals in my lifetime. I would not wish to be present at any further such gatherings unless it is I for whom the bell tolls."

I knew Roberto Tumbas to be a formal and diplomatic man with a great deal of pride. No matter how well he had rehearsed that little speech he made, it still took a measure of courage on his part to deliver it with the humble sincerity with which he spoke. It was going to be hard to ignore his heartfelt plea for circumspect behavior.

Hard, not impossible.

* * * * *

"You're an idiot, Gregori!"

Gregori Patek stood at rigid attention in the presence of his superior officer, Lazarik Kalinishkov. In spite of his Russian name and Soviet upbringing, Gregori was a product of Warsaw and Kalinishkov cursed the fact that his department was staffed almost entirely by Poles. In virtual exile in St. Petersburg for a clerical error that had cost an important agent his life during the height of the Cold War and the Space Race, Lazarik blamed all his troubles on foreigners even though he himself was from Ekaterinburg, a fact he overlooked since the last Tsar of Russia was assassinated in the small Siberian town and was therefore a representative birthplace of the Bolshevik Revolution.

Although Kalinishkov was a major in the KGB, he knew that demotion was as common as promotion as surely as he knew the fate of those who were demoted. He understood that his impeccable and promising record prior to the loss of the agent in America had saved him from a one way ticket to oblivion, but he also realized there would be no further overlooking of any failures. Proof of all this was the fact that he had not had a promotion in over twenty-five years and it was a foregone conclusion that he would end his career in his present position, a boat that Gregori Patek had just inadvertently rocked.

"Comrade Major, I. . ."

"Shut up, you stupid hunk of Polish dog meat!" Kalinishkov shouted. "I will do the talking here."

Kalinishkov walked around his desk and began pacing behind his subordinate's back. With great personal satisfaction, he noted that the man was sweating, uneasy and concerned for his own fate.

"Are you familiar with the objective of this department, Gregori Vasilov?" Kalinishkov asked. "Perhaps it has slipped your feeble mind exactly how this branch of our illustrious parent organization operates."

Gregori knew better than to answer the major when he was using a particular tone in his voice, much like the one he was employing now.

"Then I will be happy to review the purpose of our agency at this time." Kalinishkov continued.

"Our job is to secure original pieces of art, especially those items that may have a historical relationship to Russia, and replace them on the Western markets with forgeries of the highest quality."

Kalinishkov stopped pacing and spoke to the back of Gregori's head. "And how do we accomplish these lofty objectives, Comrade Patek?"

Gregori bit his lower lip.

"I will be happy to elaborate." Sarcasm was one of Kalinishkov's usual intimidating maneuvers and he used that form of contempt liberally. "We attain these goals by discreet selection of targets. That means we do not practice wholesale havoc on any of our marks. We carefully choose each and every treasure by establishing certain criteria. Firstly, we never steal more than one or two items, a fact that makes our endeavors less speculative or noteworthy. Secondly, we victimize only private collections, again to avoid being conspicuous but, more importantly, we are generally disassociating ourselves from a myriad of experts one would expect to be found in a museum or gallery."

"Comrade Major, I have no need. . ."

"Obviously you do!" The major contradicted. "Perhaps if you fully comprehend the scope of our responsibilities, you might be prompted to act in a manner more advantageous to our intent."

Gregori wished he were someplace else. It was very seldom that anyone below the rank of captain in the KGB knew the full range of any operation. Soldiers such as Gregori blindly followed orders within their compartmentalized units, frequently not knowing or caring anything about the overall picture. To be privy to information was not a privilege to a man of Gregori's standing and he feared that the major was being expansive only as a precursor to more drastic action. Gregori began to sweat even more profusely as he shifted uncomfortably.

"Almost a year ago, you and that shit-for-brains Rastov failed to get the Spaskoie Egg from the auction in Monte Carlo in spite of being in the position to make that particular one of your easier assignments. Instead, you return to St. Petersburg with a copy that is, of all things, plastic!

"So, to atone for this outlandish blunder, your cretin partner takes it upon himself to travel to South America where he enlists the aid of an embassy underling to help him break into the home of one of the most influential citizens on the entire continent without properly assessing the security risks.

"Not only does he fail, getting some poor young adventurous attaché killed in the process, he practically advertises his affiliation by running like a scared rabbit back to the embassy, very nearly creating an International Incident."

Having not made the trip to Venezuela, Gregori relaxed slightly knowing the major would not blame him for something in which he was not involved. His respite was short. The major was far from finished.

"The very minute that you and your pathetic partner are reunited, the two of you return to France on an entirely different mission where Rastov wastes no time in getting himself arrested for beating up some common street whore. He gets thirty days in the Bastille which leaves you to wander aimlessly around the capitol city instead of proceeding with your assignment or, at the very least, checking in with your control."

"I saw the Tumbas man." Gregori protested. "He appeared to be joining forces with the Americans. I followed them for two days and felt they were posing a threat to our security. I thought. . ."

"No!" Kalinishkov shouted. "That is exactly the problem. You did not use that Polish melon on your shoulders to conduct any rational thinking. Who in the hell gave you endorsement for such unauthorized extravagance?"

"I felt I was protecting the agency." Gregori insisted. "It was my intention to remove the hazard and possibly recover the Spaskoie Egg at the same time."

"Comrade," the major said, appearing to accept Gregori's explanation and empathize with his dilemma at the same time. "Why in the name of Mother Russia would you think we were any longer interested in that lousy piece of Imperial decadence?"

The major's tone had become so reasonable; Gregori thought the storm was over.

"In the four years I have worked in this department, Comrade Major, I have never failed in a mission. I felt that this was a perfect opportunity to rectify that unfortunate episode."

"So you succeed in murdering two American citizens and a Venezuelan national in order to make up for one failure that netted you a mild reprimand that did not even go in to your personnel file in Moscow." The major observed, the sarcasm returning to his voice. Gregori swallowed, his discomfort returning in an instant.

"So tell me, comrade," the major continued, "when you made your little foray into the dead man's country estate, what exactly did you find?"

Gregori winced. "Nothing, Comrade Major." He answered nervously. "The Spaskoie Egg was not there."

* * *

CHAPTER FOUR

We boarded the Second Prize less than a half hour after landing at Orly. McAllister had left the ship's crew and a small security contingent aboard during the absence necessary for us to attend funerals and less than ten minutes after we re-boarded the yacht, we were under way.

Although McAllister had attempted to dissuade Larkin from returning with us, she had insisted with determination and resolve that precluded any argument. Once she sent the twins with McAllister's daughter for a visit in California, the subject was closed and she was committed to the trip. The three of us sat on the fantail planning our next move as the Second Prize sailed down the Seine toward the English Channel.

"In spite of the circumstances, I don't see that our immediate plans have changed all that much." McAllister stated matter-of-factly.

"I agree." I said. "I think it's a foregone conclusion that we will get nowhere depending on the conventional methods used by the Paris Police. That's why we aren't sticking around, isn't it?"

McAllister nodded. "Larkin hired a local attorney." He explained. "Not because she thought we needed representation, but to act as an intermediary for us during the police investigation. So far, it has been a waste of money. The police are continuing to operate on the premise that this was a terrorist act and are examining no other avenues."

"I'm sure Anthony Wilson will keep his ear to the ground on our behalf." I observed. "After all, without him, we're reduced to using bloodhounds to try to track Antonio's egg. At least we now have a name."

"And an address." McAllister reminded me. "Mister Dorn Kublec of Westerham, England."

* * * * *

Although the British Empire is a shadow of its former grandeur, the land itself remains a testament to the pride and tenacity of its inhabitants. Slightly smaller than the State of Oregon, this tiny island nation overcame invaders from Caesar to Hitler and once controlled an empire that included much of North America, India, Australia, New Zealand, Malaysia and Hong Kong. I had never made an approach to England by sea and rising before dawn to watch the sun come up on the white cliffs of Dover to the east was a sight worth seeing.

That I was fully awake at an hour closer to my normal bedtime was a testament to nervous energy and a burning desire to be actively doing anything that would bring my flexing fingers closer to the neck of Sally's murderer.

Captain Olsen had lain off the coast, timing his entry to the port city of Ramsgate for eight o'clock when customs and immigrations would be open. The minute we docked, McAllister was off the ship and on his way into town carrying a briefcase I knew contained a false bottom. It is, of course, against the law to bring large amounts of foreign currency into most any foreign nation. As he disappeared up the ramp, Larkin came out on deck in a bikini that had last been seen on the pages of Sports Illustrated and from that point on, McAllister could have smuggled elephants into the country undetected. Also totally ignored, I watched from a vantage point on the stern deck as Larkin deftly led the officials up the ramp who were so enraptured by her beauty that they weren't interested in the possibility of any hidden treasure or the large amounts of cash stored in various places of concealment throughout the boat. I had to remind an embarrassed official that there were another nine people on board who needed their passports validated.

Immediately after they left, McAllister returned with a rental car whose keys he promptly turned over to one of his anonymous bodyguards. Larkin had changed into more suitable vacationist clothing and the four of us walked up the quay. When I reached for the car door handle, I hesitated involuntarily. My hand was shaking before I could gather my wits; I looked up to see an expression of concern on McAllister's face.

"Don't worry. Grange." He said, reading my reactions. "We're being covered."

"We were supposed to be covered at the Meurice." I reminded him.

"We're covered." He repeated, stepping in front of me to open the door. "Relax."

I got in the car, but I didn't relax.

Westerham was the summer home of William Pitt, as well as another highly respected prime minister, Winston Churchill. Pitt's cottage, a small timbered seasonal house is now a restaurant, but Churchill's country home, Chartwell, two miles south of town on a wooded hillside terraced with a series of gardens, is a tourist attraction.

Halfway between Westerham and Sevenoaks is Knole, the largest and most baronial mansion in all of England. The house was begun in 1456 by Archbishop Thomas Bourchier and was home to the archbishops of Canterbury until it was turned over to Henry VIII. Named for the grassy knoll on which it stands, the estate was given to the Sackville-West family by Queen Elizabeth I in 1603 and, of all things, enlarged even further. Nobody seems to know for certain, but the house supposedly covers over three acres of land and has seven courtyards (one for each day of the week), fifty-two staircases (weeks of the year), and three hundred sixty-five rooms (one for each day of the year).

The only reason that Knole was of any interest to me on that particular day, however, was how the present owners felt about their family home casting a shadow over the somewhat less austere home of an admitted and convicted forger like Dorn Kublec. With canvasses by Gainsborough, Van Dyke, Reynolds, and others, as well as furnishings and tapestry virtually untouched since the family was first given the house, I might tend to have circuitry on the alarm system checked frequently. I remember thinking, however, that the Knole/ Kublec connection might be symbiotic. The Sackville-West family knew exactly where the most likely source of trouble might come from while Kublec would want to protect himself by warding his peers away from his own front porch.

Just off the A225, Kublec's tudor-style cottage looked like a movie set of a country home, complete with white picket fence and separate flower and vegetable gardens.

"I hope he's home." McAllister said as the car came to a stop in front of the little gingerbread house.

He caught me off guard. Larkin replied for her husband. "We felt that the element of a surprise visit might reveal more." She smiled shyly. "Psychology 101, Professor Harrington."

I wished he were with us.

The door was answered by a plump, cheery woman in her late sixties, almost a caricature of someone one would expect to be sweeping the front porch with an old fashioned broom. She looked over our shoulders at the expensive rental car and assessed all three of us with a twinkle in her eye and an appreciative look as she dried her chubby fingers on her apron.

"Here ta see the mister, are ya now?" She asked before any of us could offer an introduction. McAllister started to reply but she continued on as if she didn't need an answer. "Well, ya did right by comin' early. He's at his best in the mornings, don't ya know. That's before he wanders in to town to waste his time drinkin' ale and watchin' sports on the telly at the Pitt Pub."

She waved a fleshy arm for us to follow her down a hallway lined with hundreds of photographs, some dating back to the invention of the camera. In a heavily beamed living room lighted only by the sunshine filtering through the heavy glass windows, sat an old man intently studying a large volume of color photographs of classic art, one of many that were scattered about the room in organized chaos.

"Some nice folks ta see ya pa." She announced in a slightly raised voice. "The car is rented and they dress too nice ta be coppers, so mind your manners and make them welcome. I'll go fix some tea." She turned to McAllister and patted his shoulder. "You'll have to speak up a bit dearie. He's a mite deaf, you know." She wobbled off down the hall to her kitchen.

Dorn Kublec sat in a beam of bright sunlight watching us through thick glasses as we filed into the room. He was clearly a very old man, probably in his late eighties, with leathery skin and thin, brittle looking arms that ended in hands that were badly misshapen from ravages of advanced arthritis. He used the side of his hand to close the book on his lap and remove the heavy spectacles with both hands.

"Come, come." He said, pointing to a threadbare sofa and a few mismatched chairs. "Sit down and tell me what brings you to see an old man who gets so few visitors these days."

"Thank you." McAllister pointed Larkin to the sofa while I sat on an imitation Louis XV chair set slightly further away. "I'm Bobby McAllister." He said, his voice raised. "This is my wife, Larkin and our friend, Granger Lawton."

Kublec waved a gnarled fist in an air of dismissal. "No need to shout, m'boy." He said, smiling and showing teeth as distorted as his hands. "The deafness the missus refers to is selective. Comes in handy when I don't care to be interrupted or when I want to hear someone talking about me." He nudged the glasses in his lap. "Don't need these buggers either, 'cept when I want to study detail. Let's see, American, but with a little Scottish blood, am I right?"

"For the most part, yes." He smiled. "But I'm not all that certain about my ancestry." He abruptly changed the subject. "We were given your name by Anthony Wilson in Paris."

"Ah." Kublec nodded his understanding. "Then I can assume you have some predetermined opinions about me an' my former profession. Anthony Wilson thinks I should be spending my twilight years in the Old Bailey rather than the English countryside."

"We haven't formed any opinions, Mister Kublec." McAllister said honestly. "However, we have been warned that your memory might be as discriminating as your hearing." He pointed to the briefcase he had set on the floor between his legs. "May I?"

Kublec squinted in the direction of the case, seeing it for the first time. When he nodded cautiously, McAllister pulled it onto his lap and twirled the combination. The snaps popped up with a resounding click. With exaggerated care, McAllister removed the Resurrection Egg and placed it on the coffee table in front of him. Kublec watched him carefully and when McAllister was certain he had Kublec's full attention, he turned the still open briefcase so it faced the retired forger. Instead of the normal protective foam packing, the case was lined with British ten pound notes. He removed a bundle of bills and broke the band that held the bills together.

"I'm going to be very frank and direct, Mister Kublec." McAllister stood and fanned himself with the spread bills. "I don't have a lot of time and therefore, not a great deal of patience either. Perhaps you might want to call your wife in here if your memory isn't quite up to snuff. It may save you a great deal of money."

Kublec looked uncertain and hesitant, but he licked his lips and raised his voice. "Katherine!" He called in the direction of the kitchen. "Be a dear and come in here, luv."

Katherine Kublec walked into the room wiping her hands on her apron. She stopped short when she saw the egg and the briefcase full of money.

McAllister was turning the informal meeting into one of his theatrical showcases. He loved having an audience and his only regret was probably that he couldn't pull off one of his dramatic presentations to a full house in Madison Square Garden. He deliberately spread the banknotes he was holding into a wider fan and placed them on the table in front of the old man. Two things were clear from the Kublec's expressions. They wanted the money and they had no idea what McAllister was planning.

"Since you probably have never heard of me, I'd like to tell you a little about myself." McAllister was warming up to his favorite subject. I could only hope he was not going to ramble. "I have devoted most of my life to searching for gold in the cargo holds of treasure laden ships that disappeared during the early years of trade with the New World. To say that I was successful would be modest. Since my extraordinary good fortune, I have become a very wealthy man and the concept of cash evolved into an abstract notion for me." He picked up one of the bills and held it delicately by a corner. From a pants pocket, he withdrew a Bic lighter and held the flame under the British equivalent of a ten dollar bill. It burst into flame and was consumed very quickly. He dropped the charcoaled remains of the note into the ashtray on the table. Larkin looked amused, McAllister looked satisfied, and the Kublecs looked positively aghast.

McAllister removed nine more fifty note bundles from the briefcase and placed them on the table. In all, five thousand British pounds, less the one now worthless ten pound note, rested in front of Dorn Kublec.

"That money is yours," McAllister continued, "conditional to me getting some honest and direct answers to some very simple questions. Do you understand what I am saying, Mister Kublec?"

Kublec, his mouth slightly agape, nodded dully.

McAllister turned the Resurrection Egg so that Kublec had an unobstructed view of the piece. "Do you recognize this?" He asked.

"That's the Faberge Resurrection Egg." He answered.

"It was presented to Tsarina Marie Feodorovna by Tsar Alexander III on Easter of 1889."

"Very good." McAllister replied, tapping the egg gently. "Now, real or forgery?"

"Mister McAllister," Kublec began, "I have no idea whether or not. . ."

McAllister deftly peeled five ten pound notes off the bundle and had them burning before Kublec could finish. "That's your money, Mister Kublec." He said, dropping the ashes a scant second before the flames reached his fingertips. "Please, Mister Kublec. Real or phony?"

"Mister McAllister, I. . ."

Before he could say another word, five more bills were on fire.

"Hesitation and evasion costs as much as a lie, Mister Kublec." McAllister was showing no emotion other than possible boredom. "One more time. Real or not?"

"Forgery." Kublec answered quickly. "The real one is a Forbes collection piece."

"Very good." McAllister drew out the words. "Now, who made this one?"

Kublec lowered his eyes. "I don't know." He said quietly.

McAllister sighed as he ignited five more bills.

"Please! Mister McAllister." Kublec begged. "You must understand. Things are different over here. British law has no provisions like your American Statute Of Limitations. I must weigh my responses to your questions carefully."

"Nothing you say to me will incriminate you, Mister Kublec."

"But, my dear lad. . ."

"Which weighs more?" McAllister asked rhetorically as he helped himself to some more bills. "Ashes or banknotes? I'm not a police officer. I couldn't care less how the law deals with forgers. I have no intentions of sharing any information with law enforcement of any sovereignty, and anything you tell me, Mister Kublec, will remain between the five of us. Now, please, who made that egg?"

Kublec looked to his wife who nodded apprehensively and almost imperceptibly.

"I . . . uh . . . did." He mumbled.

"Now we're getting somewhere." McAllister looked pleased. "When, why, and for whom?"

Kublec seemed to be searching his memory. "That would have been sixty-two or early sixty-three. I remember it was winter because the cold was beginnin' ta bother me hands a wee bit." I wondered if McAllister had noticed that Kublec had slipped back into his folksy mannerisms. "I did it for the money, of course. It was five thousand pounds sterling, is what it was. Worth much more today, of course."

McAllister was idly fingering more bills, waiting for Kublec to continue.

"Now just a moment before ya go committin' more arson in me own livin' room." He said, pointing to the stacks of cash with a gnarled fist. "The 'whom' of your last question will take some time to explain."

McAllister withdrew his hand and struck a pose of exaggerated patience.

"People like me was never house guests of them that hired us." He said, using a deformed hand to rub the side of his jaw thoughtfully. "Most of the time, the likes of me was commissioned by some barrister with a reputation for dealing on both sides of the law or some other intermediary who found a parcel of extra income for coping with artists such as myself."

"But this was different." McAllister prompted.

"That it was, Mister McAllister." Kublec nodded. "Gent by the name of Cramer. Least ways, that's what he told me. I don't think that was his real name though."

"Why not?"

"First of all, he had a funny accent. Can't rightly describe it other than to say it coulda been any foreign dialect, but I remember thinkin' he probably spoke several tongues 'cause of the way he sounded.

"Anyway, most blokes want your best work for the cheapest price. They hum and haw ' fore they tell you what they really want, they want it done yesterday, and after they take possession of the product, they never admit they ever knew ya.

"Not this Cramer chap, no sir. Drives right up to me place in Mayfair, tells me what he wants in less than two minutes, tells me ta take me time, and pays me top quid. Not only that, he supplies every bit of material, most of it top drawer stock, and he drops in every two or three days to check on me progress."

"That was the only time you worked for him?"

"Heavens no, m'boy." Kublec looked shocked. "A meal ticket like that you don't let get away. Over the next ten years, I done twelve, maybe fifteen separate projects for the man."

"What kind of projects?"

Kublec licked his cracked lips as he considered an answer, a hesitation that, fortunately, didn't cost him anything but time. "Would it suffice to tell ya that I know where all but two of the pieces are right now?"

He was pleading for a concession. "I do have a bit of reputation to protect, ya know."

McAllister allowed the compromise by asking a different question. "In a ten year relationship you must have learned something personal about the man."

"Very little." Kublec moved his body in what might have been a shrug. "Oh, I asked questions. Tried to sound casual, like I was passin' the time 'a day. He never let nothin' slip 'ceptin' this one time."

McAllister raised a questioning eyebrow.

"It had ta do with this one particular piece." Kublec looked as though he were picturing the instance in his mind. "I asked him what happened to the original piece and he said something about someone in the department gettin' greedy'. Then he said, 'let it be a lesson ta ya that we won't tolerate duplicity'. I didn't know what he meant until I saw the paper the next day.

"The police found some poor bugger hanging from a battlement at the manor of the man who owned the piece I had duplicated. They said he had been tortured. The worst thing was, the piece I had just finished was firmly fitted in an area most commonly associated with outgo instead of intake, if you know what I mean.

"When I mentioned the incident to Cramer at a later time, he acted as if he didn't know what I was talking about. Ta the best of me knowledge, that piece, one other, and the Resurrection Egg you have there, are the only pieces I did for Cramer that have been uncovered as replications. They are also the only three I had ta do without havin' the original piece to use as a model."

McAllister dug into his briefcase and uncovered the Garden Egg. "Is this the other piece you were referring to?" He asked.

"No." Kublec answered. Nevertheless, he extended his palsied hands indicating his desire to examine the piece more closely. "Good Lord, no." He said when he had the piece cradled in his claws. "Surely no one ever believed that this was a Faberge piece?"

McAllister reddened. "Never mind." He said tersely. "Can you tell me who made it?"

Kublec looked offended. "Mister McAllister, please." He said. "I can understand how serious collectors consider me as the bane of their favorite diversion, but I am still an artist who takes great pride in his work. This is not even up to the standards of a first year apprentice."

"So you don't have any idea who might have manufactured that piece?" McAllister persisted.

Kublec turned it over clumsily. "You know, there is one thing that makes this piece unique." He was slightly puzzled by his discovery. "All the materials seem ta be authentic."

McAllister seized on the observation. "You mean this piece might have been commissioned by Cramer?" He asked. "Or someone like him?"

"It is possible." Kublec looked somewhat surprised by his own answer. "But I wouldn't bet that someone the likes of Cramer would have seen this bit o' work through to its finish."

"He's an expert himself?" McAllister asked.

"He knows his text. Without question."

"So, the last time you saw this Cramer character was sometime around 1972?" McAllister changed the direction of the conversation.

Kublec hesitated just long enough for McAllister to cast a meaningful glance at the pile of money on the table. "Not exactly." Kublec said, barely averting another flare-up. "I've done no business with the man since about that time. Did a stretch at Newgate, ya know. But I seen somethin' in the Times last year."

"The paper?"

"The same." He replied. "Granted. It's been more than a summer or two since I last saw the man, but I'm certain it was him. I even made a remark to Katherine at the time."

For the first time since she had returned to the room, Katherine Kublec looked away from the money and nodded. "That he did." She said, trying to sound convincing. "It was the same bloke, I'm sure of it. The article didn't say nothin' 'bout no Cramer, though. Called him Kleinfeld, I think. "Emery Kleinfeld."

"Do you remember what the article was about?"

"Certainly, dearie." She chirped. "It was the Blair auction."

McAllister appeared to digest this information carefully. "The Blair auction." He said thoughtfully. It was clear to me that he was unaware of the details surrounding the Wilfred Blair affair. While it had been newsworthy in Great Britain and Western Europe for months, it had gotten little play in the American press. I could only imagine it was more or less than a paragraph or two in Venezuelan journalism.

McAllister looked to me to see if I had anything to address in the interrogation.

"I don't think I fully understand why anyone would go to the trouble of supplying a forger with genuine materials that make up the bulk of an item's particular worth." I said. "A copy of the Mona Lisa is, essentially, worthless if it's discovered to be a fraud. This," I leaned forward and pointed to the Resurrection Egg, "is worth thousands of dollars in its make up alone. After all, if you cut a diamond to the size, shape, and weight of the Hope Diamond, you may not have an original gem, but you still have a stone that is worth a fortune. Where is the profit in what you do?"

"Good question, lad." He sounded like a professor who had purposely created a flaw in some theory, hoping someone in his class would notice the inconsistency.

"Let me begin by making some comparisons." He pointed to the Resurrection Egg and waved a feebled hand. McAllister stood up and handed it to him, trading for the inferior piece he had been holding. "When we replicate a piece of structural art, we cut as many corners as possible." He held the egg more on his wrist than his palm, balancing it with his permanently curled fingertips. "The rock the Savior is standing on is supposed to be solid gold. The only way to know that for sure is to cut it in half. This one is gold to a depth of only about an eighth of an inch. Under that, we mixed lead and steel to get the weight exactly right.

"The pearls are counterfeit, but pearls are easy. Everything else had to be pretty much real except for the fact that a few of the diamonds are categorically flawed."

"Categorically flawed?" McAllister beat me in asking the same question.

"With diamonds, the rule is, the clearer the better. Since a flawed stone weighing more carats is less valuable than a smaller stone of higher quality, diamonds follow the dictum of the best quality within a given category.

" Faberge sold off diamonds he considered inferior. In reproductions, we can sneak in the occasional sub-standard stone as long as the prominent stones are high quality." He used a knuckle to point several times at something we could never have seen from across the room.

"Now, consider this." He gently placed the egg on the table. "In some fictional villa somewhere in almost any country, a hypothetical Mister Smith is robbed of a priceless object. Two months after the theft, an anonymous caller tells Mister Smith he has his object and will return it for a suitable reward. Mister Smith suggests ten percent of the insured value of the object, the figure most insurance companies will pay, up to ten percent; they are out less than half of the value of the item."

Larkin was quick on the uptake. "So the rightful owner pays a small fortune for the fake while the forger collects an inflated reward and gets to keep the authentic article."

"Ah." Kublec sighed. "Beauty and brains. A tantalizing, if somewhat dangerous, combination." He smiled to show that his comment was intended as a joke.

"Still," I said, not yet fully convinced, "two questions come to mind. First, how does an investment like this ever pay off?"

"Granted. It's a long term investment," he replied, "but it's part of an overall scheme that probably won't bear fruit for over a hundred years. Consider this, a great deal of the cost of the replication is recovered when the reward is collected, so the overhead isn't as costly as it seems. In the meantime, the average collector fancies himself an expert on his own collection and hardly ever consults a certified expert in attesting to the authenticity of his own property. Therefore, the replication goes undetected. Besides, I, personally, have fooled my share of so-called experts in my time.

"But that is all beside the point. The people who can afford to underwrite a project of this magnitude aren't interested in immediate returns. They're interested in cornering a market, no matter how long it takes."

"That brings me to my second question." I said. "Why wait a hundred years for a payoff? Where are the percentages?"

"Art is an investment, Mister Lawton." He smiled knowingly, "do you think Michelangelo personally sold his works for a million dollars apiece? For that matter, do you believe that anyone has sold an original Michelangelo for less than they paid for it?" He didn't wait for an answer as he followed with yet another question. "Have you ever played the board game, monopoly?" We all nodded. Even Katherine. "How do you win the game?"

"By securing all the property." McAllister answered automatically.

"Exactly." Said the old man. "And what happens when you own it all?"

"You drive the other players out of the game." Larkin answered.

"Yes, yes." He said happily. "And if the rules of the game allowed for an injection of fresh cash, what would the winner of the game be allowed to do?"

"Name his own price." I said.

"And that, my friends, is the crux of the matter. To a collector, what would the only known masterpiece by any particular artist bring on the open market?" He went on to answer his own question. "A photograph of the check would become a collector's item in its own right.

"A few years ago, your American Hunt Brothers tried to corner the silver market. Their plans failed, but let's, for one minute, assume it hadn't. Their scheme was about more than making a few dollars here and there. They would have had the potential of toppling governments. By controlling the flow of silver, they could have made the commodity more precious than gold or even diamonds. The economy of the world would have changed overnight.

"Now suppose, a hundred years from now, someone announces that they have every single item ever created by a particular artist. I don't imagine that governments would fall, but the economy as we know it today, would never be the same."

I think we all saw his point.

"Cramer was a Russian, wasn't he?" McAllister blurted it out, hoping to catch Kublec off guard.

"God, I hope not, laddie." Kublec looked shocked. "I would hate to see any more of the great works of the art world disappear into Russia." He sounded sincere.

"One final question." McAllister announced. "Why the Resurrect-ion Egg?"

"I can only guess, laddie."

"Then guess."

Kublec shook his head in bewilderment. "The only thing I can say is, I've known the Forbes Collection, and various pieces in it have been targets since the gallery's inception. Not only to would-be-thieves, but to law suits and other claims as well.

"I could have done a much better job on this had I had the original to use as a model." He continued. "All the works I have done that were replicated directly from the original have, so far, gone undetected." He held up his crippled hands. "Today it is all I can do to hold a pint o' ale."

McAllister pointed to the money on the table. "I'm sorry I had to burn some of your money, but I did need to get your attention." McAllister smiled. "That ought to buy you a few more pints and something nice for the misses." He said as he packed his two eggs back among the extra banknotes. "I hope you enjoy your retirement, Mister Kublec."

Kublec leaned forward and began scooping at the money clumsily. "Come back anytime, Mister McAllister." He said, not looking up. "A bloke of your caliber is always welcome."

I had the feeling that he had said that to far less savory characters than us.

* * * * *

"London." McAllister told his driver. "It's still early."

"Ever hear of this Blair guy?" He asked, turning to me.

"Wilford Blair." I answered. "Most Englishmen are split in their thinking that he might have been the never uncovered 'fifth man' that was part of Philby's famous spy group. He defected to Russia a couple of years ago taking a suitcase full of British Intelligence with him. Scotland Yard says it was because he killed his second wife, a woman who was forty years younger than him, when he found her in a rather delicate situation."

"She was screwing some other guy?"

"Subtlety never escapes you, does it?" I asked. He shrugged as if to say, "What did I say?"

"The Yard says he fled to Russia because he could trade intelligence for asylum. Like most Englishmen in high government positions, he was wealthy, from an old family, and titled. Knew the Queen. That sort of thing. After he took off, the government confiscated all his possessions and sold them at auction, including the family castle which was bought by that ape-shit hard rock guy from Pistols 'N Poseys. The auction was the social event of the year. What are you expecting to accomplish in London?"

"Two things." He answered. "We go to the Times to get a picture of Kleinfeld and we pay a visit to Theo."

"Theo?"

"Theodore Faberge."

"You made an appointment to see Theodore Faberge?" I asked incredulously.

"No." He answered as if appointments were a nuisance. "No appointment."

I leaned back in my seat and shook my head.

For those unaccustomed to it, driving on the left side of the road can be an adventure, but it was not nearly as hazardous as walking. When stepping into a busy thoroughfare, an American automatically looks to his left for traffic. To do that in England is to invite an enema in the form of a bright red, double-decker bus. Deep in thought and distracted, it was necessary for McAllister to save me from curbside suicide more than once.

Miraculously unscathed by the time we reached the Times building, we were escorted to the morgue files room by a bright eyed young lady who taught us how to use the computerized cross-reference system and have copies of the articles we wanted printed. The instructions took less than five minutes and McAllister had references to the Blair scandal on the screen in front of him in less time than that. I took a separate screen to cross-check against the names of Cramer and Kleinfeld.

In seconds I had the article that Dorn and Katherine Kublec must have been referring to on my monitor. According to the caption under the grainy black and white photograph, Henry A. Kleinfeld, standing to the left of Lord and Lady something-or-other, was a private bidder at the Blair auction, representing several European interests both political and private. The photo showed an average looking man, probably in his late fifties, who was totally unremarkable except for a crescent shaped birthmark, smaller than a dime, on his right cheek, just above the jaw line. While I was waiting for the printout, I searched the electronic files under every possible spelling of both Cramer and Kleinfeld, but I could not come up with anything that matched the man in the picture.

McAllister was going over the publicized list of the dignitaries attending the auction, but, instead of reading over his shoulder, Larkin had commandeered a screen of her own and was busy at the keyboard, rapidly typing instructions. When both McAllisters had pushed buttons to print their respective findings, I started to tell McAllister what I had found but he held up a restraining hand.

"Not here." He said, glancing around the crowded room. "Let's find someplace for lunch."

I was surprised to find out it was already two-thirty. We ate downstairs at Lanagan's Brasserie, uncrowded at that time of day and, after a delicious meal, McAllister was anxious to talk.

"Here's something that's a bit of a contradiction that you probably didn't know." He said, proud as a peacock that he had found some fact I was not aware of yet. "Guess who the late Lady Blair was playing the Romper Room Rumpus with when she reached the ultimate climax?"

I knew he was hoping I would have the occasion to quote him on what he considered to be a cute remark.

"A Russian National!" He said it with the same enthusiasm as NASA had used to announce that the Eagle had landed. "He wasn't a diplomat, but he was connected with the Embassy. He was a civilian fitness instructor. Blair shot them both. Emptied a 9mm automatic into them right in the middle of moment of passion."

That did seem like a strange fact. From all the books I have read, fiction and fact alike, any and every employee of every Russian Embassy is depicted as having two functions; their titled job and some kind of subversive duties. That Russian was found in bed with the wife of a government official, presumably involved in intelligence, was an indication that Blair might have been set up.

"My information may not be as indelicate as Bobby's," Larkin added, "but it's every bit as relevant, and just as interesting.

"While you two were looking under names, I was searching out items. I thought it might be interesting to see what type of things a murderer, defector, and traitor might tend to consider worth collecting." She looked at her husband with a sense of wry amusement. "And guess what?"

I would have bet the Excalibur on what was coming next.

"Two of the items were Faberge Eggs."

She had more, but she was using her husband's flair for the dramatic against him. It was nice to see McAllister squirming when his own tactics were being used to guarantee his fullest attention.

"The day after the auction, the special courier hired to deliver the eggs to their new owner had a terrible accident. The driver and the guard were both killed and the two eggs disappeared."

My little bit of information and poor quality photograph were beginning to fade in importance.

"Who bought the egg at the auction?" At least McAllister was asking the right questions.

Larkin unfolded papers she had taken from her purse. "Sir George Lancaster." She passed the papers to McAllister who spread them on the table, pushing aside plates and silverware to make room.

"He lives in Exeter." He said, looking up to me. "Where is that?"

"Southwest, I think." I guessed. "Toward Plymouth."

"Plymouth. That's a major port city."

"But far easier to drive if you're thinking of sailing over there."

"I was thinking that an old seaport is the perfect place for smuggling valuable items out of the country."

McAllister didn't leap to conclusions. He took jet propelled lunges.

"I have an idea." I was grateful to Larkin for speaking up.

"Why don't we try to find out something from the police?"

McAllister started to object but Larkin held up a hand. "In spite of what you think, New Scotland Yard has a fine reputation for excellent investigative work. A short way from here we can try to consolidate some work and maybe it won't be necessary to drive all the way to Exeter."

"Oh, we're going to Exeter." McAllister stated in spite of Larkin's reasonable suggestion. "But you might be right about seeing the police first." He started shoving the papers on the table into a disorganized pile. "Everybody ready? Good, let's go."

Halfway between Buckingham Palace and Westminster Abbey and the House of Parliament, the twentieth century concrete and glass building that houses New Scotland Yard looks unnatural among the classical architecture that surrounds it. We entered through the Victoria Street entrance into an atmosphere of systematic bedlam as four o'clock must have been shift change. People, anxious to be off duty for another day or expectant about an upcoming tour of duty, rushed in all directions and exhibited little patience for three Americans who were not sure of whom they wished to see about a case that had no bearing on them or their respective departments.

We were finally greeted politely, if not with enthusiasm, by a young female sergeant who seated us in a small partitioned cubicle where she summed up our requests in one, lengthy sentence.

"So you're asking us to help locate a man who has at least two names, no known criminal affiliation except an aging and near senile forger, who may or may not have arranged for art theft in at least two countries, who might possibly be Russian, with only a year old newspaper photo for identification so that the three of you, all Americans without law enforcement alliance, authorization, or training, can question him about the murder of a South American citizen in France."

I think I would have tried to make it sound less ridiculous.

"I think you are treading on very thin ice on this one." She continued. "Scotland Yard and the Queen frown on her subjects becoming involved in domestic affairs. I hardly think we would be eager to become involved in something as vague as this while at the same time abetting laypersons that have no jurisdiction in an International case such as this."

"Sergeant Abernathy," I said, trying to sound more intelligent than her synopsis of our mission indicated. "All we really want to know is the true identity of this man," I tapped the picture I had copied from the newspaper, "and whether or not he is a known criminal?" "Your observations about us are correct. We are not trained in the complexities of police work and only wish to gather information so that we can ultimately turn it over to Mister McAllister's attorney."

McAllister went doe-eyed and Larkin nodded convincingly.

"Since this is a case that encompasses several countries and many different laws as well as jurisdictions, we are having a difficult time getting cooperation or assistance out of anyone. We would never dream of acting on information we received from any source other than turn it over to Mister McAllister's lawyer for collation into a proper presentation for the appropriate authorities to take control."

McAllister and Larkin bobbed their heads with exaggerated sincerity.

"Just what do you expect a solicitor to accomplish on your behalf?" She asked. "That's just the point." Larkin interjected. "We won't know unless we can give him some facts. Our attorney is Ned Hoffman. He has an International reputation and, in the past, has worked with your Sir Godfrey Stewart."

She recognized the name. "Sir Godfrey Stewart? On a criminal matter?"

"Good heavens, no." Larkin amended quickly. "But Mister Hoffman is recognized for a variety of talents when it comes to the law. We have retained him because of that very fact."

At that very moment, Ned Hoffman could probably be found in some south Florida pub drinking rum punch and checking out every female between the age of eighteen and twenty-eight for their availability. McAllister had hired Hoffman originally as a diver, who knew, or cared very little about anything above water level. Hoffman became a renowned maritime attorney, as well as a reluctant criminal attorney to help McAllister out of a couple of situations, and was known, most notably for his expertise in marine salvage laws, but had utilized his talents as a diver and his eccentric ways in friendship as well. Knowing Ned Hoffman only by what McAllister had told me about him over the years, I sincerely doubted that he had even used a law book for anything other than a paperweight in the last decade. He was the epitome of wasted talent, a true beach bum whom money and prestige meant not a whit. I hoped that Sergeant Abernathy would not try calling Ned at his "office", a number that would have rung the pay phone at the Wretched Reef tavern in Key West.

Abernathy thoughtfully toyed with the copied photo of Kleinfeld. "I'll tell you what I can do." She said, indulgently. "I can run this photo through our electronic files and see how much we can get. I can't guarantee any results and I certainly can't promise any priority action, but I will do that much on one condition. I will wire the results directly to your barrister. What is his address?"

McAllister didn't hesitate. He scribbled something on a piece of paper and handed it across to Abernathy. In the brief glance I got of the hastily penned note, I firmly believed that I learned the street address of Hoffman's favorite hang-out and the probable limits of his own little world.

Larkin was the only one who thanked Abernathy for her time when we left.

"So much for your idea that the police would be of any help. Police are no different around the world; they all have their own agenda." McAllister said as we walked down the steps.

"She said she would see what the Department had on him." Larkin answered defensively. "Why don't we give her a chance?"

McAllister smiled, "Because I think I can do better on my own." He stated smugly.

"Well, it's getting late." I said, changing the subject to try to defuse a potential argument. "Perhaps we better start thinking about a place to stay for the night."

Thankfully, McAllister agreed.

The Inn On The Park has a modern exterior, but everything within is wonderfully traditional. The rooms are more than comfortable and the Four Seasons Restaurant is one of London's best. Looking over the menu made me sorry that I had eaten a hardy and late lunch. I also felt self-conscious when McAllister looked at me strangely when I ordered the petite ("ladies") filet. I got another frown when I refused dessert.

Since dinner had produced disapproval from McAllister more than once, I knew it would be useless to try to talk him out of an unannounced call on Theodore Faberge. He would tell me that anyone who didn't know how to order a decent meal in the four star restaurant would hardly qualify as an expert at calling on someone who might shed light on a mystery. The two concepts had nothing in common, but McAllister would have made it work for him. I didn't say it would make any sense. That's just the way he thinks.

If you had to describe a house that was probably part of the original reconstruction after the fire of 1666 as upper middle class, Theodore Faberge's home was a perfect example of over three hundred years of upgrading. This was a neighborhood where bowler hats and umbrellas from James Smith and Sons were still very much in fashion and the majority of homes were the residences of the merchant class, the pride and backbone of London.

The Faberge house was a walk-up with a huge door of oak and beveled glass with sheer curtains offering obtuse privacy for those inside. It was not quite dark, but the house was well lighted from inside. McAllister pulled the ancient bell chain and a raspy ring sounded from behind the door. A rotund little woman who could have been Katherine Kublec's younger sister waddled to the door, assessed us through a slit in the curtains, and opened the door partway.

"Good evening" McAllister smiled his most disarming expressions of friendliness. "We are from America and we wish to have a word with Theodore Faberge."

She blinked as if we had spoken a foreign language.

"My name is McAllister. This is my wife and over there is the famous American author, Granger Lawton."

She looked at Larkin, then at me, and back to McAllister.

"May we please talk with Mister Faberge?"

"Author, you say." She looked me over again, this time more carefully. "And what would you be writing about that you would want to talk with Mister Faberge about?"

"We're not writing about anything." I answered. "We would like Mister Faberge's perspective on some personal matters."

"You want to talk about things long past." She said. It was not a question.

"We need some insight that we believe only Mister Faberge can supply." McAllister explained carefully and patiently. "We need an expert." He was attempting to play to vanity.

"You want to talk to Theo's granddad." She pronounced Theo like T.O. "Would you like to know how many people in a given time want to talk to

Theo about the great Carl Faberge?" It was clear she was not pleased with our presence. "Read your history books." She continued without waiting for an answer. "Carl Faberge died in 1920. Theo never knew the man."

"But surely he knows something about the art." McAllister insisted. "After all, he is a master jeweler himself."

"Theo is an artist who has been ignored for far too many years because of his parentage." She stated indignantly. He is a very talented man in his own right, but he is constantly over-shadowed by a man who has been dead for over three quarters of a century. If you want to talk to Theo Faberge about an original piece of jeweled art, you'll have to contact him at work. If you want to talk about ancient history, go to a lecture at Oxford or Eaton. Don't be botherin' honest folk in their own homes."

My embarrassment was the only thing that kept me from telling McAllister "I told you so", even though I had only run those words through the back of my mind.

Before anyone of us could say anything, the door slammed with an air of finality and the bulky shadow of Theodore Faberge's protector faded from the entranceway. McAllister had dealt with two strong willed and determined women in the last five hours and came away with less than satisfactory results. It must have rankled him badly.

"Tomorrow we go to Exeter." He declared solemnly, turning to Larkin. "See if you can arrange an appointment with Lancaster when we get back to the hotel. Use Sir Godfrey's name again. That was a good idea." That was all he had said in my presence for the rest of the day. Although Great Britain has no dramatic geographical features, the wild grasses and purple heather of southwest England are lovely and lush and a calming influence on a long drive. Once outside of London it is easy to see that the island has become a nation of city dwellers with over eighty percent of the population preferring urban life. How this could be true was beyond me. We were driving through an area that was scattered with Roman ruins and a bit further to the west was the legendary birthplace of King Arthur.

Exeter stands on the banks of the Exe River, the original site of Isca Drumnoniorum, an ancient Roman fortified city. The Saxons renamed the town Escanestre when they founded a monastery there in 680, and the town became Exeter in 1068 when William the Conqueror seized it and built Rougemont Castle for himself. A port city in its earlier days, Exeter was often frequented by Queen Elizabeth's favorite sea Captains, Sir Francis Drake and Sir Walter Raleigh.

The drive from London took a little over four hours and within sight of the massive towers of Exeter Cathedral, less than a mile off the A3052, we turned onto the five or six acre estate of Sir George Lancaster. I was expecting more. The manor was small by standards of a titled landowner's home and, while not a contemporary modern structure, it had probably been built at the turn of the century. It was a two story affair, as likely as not about twice the size of the average suburban residence of any rural or country home in the world. A restored MG TD sat in the drive in front of an attached garage. The man tightened the leather hood straps of the classic car, turned at the sound of our approach and waved. Again against stereotype, Sir George was about our age, trim and fit with a full head of wavy brown hair, clear eyes, and a full set of perfectly white teeth. He wiped his hands on a monogramed hand towel as our car glided to a stop.

"Mister McAllister?" He smiled easily and extended a surprisingly clean hand. "Sir Godfrey has told me about how you were such a wonderful host to him during the recovery of the Hacha. He didn't mention that you also had excellent taste in traveling companions."

He wasn't talking about me.

McAllister made the introductions which elicited a deep bow for Larkin and a short but polite handshake for me.

"Won't you come in?" He said, pointing to the front door.

"Rebecca is in the village doing a bit of shopping but I'm certain I can scare up a spot of tea and cake."

We walked through a spacious living room and formal dining room to the kitchen where we sat on bar stools at a breakfast bar while Lancaster put a tea kettle on the stove. He began searching through cabinets as he talked over his shoulder.

"So what does a treasure hunter, a beautiful woman, and an author of adventure novels require from a humble country doctor?"

"You're a physician?" McAllister asked, surprised.

"Why not?" Lancaster countered. "You don't approve?" He was smiling.

"It just surprises me that you could make a decent living this far from any real population center." McAllister answered.

"I spent twenty years as a surgeon in London trying to live up to my father's expectations. When the old man finally departed this dreary world, I took leave from the sixteen hour days, the pressure, and city life to get to know the woman I married nineteen years ago and enjoy life in general. I donate a day a week in a clinic in Dorchester and spend the remaining six days of the week spending my savings and my inheritance at an alarming rate."

"Which brings me to why we're here today?" McAllister informed him.

"Oh, dear." Sir George said with mock consternation. You're about to tell me you have a social disease or you want me to invest in your latest quest for sunken treasure."

"Actually," McAllister smiled politely, "we need neither your talents nor your money. Just the answers to a few questions."

"Well, I find that very disappointing, Mister McAllister. I'd fancy an offer to invest and maybe participate in one of your treasure hunts; Sir Godfrey absolutely enthralled me with his stories."

"I'm flattered, Sir Lancaster. But I'm afraid I'm not exactly hunting for treasure at this time."

"Just answers, you say?"

McAllister nodded.

"In that case," Sir George continued his light banter; let me see if I can save you some time.

"I'm fifty-two years old. I don't miss practicing medicine. I'm boringly faithful to my wife. I touch up my hair a bit because I'm vain, and my golf handicap is seven. What else?"

I could tell McAllister was reluctant to break the mood. Nevertheless, he plowed ahead, instantly changing the atmosphere in the small kitchen.

"Last year you bought two Faberge Eggs at the Blair auction."

A veil dropped behind Sir George's eyes and his expression changed to one of annoyance and distrust. The tea kettle picked that moment to begin its shrill whistle giving our host something to do while he thought of a response. As he poured the boiling water into a tea brewer, he took the opportunity to study each of us a little closer. He set tea cups in front of us slowly and deliberately.

"If Sir George hadn't vouched for you personally, my next question would be if you represented the police or some other consortium of the like. Since your affiliation seems to be other than law enforcement, I find myself curious that three Americans would appear on my doorstep asking about something that has caused me nothing but trouble since that bloody auction."

"Bloody. Figuratively or literally?" I asked.

"Both." He answered disgustedly. "But you haven't answered my question."

He hadn't really asked one, but McAllister replied anyway.

"I'm a collector myself." He said. "I became interested in Imperial Eggs about a year and a half ago through the indirect actions of my late brother-in-law."

"Then our interests are somewhat similar." He replied, pouring tea into each of our cups. "While I am partial to all items of Faberge art, I cannot afford the Imperial aspect of the art. My collection is limited to the comparative mundane articles of jewelry and objects created for the less prestigious customers of the master."

"But you successfully bid on two eggs anyway." McAllister observed.
"Yes, I did." The doctor answered. "But my selections were never owned by the Czarist families.

"The first piece was a miniature clock within an egg made from silver gilt, enamel, and pearls. It was a gift from Siberian mining magnate Alexander Ferdinandovitch Kelch to his wife Barbara on Easter in 1898.

"The second egg contained nesting vodka glasses. It was an unremarkable piece except for the clever way it was constructed and bore no precious stones and just a minimum of gold and silver gilting. It was purchased by Alexi Ivanovich Putilov who was the chairman of the Russo-Asiatic bank.

"Both pieces were most likely designed and crafted by senior apprentices or first year journeymen and probably never even seen by the Master himself.

"I share your attraction to the Faberge art but, unfortunately, not the means to indulge myself as you might have. How many eggs do you own?"

"Nine." McAllister corrected himself immediately. "Seven."

Sir George seemed unconfused by the self-contradiction. "I could only hope to, one day, view such a marvelous collection."

"You have an open invitation." McAllister offered graciously. "Any time you're in the neighborhood of Savannah, Georgia, give me a call."

"Thank you, Mister McAllister. That is a kind inducement to someday visit your beautiful city. I have seen pictures and read many articles on Savannah, which, if my memory serves me, our General Oglethorpe designed, settled and built."

"Your memory of your history is correct, Sir George. Seems we share a distant, but common heritage. You have an open invitation."

"Indeed, Mister McAllister. You are most gracious."

"In the meantime," McAllister continued with his sincere lack of subtlety, "you were never able to take possession of the eggs."

The cordial smile instantly disappeared. It was a good thing that we were not connected with the police because it became immediately evident that Sir George was hiding something. He acted both suspicious and distrustful and if he had attempted a lie at that time, it would have been transparent.

McAllister saw it too and put him to the test.

"What do you know about the accident?"

"The accident?" Sir George looked slightly relieved. "Very little. It happened on the coast road near Lyme Regis. A rollover that broke the necks of both men. The van was empty when it was found by a passing motorist."

McAllister's line of questioning was getting us nowhere, so I decided to try my hand.

"Sir George," I began, "sometimes in the art world things happen that, on the surface, do not appear ethical or honest, but in reality, cause no laws to be broken by an otherwise innocent collector. Art cannot be fully appreciated unless it is shared among those who fully recognize and cherish the true creativity of the profession." Even though it was double talk, I think I was making an impression. "While we have been engaged in our particular pursuit for only a short time, we have discovered and become privy to information that you might find very helpful."

"What kind of information?" Lancaster remained guarded but curiosity proved more enticing than caution.

"Let me put forth a purely hypothetical situation." I suggested. "A prospective buyer attends an auction where he becomes a successful bidder. He is happy with the particular items he purchases and anxiously awaits delivery by a bonded courier. The courier, however, meets with an unfortunate set of circumstances and loses the items in transit. Since neither the buyer nor the seller is responsible, the courier, or their insurance company, must stand the loss. Three months later, the buyer receives a telephone call asking if he is still interested in the lost product. The buyer is offered a deal in which he can recover the items for the bargain price of fifty cents on the dollar or, your purely academic case, pennies on the pound."

"The caller explains that his offer is contingent on the buyer remaining silent about the deal since the insurance company for the courier has a legitimate claim in the item. The buyer, concerned only with a collector's mentality, agrees and a pact is made. He takes delivery of the pieces and remains silent about the transaction, happy to make the tradeoff of the money he saved for the anonymity of the deal."

"Interesting." Lancaster conceded. "Even plausible. But how would this information affect me or help you?"

"I know a way that the buyer could not only keep the items he purchased without further expenditure, but avoid any litigation with anyone who thought they might have a claim on the items."

McAllister's eyes went wide at the audacity of my proclamation but Lancaster was watching me carefully for any – sign of deception. Apparently I passed his scrutiny because he beckoned us to follow him back through the dining and living rooms to the front hallway where he stopped next to a thermostat set in the paneling on the side of a staircase. He removed the cover of the thermostat to reveal a combination dial which he worked quickly, pushing the dial after spinning the appropriate numbers. A section of panel popped outward exposing a narrow stairwell set on a curve that corresponded to the stairs that led to the second floor. We followed him downward to a windowless cellar about the size of a basketball court. It bore a striking resemblance to McAllister's gallery at his plantation in Georgia except that it was woefully lacking in substance. Aside from a few paintings that were old but familiar, the room contained two velvet lined display cases that contained their own lighting.

“My family was well-to-do by any standards, but not overtly wealthy.” Lancaster explained. “What you see here is the humble beginning of a collection, something my forefathers would have considered extraneous. I admit that I began this collection because of the associations I made when I became a Knight of the Realm, a snobbery I personally used to condemn. But I found an area of genuine interest in decorative art. I know my acquisitions are miscellany and varied, but I hope someday to have a gallery of special interest.”

He led us to the first case which held about fifty pieces of personal jewelry from cufflinks to necklaces all mounted proudly next to a simple printed placard describing each particular item.

“As you can see, my pieces are a bit diverse. The pocket watch once belonged to Winston Churchill. It was said he claimed to have spent seven pounds sterling for the watch which he put on a solid silver chain which was a gift. I paid two thousand for both. The gold choker once belonged to a minor queen of Egypt whose tomb was discovered by Napoleon's men. To date, it's my most expensive piece. Those shirt studs belonged to Laurence Olivier. He wore them when he accepted his Academy Award in 1948. As I said, a varied and unconventional grouping. “

We worked our way in the direction of the second case where, on a raised section in the middle of the case, there sat two eggs Sir George Lancaster had described earlier.

They were surrounded by lesser items, all unmistakingly Faberge, from cigarette holders to picture frames. There were about forty items in all, some functional, many frivolous in nature. There were several items which were miniature replicas of animal life including bulldogs, pigs, frogs, and bears. Other than the eggs, he was apparently proudest of a pair of diamond studded opera glasses which also rested on a raised platform, a half step lower than the eggs.

“It was exactly as you described it, Mister Lawton.” Lancaster said, leaning against the case. “Three months to the day after the accident, I got a call offering both eggs for exactly one half of what I bid for them at the auction. Since the auction officials retained my marker uncashed, I felt I was getting a tremendous bargain. At first I balked, concerned of course that I was dealing in stolen property and when I voiced my reservations, my caller reminded me that there were at least three other bidders at that auction. His veiled threat was enough. Later in the week we met at the Hole In The Wall Pub in Plymouth. I must admit I felt a bit strange carrying all that money into a pub that was formerly a debtor's prison. The deal was complete and the man was gone even before our drinks arrived.

“Distinguished looking man?” I asked. “Crescent shaped scar on his jaw? Slight accent”.

"No." I knew Lancaster thought he was being tested. A thug. Mean looking. Short and stocky. A thick Slavic accent."

I nodded as if he had passed his test.

"Now suppose you tell me how I can keep these eggs without fear of legal reprisals or further payoffs."

McAllister smiled at me as if to say "Now whatcha gonna do".

"It's fairly easy, Sir George." I said. "Report this incident to the courier's insurance company and let their experts examine the eggs."

"And?" He still didn't get it.

"Your eggs are counterfeit, Sir George." I said as gently as possible. "Probably not worth half of what you paid."

The wind went out of Sir George's sails in an instant.

"You seem to be sure of yourself." Was all he could say.

McAllister was looking at me as if I had just told his kids there was no Santa Clause while Lancaster spent a good minute and a half staring into his display case. When he lifted his head, he regained his composure.

"Shall we go back upstairs?" He suggested.

When we had reassembled in the kitchen, Sir George offered us more tea.

"I have forty-three items in all including some opera glasses that were supposed to have belonged to the actress Vera Komissarz-hevskaya, given to her by Olga Knipper who was Chekov's wife. How many more pieces in my collections are mere fakes?"

"I have no idea." I answered. "I would suggest you find yourself an expert and have your entire collection evaluated."

"Of course." He said fatalistically, already expecting the worst.

We spent another twenty minutes discussing the merits of employing an independent expert when purchasing a major acquisition which was really a polite way of easing ourselves out the door. We had driven almost two hundred miles to get confirmation of what, in our hearts, we already knew, learning only that we had yet another suspect who may or may not have been with the man who planted the bomb in McAllister's car in Paris. I felt we were being pelted with background information and nothing of any substance that would lead us to the murderer of Sally and Antonio.

I was tired of McAllister's shotgun approach to everything and was hoping that he would lead us in a more focused investigation that I knew him to be capable of. I had seen McAllister pull off miracles before. Many times.

McAllister snapped me out of my reverie. "Why did you tell him about the eggs?"

It was a question I had known was coming and, although he felt that silence would have been more benevolent; I vehemently disagreed and told him why.

"What if, ten years from now, Sir George fell on hard times?" I said. "Just say he offered those two eggs to you for sale and, not knowing they were phony, later discovered they were relatively worthless forgeries. What would you do? Say 'that's all right, Sir George, you need the money'. I'll be a good chap and take the loss?" No, I don't think so. You'd be hollering rape loud enough to be heard in Atlanta. I saved the man possible embarrassment and probable criminal prosecution. No man likes to be made a fool of. Especially you. He can be thankful it happened in front of three sympathetic persons, two of whom suffered a like experience, instead of having to listen to the interrogation of a suspicious cop."

I think he thought more about the way I said it than the words.

McAllister nodded. "I see."

* * * * *

That night back at my hotel room in London, the phone rang.

"Yeah."

"Grange, I have an idea." McAllister announced.

"Would you like to share it with me?"

"Come on over to our suite."

I obliged.

Larkin had already retired for the evening. I sat across from McAllister in the parlor waiting for him to astound me with his great revelation, but before he got around to it the phone rang.

"Pick up the other line at the same time as I lift the receiver." He pointed to the other phone near the bar. "And be real quiet."

"Hello."

"Mister McAllister, please."

"Speaking."

"Bobby McAllister? The anti-terrorist and treasure hunter?" The voice sounded amusingly surprised. "After all these years this is indeed an unexpected pleasure. How are you, my friend?"

"Fine, thank you, Mister Camper. It has been awhile." McAllister answered with a genuine smile on his face. It also reflected in his voice.

Camper? With a 'G'? I wondered.

"Yes, it has Bobby. Are you staying out of trouble?" He asked, followed by a chuckle.

"More or less. How about you, Mr. Camper?"

"Well, compared to the circumstances involved in our very first meeting in Jackson Hole, and what I heard from Jeff about your little adventure in Venezuela, my life is boring." He chuckled again. "Yes, I'm enjoying life to the fullest thanks, in part, to you. I'll forever remain in your debt."

"Nonsense! I'm in your debt."

"Well, who's keeping score, my friend? Is there anything I can do for you? Just name it."

While I had never met, nor heard Geoff Camper's voice before, he seemed familiar to me. McAllister recounted the story of how fate placed him in Jackson Hole, Wyoming at the right time and place to thwart an assassin's attempt on his life.

I was also thankful to Uncle Geoff for sending his nephew to Venezuela a few years ago to reciprocate in kind by helping us out of a tight spot. Probably saved our lives. I met his nephew Jeff with a 'J', but not our real benefactor.

"Well, since you asked." McAllister teased. "I could use your advice."

"It must be very important for you to be calling all the way from

London, England."

"It is. But how did you know I was in London?"

"Just a minute m'boy." We were put on hold while McAllister and I listened to the hum and cackle of transatlantic noise for a full sixty seconds.

"Are you familiar with Ye Olde Cheshire Cheese?" Coming back on the line so suddenly had startled me.

"What is it, a pub or something?" McAllister asked.

"Yeah, on Little Essex Street, just off Fleet Street."

"I'm sure I can find it."

"Great. Find it by two o'clock tomorrow afternoon. Good to hear from you again, Bobby." The line went dead.

"Looks like we have something to do tomorrow afternoon, Grange."

"We?"

"Why not? You're my Sancho Panza." Great. I thought.

* * * * *

Ye Olde Cheshire Cheese was right where Camper said it would be, a seventeenth century pub with dark paneled walls and sawdust on the floor. Though barely two o'clock, it was crowded with a yuppie clientele who, every time they purchased a fresh drink, saluted the empty table where Doctor Samuel Johnson was said to have held court with the literary giants of his day. Only blocks away, in nearby Gough Square, was Johnson's home where he wrote his famous dictionary, long before Noah Webster was about off of knee breeches. I ordered iced tea as I waited at a separate table at the opposite end of the pub from where McAllister awaited his friend. The look on the bartender's face persuaded me to change my mind and order a beer. It was barely in front of me when I saw the man approach McAllister. The man was my age with a push broom moustache and wire rimmed glasses. He was wearing a three button suit with all three buttons fastened and while he wasn't wearing a bowler hat, he would have looked comfortable in one.

The two men exchanged greetings, but didn't seem to know each other. McAllister glanced in my direction and the man turned his attention toward me, nodded, and McAllister beckoned me to join them.

"Mister Pagliossi, please meet my good friend and traveling companion, Granger Lawton." McAllister said.

"Pleased to meet you, Mister Lawton." The stranger said.

"Likewise Sir." I didn't want to attempt to pronounce his name.

"Shall we take a walk, gentlemen?"

I looked at McAllister. He smiled reassuringly and said, "Sure, a great day for a walk."

In silence, we walked along the sidewalk until Pagliossi saw a taxi. He flagged it down and motioned us to get in.

"Where are we going?" Asked McAllister.

"All in good time, dear fellow, all in good time." As we made a series of turns, I noticed that he was carefully watching the rear-view mirror. I don't think McAllister noticed, he was sitting in the back seat next to his host while I sat in the front passenger's seat.

"Mister 'C didn't know the extent of your little problem so he thought it best that any talking take place in a spot where the walls didn't have ears. Since certain offices in the colonies were most probably listening to your call last night, it's a safe wager that the Cheshire might have been, shall we say, audio/visually compromised. One can't be too careful in this day and age."

"Would it be out of line to ask who the hell you are?" McAllister asked in a less than charming way.

"Of course not, old chap; Boylston Pagliossi." He said as if everyone knew who Boylston Pagliossi was. "But I'm just a messenger. An escort, so to speak."

At Boylston Pagliossi's command, our taxi made a sharp U-turn in the middle of a busy avenue. While I was still rocking from the suddenness of the maneuver, both McAllister and Pagliossi turned in the seat, watching out the rear window.

"Your paranoia seems to be a little contagious." McAllister said.

"Nonsense, my friend." Pagliossi said. "Just a mite precautious."

"Well, I'm not having a whole lot of fun." McAllister said.

"Okay, that should do it." Pagliossi said, quite satisfied. "Eighteen Wilton Row." He told the driver.

The Grenadier was, quite possibly, the poshest pub in town. Just off Belgravia Square, it was much more subdued than the Cheshire and far more private. In a booth at the rear, with a clear view of the entire establishment, sat Geoff Camper. He didn't seem all that thrilled to see me, a total stranger, but when McAllister made the introductions and assured him that I was a "dear trusted friend", Camper with a "G" relaxed.

Camper was a broad shouldered man, tan and healthy for his age which must have been somewhere in the middle sixties, and he smiled easily, something I didn't think someone in his profession did. Seated next to him was a non-descript man in his forties, average looking but well dressed and probably European. Pagliossi stared at me, making me very uncomfortable.

"Grange is my friend, Mister Camper." He said again.

Reluctantly, Camper released me from his glazing stare, leaned over and spoke to his companion who nodded immediately and excused himself.

"Have a seat, Grange, you too, Bobby. Pardon me for not making introductions." He said, nodding toward his departing associate who had Pagliossi in tow. "But circumstances sometime dictate that some of my colleagues would prefer to remain unacknowledged." Camper looked me in the eye, then smiled. "If Bobby McAllister says you're his friend, then..." He paused, ". . . you're my friend too." He offered me his hand, we shook, and the tension was eased.

"Have you been to Jackson Hole lately, Mister Camper?" Asked McAllister who was displaying his trademark smile.

Camper caught the humor, smiled, and said. "Not lately, my friend."

"Neither have I." Said McAllister.

They both laughed at their own private joke, which for some reason I didn't find humorous.

"It's great to see you again, Bobby." Said Camper as he signaled for a waitress who hurried over to our table. "What would you gentlemen like to drink?"

I finally spoke. "I'd like iced tea, but every time I order it in this country, I get treated like a leper."

"I'll have iced tea." McAllister said. "Long Island Iced Tea."

Camper smiled. "Two regular iced teas and a Long Island Iced Tea for my friend there." He said, nodding at McAllister. "With plenty of ice." He added as she wiggled away.

"I certainly didn't expect to see you here." McAllister told him.

"Well, you asked for my help." He reminded him.

The waitress returned with our orders. I couldn't see any ice.

"Still," McAllister continued. "To just jump up and fly from Chicago to London in answer to an ambiguous phone call seems rather, we11, impulsive."

"You have a lot of nerve calling me impulsive, Bobby." He replied. "Besides, throwing a beer bottle when it's not part of an Olympic event seems somewhat spontaneous too." He continued, still smiling. "So we're both guilty of impetuous behavior, aren't we?"

"How did you know I was in London when I first called you last night?" Asked McAllister.

He chuckled. "You would be surprised what you can buy over the counter these days." He said. "Manufacturers have found that the government isn't the only customers in the market for their surreptitious devices. They even have their own retail outlets now.

"There's this box you can attach to your telephone. It displays the number of the person calling you. If you don't want to talk to whoever is calling, you simply don't answer. I go into this shop once a month just to see what's new on the market. You wouldn't believe the things they have for sale. The place is even called the Spy Store."

"For a number of years you have resisted coming to me." He said to McAllister, growing serious. "I could have helped you in a number of ways. Not all of my pursuits are made of the stuff that gets reported in newspapers. I do have legitimate enterprises as well as connections."

"You were very helpful by sending Jeff and his friend Scott to Venezuela just in the nick of time." McAllister answered.

"Okay, Okay." He conceded. "We're even." Then he finally spoke to me. "Granger Lawton, the author?"

"Well, yes. . ." I tried to answer modestly, but he cut me off.

"I read Fool's Paradise. Bobby sent me a copy. You did a fine job, Grange." He paused to scratch his ear. "But I don't have your autograph. Why didn't you have him autograph my copy, Bobby?" He asked, turning his attention to McAllister.

"Grange sent me a few copies, unsigned of course, to Venezuela, which is a million miles away from where he lives in Arizona."

"Payson, isn't it, Grange?" Camper asked me.

"That's home."

"Fine place." He then focused on McAllister with a serious expression. "Well, I have come all the way to London to listen to your story, Bobby. Are you going to keep me in suspense?"

"A friend of ours, actually, Grange's fiancé, and my brother-in-law were killed. Murdered." McAllister said. "I . . . we want the man who did it, as well as the people responsible."

If McAllister was waiting for a reaction, he was due for a letdown. Camper remained motionless and unmoved as if McAllister had just asked for something as simple as the loan of a dollar. I was a little confused myself.

After a few seconds, he leaned forward and laced his fingers together on the table. “Start at the beginning.” He said. “Tell me the whole story. Don’t leave anything out.”

McAllister spent the next thirty minutes telling Geoff Camper what had transpired over the past summer. Surprisingly, McAllister didn’t ramble and he left out nothing. Camper listened intently, without interrupting, and when McAllister had finished, he looked at me as if to ask if he left anything out. I slowly shook my head, suppressing my desire to chastise McAllister for the way he had cavorted all over Europe as if he were on his own private Easter egg hunt. After all, I was there with him.

Camper ran his fingers through his thick, wavy hair and looked at us sympathetically.

“So you thought your old friend with a penchant for bad publicity could help you find the guy that ruined your vacation in Paris.” He said to McAllister. It sounded like an accusation.

McAllister studied his Long Island Iced Tea, which he had barely touched. “I honestly don’t know.” He said guiltily. “I just thought that.

“Never mind what you thought.” He said to McAllister.

I was having a hard time reading him. He seemed disappointed, almost resigned to his role of a Godfather, dispensing his own kind of advice and justice. McAllister continued his study of his drink as Camper was tapping his fingers on the table top almost soundlessly.

“This is not an easy thing.” He said, after what seemed like a long time. “If we were talking about Chicago, I could have a name for you by tomorrow morning and the man himself by nightfall. While I have many connections in this part of the world they are, for the most part, accredited business interests that are unfamiliar with methods that may exist in other parts of the world.”

“I’m really sorry I dumped my problems on you, Mister Camper.” McAllister said, losing interest in his Long Island Iced Tea. “I should have known that this is a world apart from Chicago and Arizona.”

I tried to hide my own disappointment.

“Difficult,” Camper said as if McAllister had not spoken, “but I will see what I can do.” He reached in his shirt pocket and found a business card. He studied it as he said. “Call my attorney every other day. I will leave a message. Follow my instructions carefully. I would hate to see that Mister Lawton’s next book was a firsthand account of European prison life.” He handed the business card to McAllister who studied it carefully, smiled, and handed it to me.

It read: Jeffrey Camper, Attorney At Law. Offices in Chicago and New York.

* * * * *

"Hello?"

"Is all this really necessary, my friend? I've been running from phone to phone for almost two hours now."

"I suppose you could call me at home." The voice changed very subtly. "Then we could both risk being discovered by people we would rather leave in the dark."

"I just think you're being over cautious." The caller responded. "In five years now we have not aroused suspicion from any quarter."

"All that proves is that my system is working." Was the response. "What have you got to report?"

"The Americans are in London. They went to see Kublec yesterday morning and tried to see Theodore Faberge last night. Today the treasure hunter left his beautiful wife at their hotel while he and his author friend went sightseeing in a taxi. They were not followed."

"Why were they not followed?"

"Well, the taxi . . . uh . . . made an unexpected U-turn in the middle of the boulevard, and they were . . . gone."

"Gone? Gone where?"

"They were lost."

"You lost them?! Where did they go?"

"If I knew that, they wouldn't be considered to have been gone, would they?" It was the caller's turn to exhibit sarcasm. "I'm only one person out here, you know?"

"Were they on to your shadow?"

"Can't tell, really? I don't think so. I'm all alone out here, like I said."

"Surely you're not going to blame that on me." The tone was self-righteous.

"Of course not. I'm simply reminding you that I can't be everywhere at once."

"Speaking of being everywhere, why aren't you concentrating on the real objective in this matter?"

"I told you how I operated when we first met. You haven't had occasion to question my methods in the past. Why start now?"

"It just seems that this is the perfect opportunity to act." "This would be the perfect opportunity if I had a division of men at my disposal. Have you had a chance to see this treasure hunting fellow's security arrangements?" "No."

"Well, I have. And I don't mind telling you, his people really know what they're doing. They're professionals, they're good, and they're practically invisible. I know you expect a big payoff on this one, but I still think your reasoning is faulty."

"Why?"

"Do it my way and you will never have to work again."

"That's where you and I differ. I like my work."

"Wrong again. The caller corrected. "I love my work."

* * *

CHAPTER FIVE

Did you guys get your business taken care of?" Asked Larkin who was suffering from an overload of curiosity.

The Savoy Grill was constructed to resemble the first class dining room of an older luxury ocean liner and, although it was purportedly frequented by celebrities from the performing arts to politics, I saw no one notable. One of the army of staff serving our table told us that the dignitaries usually started coming in after the theatre.

McAllister, for some reason, did not want to let Larkin know that he had resorted to contacting a mafia don to find answers that he should have already found on his own. McAllister was definitely difficult to understand at times. Most of the time.

"It was actually an opportunity to see an old friend." He semi-lied.

"A friend? Why didn't you invite him to dinner? It was a him, wasn't it?" She asked with mock jealousy.

"He actually arrived unannounced for the afternoon." He said, and then changed the subject. "What did you and Gary and his shadows do today?" McAllister asked feigning jealousy in return.

She looked at me. "Grange, is Bobby telling me the truth?"

"Well, as best as I can tell." I don't think I answered that to her satisfaction but she just smiled.

"We went to the Tower of London." Larkin said, exuberantly. "It's much more than I thought. Do you know how many different things the Tower has been?" She asked me. McAllister seemed indifferent to her excursion.

"Let's see," I said, shifting my attention to a more pleasant view. "A fortress, a palace, a prison, a museum." I ran out of options so I shrugged.

"Aha!" She said gleefully. "I'm actually one up on the great Granger Lawton?" She then turned to her husband. "Do you know?"

McAllister shrugged.

"Well, it was also a mint and an observatory. It's much more than I had pictured. They have the Crown Jewels there and a couple of museums that have things like armour and instruments of torture." She shuddered on purpose. She looked at McAllister. "Do you really think they used those things, Bobby?"

"Of course. They'd probably use them in Arizona today if they could muster up enough votes."

"My goodness. I could never imagine anyone being so cruel." She said.

I didn't know whether she meant Arizona or medieval London.

"Well, you're talking about the ancestors of people who murdered two innocent princes on that very same spot in 1485 and where Sir Walter Raleigh spent twelve years chained to a wall in the seventeenth century, not to mention, it was the place where at least two of Henry VIII's wives were beheaded." McAllister reminded her, which impressed me that he was still up on his history.

The next time she shuddered was less voluntary.

"It would have been nice if you could have seen the Ceremony of the Keys. It's really something to see." I added.

"Yeah, I read about that in one of the Richard Sharp adventures. But I think you have to get a special invitation or tickets months in advance." McAllister said. Then, "This has been a pleasant little interlude and history lesson, but don't you think we should be talking about our next move?"

McAllister was not the tourist type. He'd rather participate in making history rather than reliving it. If it wasn't his beloved Savannah, the site of a possible shipwreck, or a project that was of special interest to him, the Seven Wonders of the World would not have been worth more than a passing nod of recognition. While McAllister had never enjoyed a close relationship with Antonio, he was not beneath using the excuse that his precious eggs were the means to finding his brother in-law's murderer to Larkin. If that wasn't enough, he would remind her of Sally's murder and what a dear friend and sweet lady she was to them. All I knew was that I had my own reasons, which were just as valid as McAllister's, to achieve our common objective. I wanted to find the murderers.

I was tiring of McAllister's self-serving methods.

"Just what is our next move?" I asked, a little testier than I planned.

Both McAllisters noticed the edge in my voice but Larkin looked away as her husband stared at me for a two count before answering. "We're going to Switzerland." He said. "We leave in the morning."

Why not? I thought.

* * * * *

Zurich is Switzerland's largest city and one of the most expensive cities in all of Europe. In the northern part of the country, very near the German border and in view of the Alps, Lenin wrote Imperialism, The Highest State of Capitalism and James Joyce penned his novel, Ulysses.

We landed at Kloten Airport a little after eleven o'clock and twenty minutes later checked into the Kindle, an extremely small hotel whose five hundred year old exterior hides a modern and tastefully furnished interior. The nightclub at the Kindle features a folklore show that, under different circumstances, I would have attended without a second thought no matter what McAllister had planned. Instead, I ignored the in-house literature promoting the show and went directly to my room to shower and shave. McAllister had told me that we had a two o'clock appointment at Euro-Bank on Banhof Strasse and I wondered what a Swiss bank had to do with what we supposedly had to accomplish. I doubted that we would be finding a murderer in the lobby.

At one forty-five, I met McAllister in the lobby. He had one of his familiar aluminum attaché cases at his feet and his usually amiable smile on his face.

"Larkin won't be joining us?" I asked.

"You think I would bring her anywhere near the 'most beautiful and expensive shopping street in the world'?" He tried to make it sound like a joke but I knew there was something behind his flippant remark.

"There's an organ concert at the Fraumunster Church this afternoon and you know how much she enjoys that kind of thing."

No, as a matter of fact, I didn't.

Nevertheless, ten minutes later, the two of us were breathing the intoxicating scent of the Linden trees as we stepped out of our taxi in front of Euro-Bank, Zurich. On the site of the ancient moat, Banhoff Strasse runs from the lake to the main railway station and is the center of Zurich's business district. The clientele pays for the address on labels in this shopper's paradise and often the people watchers far outnumber the paying customer.

Euro-Bank is a newer building near the intersection of Kuttel Fortunagasse, the road that leads to Lindenhof, a lookout point that offers a lovely view of the old town.

The panorama from Lindenhof had to be more pleasing than the lobby of the bank, a three story open warehouse of tile and fake marble pillars and the personality of a Greyhound Bus station. At McAllister's query, we were directed to the second mezzanine level office of Herr Docktor Joseph Heinz where McAllister erased his easy smile as he entered the office and came directly to the point.

"You and your little scheme didn't work, Herr Heinz." He said, slamming his case on the bank executive's desk. I wondered how long he had rehearsed this scene. "Now we have to decide if your bank is going to make good on this deal or if I'm going to have to carve some satisfaction out of your ass."

I believe I've already mentioned that McAllister was not a candidate for the position of ambassador to any foreign country.

"Herr McAllister," The Herr Docktor was surprised by the outburst but somehow managed to maintain his composure, "perhaps you owe me an explanation for this unwarranted and unwelcome intrusion."

Heinz was in his mid-fifties with thinning blond hair and the build of someone who spent his lunch hours in the health club. He would not be intimidated by McAllister, either intellectually or physically, no matter how tough McAllister acted. He spoke English with a Schweizerdeutsch accent that was indicative of the area.

Continuing his act, at least I hoped it was an act, McAllister angrily snapped the case open to expose the Resurrection and Lilly eggs. "You and your bank brokered these eggs to me on behalf of Luigi Paretti. They are both imitations and one of them isn't worth the effort it took to make it."

Heinz allowed himself a hint of a smirk as he slowly lowered himself back into his chair. He pressed his fingertips together and spoke from behind his hands. "You make a very serious accusation, Herr McAllister." He spoke slowly, almost threateningly. "You come into my office, now almost a full year after concluding a sale that this bank discouraged our client, Senor Paretti, from making, and accuse me and one of the most respected banking institutions in Europe of intentionally perpetrating a fraud on you."

He pressed a switch on an antique intercom box. "Miss Kleinhoff, please bring in the file on the late Senor Paretti."

He leaned back in his chair and studied the two offending eggs, still in the case in the middle of his desk. As usual, McAllister had burst headlong into a situation and a course of action that was doomed from the beginning. Although he would never admit it, I'm certain he knew that he had erred badly in thinking he could intimidate this man and had left himself no room for a graceful retreat. When the door opened and Miss Kleinhoff came in with a thick file folder, McAllister utilized the distraction to turn to me and silently offer me a chance to intervene. I declined by shrugging helplessly and leaned back to watch him try to wiggle off his own hook.

"Senor Paretti asked us to broker eggs to you on his behalf." Heinz read from his file as he refreshed his memory. "The descriptions are listed here if you care to review them yourself." He tapped the file.

"As is customary, the bank marked and photographed each piece individually and stored them in our vault until you yourself arranged for secure delivery to you in Venezuela. Here is a copy of the receipt you signed for that delivery in August of last year." He slid the paper partway across the desk and pointed to a space on the form. "This box here, with your initials, certifies an acceptable delivery and your signature at the bottom releases the bank and the messenger service of any further responsibility."

McAllister stared dully at the receipt.

"Now," Heinz leaned forward as he pushed the paper closer to an unresponsive McAllister, "suppose you explain to me, Herr McAllister, how you believe our institution should be held responsible for any of the irregularities you are suggesting."

McAllister looked sheepish and hopeless which I'm sure he didn't realize anyone noticed.

"You said the eggs were marked by the bank." McAllister wasn't giving up. "How?"

"The bank uses a die stamp to mark the underside of the pedestals." He explained, returning his attention to the file. "The eggs themselves, of course, cannot be marked in this fashion without being damaged, so they are tagged with adhesive labels for the photographing and the tags are not removed until the new owner removes them." He withdrew a stack of five-by-seven professional photos from the file but didn't offer them to McAllister.

McAllister stood up to remove the eggs from the case he had ceremoniously plopped on Heinz's desk. After turning the pedestals over several times he passed them to me. I saw no unusual markings. Heinz passed the photographs to McAllister with an air of superiority and McAllister shuffled through them quickly before thrusting them in my direction.

"This doesn't prove anything." I couldn't believe McAllister was continuing to act like a damn fool. "Anyone could have switched these at any time."

"Exactly my point." Heinz was completely unruffled. "The difference is, I have the necessary documentation to refute your unfounded allegations and you, Herr McAllister, have nothing but an objectionable presence in my office."

McAllister fumed but thankfully stopped short of exploding. He was no longer acting, but he knew he had run out of ammunition. Heinz, however, was not finished.

"I have indulged you graciously," he continued, "but I strongly suggest that, in the future, you assemble all your facts before you begin to cast aspersions against the character of this honorable institution or its associates. People with less patience than me might take your emotional outburst personal and have you physically thrown out of the building." He snapped his fingers annoyingly in my direction indicating he wanted his pictures returned. "I sincerely hope you can find the door on your own accord."

Despite the humility McAllister must have felt, he regained his composure, smiled, and said, "Well, I've decided not to open an account with your honorable bank at this time."

I doubt that McAllister had ever been talked to by anyone in that manner, at least since he was released from prison in Arizona, which is another story. Even though I knew that McAllister was livid, he covered it up well. He silently repacked his forgeries while putting on a smug front. I followed McAllister out of the bank hoping he wouldn't release his hidden anger on me for not stepping in to somehow buffer some of the humiliation he suffered during his confrontation with the banker. He curled himself into the back seat and fortunately, didn't say a word on the way back to the hotel and when we separated in the lobby, I asked him if we would be meeting at dinner."

"Grange," McAllister said slowly and ominously, "if you utter just one word to Larkin about our little meeting at that fuckin' honorable bank, you will be joining the piranhas for dinner when we get back to Ciudad Bolivar." He accentuated his statement with a sinister smile.

So much for diner, I thought.

If I had been traveling on my own, researching a book, or just following McAllister around as I have done many times in the past, I would have spent the afternoon in the museums, churches, and historic locales of the area. Instead, I sat in my room at the Kindle, quite possibly the smallest hotel in all of Europe, staring at the Old Town, the church towers, the bridges, and the medieval facades without seeing anything. Since I had not marked the time when we had returned from the Euro-Bank office of Herr Heinz, I had no idea how I had been looking fixedly at the lengthening shadows of the Alps when a gentle knock brought me back to the present. Larkin stood in the hallway in front of my door looking very unsure of herself.

"May I come in?"

"Of course." I automatically looked around to make certain the room was presentable.

When Larkin McAllister entered a room, her passage was a film director's dream. In a crowd, heads turned, conversations stopped in mid-sentence, and drinks stopped halfway to waiting lips. She flowed rather than and the proud but unconceited way she held herself spoke of breeding and panache. This was different. Since the first time I had known her she seemed unsure of herself and tentative as she lowered herself in the chair I had recently vacated. She even sighed.

"Bad day for organ concerts?" I asked.

"No," she lifted an eyebrow cynically, "but the music in church apparently sounded much better than the tune you two heard at the bank."

McAllister seemed to enjoy putting me in the creek without a paddle. I had no idea what he had told her, I only knew that I was strongly admonished into silence. She was acting as if she knew exactly what had transpired that afternoon at the bank, but I suspected, or at least hoped she was on a fishing expedition. It wouldn't have been the first time.

"It was not the best of times for your charismatic husband." Was all I was prepared to say, except, "He wasn't all that communicative the last time I saw him."

"All right," she conceded, sensing that I knew she was baiting me, "he does tend to be a little stubborn sometimes."

"My goodness, Larkin." I said in mock surprise. "I've never noticed."

She smiled and said, "I was hoping it wasn't contagious."

"Being stubborn isn't contagious," I replied, "but coming between a husband and wife is not being tenacious, it's downright stupid."

"Women do it all the time and call it harmless gossip."

"Bobby doesn't believe in harmless gossip."

"Bobby doesn't believe in murder either."

"Well, I think he wants to solve one." I continued with her chosen game of mental ping pong. I was getting dizzy. We could have served back and forth like that for hours but when she started to make another argument, I held up both hands.

"Okay, Larkin. You get him to come to dinner tonight and I'll try to draw him out. I promise . . . I'll try." I conceded. "That is all I can do, I'm already in a shaky position here. Bobby wants me to help him find another Prize and you want me to tell you how he thinks every step of the way. Quite honestly, I haven't figured out down to a science just how Bobby thinks, myself. I got lucky with the Prize, but most of that was attributed to Bobby's luck." I paused to ponder, "And to some degree, his stubbornness."

"But you know Bobby. You two have been friends for a long time."

"Yes, Larkin. And I'd like to keep it that way. Not only do I not know what goes on in his mind, he can't even tell you how he assimilates his own thoughts.

"Your husband has a habit of going into a situation headlong, without being concerned with anyone else's opinions or information other than what he has concluded. You have to admit, he does come up with some far-out notions. Then, on occasion, when things blow up in his face, he can't understand why bad things could possibly happen to him."

Larkin lifted her head as if she was going to defend her husband but she knew I was right and couldn't find the words or justification for a decent argument.

"This whole project was doomed from the beginning. What did he think he was going to accomplish when he started this scheme? This isn't about Faberge, his eggs, or any insults, real or imagined, because of forgeries. Your brother and my girlfriend died because Bobby got bored."

"That's preposterous, Granger Lawton!" She said it sharply, and she meant it.

"No it isn't." I was more convincing than Larkin's feelings. Although I had known McAllister only slightly longer than her, all my associations with him involved chasing his dream, and as a result, finding Larkin. "I'm not blaming Bobby for two unnecessary deaths." I rethought my position. I didn't like piranhas. "But what I am saying is that when other people die, Bobby lives a little bit longer." I wasn't trying to be cruel, or provoke Larkin, but the words just flowed right out of my big mouth.

However, Larkin was provoked. "Why do you stick around if you feel that way?" She asked. "Aren't you afraid you might be next, Grange?"

"I do know Bobby. And I do know that he would never deliberately harm anyone or allow anyone to be harmed if he could prevent it. And I don't think anyone anticipates their own death or personal safety by association. Right now, that's not the point. However questionable his methods have been in the past, he has always managed to prevail. His greatest achievement was finding you, Larkin. I knew what he was looking for before we ever showed up at your father's estate in Venezuela. I watched him do the impossible many times, but that was in the past. He has depended on luck which, fortunately seldom let him down. I'm just afraid that someday lady luck just might not be there for him when he needs her the most. Then what?"

Larkin didn't respond.

"It's time, Larkin, for Bobby McAllister to pull another rabbit out of his hat. Maybe get in tune with his subliminal orbital parity or whatever it is that guides him. He needs to step back a pace, re-evaluate what he's doing, then step back up to the plate and hit a home run. When he does that, I might be closer to my objective."

"Which, I suppose, is finding out about the only egg we have yet to have authenticated by an expert? Yours."

"To hell with my egg!" Larkin cringed and I felt bad because I then realized that I had spoken a little more harshly than I had intended. "You're getting as bad as Bobby. Not everything I do is for profit, you know.

"I'm sorry for raising my voice, Larkin, and please don't get me wrong." I moderated my tone substantially when I saw the shocked and somewhat hurt expression on her face. "The egg was a very thoughtful and generous present. I cherish the gift and the sincerity which it was given, but it isn't worth lives. It's just an inanimate object that, right now, has caused me far more grief than pleasure. Bobby has long had a difficult time getting his priorities in order and his attitude is wearing off on you."

"Maybe so, Grange," Larkin began defiantly. "But that's Bobby. His goodness outweighs his sins. I'd rather be compared to Bobby McAllister than anyone I know. Anyone!"

Two McAllisters. One Granger Lawton. The deck was stacked.

"I'm sorry, Larkin." I wanted to quit while I could.

"How do you think things could be better, Grange?"

"I don't know." I answered. "Let's see what Bobby's friend finds . . ." I stopped in mid-sentence. Did I ever mention my big mouth?"

"What friend? Find out about what?" Larkin asked surprised and suspiciously.

"Never mind."

"What is Bobby up to now, Grange?" She demanded.

"Please, Larkin. Give me a break. Let's talk about it at dinner."

As Larkin departed the room, her eyes never left mine. She kind of walked out backwards. I couldn't seem to win for losing. I returned to my chair and stared at the phone. I have no idea why I felt intimidated by an instrument I had used all my life, but the mere thought of it ringing at any moment with McAllister on the other end made me dreadful of having mentioned McAllister's "friend" to Larkin. I knew I had inadvertently opened a can of worms which I could not put a lid back on. My big mouth!

The phone rang . . .

"Hello."

"Mister Lawton?"

"Yes."

"This is Mister Camper's secretary. Mister Camper is an attorney here in Chicago."

"Yes."

"Well, we've been trying to contact Mister McAllister but he hasn't returned our call. Mister Camper, Jeff Camper, that is, has a message for Mister McAllister from the elder Mister Camper. Can you please have Mister McAllister contact this office?"

"I certainly will."

"It's quite urgent, Mister Lawton."

"I understand."

* * * * *

"Call Jeff's secretary back and inform her that I appreciate Mister Camper's concern, but we have solved our own problems." McAllister said to me in a less than pleasant tone." Apparently his ego was ruffled after Larkin's obvious query.

"But, Bobby, she said it was important."

"I don't give a damn, Grange!" He shouted. "Please do like I ask."

He hung up.

"Law offices of Jeffrey Camper. May I help you?"

"Yes, this is Granger Lawton. May I speak with Jeff?"

"Mister Camper is not in at the moment, but he has asked me to convey an important message to either you or Mister McAllister."

"Well . . . uh . . . that will be fine."

We ate at Belchanto in the city's Opera House, a restaurant that would have been packed on the night of a performance but was quiet and almost intimate when the theater was dark. McAllister picked at dinner while Larkin anxiously threw glances in my direction, hoping I would start a conversation that would draw her husband out of his self-induced funk. I was trying to focus all my attention on my fondue.

"So," Larkin ventured, after the waiter had cleared the dishes, "what are we going to be doing tomorrow?"

McAllister looked at me with quiet disdain, then to Larkin. "I'm working it out now." Whatever that meant.

I definitely did not want to bring up my conversation with Jeff Camper's secretary, and ultimately with Jeff himself, so I tried to be invisible. I did, however, notice Larkin's disappointment in my cowardice.

McAllister actually smiled. I think he knew what was going on. "Nothing comes easy in the treasure hunting business." He said with a straight face. "Sometimes you have to make some waves before the water gets clear."

I was concerned with McAllister's flippant attitude. I had seen it many times in the past. I knew his splashy metaphor was going down for the third time, but I did not say as much. I thought it though.

"So what in the name of the Seven Seas and the Great Lakes caused such a cloud of doom to settle over my closest friends?" He asked both Larkin and me. "I learned quite a bit at the bank yesterday." He continued. "It follows that between the times I purchased those eggs until the time they were delivered to me at El Empleado, a clever switch was made."

Larkin looked bewildered.

"Uh . . . I have to disagree." I interrupted, unsure of what he was trying to say. "I'll stipulate that you were probably not robbed at the ranch in South America, but look how much traveling those eggs have done since then. They went from Venezuela to Georgia where they sat for a few months in your fancy basement before they were loaded on a boat in a safe you yourself admit is less than Fort Knox, and run up and down the coast of Europe. You can't vouch for the integrity of your security, no matter how sophisticated, under those conditions."

"Logically, I can." He got my attention. "First of all, when those eggs arrived in Venezuela, I lovingly and carefully unpacked each and every one. I remember the die marks on one or two of the pedestals and all of them had adhesive stickers on the actual egg, but those could have been added at any time.

"The showroom in Savannah is secure. I'd bet my life on it." He paused to flash a reassuring and self-confident smile. He then continued. "The hidey-hole on the Second Prize isn't the most impregnable spot in the world, but it is constantly under guard. A switch under those circumstances would be next to impossible. That means the eggs were switched someplace between Euro-Bank and my front door."

"Unless, of course, it was an inside job." I suggested.

McAllister rolled his eyes. "I won't even consider that." He said emphatically. "The benefits of working for me far outweigh what anybody could get from a fence for something like one or two of my eggs."

I let it pass. Sometimes it's better to let certain people live in their own private world.

McAllister wasn't finished with his fairy tale. "Besides, Grange, you're forgetting one important factor."

"Okay. Which is?" "The head of my security is Gary Caldwell. My former squadron commander. A man whom I grew up with, who listened to my whacky dreams way before I realized they were dreams."

"Bobby." I began. "That may be true, but you've made him primarily responsible for the protection of Larkin."

"Exactly!"

"Exactly?"

"I trust Gary with my most valued treasure."

Of course. I'm sure that was supposed to make sense.

I always found it unsettling when McAllister wound up persuading me to at least consider his soundless ideas. But a question came to my mind. "Well, I would like to know one thing ..."

McAllister stared at me. Larkin stared at her husband.

"Let me guess, Grange. McAllister assumed his irritating smug pose. "You'd like to know why just two? Why not the whole kit and kaboodle?

Right?"

I could hear the sound of fingernails scratching against a chalkboard in my mind. He was so dammned smug! "Well, come to think of it, yes."

"Well, I'll tell you why." He sensed my discomfort and softened his condescending sneer. "Because whoever took them only had two placements."

"Am I missing something?"

"Which only indicates to me that they were switched before they were delivered to me?" He said it as if he had proven a point.

"Also, they haven't travelled the Coast of Europe. They were appraised almost as soon as we arrived in France."

"Good heavens!" I blurted.

McAllister smiled tolerantly. Larkin shook her head in amazement.

"Damn you, Bobby!" He did it again to me. "Your little temper tantrum at the bank was planned!"

"Well." He looked slightly embarrassed. "Sort of. Actually, all I wanted to do was getting noticed. I figure someone in this neighborhood is the person or persons who made the switch. It's the squeaky wheel that gets the grease." My big mouth wouldn't open.

Larkin placed her hand on her husband's arm and patted it softly.

"Yeah, but. . ." I was still confused to some extent.

"By coming to Europe we've put those people on notice, Grange." He leaned forward and almost whispered as if planning some great conspiracy. "You did get a hold of Jeff, right? I nodded. "You told him thanks, but I had things under control. Right?"

"I spoke with him. . ."

McAllister cut me off. "Good." He placed his hand on Larkin's arm. "Now, all we have to do is sit back and wait for the bad guys to come to us."

"Bobby. . ." I wanted to elaborate more on my conversation with Jeff Camper concerning the message he relayed from his uncle.

"What?" He asked before I could continue.

"Bobby. . ." I decided to keep my exchange with Jeff to myself for the time being. ". . . Why would they come to us? If I were the guy that ripped you off, I'd say that I was sitting pretty right now. So what if you found out you were robbed? If you are right, the theft happened a long time ago. If the trail to the crooks isn't dead, it's pretty damned cold. If I were the thief, I wouldn't touch you with a ten foot pole. I'd let you prance around naked in every capitol of the continent crying your eyes out while those who watched pitied you."

"You don't paint a pretty picture."

"Well, at least we agree on something."

McAllister leaned back and studied me carefully. Uncharacteristically, he wasn't giving me an argument. He just sat there smiling, looking back and forth between Larkin and me. When he finally spoke, it was his turn to inject sarcasm into his question.

"I suppose you have a better idea as to how we should proceed."

I steeled myself for a battle.

"As a matter of fact, I do."

McAllister looked at his cherished Larkin with some sort of self-satisfied expression and, without turning to face me, waved a hand for me to continue.

"In Savannah, you said we were going to fire a pre-emptive strike. Well, so far, you've been firing blanks." I got his attention again.

"All we have been doing on this trip is better educating ourselves. Sure, we found the guy who manufactured one of your bogus eggs. We even have a poor quality photograph of someone who may or may not be pulling the forger's strings. But the fact remains that, as investigators, we are not Sherlock Holmes and Doctor Watson."

"So, what are you suggesting, Grange?" He said after completely returning his attention back to me.

"Our focus thus far has been on the eggs." I said. "While they are a part of the overall problem, they are not necessarily the way to get answers. I know you think I've developed a one track mind on the subject, but we need to find out who murdered Sally and Antonio. Buying and selling Easter eggs is no crime and, in the art world, dealing in forgeries is sometimes an honored profession.

"Murder, however, is another story." McAllister interjected.

"Let's assume something we have no right to adopt as absolute fact. Suppose we have two separate entities involved here. One is benign, the other dangerous."

"You lost me, Grange." McAllister said. Larkin nodded agreement with her husband.

"All along, we've been taking the position that there has been a single conspiracy working against us. What if we are fighting two separate existences that have different ideas about how to attain their objectives?"

"Go on." He sounded bored.

"Try to imagine that there are people who want to collect eggs by bidding for them at auction, burglarizing homes, or surreptitiously switching authentic pieces for replacements, all no violent acts. The other faction consists of thugs. For whatever reason, these people will go to the furthest extreme to reach their goal."

"Grange. . ." McAllister was losing patience. "What difference would that make?"

"Look," I said, realizing that my mouth was getting ahead of my brain, "if we have two different mystery groups to deal with, we might not know which group we're reacting to at any given time."

Larkin was paying attention. "You mean that we're the victims of some kind of 'divide and conquer' scheme?"

"Only they don't know we're divided and we don't know what group we're dealing with at any given time." I elaborated. "One minute, we're chasing one set of clues and, without knowing it, the next minute we switch horses in mid-race. Add to the fact that we get sidetracked yet again by getting into arguments with innocent and unconcerned parties," I looked pointedly at McAllister, "and we wind up chasing our tails in circles."

McAllister didn't like the analogy. "You have absolutely nothing to support a theory like that."

If he only knew.

"No proof," I kind of fibbed, "but some very good logic. If we are dealing with two distinct personalities, one is a man who spends time and money to get what he wants. He hires forgers, attends auctions, and operates discreetly. The other uses strong-arm tactics, terror, and doesn't care who gets hurt. It doesn't make sense that they might be working together. It's like mixing oil and water.

"One minute we find ourselves chasing after the guy who did things like bid against Antonio for the Spaskoie Selo egg and hired the likes of Dorn Kublec, and the next we are up against the gangsters who threw a bomb into the car in Paris."

McAllister held up a hand. "You seem to forget my idea." He said. "That the KGB is behind all of this. It stands to reason that if we're dealing with a secret government organization, especially the KGB; we might have to face such diverse obstacles as finesse and force. Why should we be concentrating our efforts on a single area?" A twinkle came to his eye as he realized what he was going to say.

"You want us to put all our eggs into one basket?"

Larkin was amused. I ignored his pun.

"But I think we need to do something different."

"Like what?"

"I think we need to go to Russia."

"Grange." McAllister became patronizing. "You are no doubt my best friend. But I must say that you have either written too many fiction novels, or you know something I don't. Which is it?"

I shrugged.

"I know I am the perfect example of advocating going to the experts, but. . ."

I found a soft spot.

"And that's why you wanted to talk to Theodore Faberge, Bobby."

"Yeah, but. . ." He scratched his chin. "The grandson of the old man is probably as expert as they come, but still. . ."

"Still, what?"

"Still, Grange. In case you have forgotten, there are no more jewelry stores in Russia. Theo Faberge and Anthony Wilson are as close to an expert as we are going to find. We don't have to present ourselves in the enemy's doorstep in a police state to accuse the government of fraud. That would be like walking into the gates of hell and accusing Old Scratch of being a sinner."

"It's a new Russia." I argued. "Do you think that in this day and age of Soviet/American relations, the breakup of the USSR, and the unrest in the satellite states, the government is going to worry about three pesky Americans who can't even speak Russian? Of course not."

"If we don't speak Russian, how are we going to communicate with anyone?" He asked. "We won't even understand our Miranda rights when we get arrested. McAllister added facetiously.

"We can hire a translator. It wouldn't be the first time."

"Listen, Grange," McAllister leaned forward again. "I came to Europe to make waves. It's what I do best. I figure there ought to be people who want me to shut up and go back home and as long as I stick around making waves, unfounded or otherwise, someone is going to take steps to cut me off. If and when that happens, I want to be prepared, and I want to be in a place that doesn't have barbed wire on the borders making it difficult to leave when it becomes expedient to make a tactical retreat."

"You make a good point, except for one thing." I said.

"Let's hear it, Grange."

"If I were the person responsible for making your life miserable right now, I would get as far away from you as possible. You're at an impasse. As long as you stand at the dead end we face right now, you remain harmless. If you show up in your antagonist's back yard, I would think they would begin to worry."

"My point exactly." He concurred. "And if I were a powerful, semi-secret agency worried by some pesky foreigners, I would be sorely tempted to make me disappear into some frozen Siberian gulag."

"I can't believe' it." I banged on the table in exasperation. "You of all people are, by virtue of doing nothing, are giving up on this project."

"Don't give me that crap, Grange!" McAllister banged on the table right back. "Give me facts, not something you dreamed about. You came along on this little junket because you're supposed to be the one with all the deductive powers. Well, start being deductive. Give me facts. Impress me, Grange."

Like his wife earlier, McAllister was baiting me. His way of testing someone's mental capacity was to argue pigheadedly until his verbal sparring partner became so frustrated, they either blurted out something stupid or incredibly brilliant. I took a deep breath.

"The two guys who attacked Antonio in Monte Carlo were Russian. Antonio caught somebody's name that was definitely Russian and the same bastard that he heard speaking Russian killed three people including Sally and Antonio in Paris.

"If your assumption about KGB involvement is anywhere near correct, my guess is that these two guys are part of the goon squad for the department. You and I can identify them and if they are part of a conspiracy, we are a threat. If we show ourselves in Russia, they are going to reappear."

"Russia is a big country."

"Not if you're not Russian."

"Then why not have someone who we couldn't recognize do their dirty work? After all, it's a very big department. Why should we be forewarned because we can identify one of thousands of operatives?"

"First of all, I don't think there are thousands." I responded. "I think the operation is very compartmentalized."

"I suppose you have a reason for thinking that way."

"I do." I replied. "If there were more than a few, why would they risk being recognized when a stranger could have waited patiently next to the car in Paris and blown us all to Kingdom come?"

"They might be short of field operatives."

"It's a big organization." I threw his own words back at him.

"Okay," McAllister was willing to accept my idea as conjecture only, "but we still have another piece of the puzzle that seems to be missing. Where does the guy who operates with all the savoir-faire and tact fit into the picture?"

"Our suave and sophisticated friend has a problem. Communism has flourished far too long in Russia and he finds that the skills of his country's craftsmen have dwindled considerably. That's why our basket of lilies is pronounced a total disaster by everyone from Anthony Wilson to the busboy at the Russian Tea Room. He has to leave his own country to find an artist that can replicate masterpieces with convincing authority. However, he cannot allow his affiliation to be discovered. He has to represent himself as anything but Russian to protect the overall operation, which means assuming another identity. What better way to hide his true heritage than to pose as a Jew?"

"Jew? You mean Kleinfeld?"

"Of Course."

"He is a Jew."

"Huh?"

"Tell him, honey."

Larkin looked at me sympathetically. "I spoke with Ned Hoffman this afternoon. He got a call from Sergeant Abernathy. Mister Abraham Kleinfeld is a citizen of Israel. Although a private person, he comes from undetermined wealth and travels Europe buying and selling art treasures. Word has it he even deals with royalty."

"Royalty?" I was stunned. "You mean the Queen of England? The security involved in dealing with the Queen should be able to expose a Russian spy."

"I don't know about that. Larkin answered. "I'm just telling you what Scotland Yard told Ned. Either we have the wrong Kleinfeld or the wrong tree."

"This is nuts." I was flabbergasted. "We talked to a known forger and ex-convict who positively identified the man. If we could get that kind of information for a few thousand bucks, why couldn't the cops get that same information with thumbscrews or the weight of the law?"

"I don't know." McAllister shrugged. "Maybe he's kept a low enough profile to fall through the cracks. It could be that we just got lucky."

"Get a phone." I demanded. "We need the answer to one more question."

Apparently my expression was enough to tell Larkin I meant business. She went in search of our waiter and took the opportunity to have another round of drinks delivered to our table. When the phone was brought. I instructed that it be placed in front of Larkin.

"Call the Sergeant." I told her. "I want to know how long Mister Kleinfeld has lived in Israel."

Larkin looked toward her husband as if to ask for permission and McAllister nodded almost imperceptibly. She opened her purse and withdrew one of those two inch by three inch personal telephone books, located the number, and dialed. McAllister and I only heard half of the conversation.

"Sergeant Abernathy, please. Extension six-four-oh-eight." While on hold, Larkin hummed, McAllister sat expressionless, and I fidgeted with a napkin.

"Yes, Sergeant. This is Larkin McAllister . . . Fine, thank you. I wanted to personally thank you for calling our attorney with the information we requested. It was most helpful. However, my husband wanted me to ask you if you could help us with one more tiny thing." She made a gesture with finger and thumb as if Abernathy could see her.

"Yes, I know. But this is related and I'm certain your department would understand if you didn't expend the time and money to make another International call. . .Well, we were wondering if Mister Kleinfeld was born in Israel. . .Yes, I told you it wasn't much. . .Certainly."

She covered the mouthpiece and mouthed the words. "I'm on hold." It was a full minute during which time I finished one drink and signaled for another.

"Yes." Larkin said suddenly, startling all three of us. "I see. Well, thank you, again, Sergeant. We really appreciate your cooperation."

Larkin replaced the receiver gently and shrugged.

"He emigrated from Russia five years ago."

I allowed a self-satisfied smile to creep onto my lips.

"What?" McAllister had not yet caught on to what I knew.

"This is helping to prove your theory." I said. "You should be pleased."

"Okay, I'm pleased." McAllister said. "Now, tell me why I'm pleased."

"In all likelihood, Comrade Kleinfeld is some kind of KGB plant."

"Now how the hell can you tell that just by knowing that the man came from Russia five years ago?"

I smiled broadly. "When was the last time you heard about a millionaire Jew being allowed to emigrate from Russia?"

Realization caused McAllister to look at his wife with the same stunned expression she was using on him.

He looked back at me. "Okay, Grange. You've impressed me."

I wanted to gloat a little, but I didn't want to push it. "Should I start packing, Bobby?" Asked Larkin.

"Please do. We leave for the Motherland first thing in the morning."

* * * * *

Even though Amsterdam is the official capitol of the Netherlands, The Hague is the country's seat of government and a remarkably modern city of over a half a million whose roots were of the villages surrounding the Count of Holland's thirteenth century hunting lodge. As we waited the arrival of the Second Prize, we checked into the landmark Kurhaus Hotel on the city's lively and recently renovated seafront, Scheveningen. McAllister planned a three day stay in the cosmopolitan city to take on provisions and stock the Second Prize with everything he felt we would need for our excursion into what was left of the Union of Soviet Socialist Republics.

The entire crew spent the afternoon on fragrance-filled, tree-lined embassy row, where the Russian consulate is one of sixty elegant and stately palaces, obtaining our visas. That left me with two days to wander the city while McAllister attended to other details.

I asked McAllister what I could do to help and he told me that errands could be handled by the hired help. He wanted me to keep my mind open and fertile for the days ahead, so I spent two days taking in the sights.

I could never find a definitive reason why they didn't call the city "Hague" Why did they call it "The Hague"? I wondered how many Hagues there were. The Hague is probably best known for Madurodam, a five acre miniature city of meticulously crafted reproductions of real structures. The 1:25 scale town includes a working two mile railroad, canal locks, and harbor fire boats. At night the entire display is lighted by over fifty thousand tiny lights, making it look like a huge metropolis viewed from a high flying airplane. I visited the panorama Mesdag with the world's largest painting, the Royal Residence at Huis ten Bosch Palace, and the International Court of Justice, or the Peace Palace, a gift bestowed upon The Hague by Andrew Carnegie.

The only justice I was concerned with, however, was on display at the Gevangenport (prison gate) Museum where a medieval horror chamber, complete with torture rooms and working unpleasurable instruments caught my eye and sparked my imagination of how those accommodations would do nicely for Sally and Antonio's murderers.

Nightly, I joined the McAllisters for dinner at one of the two first class French restaurants at the Kurhaus, after which they would go into the casino, Larkin to show off her latest gown and McAllister to show off Larkin. With nothing or no one to show off, I sat at a corner bar playing video poker and seriously depleted the casino's supply of rum as I watched half the male population in the room lust after Larkin while trying to appear nonchalant.

On the morning of the fourth day in The Hague, McAllister called me early and asked me to meet him at the breakfast bar in the solarium. Since he knew there was little that could entice me to eat at that time of day, I assumed it was to talk. I was right.

McAllister didn't bother to stand as I approached and neither did his guest, a young man dressed in a sports coat and no shirt. He had sun bleached hair, an earring, and two days growth on his face, a pathetic attempt to resemble every out of work actor in Hollywood. In spite of his feeble attempt at what he considered to be the current fashion of sane men, I probably would have liked him except that he reminded me of another young man from Seville. The comparison became even more eerie.

"Grange, meet Artur Ladvick." We shook hands over the table. "I found him at the University sweeping floors for the summer. He speaks perfect Russian and English as well as five other languages.

"How do you know what perfect Russian sounds like, Bobby?" But before he could answer. . .

"Hello sir." At least he had some manners. "Mister McAllister has told me so much about you." His accent was European-Slavic, but not thick.

"How come you speak so many languages?" I asked, trying to sound like a concerned employer even though it was obvious that McAllister had already hired him.

"I'm a political science major." He replied as if he were embarrassed. "That probably means I'll get a job translating at the United Nations after I graduate." He shrugged fatalistically. "A sign of the times."

I found myself nodding sympathetically. "Did Mister McAllister tell you where we plan on going?"

"Yes sir." He straightened as if he were going to tell me something he was proud about. "I've been in Russia before. I acted as a translator for the Kushman defense team. We spent almost three weeks in Moscow."

I raised an eyebrow. I couldn't remember the Kushman kid's first name, but I knew he was a teenager who drove a stolen Mercedes from Hamburg, Germany all the way through the gates of the Kremlin without so much as being challenged once. He was actually less than ten feet from Gorbachev's office door when he was finally arrested. The kid was two or three years into a ten year sentence.

"I don't suppose Mister McAllister told you there might be some danger involved on this trip?" McAllister glared at me but Artur didn't flinch.

"Russia has always held a measure of instability." He said. Especially for someone who has defected and dared to return."

I raised an eyebrow.

"Czechoslovakia." He answered my unasked question. "At least what used to be Czechoslovakia?"

There wasn't anything to say about that which could be said in less than a billion words so I struck what I hoped was a scholarly pose and nodded.

"Artur has already proven his worth." McAllister probably interrupted because he didn't want me divulging any more than I already had. "He gave me a list of things we won't be able to buy freely in Russia as well as a few other things. I've already given a shopping list to Captain Olsen."

"Things like what?" I asked. I had a few ideas of my own on that subject.

"Cigarettes, food, chocolate, dollars."

"Dollars?"

"The black market is the most successful form of capitalism in Russia, Mister Lawton." Artur informed me. "The only place to spend rubles is at a state owned facility. The black market offers a wider selection of goods and operates as openly as your American Swap Meets."

"What happens if you're caught trying to bring this stuff into the country?" I asked.

"What happens if you get stopped for speeding by a Chicago Police Officer?" Artur had an excellent grasp of the free enterprise concept.

"It sounds like we're just about ready to leave." I observed, now uncertain about where our mission was taking us.

"Yes." McAllister said, a little hesitant himself. "At checkout time."

I wished he would have used different terminology.

* * * * *

We didn't see land again until we turned east to enter the Skagerrak Strait and came within sight of the northern tip of Denmark. We hugged the west coast of Sweden to avoid the commercial traffic in and out of Copenhagen. As if it were a bad omen, it began raining when we turned north, entering the Baltic and open sea again and, even though Stockholm and Helsinki lay ahead, we saw fewer ships as clearer skies and dawn greeted us on our third day since leaving The Hague.

Artur would have been happy if the cruise had been scheduled for a lifetime. It was obvious that he had never lived as comfortable as the amenities that were offered that the Second Prize allowed. He adjusted nicely, however, spending most of his time in the lounge playing video games in front of the big screen television and devouring food as if he had just discovered the concept of eating.

Larkin and McAllister had changed too. We no longer consumed Savannah's Artillery Punch on the fantail and, in spite of the mild weather, Larkin avoided her fashion shows and seemingly endless supply of bikinis, probably out of respect for her husband and crew, and McAllister ventured above decks only after dark.

Even Captain Olsen was profoundly affected by his proximity to his homeland. He stood on the bridge from dawn to sundown, staring in the direction of his beloved Scandinavia and nightly, after dinner, sat in the lounge regaling us with stories of his country's history and how his family participated in Norse heritage. The McAllister's were intrigued by his stories and culture and promised to have their Captain take them into a reasonably nearby Scandinavian port and afford him a few days shore-leave if everything worked out wherever we were headed. The Captain even offered to act as their host in his homeland.

To keep my mind from turning as dull as the gray waters of the Baltic, I began keeping a journal of our progress, not as a pre-cursor to a book, but as a diary of idle observation, which, I must admit, came in handy at a later time. At that time I felt that there was more of a purpose to our journey than finding a few trinkets or exacting justice on behalf of Sally and Antonio. I kept telling myself that I wasn't looking for revenge, only answers. But I wasn't being convinced.

Late in the evening of the fourth day, the powerful twin diesels of the Second Prize suddenly ceased their incessant vibrations and the clanking of chains signaled a long drop for the anchors.

The silence that followed was like a cue for McAllister's security force to spring into action. Numbering five, the walking advertisements for physical fitness began a series of exercises that appeared to include little more than hurrying from one point to another aboard the ship. Only one man seemed to have any real purpose as he donned a wet suit and scuba gear but before he went over the side and I could ascertain his intentions, McAllister summoned me to the lounge.

"We're in the Gulf of Finland, right about here." He pointed to a spot on a chart from the Russian coast. "We stopped here to make some final preparations before entering Russian waters."

"What kind of preparations?" I asked.

"Security." He said with a finality that discouraged further discussion. "You better think about retiring early tonight. Who knows how long it will be before we can rest easy again."

And with that, he expected me to get a good night's sleep.

* * * * *

I must have got some sleep because when I opened my eyes, sunlight was streaming through a porthole and the Second Prize was again in motion. Since I had no way of knowing how long we had been underway, I bolted out of bed, dressing myself as I headed up the companionway. It took me a couple of minutes to locate anyone as everyone was one deck above, standing on the bridge, looking over the bow.

"So what do you wish to do, Mister McAllister?" Captain Olsen was asking as I approached.

McAllister was standing with his hands on his hips, trying to look unconcerned.

"Nothing." He answered after a lengthy pause. "We're doing nothing wrong. We all have visas, we're here legally. Let's just see what happens."

In the distance, two boats were converging on the Second Prize from opposing forty-five degree angles. Without binoculars I could not make out any markings, but the squat, gray appearance of both boats made it unlikely that either ship was a pleasure craft. The three boats merged quickly and as one of the nearing ships turned slightly, a large red star on its side became visible.

Identical, I would have to say they looked like a combination of a World War II P.T. boat and a harbor tug. Dull gray, except for the red star, they looked ungainly and top-heavy, a misrepresentation considering the speed with which they closed the distance between us. At about a hundred yards, one of our uninvited escorts throttled back while the other circled us at half that distance. An armed contingent of six men appeared on deck and, although they didn't actually point or aim, their attitude wasn't what I would describe as hospitable. The radio next to Captain Olsen crackled to life.

"They want us to heave to." Artur said. "They intend to board."

Captain Olsen stiffened visibly.

"All stop." McAllister ordered. Nobody moved.

"All stop, damnit!" He repeated. Olsen reluctantly reached for the telephone. McAllister handed Artur the radio microphone. "Ask them their reasons and instructions."

Arthur hesitated.

"What the hell is going on?" McAllister shouted. "Has everyone forgotten who the hell's in charge around here?"

"It might not be a good idea to question authority at this point, Mister McAllister." Artur said, rather uncertainly. "They might take it as a sign of us being uncooperative."

McAllister snatched the microphone from Artur and looked at it as if he thought he could speak Russian or something.

I suppressed a smile.

"It may be a good idea to listen to Artur, Mister McAllister." Captain Olsen said.

"That's right, Bobby." I got my two cents worth in too. "After all, he has been through this before. Let's not blow this before we even come within sight of land."

McAllister looked back and forth between Captain Olsen, Artur, and me. When he got around to looking in Larkin's direction, she nodded in a common sense manner.

As the Second Prize slowed, the Russian craft sided up to the starboard boarding ladder. Captain Olsen watched and, with no enthusiasm whatsoever, lowered the stairs by pressing a switch on his console. Bumpers were thrown out by Russian sailors as we descended to the main deck and a young lieutenant and three enlisted men rose to meet us. They looked serious and determined and it didn't take any time for our mixed community to push Artur to the front of the group. The lieutenant began barking orders before Artur could say more than two words of greeting.

I like the sound of the Italian language because of its familiarity with classic Latin, French because it's romantic and even German because it's so easy to make fun of, but to me, Russian sounds like someone choking on three day old borscht. It was as if Stalin himself had invented the language to be intimidating, rude, and threatening.

"This is Lieutenant Penko. He would like us all to join him on the afterdeck while his men inspect the ship." Artur informed us. "He asks that we have our passports and visas ready for inspection as well as the Captain's log and ship papers."

McAllister smiled through clenched teeth. "Tell the smug little bastard that everything we have is inventoried. We'll know right off if anything is missing or damaged."

Artur started to turn, but I stopped him.

"Tell them that we will happy to cooperate in any manner." I said. "We, as friendly American tourists, would not wish to run afoul of the authorities before we had the opportunity to visit their lovely country."

McAllister looked at me scornfully but nodded to Artur.

Penko's men slung their rifles over their shoulders and disappeared to pre-assigned positions as we followed the lieutenant to the fantail. As we made the short walk, I fell in next to Artur.

"Regular army?" I asked sotto voice. It was a question within a question.

"Good observation, Mister Lawton." Answered Artur. "The Army guards the borders here. At more conspicuous places like the airport, they might wear different uniforms, but they are still the same."

"What can we expect from this guy?"

"Not as much as we can expect on the way out." From his tone, I would have said he was as serious as his words indicated.

"This man is a lieutenant. If he were a major, we might have cause for alarm. He is just doing his job and probably enjoying the fact that he can see all this capitalistic decadence first hand."

Penko seated himself at the outdoor breakfast table and removed a stamp and pad from inside his tunic. Meticulously, he placed his tools on the table and looked up expectantly. Artur obediently presented his papers and said something to which Penko immediately replied.

"I told him we were tourists." He said. "He says he will not detain us long."

True to his word, Penko examined our documents with the bored and indifferent attitude of civil servants everywhere. One by one, his men returned, each saying nothing as they took up a position and remained at rigid attention, staring at an unidentified point on the horizon. Penko gave us each a final appraisal before turning to Artur and beginning a monotone dissertation. From the colorless tone, it sounded memorized.

"We cannot take the boat past the Ostrov Kanorerskiy." Artur translated. "Our hotel is the Evropeiskaya and. . ."

"Wait a minute." McAllister interrupted. "We're staying at the Astoria."

Artur held up a hand and shook his head. "He wants to know if we have foreign currency, weapons, or other contraband."

"What does he consider, contraband?" McAllister asked, and then said, "Never mind. Tell him we have no contraband, and what does he mean, we aren't staying at the Astoria? We already paid for our accommodations there."

"In-tourist arranges all accommodations." Artur explained. "If they want to change your itinerary, it is their prerogative. It is very unusual that you were told that you would be staying at the Astoria. It is probably for that very reason that some mid-level bureaucrat changed your expectation without notification. Every pencil-pusher in government service believes he or she is more important than the next person and takes it upon themselves to decide what is best. If the Premier were to travel under an assumed name, most of the civil servants would find themselves in a gulag."

Penko stood up and began returning our validated passports one at a time, comparing person and photo one last time. He slapped them into each of our hands in a manner I can only describe as truly Russian. When he got to McAllister, he smiled cynically. "Enjoy your stay in Mother Russia, Comrade McAllister." His English was heavily accented, especially in the pronunciation of Bobby's last name. "Da Svedahnya." And broadening his smile and snapping his fingers, he retreated down the stairs. His men followed without making eye contact with anyone.

"Relax, Mister McAllister." Artur said. "It's probably the only English he knows."

"Just the same," McAllister said, regaining his composure "Let that be a lesson to all of us. We can never assume that these people do not understand us." He made a gesture toward the deck. "Loose lips, sink ships." He tried desperately to say with a straight face.

"Cute." I said, smiling at a situation that had to be written into every movie ever made that addressed the language barrier. McAllister me in a reproving manner while the normally unflappable Captain Olsen stifled a snicker as he returned to the bridge. In minutes, we were up to speed again, but not without an escort. Penko's sister ship stayed off our port beam, maintaining a respectable distance but matching our exact speed to a point where we were well within the territorial waters of the one-time capitol of what was once the largest country in the world.

Although I neglected to check with Artur, I suspect that Ostrov is the Russian word for island. Side by side, Ostrov Kanonerskiy and Ostrov Gutuyevskiy effectively blocked the entrance to the river Neva with its three distinctive areas. The southeast basin of Gutuyevskiy was the berthing enclosure of the Russian fleet and Artur informed us that picture taking in that region was strictly forbidden. With satellite photography that can read license plates from miles above the Earth, the precaution seemed expendable, but typical. Kanonerskiy was divided equally between commercial boats and private craft and both marinas were woefully lacking in business. Still, Captain Olsen had to call on his considerable skills to maneuver the Second Prize into our narrow assigned slip at a pier that extended only halfway along the side of the ship. From the tip of the island, we could see the Fortress of St. Peter and St. Paul with its tall, extremely slender golden spire, reflecting sunlight from the center of the fortress. We were so captivated by the view; we almost failed to notice the diminutive woman on the dock, anxiously trying to attract our attention.

Irina Denikoff was more American than Russian in dress, stature, and attitude. Just under five feet tall, she wore distinctively California clothing on a well-shaped frame. Her English was flawless and only accented and her smile was radiant and sincere. She waved tentatively, trying to imagine how she was going to board when the dock did not reach to the boarding ladder. There was some brief confusion on the Second Prize also until one of Captain Olsen's men appeared with a secondary ladder which, when attached to the starboard side, proved not only serviceable, but only mildly inconvenient. When she reached the deck level, she smoothed her skirt unnecessarily and looked at McAllister expectantly.

"Good morning." She said, extending a delicate hand. "I am your In-tourist guide."

"Guide?" McAllister looked confused. "We didn't request the services of a guide."

Irina blushed self-consciously. "All foreigners are assigned an In-tourist guide." She explained. "It is part of the hospitality that Russia is pleased to extend to all of her visitors."

McAllister eyed her suspiciously, but at least he responded politely. "Well, thank you very much Miss Denikoff, but we have made our own plans for tour guides."

She hesitated slightly but didn't lose any of her enthusiasm and charm. "I don't believe you understand, Mister McAllister. All tourists are required to have an In-tourist guide with them at all times. It is a courtesy to insure that you are able to cover all aspects listed on your itinerary."

"That's just the point." McAllister was losing his patience and showing it by responding with exaggerated politeness. "We generally do not adhere to a strict schedule. We like to have the freedom to change our plans from day to day."

Irina looked distressed. "But I am afraid that is not allowed." She said. "Any changes in your plans must first be approved by In-tourist. We do this for your safety and protection."

"Protection?" McAllister's composure was dissolving. "What is that supposed to mean?"

It was obvious that Irina was having a difficult time thinking of a reply so I stepped in with a question of my own. "What if we do ask In-tourist to alter our schedule? How long does it take to get an approval?"

Irina looked confused. "I don't know." She answered honestly. "I have not known it to ever happen."

I looked at McAllister and raised an eyebrow. "Looks like we have our work cut out for ourselves."

"Work?" Irina still appeared perplexed. "You are here to work?"

"It's an American expression." I said, probably a little too quickly. I was going to have to be a little more careful in front of someone who spoke English so well. "It probably loses a lot in translation. What are we going to be doing first?"

"Well," Irina shook her hair in what I am certain was a western affection, "I suppose we had better see you to your accommodations. I am told that three of your people will be staying aboard your ship." She couldn't help looking around appreciatively. "I must caution your workers that their movement is restricted between the boat and your hotel. They must surrender their passports to the In-tourist representative at the hotel and to be outside of the prescribed areas without papers is a very serious offense in Russia. Again, these rules are for your protection."

I wondered why it was that every time anyone said that rules were made for the protection of others, it really meant that it was for the security of those making the rules.

"So that means that eleven of you will be going to the hotel." Irina said as she checked her facts in a small notebook.

McAllister shot me a warning glance when he saw I was doing some mental arithmetic. "Yes," he answered, "Captain Olsen, Mister Carter, and Mister Hart will remain on board. The rest of us will be depending on your kind hospitality to see the sights of your glorious homeland." To my way of counting, someone was missing. I immediately thought about the previous night and the man in the wet suit. I felt a mild shiver crawl up my spine.

"You will enjoy your stay at the Evropeiska." Irina said as she gathered passports and visas from everyone grouped around her.

"It is small but grand and has much of what you would call charm. It has a good restaurant and a late night bar. Much like your American Hiltons. You will see."

The Evropeiskaya is on one of St. Petersburg's most famous streets, the Nevsky Prospekt. It is old and definitely not as well kept up as any Hilton I have ever seen, but the rooms were clean and the service adequate. The lobby had a bank, barber and beauty shops, newsstand, and a gift shop that carried little more than postcards and stamps. The rooms were high ceilinged and spacious and McAllister inspected everyone's, hoping to find one bigger and with more amenities than the one assigned to him. An English speaking porter took up a position at a desk at the end of the hallway, presumably to act as a guard as well as an attendant.

I had not even begun to unpack when McAllister appeared at the door.

"You hungry?" He asked. He put a finger to his lips, pointed to an ear, and circled the room with a finger, indicating he thought the room might be bugged.

Since I didn't know if I was supposed to answer even an innocent question like that out loud, I nodded.

"Next door in ten minutes." He announced. "The hotel already made reservations for us."

Next door was Sadko, supposedly the best restaurant in the city. From a prix fixe menu supplied by the hotel, Larkin ordered blinis stuffed with caviar and smoked salmon, McAllister had beef stroganoff, and I had skewered meatballs which I thought was shish kebob but was called Lyulya Kebab while shish kebab was shashlik. Go figure. No one else from our shore party was joining us.

A balalaika orchestra complete with singers, entertained while we ate and during a particularly loud rendition of some folk number, McAllister leaned close and spoke directly in my ear.

"I don't want to talk about anything important while we're inside any building." He said. "I don't trust anyone around here."

"From what I understand, we won't be alone even when we're out in the open." I shouted over the music. "How can we communicate when we're either inside or being led around by Russia's version of the State Department?"

"I thought that she was kind of cute." McAllister hollered back. "I was hoping you two might hit it off."

"What the hell are you talking about?"

"C'mon," McAllister nudged my ribs, "a nice looking young lady meets a successful and well-to-do distinguished author. It shouldn't take much to convince a struggling and educated woman into realizing what a rare find you would be, and, a man of your esteem, semi-world famous mediocre good looks," He smiled at that comment, "who just might be inclined to sponsor her on a trip to the Land-O'-Liberty and the Land-O-The-Free."

I blinked. Several times.

McAllister winked in a conspiratorial, knowing way. He was enjoying himself at my expense.

"You want me to seduce our guide?" I couldn't believe my own ears.

"It would be only natural, Grange." He smiled. "As far as I'm concerned, anyway."

Although I never considered myself a prude, McAllister considered me one. I was speechless.

"Relax, Grange." McAllister looked around, afraid we might be overheard. "It's not beyond the realm of reality."

"How long and how hard did that brick hit you on the head?" I couldn't believe he was pursuing the matter. "That girl is easily twelve or fifteen years younger than me. You yourself just said she's intelligent. She officially works for In-tourist but she probably fills out a standard form of our daily activities and drops in it the night slot at the nearest drive-thru window of the KGB outlet.

"You're also the one who just said that you suspected our rooms might not only include running water, but live microphones. How do you expect me to deal with the fact that I might be making a fool of myself while, at the same time, making some kind of entertaining audio, or possibly video? You're talking about me! A guy who thinks foreplay is thirty minutes of intense begging!"

"It never bothered James Bond."

"Well, I'm no James Bond."

"You got a good point there."

McAllister was so damned smug. "Besides, Bobby. . ."

"Besides, what?"

I was quiet.

"Sally, right?"

I lowered my head.

"Don't even try that angle, Grange." McAllister's smile disappeared.

"Sally's gone. She was a sweet girl, but you weren't in love with her, not that way. So don't even try it."

"I . . . Well . . . I guess you're right, but . . ."

"Damn, Grange. I didn't know you were so sensitive. You can sleep alone for the rest of your life. Be a hermit if you like. But it wouldn't be fair to poor little Irina."

"You can sure pour it on thick, Bobby McAllister. In fact, you're nuts!"

The music picked that very second to come to an abrupt stop and my last three words echoed throughout the room. I hadn't realized how loud I had been talking.

Larkin's head spun around as McAllister pretended that he didn't even know me. Several other diners turned, not because of what I had said, but because of the volume with which I had said it.

McAllister gave me a triumphant sneer as he studied the bill, apparently trying to figure how many rubles equaled a dollar. His smirk turned to a pleasant smile as he said. "Outside."

Since the restaurant was only steps away from the hotel lobby, McAllister didn't have time to pursue his wild match-making scheme, but when Irina met us in the lobby, he wiggled his eyebrows suggestively and presented me with one of his famous smiles. I groaned inwardly.

"How did you find your luncheon, Mister McAllister?"

"I just moved a piece of lettuce and there it was." McAllister laughed, I cringed, and Irina looked confused.

"That's a joke, Irina. My husband is trying to be cute." Larkin came to the rescue.

Irina forced a smile. "I see." It was evident that she didn't though. "Well . . . Our first stop this afternoon is the Summer Palace. Is everyone ready?"

We sent for the porter to gather the rest of our party.

That McAllister's normally invisible security contingent was obviously evident was something that irked McAllister to no end. He didn't like it one bit. We traveled in three separate Mercedes limos, none of which McAllister's men were allowed to drive. We resembled a short funeral procession as McAllister, in the lead car, would not allow his Russian chauffeur to exceed forty miles per hour, afraid that the cars behind us might be lost. We arrived at the Summer Palace, nearly bumper-to-bumper, and parked next to the unpretentious palace built in the Dutch style for Peter the Great. When we had grouped at the entrance at Pestelya U1.2., Irina gave a short, uninspired speech about the grounds, originally laid out in 1704, and invited us to stroll the thirty acre park to enjoy the classical sculptures.

In a city of such great beauty, where virtually every downtown building has a bronze plaque imbedded next to the cornerstone noting its historical significance, it seemed strange to spend our first day in the wide open spaces of the Garden of Peter. Perhaps it was Irina's or In-tourist's way of showing us that, even in Russia; people can stroll arm-in-arm in the streets and relax in the parks, enjoying life as if care were only the name of some cartoon bears.

As the two McAllisters and I sauntered through the underpass below Sadovaja Street, discreetly followed by four unarmed but attentive bodyguards, Larkin looked to her husband for permission to talk openly.

"Here we are." She said, turning to me. "Now what can we expect?"

"I haven't the faintest idea." I admitted. "But I still think we're on the right track. Somebody has got to believe that we know more than we do, but in order to confirm that belief, we're going to have to act like more than mild mannered tourists. We have less than ten days to try to make something happen.

"So how do we go about making something happen?" She persisted.

"I don't know, yet." I said, stopping in front of one of the park's marble statues. "But I'd be willing to bet that within forty-eight hours that man you married will be goading me into making some kind of suggestion."

McAllister smiled. "And in the meantime, you can work on getting the little Miss Collective Farm on our team." He jerked his head toward Irina who was explaining something to our rear guard with exaggerated motions. "That's my first bit of needling."

I looked to the sky and silently damned every author who ever wrote a spy novel.

* * * * *

Other than theater and concerts, nightlife in St. Petersburg is limited to the scant fare offered at the hotels catering to foreigners. In stark contrast to the days of dazzling court life and lavish socialization, the foreign-currency bar at the Evropiskaya was dismal, but since all I wanted to do was think and drink, the quiet, late night answer to a Western night club suited me nicely. Maybe somewhere deep down I had expected Irina Denikoff to make an appearance at that lonely bar that night but, five or six drinks into my first full night in St. Petersburg had my feelings and reactions as dull as my surroundings. When she laid a gentle hand on my arm, I was taken off guard and I experienced a sudden physical start.

"Forgive me." Not expecting my reflex action, she jumped back, nearly as startled as I had been. "I'm very sorry."

"No." I apologized. "It's my fault. I wasn't expecting anyone."

"Oh, really?" She said, looking somewhat bewildered. "Mister McAllister said that you wanted to see me."

I should have known.

"Well, that's true." I lied, I think. "I just wasn't expecting you to work overtime."

"Overtime is a word that has no meaning in a people's republic." She said idealistically. "We are always available to make your stay pleasant and comfortable." She smiled as if she had made an important point. "So, what did you wish to talk about?"

"Uh. . . Background information." I said, almost as automatically as her rhetoric had been. "Authors are always looking for background information, even when not working on a specific project." I interjected. I didn't know how much she actually knew about us so I had to choose my words carefully. "I often do special projects for Mister McAllister and, even though we are supposed to be on vacation, he always expects me to be developing ideas for some future reference he may put to use."

"You are writing a book about St. Petersburg?" She asked. I couldn't tell if she was impressed or concerned.

"No, of course not," I assured her, "just sort of keeping notes so I can share my experiences in your lovely country with friends back home who are less fortunate than me." The charade called for me to act more interested in her dreadful country and asks some insightful questions but, much to my own surprise, I found that I was actually attracted to the lady. Technically, off duty, she had allowed her shoulder length dark hair to hang loosely around her shoulders and, wearing a tight fitting and provocatively cut blouse instead of her In-tourist blazer, a tantalizing figure became obvious. She had dark blue, Scandinavian eyes that registered amusement and natural curiosity. "How long have you worked for In-tourist?" I asked lamely.

"Four years." She answered as if she had known the question was coming. "It is a wonderful job. I get to meet many fascinating people like you and Mister and Misses McAllister."

"You speak English better than most Americans I know." I observed. "Where did you learn?"

"Lononosov University." It was another question she had apparently expected, or she was just very quick. "The Moscow State University is the largest University in the world and those of us privileged to attend feel it is the most comprehensive in all of its course offerings. My own professor of English was from Louisiana, in your country."

"Have you ever been to the United States?"

"No." She shook her head sadly. "But after I attain ten years of tenure with In-tourist I qualify with our cultural exchange program as an official translator. I hope I may see your country at that time."

I reached into a pocket for a small notebook I keep handy in case I come across something worth writing down. I wanted to look sincere. "If I were able to give you free rein, what would you want to tell me about St. Petersburg or Russia in particular?"

She smiled again. So far I had kept our conversation on grounds where she felt comfortable. "St. Petersburg is the jewel of Russia's crown." She said proudly. "It has everything that every other European city has; beauty, culture, political heritage, yet it is a young city by comparison. Nowhere else in the world has a city affected world history as much as St. Petersburg.

"Peter the Great recognized the Neva River as an important trade artery between Europe and Asia and designed the city in well planned stages. Even today, new construction in the downtown area must be completed within existing facades. Modern skyscrapers are not permitted to mar the horizon and industrial expansion is restricted to outlying areas, thus preserving our ties to the past.

"More than seven hundred thousand men, women, and children lost their lives during the nine hundred day German siege of what was then Leningrad during World War II and over ten thousand buildings were destroyed. Still, the city has restored itself to its original grandeur in remarkable time, becoming eminently more functional in the process.

"We are a city of more than four and one half million people yet we have less than ten percent of the crime and political and domestic unrest as Moscow. We are the home of the excessiveness and indulgence of the czars and nobility, yet we speak eloquently of our past. We were once the capitol of all of Russia, but we remain politically aloof of the power struggles and petty infighting in the Kremlin. In short, St. Petersburg is a combination of the best cities of Europe. With the rivers and canals and our wide boulevards we have the beauty of Venice and France. Our churches rival those of Rome and Spain and our architecture is the finest of France, England, and Scandinavia. You will find us politically astute and economically better off than any area of what used to be the Soviet Union, including the capitol."

Her pride and admiration of her homeland made me smile, even though her little speech sounded something straight out of the chamber of commerce propaganda handbook or the tourism guidebook. Tactfully, she did not liken anything she was espousing to the United States, proving to me she was indeed, not strictly political in her thinking.

Still, I was only listening to the canned stuff so I decided to try to make something happen. "What can you tell me about Russian art?"

She beamed at my question. "The Gosudaratvenni Russky Gallery in Moscow, the former Mikhailovsky Palace holds the largest collection of Russian art in the world. There are over three hundred thousand examples of paintings, sculptures, decorative art, and folksy art in the Russian State Museum. Much more than you can see in a day."

"I was thinking of something more specialized." I said, passing her the drink I had signaled the bartender to make. "Bobby-Mister McAllister and I have a more exclusive interest." I was stretching my own involvement. "We collect Faberge eggs."

A dark cloud formed behind her beautiful eyes and she stiffened noticeably. When she saw that I had caught her hesitation, she relaxed visibly and sat down for the first time. She had to literally climb into the barstool next to me.

"You would do well not to mention that fact in the presence of Russian citizens." She said her voice lower as if afraid of being overheard. "Many people in this part of the world believe that Faberge eggs are the select property of the State. For someone of a different nationality to possess these ethnic treasures is tantamount to theft, regardless of how they were acquired."

"You seem very opinionated on the subject." I noted. "You seem to have forgotten that Faberge once had a shop in London."

"Carl Faberge created his eggs exclusively for the Imperial Families and the nobility." She replied, growing a bit testy.

"And for the Royal families of half the nations east of the Greenwich Time Line." I said. "Face it, the old man was a confirmed capitalist. He sold to anyone who had the price he was asking. He took over a failing business from his father and made it successful, not because he was a better jeweler, but because he was a better salesman. If he were alive today, he would be tickled pink to know how much his little trinkets were getting on the open market."

"Faberge was an artist." She insisted. "He was a master craftsman without peer."

"That may be so, but he was a businessman as well." I argued. "He employed other people to use methods he perfected to conceive and design pieces he put his name to and sold for an inflated price because his name was on the product. Come on, Irina. How many people helped Rubens when he painted a nude Helene Fourment? Do you think Van Gough had an underpaid apprentice paint his self-portrait and he signed it after the guy went home? Did Leonardo da Vinci have twelve different men paint the disciples at the Last Supper while he concentrated on Jesus?"

"That is not fair." She said, finishing her drink with a flourish. I automatically pointed out the empty glass to the bartender who refilled it straight from a single bottle. "You are making with oranges and tomatoes."

That was a cute misquote, but I let it pass. "Don't fool yourself." I said. "How much would 'The Anatomy Lesson' be worth if it was painted by Irving Schmuckenduck instead of Rembrandt. For that matter, how much more would King Tut's treasure be worth if we put a name to the person who crafted them. It's not a matter of supply and demand, it's strictly salesmanship.

"Americans are obsessed with culture." I said. "Alex Haley proved it when he wrote 'Roots'. Now every college department that not only tells us unwanted facts about everything from ethnic back-grounds to why heroes of the past were really villains and should not be held up as role models."

"I have two questions for you." She was loosening up a little, I thought. "If Carl Faberge was an anti-hero, why do people vie to collect his works? She thought she was making an important point and I had an answer ready for her, but she continued.

"And why did Mister McAllister exploit the looted and pirated treasures of the Church of Spain?"

She caught me completely off-guard. First, I didn't realize that she knew anything about McAllister's exploits. Secondly, the wording of her question was confusing.

She caught the surprised look on my face and it pleased her.

"Irina . . . . Wait a minute. Okay, first let me say that Mister McAllister didn't exploit or plunder any Spanish treasure. He discovered it after, in fact, centuries after the pirates had plundered it from Spain. And since we're on the subject, how do you know about Mister McAllister's past?"

"I read your book, Mister Lawton." She smiled and answered with a very coy expression.

"You read it here in Russia?" I asked, completely shocked.

"Well, since I have never left Russia, where else would I have read your book?"

"But . . . I. . ."

She was enjoying her advantage. "I know a lot of things that would surprise you, Mister Lawton."

"Please call me Grange."

"Very well, Grange."

"Well, still, Bobby – Mister McAllister didn't exploit any treasure."

"Well, I hope not. And I sincerely hope he has no intentions of exploiting our cherished Faberge art."

I had to think more in-depth about Irina's startling new edge she had gained over me, so I changed the subject back to more safe grounds. "As far as your 'anti-hero' theory." She knew she had me squirming. "There are three very simple reasons." I began, trying to remember her earlier question. "People want investment; they want to convince themselves that they are closer to something or someone than they really are. We Americans call that living vicariously. Columbus. . ." She held up a hand to cut me off.

"Mister McAllister didn't have to live vicariously, did he?" She smiled. A smile that kind of reminded me of McAllister. Why was she so interested in McAllister, anyway?

"Well, no." I gulped the contents of my glass. "Mister McAllister. . . uh . . . we actually had our own true life adventures; we didn't have to live vicariously through anyone else's dreams." I found myself sounding like McAllister himself. Where was this conversation leading?

"So." She began smugly. "Why would Mister McAllister want to share anyone else's glory? Seems to me like he was a hero himself." Don't forget me. I thought.

"I can't say for sure, but like I was saying about Columbus."

She was amused.

"Columbus was a hero until someone described him as a slave owner and a greedy and cruel tyrant, yet those same people would pay millions for the sextant he used. Then you have the case where that guy bought the brick wall of the garage where the St. Valentine's Day Massacre. . ." She interrupted.

"Do you suppose that it would be inappropriate for me to speak to Mister McAllister about his adventures?"

Damn McAllister! I thought.

"Well, no, not really." I ordered another drink, she declined.

"But I am his biographer, and. . ."

"Would Misses McAllister object?" She wasn't listening to me.

"Of course she wouldn't."

"Great!" She sounded like some teenage groupie.

"Now, what were we discussing, Mister, uh, Grange?"

I didn't feel like defending McAllister any longer, but I had already started the ball rolling that I could not stop.

"Mister McAllister is a historian at heart. He is also convinced that his destiny is predetermined by whatever powers make such a determination. He somehow draws from the past to pave his way into the future. He comes from a city not unlike your precious St. Petersburg. That city was built by an English nobleman on the edge of a river sort of the same way your beautiful city was built by Peter the Great on the banks of the Neva river. Rivers of dreams." We continued our discussion, leading to where I explained to her what the 'St. Valentine's Day Massacre was.

She thought it was macabre that anyone would want to buy a brick from a wall where such a bloody massacre occurred. Then I told her that it was no more macabre than trying to find the remains of Alexander the Great in his golden casket. I shouldn't have been surprised that she was also familiar with the Russian archaeologist, Pyaim Zagorski who had spent a career of forty-five years, funded by Moscow, with that one and only aim. Irina maintained her spunk and insisted that there was a great difference between archaeology and art, but instead of gaining any insight or information other than her mysterious interest in McAllister, our conversation was turning into an ideological discussion so I tried to steer the talk back on track.

"Do you know where the Faberge store used to be?"

"Of course." She said. I looked at her glass and this time she nodded. I signaled the bartender for a re-fill. "The site of the salon was among the fashionable shops on Morskaya. I believe the exact location is now part of the offices of the Ministry of Finance."

"It might be nice to see." I hinted. "A picture of us in front would be fun to add to our collections."

She smiled again and sipped her drink. "I will see if it can be arranged. Is there anything else you might want to see that you think is fun at the expense of the people?"

It was the first flaw in the sparkling smile of the lady who intrigued me. For some reason, I knew that there was more to Irina than simply being an In-tourist guide. While it didn't make her any less attractive, it sure made me hope I was only being affected by the Russian vodka.

I didn't know when to quit. "You say you're not political but you seem to have some narrow opinions of the art and science of the administration of government. Ideology has its place, but not on vacation. If I had come here to discuss or debate statesmanship, I'd be surrounded by the press, and Dan Rather and Connie Chong would be calling this a summit."

She finished her drink and smiled. It appeared genuine this time. "You're right." She said. "And lucky."

"Lucky?"

"Lucky that I know who Dan Rather and Connie Chong are."

I somehow knew that I did not make a great impression on Irina, wondering who, in the long run would be more disappointed, McAllister or me. We talked another ten minutes before she excused herself, citing her pressing duties in the morning. When she stood up, she laid a gentle palm against my chest. "Thank you for an enlightening evening, Grange."

That damned McAllister. I thought. But I knew I couldn't blame him for my big mouth.

Making a phone call to anywhere out of the country required at least a one hour advance booking, presumably, to suspicious Americans, to arrange for an English speaking KGB agent to monitor the call. I knew that McAllister didn't want me to accept any help from his old friend, Jeff Camper, and I sort of promised him that I had conveyed his message to Camper, saying thanks, but no thanks. McAllister and Camper were old friends. It wasn't a matter of trust or lack thereof, but instead, it was because of McAllister's ego and determination to 'not let the facts stand in the way of making any type of decision'. In other words, McAllister was just plain stubborn.

I decided to procrastinate.

The porter manning the desk at the end of the hall was the same fellow that had been at the post when we had checked in and I wondered if he had a twenty-four hour a day job. At first he acted suspiciously and even fearfully, but when I finally conveyed the fact that all I wanted was a bottle of rum, he suddenly became very businesslike. In broken English, he told me his name was Mikhail and how much he would be happy to serve me as he helped himself to forty bucks worth of Russian currency. Twenty minutes later I had a quart bottle of dark brown liquid that smelled faintly of alcohol and tasted terrible.

I drank it anyway.

* * * * *

Irina had survived the evening better than I and her knowing smile and my disheveled appearance prompted McAllister to make one of his famous and outlandish speculations.

"Hey, Grange!" He said as we waited for the cars, "did someone embrace the Russian Bear last night? Maybe making new definitions for the word 'detente'."

"For Christ's sake, Bobby." I involuntarily looked toward Irina who, for no apparent reason, blushed slightly and looked away. "I've known the woman for twenty-four hours. This is Russia, not Woodstock."

"Politics makes strange bedfellows." He said suggestively.

"Sanity makes abstinence practical."

"You would have to be insane to abstain."

"Damnit, Bobby! Would you quit trying to play cupid." I said a little too loud.

"You snooze, you lose." He wouldn't quit.

"Get in the damn car, Bobby." I pushed him gently. He climbed into the back seat almost convulsing in laughter.

* * * * *

Fearing hostile action from the Swedish fleet, Peter the Great built a fortress that must have been a great deterrent because it was never used for the protection of Peter's new capitol. Established in 1703, the fortress came to be used as a prison for opponents of the czarist's regime and prisoners included Peter's own son, Czarevich Alexi, Dostoyevsky, and the anarchist Mikhail Bakunin. The Cathedral of Saints Peter and Paul stands in the center of the fortress and is the burial site of the czars from Peter I to Alexander III, with the exception of Peter II. The Petropavlovskaya Krepost, as it is known locally, is all that occupies the island at the junction of the Neva and the Mataya Neva and, since Peter's decree that no structure should be taller than the spires of the Cathedral, an edict still honored today; it is impressively visible from most anywhere in the downtown area. Only an autocrat and a visionary could have begun such a truly European city out of Baltic marshlands and drag a backward giant into the modern world at the same time.

In 1924, the fortress became a museum and a footbridge was built to allow tourists easier access to the island. As we followed Irina across the bridge, McAllister had the courtesy and foresight to get off the subject of Irina's defection by Lawton.

"How long are we going to have to act like we're enjoying ourselves? Are we going to stop somewhere and have fun, or is this it?"

I rolled my eyes, and shook my head.

"We can't afford to waste all our time sightseeing, Grange. Our chariot will soon turn into a pumpkin."

"Why don't you try to enjoy yourself, act a little enthused, Bobby." I didn't mean to try to sound rude or sarcastic, but I'm sure it came out that way. "I think we have to consider the fact that nothing might happen. We may spend the full ten days here without finding out anything except when this czar died or who painted what painting?"

"Then you must be in an artisan's heaven." He suggested, exhibiting his impatience.

"Loosen up." I advised. "As soon as we get the routine down we can start testing the limits of our circumstances."

"Was that statement supposed to mean something?"

"For every action, there's a reaction." I reminded him. "We push and wait to see who pushes back."

"And who decides whom to push and how far?"

"If we plan this thing down to the last detail, we leave no room for flexibility." I answered. "We have to be able to improvise."

"You don't have any idea what you're talking about, do you, Grange?"

"Not a clue."

Since we had witnessed first-hand the lavish and opulent style in which the Czars were sent to meet their makers; I guess that Irina felt we should see how the common folk made the same trip, so our afternoon stop was Alexander Nevesky Monastery.

On the way, we stopped at a street vendor's stand where we bought tasty meat, mushroom, and cabbage filled pastries called pirozhki, morozhenoye, which looked and tasted like ice cream, and kvass, a drink made from fermented black bread. It was delicious and as we ate there on the sidewalk, Larkin remarked that we could have been standing on practically any corner in any major city in the world.

"Except for one thing." McAllister noted, looking around. "This is a city of almost five million people. Where is everybody?"

He was right. The wide avenues had only minimal traffic and pedestrians were few and far between giving the entire downtown area the appearance of some sort of attraction frequented by a few curious out-of-towners.

"Unlike urban areas you might be used to, St. Petersburg has only a few places in the metro area that require the presence of the greater amount of our population." Irina informed us. "To the east are modern apartment complexes that rival the finest part of any Western suburban center as well as their work places of ship building and factories that produce hydro generators.

"By nature, Russian people are not of a mind to walk around for the sake of idle recreation. When not working, the family and togetherness are far more important than aimless wandering."

The McAllisters and I had an unspoken agreement to assimilation of information with as little comment as possible. Diplomats did it all the time, but McAllister was not the best of ambassadors of goodwill.

"In other words," McAllister said when he thought Irina wasn't listening, "they stay at home until they have to stand in line for food."

He didn't see it, but Irina looked at him over her shoulder with an expression of reappraisal of McAllister.

Aleksandr Nevskaya Lavra contains Trinity Cathedral built in 1722 to house the remains of St. Alexander Nevsky. In 1922, however, the saint's silver sarcophagus was moved to the Hermitage and the monastery began charging a small fee to those wishing to tour the grounds and its ten churches and four cemeteries known as necropolises. Also on the grounds, but considerably less interesting are the seminary and the museum of Urban Sculpture.

We walked among the graves of Mikhail Lomonosov, the founder of Moscow University, and Peter I's sister. In more modern necropolis next to the eighteenth century graveyard, are the remains of Dostoyevsky, Mussorgsky, Rimsky-Korsakov, Borodin, and Tchaikovsky. Among the unusual grave markers are miniature oil rigs for deceased oilfield workers and a propeller for a departed pilot.

At dinner at the Azerbaijani restaurant that contained an upstairs room for after dinner dancing, Irina proudly announced that she had obtained tickets for us for a performance at the Gorky Academic Boldhoi Drama Theater whose Russian name was far too long and incomprehensible for me to remember. Since alternative nightlife was at a minimum, we feigned enthusiasm and two hours later, tried desperately and unsuccessfully to show interest in the presentation. To this day I have no idea what the show was about but it looked like an analytical study of Death of a Salesman meets Zorba the Greek. McAllister paid a bartender a double fist full of rubles to be able to stay in the lobby drinking champagne while the rest of us suffered through the entire second act.

When we returned to the hotel I didn't bother Mikhail for another bottle of overpriced and under flavored rum as I still had a half bottle of the vile stuff left. I simply traded my poker chip chit for my room key and walked innocently and unsuspectingly into my room. The hotel was not much for having wall switches so I struggled in the dark to reach the table lamp when the glow of a cigarette stopped me in mid-reach.

There was a feminine voice from behind the incandescence.

"Good evening, Citizen Lawton."

* * * * *

"What do you have to report?"

"Nothing. They are taking in the sights like school children on a field trip."

"They are up to something." The disembodied voice replied. "I want to know their every move."

"How about I call you if and when something happens." The caller suggested. "Your elaborate game of telephone tag takes too much time from my duties here."

"I have to know what happens at all times. I do not want to miss any opportunities should something take place."

"Maybe I can force something to happen."

"Like what?" The voice was skeptical.

"I don't know. Give me time to think."

"God help us." The man at the other end of the line was exasperated.

"It should not be hard." The caller insisted. "The American has no fancy weapons to protect him in this part of the world. His so-called deluxe security force is impotent except for bulging muscles which do not stop bullets."

"What do you suppose he did with all that firepower he had on board?" The man asked.

"How the hell would I know?" The caller responded irritably. "He probably dropped them to the bottom of the Baltic on the way here. All I know is that my sources tell me that there is no way he could have smuggled his personal armory into the country. The boat underwent a complete and careful examination."

"Then why did he keep three of his men on board?"

"Because he still has seven authentic eggs in that silly little safe of his." The caller said contemptuously. "As if we could not crush that ten box at our leisure."

"No." The man said emphatically. "I told you not to be shortsighted. I have a feeling that McAllister is going to lead us to something important."

"So you expect me to continue following this band of ignorant tourists?"

The man hesitated while he considered his options. "Do what you wish," he finally said reluctantly, "but be discreet. You may try to force their hand, but only if you are able to do so without tipping our hand. My people tell me that McAllister can be a very formidable opponent if he is ruffled. I do not wish to invoke his wrath unless I am certain I am in control of the situation."

"As you wish." The caller conceded. "Just remember that I do not have the luxury of time that you enjoy."

"I have not forgotten." The man replied. "McAllister's visa expires in eight short days. One way or another, I think we will have some answers by then."

* * *

CHAPTER SIX

Somewhere I had read that the Russian language contains no word that could be considered an honorific. On the street, A Russian greets his fellow countryman with a common name and a patronymic. An official addresses his contemporary as comrade, and a jailer or custodian of a re-education camp refers to his wards as citizens.

The only thing I could think of as I stood before the shadowy female figure making herself comfortable in my room was that she had used the latter form of address to greet me. My mind went nowhere at warp speed.

"By all means, please turn on the light." She prompted. "Had I left it on, someone might have come in to turn it off. Russians are very conservative when it comes to energy consumption and it is your porter's job to see that the hotel's resources are not wasted."

Her tone was reassuring, but I wasn't able to equate this encounter with any other experience in my past, not even the time I discovered the uninvited presence of Agent Frank Kipper in my hotel room in Savannah. I did what I was told, however, and when the light came on, I found myself in the company of a strikingly beautiful woman with the reddest hair I had ever seen tied tightly behind her head in a bun. She was in her mid-thirties, slim waist and long legs which were covered in a peasant's dress resembling some sort of costume fresh from the wardrobe of a movie studio, and was rolling something between the thumb and first two fingers of her left hand.

"We do not have much time." She said in perfect English while rising. "They will expect to be hearing you move around and when they don't hear anything, they will investigate."

"Sounds?" I said stupidly. "They?"

She held up the small ball of glop that she had been twirling between her fingers. "Potter's clay." She said. "A little dab on the microphones and we may talk freely for a short time. If we remove these listening devices," she pointed to a picture frame and a spot on the bed's elaborately carved headboard, "they will be very upset. There is no telling how they might react."

"Who are you?" Information was not reaching my brain in the order I would have preferred.

"You have a friend in Chicago in the American State of Illinois." She pronounced the "s" in Illinois. "I am his messenger, Sanya Roskovin."

Jeff, or Geoff Camper, I was wondering. But that was not my primary concern at that time. McAllister's wrath was.

"You have a message for me specifically? Or. . ." I began, as anxious as I was surprised.

"For Mister McAllister." She said, and then smiled. "But I was informed that he might not be receptive to any messages at this time and that I was to speak with you, Mister Lawton. Is that not so?"

"I, uh . . . Well sure. That is, yes you can communicate with me." I stammered. "Mister McAllister is a very busy man, and, well, you know..."

I was cut off mercifully. "Perhaps I used the wrong word to describe my responsibility." She looked somewhat disappointed that her own importance had suddenly diminished. "Alas, I know nothing of your purpose here in St. Petersburg. I am to take you to a man who has the information you desire."

"When?" I asked. "How? Why doesn't he come here?"

"I will come for you tomorrow night." She answered. "We will meet in a place that is safe for both of you. Wear dark clothes and be ready to go any time after nine o'clock. I will knock three times."

"Is what you have planned in any way something that could cause embarrassment to Mister McAllister or jeopardize our welcome here in Russia?" Or worse, I thought but did not verbalize. I know I sounded lame.

Sanya frowned. "I was told you were a very determined man." She said. "You are a foreigner and everything you do or say is suspicious. There are very few rewards in this country and the only way to obtain anything requires risk. You either take your chances or remain without."

I wished McAllister had not been so adamant about not wanting the Campers' assistance and that he would be a little more receptive to this cloak and dagger situation.

"Okay." I said, trying to cover for my underworld social blunder. "I'll be ready. Is there anything else I should know?"

"Say nothing to anyone from this point on." She said. "Follow instructions without question and be prepared to move quickly at all times. Mister McAllister and his, what he believes to be his invisible, security force is being watched very closely. I would have preferred to deal directly with Mister McAllister in this matter, but I am not to question my instructions. I do know that Mister McAllister has a very concerned friend in Chicago, USA."

"Do you know this man, uh, person I am supposed to meet?"

"Your answers will come tomorrow night." She said. "Tonight is for making the preparations and precautions. We need to know that you will act as you are told. This is not a game. Several people are going to great lengths to help you in this matter."

"What do I do in the meantime?" I asked, lamely attempting to show my willingness to cooperate.

"I must go now before your porter comes to see why they cannot hear you downstairs. Remove the clay from the microphones very carefully and flush the bits of clay down the toilet. Stay in the bathroom for five minutes making bathroom sounds. If no one comes to your room, we can assume that they suspect nothing at this time."

"What if someone comes?"

"They would probably send the porter with an excuse like the maid has lost something or another. Volunteer nothing. If they ask how you have been spending the last few minutes, tell them you were sitting here quietly thinking about something or maybe reading."

I nodded my understanding and carefully peeled the clay from the two microphones and did as I was told. I flushed the John two or three times, ran the tap, brushed my teeth, and coughed several times. When I thought the appropriate amount of time had passed, I went back into the main part of the room. Sanya was gone, but I couldn't help feeling I was not alone.

* * * * *

The Italian architect Rastrelli designed the Winter Palace as a home for the czars and czarinas of the eighteenth century reigns of Elizabeth and Catherine the Great. Today, the Baroque palace and four adjacent buildings house the Hermitage collection. One of the finest art collections in the world, da Vincis, Raphaels, Titians, Rembrandts, and hundreds of impressionist and post-Impressionists paintings hang in rooms with patterned parquet floors, molded and painted ceilings, and decorative objects of malachite, lapis lazuli, and jasper. The highlight of the tour was the Gold Treasure Room, the repository of Catherine the Great's jewels and an incredible collection of Scythian Gold.

Elsewhere is the St. George's Salon with its white marble Corinthian pillars and its six chandeliers of crystal and gold and the throne set against a background of the Imperial Coat of Arms embroidered in gold on red velvet.

The Jordan Staircase, Pavilion Hall, and even the mythological figures that silently stare across the Neva conjure up visions of Cossacks in crimson or sapphire blue, Caucasians in white tunics, and members of the Rifle Brigade in magenta shirts and dark green fur-trimmed coats, all walking among the corridors, attending to royal families in excessiveness never equaled.

Catherine the Great once wrote, "I have a whole labyrinth of rooms... and all of them are filled with luxuries." To the semi-enslaved serfs of her time, that missive must have been the understatement of all time. Even the individual apartments were examples of a lifestyle that billionaires of today would consider extravagant and lavish. I have been to such places as San Simeon in California, and the Vanderbilt mansion in North Carolina and I can say with authority that those splendid homes pale in comparison to the self-indulgent taste of the Romanov dynasty.

In spite of the art, history, beauty, and ostentatious display of wealth that surrounded me, Irinia's incessant lecturing took on a droning quality, the canvasses of the great masters began to blur, and McAllister's cute little quips about everything from innuendo about our guide to the state of the world today took on a boring and slightly ridiculous element. I was anxiously waiting to take one step closer to the man who had heartlessly and deliberately thrown the bomb that ended Sally's life in a flash and a bang. My fantasy about ending his life slowly and painfully mingled with my fear that I was chasing a ghost in a blind mist and then merged with my misgivings about taking another human being's life no matter how reprehensible and disgusting that life had been.

I remember McAllister telling me once that if one tried to play God with him, that McAllister would play the devil. Even though McAllister suffered no real personal loss, I dreaded the thought of being the man who threw the bomb that took Sally and Antonio's life. McAllister was the poorest loser I had ever known existed. But still . . .

My apprehension included the facts that I was an amateur tough guy in a foreign country with no weapon to carry out any threat as well as, since I didn't know Sanya from Natasha Badinoff, I could have been helping set myself up as well as the McAllisters for a major plunge. I remembered another quip that McAllister once said to me: "You're only as strong as your weakest link." I shuddered.

I had already admitted to myself that it was strange that Sanya had entered and exited my hotel room supposedly undetected, that she apparently knew me by sight, and that she was willing to help an unwitting McAllister using me as a conduit, on the word of an American underworld boss whose interest and influence in Russia had to be questionable at best.

And finally, I worried that my personal quest might not only endanger McAllister's mission, but place a strain on our friendship, not so much because he might not be able to make some kind of recovery on his investment or solve his mystery, but because I was not succumbing to his every wish and disregarded his order to reject the Campers' kind assistance. McAllister despised being second-guessed; no matter how trivial the matter appeared to be. His priorities were sacred to him.

McAllister would forgive my motives but not my methods.

With McAllister's full entourage, including Artur Ladvick, who was proving to be an unnecessary asset as far as I was concerned, especially considering how many people spoke English in this country, we appeared to be members of a typical tour group except that Larkin was our only female member. She didn't seem to mind, however, as she would have been happy to be a simple tourist instead of part of a double edged conspiracy. Since fiction writers everywhere wrote spy novels about Russian subversion, our combined missions caused me to wonder if common Russian citizens thought in insurgent political terms of an American plot against their way of life. It was the first mildly amusing thought I had all day.

"What's so funny?" Larkin had sided up next to me as I was staring without seeing Van Gough's version of Eternal Damnation. She pointed to the canvass. "Van Gough was much too sensitive to be laughed at, even posthumously. Besides, that's not exactly the Sunday comics."

"Actually, I was a million miles away." I confessed. I looked at my watch. "I guess my mental floppy disc has reached its capacity. We've been here almost six hours now and I figure we're only halfway through. When someone wanted to see someone from one end to the other of this place they probably had to obtain a travel permit."

"It is rather overwhelming, isn't it?" She ran another glance around the high ceilinged room and smiled. "I'm surprised that Bobby hasn't made someone an offer for this place. Maybe he thinks the zoning laws are too tough."

"He would make his changes anyway and dare the government to defy him."

She would have made an appropriate comment if she had thought I was wrong. Instead, her expression changed to one of concern. "Are you all right, Grange?" She asked. "You seem a little preoccupied."

"I'm okay." I said, trying to look unconcerned. "It must be the water."

"We're not in Mexico, silly. We're in Russia."

"Read your travel Funk and Wagnall's." I said. "It's a parasite called giardia lamblia and it lives in the water system."

"Is it a communist parasite?" She asked with amusement in her eyes. She had definitely been around McAllister too long.

I sneered at her question.

"I think I need to get to bed early tonight." I said. A little extra rest will have me back on my feet in no time."

Instead of answering, she seemed to hesitate a second as if she wanted to say something, but turned quickly to rejoin the bulk of the group. I saw her whispering something to McAllister who shook his head emphatically in response. To his credit, McAllister studied a half dozen more paintings before he casually made his way over to me.

"This is far out stuff, Grange." He smiled. "Well, maybe not as far out as maybe, Long Beach, California, but it's far out."

This time I flashed a more cultivated sneer.

"You're an ass, Grange." His smile turned to a frown.

"Me?" I answered innocently. "Because I warned Larkin about the water?"

"No, you jerk-off. There's nothing wrong with the damned water here. How would you know anyway? All you've been drinking is that god-awful potato vodka. You're just trying to get out of another night at the Ballsy Teatar Coocoo."

"What?"

"You heard me."

It took me a second. "You mean the Bolshoi Teatr Kukol. I think you might enjoy that. It's the Bolshoi Puppet Theater. It's world famous."

"Yeah?" His attitude changed suddenly. "Puppets, huh? What makes you think I would sail halfway around the damned globe to enjoy a bunch of damned Russian puppets?" He shook his head. "That sounds like a whole bunch of fun."

"Most of the stories are pantomime." I was winging it. "It's really a great show."

"How could a Russian pantomime sound any different than a Swahili pantomime? You really are feeling sick." McAllister would never understand why someone else would not enjoy the same things he might relish.

"I just need a night to myself." I lied. "And you need a night out on the town with your wife."

McAllister studied me for a few uncomfortable seconds before looking me directly into my eyes. "Grange," He began slowly. "Do you remember me telling you the story about Captain Jim and me and the kidnapping of my daughter?"

"Of course, I remember. It's documented in Fool's Paradise."

"Remember I told you how Captain Jim ceased to be my very best friend, and now is only one of my cherished, but distant friends?"

"What. . ."

"Do you know why I sent Captain Jim out to the great blue pasture to live out his legacy without me?"

I was beginning to see where McAllister was coming from.

"In other words, Grange, do you know why Captain Jim is no longer among my traveling band of adventurers?"

"Because he lied to you once?"

"No, Grange. It was because he didn't tell me the truth."

I had no reply.

"Better get some sleep, Grange. You have a bug to get rid of."

I stared noiselessly at the ceiling awaiting nine o'clock. Sleep was the farthest thing from my mind.

* * * * *

At exactly nine o'clock, I soundlessly moved a chair next to the door to wait for Sanya. By ten fifteen I was about to give her up as a welcomed no-show when a three-knock sound, much like a pen tapping on a wooden desk, caused my breath to catch and my heart to skip a beat.

Sanya was unnecessarily holding a finger to her lips as she nervously glanced back and forth along the length of the corridor. I stepped into the hall, silently closing the door behind me while noting that Mikhail was absent from his post, and followed Sanya as she led me in the opposite direction of the elevators and Mikhail's deserted checkpoint. We descended two flights of stairs to the second floor of offices through a hotel corridor. We entered a cubicle and stopped next to an open window.

"It's a five foot drop to the pavement." Sanya whispered. "If you hang by your fingertips, it is only half that distance. Do you think you can manage without hurting yourself?" She asked trying to suppress a chuckle.

Damn! James Bond would have already seduced Sanya, dropped the distance and disappeared out of sight. All I had was a slightly amused beautiful redhead staring up at me from the uneven brick pavement of a back alley.

"No problem." I said, figuring even if I could survive a seven or eight foot drop. Having a good understanding of the forces of gravity, I was more worried about getting back up. I landed hard but relatively painlessly but not quite ready for the Olympics. Sanya grabbed me by the arm, assisting me off my butt and almost dragged me toward the dim lights at the Nevskiy Prospekt.

I followed Sanya through a labyrinth of alleys and back streets, rushing blindly, not having any idea where I was headed. It was a helpless feeling, being led by a complete stranger, and a beautiful stranger at that, through unfamiliar territory on a moonless night, and when we finally emerged from the shadows next to a canal near the Moscow Station, I was only marginally relieved. A battered yellow Yugo was idling noisily at the curb, dirty gray smoke coming from the tailpipe.

"Do not speak with the driver." Sanya said, standing at the rear of the car. Her beautiful red hair reflected the light of a slowly passing car. "He is not a part of this and is only helping us as a favor to me. You will never see him again."

Did that have a double meaning? I wondered.

To insure we had no eye contact, Sanya herded me into the back seat and before she had fully seated herself in the front, our driver ground the transmission into gear and headed what I presumed to be north. From then on, I could have been on the planet Mars. Without street signs, I could not tell where we were going except that we turned east at one point and seemed to travel in a straight line from there. We must have gone about four miles through nearly deserted streets when we began a series of twists and turns designed to take us to our final destination.

Or to keep me from finding my way back.

We stopped in front of a non-descript house next to a stairway that went down to a basement a half story below ground level.

"This is a neighborhood traktir." Sanya explained. "You would call it your friendly neighborhood bar. Do not talk to anyone other than the man we are here to see."

The heavy door creaked to admit us to a smoky room maybe three times the size of the average American living room. About a dozen customers sat at tables and an old wooden counter ran the entire length of one side of the room. Bottles, glasses, and plates of sausage and ham were piled on the bar which seemed to exist solely for the purpose of display as no one was lounging at the bar. A waiter in white blouse, white trousers and a white apron ran from table to table, taking and filling orders. The people at the tables were all apparently workers, dressed in clean but shabby clothing.

"Traktirs have been in existence for over three hundred years." Sanya said. "While they have always existed for the workers, they were also frequented by scholars and philosophers in time of revolution or political unrest. Normally, I would not be welcome here among the working family men, as they consider women to be domestic creatures." She smiled.

For some reason I couldn't picture Sanya as domestic; A spy, maybe.

She continued. "They are still the closest thing to a public forum today and barely tolerated by the government. "This particular place is owned by my brother-in-law." She smiled again. "So I know it's safe."

We walked to the corner of the room where worn and dirty worn blankets were strung from wires that were embedded in the walls near the low ceiling. Sanya parted the ragged curtain to reveal a small wooden table and three chairs. A shriveled old man sat at the table looking frightened, suspicious, and cautious. Sanya said something to him in Russian but the man looked no happier as he finished the drink he had in front of him and wiped his mouth with the back of his hand.

"This is my uncle, Serge Byachev." Sanya said, seating herself in one of the rickety chairs. "He speaks English, but not very well. He would prefer me to stay and translate."

"Good evening, Mister Byachev." I said. "My name is Granger Lawton."

"Da, da." The old man held up his glass. "You buy vodka?"

"Of course." I said to Sanya who stuck her arm through the curtain and waved her hand. "Do you know why I am here?"

"Da." Serge rested his forearms on the table and looked up. "You sit." He said, nodding toward the empty chair. "I will tell you things."

I sat just as the white clad waiter brought us a bottle and three glasses. Serge poured us each a measure of the clear liquid, helping himself to a slightly larger portion. Serge was a man who was older than his chronological years. He had a large, bulbous nose and his wrinkled skin reminded me of old, cracked leather. Everything about him drooped including his eyes which were rheumy, betraying years of alcohol abuse. He held his glass up in a silent toast, downed the contents in a single gulp, and immediately reached for the bottle for a refill.

"You want Rastov." He said, without preamble. "A very bad man."

"How do you know?" I asked, surprised at the suddenness with which I received the information.

Bayachev looked to Sanya who nodded silently. "Many years I work now." He began. "I work as, how you say," he said a word in Russian.

"Custodian." Sanya said. "In Russia it is more than a janitor or security guard. It is many jobs in one."

Serge was nodding. "I work at Ermitazh, the Hermitage, only not in the public. In basement, like this." He pointed at the table as if it were the room we were in. "Many secrets there." He said, pounding his chest with a closed fist. "I know. I work hard to see things move calm."

He raised his eyebrows to make sure I understood what he was saying and that he was an important man. "Go on." I said, bobbing my head.

"KGB have office." He continued. "Five, sometimes six men. They work in secret room even important man like me know nothing about. Many other men come and go this secret room every day.

"One day I see man from secret room in traktir near Puskin. Very drunk. He see me and say 'come, I buy you a drink. Many drinks so you will not tell Kalinishkov I am drunk and fearful.'"

"He means scared." Sanya interrupted unnecessarily.

At the mention of the man with the name that was almost the same as that of the Russian gun, my heart froze. Impatiently, I waved Sanya to silence; hanging on Serge's every word.

"I ask him what is bad that he is fearing." Serge went on.

"He said he was crafting work, work with gems, I think, when Kalinishkov and Rastov come in to talk to man at work table next to him. Kalinishkov very angry. Says man did bad work. Knows nothing of . . ." He searched for a word and not finding one, turned to his niece and said several words in Russian. Sanya looked confused but held a hand to Serge and turned to me.

"It sounds as if he wants to say 'waxed painting.'" She said.

"Enameling!" I said it so loud that the low murmur of conversation in the rest of the small bar stopped momentarily. Sanya translated the word to Serge and he nodded vigorously.

"Da, da." He said as he tried to pronounce the word in English. "So bad man Rastov asks man where is real piece. Man is crying and telling Rastov he has lost it. Rastov calls him a liar! Rastov drags man away from bench.

"Man in traktir thinks poor man is fired for being stupid and goes back to his work.

"Two days later, man in traktir leaves Ermitazh by secret door and sees many people standing by River Neva. When he looks, he sees man who was dragged away from work place pulled from water. Dead man has bullets in knees and elbows and many fingers are broken."

"How do you know this has anything to do with the man I am looking for?" I asked.

He shrugged. "I know that two, maybe three weeks later, I hear Kalinishkov talking." He said. "He is telling Rastov that they have chance to make money," he held three fingers, then changed to four, "returnings." He looked to Sanya and again spoke in Russian.

"Recoveries." Sanya said simply.

"Da." Serge said, bobbing his head eagerly. "But Rastov must go to France and find out what some Americans are doing at home of man from Spain."

"How long ago was this?" He had me on the edge of my chair.

Serge shrugged. "A month, maybe six weeks. But Rastov say he barely get out of South America alive after last dealing with American. He tells Kaliniskov he needs more men. Kalinishkov say they work in secret so there is no need."

Pieces were falling into place so quickly that my head began to swim. I felt dizzy and elated at the same time. The room tilted slightly and I heard a dull roaring from inside my head so I reached for my drink and tossed it down quickly. It was vodka and it must have been a hundred and twenty proof. I choked.

Sanya began slapping my back, hard at first, then soft and sensual. "Are you all right?"

I held up my hands in a gesture of surrender. When my head cleared and my eyes stopped watering, I turned back to Serge.

"This man, Rastov." I said. "A big man? Bad clothes? Rubbery looking nose? Dirty brown hair and big hands?"

Serge looked confused. "Nyet." He said, wondering if he was being tested. "Big man, da. But dark, like Jew. Very black hair. Face looks like rock."

I sighed heavily. As quickly as things had started to fit together, they were now blowing apart. It sounded very much like I was hearing a partial confirmation of McAllister's wild theories, but the very moment I started thinking I had put a name to Sally's killer's face, my ship was blown out of the water. I began grasping at straws.

"This man at the bar in Pushkin." I said. "Do you know his name?"

Serge squinted his eyes in an effort to think more clearly.

"Da, I think." He poured himself another drink. "He is Sarzanov." He said after a pause. "I do not know more. I am sorry."

"How about the man that was killed?" I asked.

Serge shook his head. "Nyet." He said sadly. "This is important?"

"I don't know." I said honestly. "What else can you tell me?"

Serge looked to Sanya with a slightly disgusted look on his face. She sipped her drink and made a non-committal gesture.

"I make special way to talk with you." He said. "Very dangerous for man in my place. I think to talk more would be to give you what you do not need to know and to me, much trouble."

I nodded sadly. I knew what he was saying. Still, I felt I had to make one more try.

"Do you know anyone who resembles the man I described earlier? Maybe Rastov had a partner. Maybe someone else who works for the department?"

Serge shook his head as he drank then exhaled as if he really enjoyed the vile stuff we had ordered. "You tell me what looks like many Russian men." He said. "If you have a picture maybe?" I shook my head again. "You must know that I would tell you. Secret room have many I do not see. Sometimes I hear. I know Rastov in much trouble."

"Why?"

"Rastov have big trouble in France." He said. "Kalinishkov wishes to see him much. Kalinishkov yell at another man about Rastov."

"Thanks, Serge." I said, slowly getting to my feet. "You've been very helpful."

I reached in my pocket and withdrew a fist full of rubles I had brought along, hoping that it was going to buy me more, but still grateful for what I had learned. It was equivalent to a couple of hundred American and I sadly extended it to Serge. Instead of taking the money, he looked questioningly at Sanya who placed a restraining hand on my arm.

Serge looked insulted. I couldn't tell if it was because Sanya disapproved or if my offer was in bad taste.

"It's okay." I told them both. "This is a time honored tradition in my country. Please accept my offer as a sign of my sincere appreciation."

"But you do not have information correct." Serge said, unwilling to believe I could be so disappointed and still be willing to part with what was, to him, a small fortune.

"I'll get it back when I tell my friend what I learned tonight." I said, hoping that he would feel better if he knew I was not going to be out of any money.

Serge paled visibly. "You tell someone?" He asked. It almost came out in a squeak.

"It is all right, Uncle." Sanya was reassuring. "Our friend said this will be very confidential. We are not talking for other's ears."

"You're right." I said quickly. "I know it sounds like a contradiction, but you both have been very helpful, really. My friend and I have similar purposes for coming here and I can assure you that what I have learned here tonight will be put to use to solve my mystery. Our mutual friend who somehow directly or indirectly put you and your lovely niece, Sanya and me together is definitely aware of my absent friend."

Serge looked to Sanya with questioning eyes.

"It is true what Comrade Lawton is saying, Uncle. He and his friend can be trusted." Surprisingly, she placed her hand on my arm again to demonstrate a gesture of trust.

Serge seemed to be reassured, but looked me over with undisguised suspicion. Nevertheless, he accepted the wad of bills and poured himself another drink.

"Good." I said. "Thank you for your help, Serge. I extended my hand over the table.

"Da svedahnya, American." He said, shaking my hand curtly. He added something in Russian.

"What did he say?" I asked Sanya as we ascended the steps.

"He quoted an old Russian proverb." She said. "Only the czars know the truth, and they are still dead."

"Yeah, well I've read somewhere that 'only the dead know the truth' "I added. "I guess that applies to the czars too." I had never heard of an optimistic Russian proverb. For that matter, I don't recall having ever heard one and I was sure that if I had, I would never understand it. I'm still pretty sure of that.

We made the return trip to the hotel in an Audi. Sanya drove without headlights.

"I don't suppose you'd like to climb up to my room for a nightcap, would you?" I asked half-heartedly, trying to think what James Bond would have done at that particular time. I was reeling from an overdose of adrenalin and found myself not wanting the evening to end so soon. I had no idea what time it was, I forgot to bring my watch.

At first she smiled. I couldn't tell whether she was amused or tempted, but her smile faded as she looked at me as if I were something distasteful.

I tried to save face. "Is there some way I can call you if I need you again, Sanya?" I asked meekly.

"I understand that you may have been disappointed tonight." She said. "But I have exhausted my resources in this matter. However, since our friend in Chicago is your patron, I cannot refuse. If you feel you must see me again, hang a bright yellow shirt so it can be seen from your window. I will contact you when I am able."

She stopped the car two blocks from the hotel and shut off the motor.

"Watch me when I drive away." She said. "I will park beyond the hotel entrance. When you see me flash my headlights, walk quickly and directly to the hotel. Take the stairs on your left and go to your room. If you see anyone, do not talk. Good luck, Comrade Lawton."

I felt dispirited but thanked her and got out of the car.

Five minutes later, I was quickly back in my room having encountered no one on the way. I fell into bed semi-exhausted, hoping I would snore for the benefit of the microphones.

* * * * *

"Feeling better?" McAllister asked when I stepped off the elevator.

"Not much." I admitted honestly.

"Well, take a pill or something." He said suspiciously. "I want to talk to you."

Here it comes. I deserve it.

He walked over to Larkin, took her by the elbow and guided her to the waiting car. His curt greeting indicated displeasure, but, knowing, McAllister that could have been about anything, so I followed with the fatalistic attitude I learned to adopt when dealing with him.

Between the Winter Palace and the Admiralty is the Dvorcovyi Most Bridge that leads directly to the Peter the Great Museum of Anthropology and Ethnography. It is two separate buildings under the same roof and the home of the famous art collection Irina had mentioned during our meeting at the Evropeiskaya's late night bar. It was everything she said it would be but to three distracted Americans; it served only as a place to talk in low voices.

"We're leaving tomorrow." McAllister announced abruptly. "Larkin and I talked it over last night and we think this museum hopping is a waste of time." I looked to Larkin for confirmation. She tilted her head slightly and shrugged as if to say she was merely going along with her husband.

"But, we can't, Bobby. Not. . ."

McAllister cut me off with his glaring eyes. "Oh, then you must know something I don't, Grange. Could that be?"

"No. I mean no we can't leave now." I said far too quickly.

I knew at that moment that McAllister knew something. Exactly what, I didn't know. "And why is that?" Continued McAllister.

"What brought you to this decision?" I ignored his question and posed my own, stalling for time, wondering if and how I should tell him about the previous night's excursion.

"The simple fact that nothing is happening. We're wasting our time here, Grange. So, we just hoist anchor and sail out of the harbor." He said as if he were talking to a child.

"I don't agree." His next question was going to force my hand. I knew McAllister, and I knew that he was tiring of my little dance, but I forged ahead. "Tomorrow we're scheduled to go to the Czar's Village and the Yekaterinsky Palace. I have a feeling that going there could be important."

"A feeling, Grange?" We were walking the corridors slowly, giving only cursory inspection to the art treasures that surrounded us. McAllister took on the appearance and pose of an arrogant Russian officer or a Captain Bligh as he strutted, hands clasped behind his back, pretending to be interested in the canvasses as he questioned me. "So, you suggest hanging around here for another couple of days because you have a feeling?"

At first I was going to try reasoning with him, but his ridiculous pose and his attitude suddenly burned a hole right through any willingness I had to endure his pompous behavior.

"Yeah, a feeling." I cranked myself up for an argument. "Sort of like the dreams of a ten year old boy, an underage beer swallowing teenager, and a modern day reincarnate-apparent pirate who nobody took seriously until his dreams come true.

"Who the hell are you to deflate anybody's balloon when it comes to a hunch? Just what the hell is so important that you think you have to leave tomorrow? Is someone expecting you at the office Monday morning? Do you have some plan that relies on some sort of schedule? And finally, do you always have to be in charge of every God damn thing that has the least remote thing to do with what you decide is your business?"

McAllister stared at me with his mouth slightly agape and his eyes showing amusement and, of all things, admiration.

"Why, Granger Lawton." He said without sarcasm but with an exaggerated show of respect. "What, pray tell, has caused this sudden onset of stiffened backbone? Such conviction of principles makes me think you know something you're not telling your old friend."

I sighed, realizing what must have happened.

"How much do you know?" I asked, resigned to the embarrassment I was going to suffer.

"We know that you look silly when you climb out of hotel windows."

I sighed again.

"All right." I said. "I didn't exactly follow your instructions to the letter. But . . . I intended to."

"Who was the redhead?"

"Sanya."

"Sanya?" McAllister asked in feign shock.

"Yeah." I said in a tone of resignation. But, Bobby, please don't ask me any more questions. Just give me a free-hand on this one and let me see if I can solve a mystery just once. Humor me, okay?"

"I'm amazed. Simply amazed. I knew it all along." McAllister said to no one in particular.

"Amazed at what, Bobby?" Larkin asked. She looked bewildered.

"I knew that the Russian ladies were no match for the charms of our esteemed friend, Granger Lawton."

"This is serious, Bobby." I mentally cringed. "It seems that there is some validity to your theory about the KGB."

"When are you going to learn not to doubt my theories, Grange?"

I had that coming.

"I, uh, ran into someone who thought he could identify the man who bombed our car in Paris. He was wrong, but he did have some information."

McAllister looked bored.

"I met with somebody who says he works in a special department at the Hermitage. He says that there are some very distinctive projects going on that are overseen by some very bad men."

"What kind of projects?"

It was obvious that we were focusing on two entirely different priorities. I had just told him that fierce alligators were guarding the swamp and he asked me what they were guarding.

"The guy barely spoke English." I answered, still unsure of how much to tell him. "I got the impression he had no direct knowledge of what exactly happens there, but he did give me a name; Sarzanov. He supposedly hangs out in a bar in Pushkin."

"What bar?" He asked. "What's his first name?"

"I don't know, Bobby." I said. "On both counts. From what I can tell, bars don't have names around here. The only thing I have is Saranov's name and the village of Pushkin. I think I was pretty lucky to get that much."

"How did you?"

"How did I what?"

"How did you exactly stumble on to this bit of enlightenment?"

I thought about lying for about one second, "I got a call from Camper's secretary."

"I see." McAllister looked like a judge about to pronounce sentencing. "How long was it going to be before you got around to telling me about all of this?" His tone shifted to sound like he was hurt more so than accusing.

Fortunately for me, Irina picked that moment to see how we were enjoying our vacation.

"You have been standing here for ten minutes." She said. "With so much to see, I would have thought I would have had a hard time keeping up with you."

"Sometimes you have to stop and absorb it all." McAllister said dryly.

I shrugged.

For someone who spoke English so fluently, Irina was seriously lacking in common expressions. She looked at the painting of peasants working in a field behind us and shrugged. "You will enjoy the Ethnographical Museum." She said. "It has a beautiful collection of clothing, household goods, and folk articles associated with the daily life of the people."

Irina was wrong. It was the most boring part of our sightseeing to that point and Irina insisted on staying at our sides, preventing any further conversation about our alternate mission. It was after dinner before we had an opportunity to talk again, dismissing our car to walk back to the hotel.

"What was the name of that place?" McAllister asked.

"Kavkazy." I answered, thinking he was talking about the restaurant.

"No, no." He said. "The bar in Pushkin." He was testing me, hoping I would make a mistake.

"No name." I said. "I told you that."

"Oh."

I looked at him and shook my head at how casually he had accepted my answer.

"How do you think we should go about getting to this Sarzanov guy? I don't suppose they have telephone books in this part of the world."

I shrugged.

"Let me think about it." I said.

Before I went down to the late night bar, I hung a bright red shirt in front of my window. Even though I knew that Mikhail was commissioned to monitor my utility consumption, I left the light on and spent another boring night in the hotel lounge with a couple from Sioux City, Iowa who were happy to find another American who had strayed so far from home. When I returned to my room, the light was off and the curtains were closed.

* * * * *

McAllister greeted me with a questioning look for which I had no answer. When he made what must have been a prearranged signal, the other members of his contingent, including Larkin, immediately found something else to do, a feat made even more obvious by the lack of anything of interest in the hotel lobby. McAllister put his arm around my shoulder and guided me to the door.

"Perhaps it's time we had a little talk." He said as we emerged to a gray and unseasonably cool morning. "I think I had better take this time to remind you of how much I despise being second-guessed and left in the dark. I also think you should consider getting your priorities in order, Grange."

"Priorities?"

"Yes. Priorities." McAllister said. "Which means you should remember who's in charge here."

"In charge?" I turned to face him. "I didn't know I was one of the hired help."

"Come on, Grange. You know what I'm talking about." He said as if trying to soothe ruffled feathers. "We've already established the ground-rules. I must be kept informed of whatever you're up to. It's for your own good as well as the overall project's. No matter how smart you think you are, Grange, you're not as smart as me."

"Smart ass, maybe."

"Thanks." He smiled which surprised me.

"Bobby, listen for a minute. Okay?" I tried a different approach. "You're talking about the difference between cracking a walnut with a nutcracker or a sledgehammer. I know all about your unique logic. But please, give me some credit." I sighed. "People in this part of the world don't part with information easily and, from what I understand, rightfully so. We need whatever outside assistance we can get. We definitely don't need to be employing the methods you used in the past to announce to the entire Eastern Bloc that you want your Easter eggs."

"I know how to be discreet." He shot back, the smile gone. "May I remind you that you came along on this expedition as an advisor.

I'm the one who assimilates information and decides which course of action, or who we will deal with or won't deal with."

"Three people dead and the front line of the Rams walking around the second largest city in Russia isn't exactly discreet."

McAllister glared at me. I flinched. "God damned it, Grange! You're the one who convinced me to come to this God forsaken country. Are you holding me responsible for Sally's death? Is that what it is, Grange?"

"Bobby, I. . ." "I don't want any more fucking surprises, Grange. Do you understand me? None!" McAllister tried to compose himself. "We are not individuals in this; we're a team, Grange. Everybody should know precisely what is going on at all times."

"Exactly."

McAllister continued as if I hadn't replied. "... And I'm getting sick and tired of every time I count the members of our little group, I run out of people before I run out of fingers and toes!"

McAllister unconsciously clenched his fists while I remained silent avoiding eye contact with him. He paled slightly before continuing. "This has nothing to do with gathering information." He placed a hand on my shoulder. "Just be happy that I'm on top of things, Grange." He took a deep breath as if he was going to say more, but just then our cars pulled up and Irina appeared at his side.

"We have an interesting day before us." She said. "I hope you are ready for some unusual surprises."

I looked at McAllister, ready to hear his comment.

"Great. I love surprises." He said without conviction.

But my first surprise was when we got into the car. For some reason, my attention was drawn to the rear view mirror where another pair of eyes was staring back at me intently. Our driver for the day was Sanya Roskovin.

* * * * *

I was even further surprised that our trip was only about twenty-two kilometers south of the city along Moscow Prospekt. To save someone from breaking out a calculator, that comes to about fourteen miles, so I was surprised that this was to be an overnight stay away from Evropeiskaya. Pushkin is a village that was originally known as the Czar's Village and the site of the Yetaterinsky Palace, named for Peter the Great's wife, Catherine I. It was built during the reign of Elizabeth and Catherine II in a park of almost fifteen hundred acres. The palace itself has an eye-opening facade, decorated with gold and white ornaments. There are two separate museums in the palace; one exhibiting furniture, china, and the palace's history. The other, containing manuscripts, rare books, and personal belongings of the poet Alexander Pushkin, who studied at the school of nobility attached to the palace. It was in 1937 that the village was renamed for the literary genius on the one hundredth anniversary of his death.

Unlike its parent hotel in St. Petersburg, the Moskva maintains a small, single story motel-like facility in the village proper and after our overnight bags were dropped off, we began our tour of the grounds. I watched the cars pull away from the gates, wondering how Sanya intended to renew our contact. My apprehension was to be an all-day affair and when we finally returned to the motel after a physically exhausting day, the cars were nowhere in sight.

The Moskva had a buffet dinner attended by about forty of their guests, all presumably tourists as we had seen most of them at one time or another on the palace grounds. The bar closed at nine o'clock in spite of our efforts to bribe the bartender into working overtime and we went to our rooms which, for some reason, were widely dispersed. I was only in the room long enough to brush my teeth when a sound like pebbles striking my first floor window caused me another onset of paranoia. I crept over to the window and parted the curtains a quarter of an inch. Nothing.

I pulled on a shirt and opened the door slowly. Still nothing. I was at a loss as to what to do.

"Shut the door." The voice was harsh and insistent. I turned quickly and did as I was told. The pathway that fronted the short row of rooms fell into darkness.

"You are not very good at being secretive, Comrade Lawton." I recognized Sanya's voice before my eyes adjusted to the dark so I didn't see where the sound had come from.

"I'm not in your line of business." I answered. "If there were a manual, I would have read it."

Sanya either did not understand my ironic comment or did not care to comment.

"You have no secrets now, you know."

"I only passed on the information that I learned at the traktir to the intended recipient. I assured you and your uncle that we were all on the same side. You agreed with me then, Sanya."

"You are such an amateur, Comrade Lawton." She said shaking her beautiful head while tossing her red hair back over her shoulder.

I was confused.

"That is what Stalin told the people he had arrested." Sanya continued cynically. "Those citizens did not believe him either." She took me by the arm and guided me off the path into darker shadows. "Perhaps we should approach Mister McAllister at this time. Let him decide for himself what he thinks he should know."

"He's already deciding." McAllister stepped from behind a tree, startling both of us with his sudden appearance. Far more disturbing than his unexpected manifestation was the tiny automatic pistol he held pointed squarely at the bridge of Sanya's nose. "I would never believe the likes of Stalin," he said, "but what Comrade Lawton tells you is true." He lowered the gun and smiled. "He's not in your line of business. He is an amateur." He glared at me and shook his head. "I'm Bobby McAllister. Pleased to meet you, Sanya."

If looks could kill I'd be dead.

"You and your friend, Mister Lawton, have placed my uncle and me in great peril, Mister McAllister." Sanya said.

In spite of the cryptic statement which he obviously did not understand, McAllister came to my defense. "Mister Lawton had the greatest of intentions I can assure you, Sanya." He glanced at me again. "He just doesn't understand that I'm just a little bit smarter than he gives me credit."

"I don't care what kind of game you two are playing with each other, Mister McAllister, but you insult me with the presence of your offensive gun. Is this a common practice in your country?"

McAllister picked the perfect time to be eloquent.

"In my country, it's called laying all my cards on the table." He answered philosophically. "What you see is what you get. I am offering my considerable experience and knowledge while at the same time, demonstrating that I am willing to go to any length to protect my friends." McAllister smiled. "A pretty friend at that."

Sanya was not impressed. "To obtain a gun in Russia is very difficult for someone here for so short a time."

I had a hunch that McAllister's next response would be critical to his believability.

"I am certain, Sanya that you have methods of obtaining equipment necessary to run your operation that you would not want me to know about." McAllister smiled again as if he had just revealed the secrets of life.

"I do not object to your participation, Mister McAllister. In fact, I welcome it. But not your weapon."

McAllister just smiled.

"But we do have mutual friends in your country, and. . ."

"Great! That settles that. What are we doing tonight?" He asked Sanya. "What do you have in store for us?"

I was being completely ignored.

"I have found someone that I think you will be interested to meet." Sanya said.

"Sarzonov?" Asked McAllister rather smugly.

Sanya was surprised. "How did you know?"

"Please let me ask the questions, Sanya." McAllister said with all the charm he could muster.

Sanya did not reply.

"Where?"

"Uh, well, we can walk to his home now." Said Sanya with obvious confusion. "It is about a four kilometer walk from here."

"Walk?" McAllister felt that physical exertion was to be done for recreation or profit. Information gathering was a job for telephones and computers.

Sanya looked perplexed. "You would prefer to draw a great deal of attention?" She asked.

"All right." In turn, McAllister's expression indicated impatience and disdain at being patronized. "But let's get going. We haven't got all night."

Sanya agreed. "Follow me." She stepped back onto the path and began walking purposefully. "Please try to keep up."

We walked around the motel, giving a wide berth to the parking area and the front entrance, and turned what I thought to be east. The neighborhood changed quickly from the marginally prosperous area around the touristy section of the Czar's Village to where two or three short streets made up a market of shops. Behind each stall was a motley collection of vehicles and horses which carried the itinerant traders. Although the shops were closed, it was still a windowless display of drapers, clothiers, boot makers, cobblers, and saddlers. Further on were rails and posts where livestock was tethered, waiting to be sold in the morning. Nearby were stacks of carts and sledges, agricultural implements, household goods, and pre-fabricated timber houses. A couple of open air traktirs remained open with old men quietly haggling over future transactions and celebrating successful deals with the ever present bottle of vodka passing amongst them.

The market-place gave way to a residential area of three storied apartment houses that looked more like abandoned factories. Tall windows were backlit with occasional wavering lights, evidence that the interiors were lighted by candles or kerosene lamps. Without exception, the wide doorways were dark and cavernous, much like the hopes and dreams of those housed within.

Abruptly, the rows of tenements ended and we were walking along a dirt road with fields stretching into the distance. It was remarkable that the farms abutted the small city so closely; giving the impression of ancient fields that may have stood outside some archaic walled fortress. We walked for almost a half hour, conspicuous because we were the only humans within miles, hidden only because of the enveloping darkness.

In a darker corner of the night stood a lonely cabin of logs stacked closely together and waterproofed with oakum packing. The roof was made from the outer layers of bark of lime tree and a crude cross was etched into a door of scrap planking that seeped deep yellow light from inside. Sanya paused at the door.

"We are only expected to be two." She said quietly. "I do not know how our friend will react to having an additional stranger in his home."

"Maybe Grange should wait outside." McAllister suggested.

Gee thanks. I thought.

"Too late." Sanya said as she knocked on the rickety boards. "He will already know we are here."

"Then why bother to bring it up?" McAllister uttered under his breath. Sanya turned, but I don't think she heard the sarcastic remark.

The door was answered by a young boy of about twelve who was dressed in clean but threadbare clothes, loose white blouse, baggy pants, and mid-thigh boots that were so old, they would not have held a shine. He looked like a young Cossack in dress but not in attitude as, recognizing Sanya, he humbly lowered his eyes and stood aside, allowing us to enter the small and unassuming abode.

It was obvious that the whole family lived, ate, and slept in the single twenty by twenty foot space. It contained a large stove, blackened with smoke, a rough table, and benches around the walls. In the corner closest to the door were icons, lit by night lights, and nearby on a shelf, lay a dusty, mildewed, much thumbed Bible, testimony to deep and long held religious beliefs. A few earthenware pots and plates, wooden spoons and other utensils, and goatskins hanging by nails completed the meager furnishings where flies flourished in the overcrowded space.

Sanya curtsied before the array of icons before turning to our host and greeting him in Russian. The old man at the table acknowledged her by closing his eyes for a moment only slightly longer than a blink. He looked with a stern expression at McAllister and me. I raised an eyebrow slightly as he returned his gaze to Sanya.

"Citizen Sarzonov expects the same courtesy he would extend to you in your home." Sanya translated the unspoken message, nodding in the direction of the icons.

He took the hint and turned toward the makeshift altar for a quick bow. I felt more like I was in a Japanese Temple than in a peasant hut in northeast Russia. Even Sarzonov had a slightly Asian cast to his eyes, eyes that did not betray the fear that Serge had described. He poured liquid into four mismatched mugs and motioned us to join him at the low table. As I sat, I remembered the potent alcohol from the night before and gently sipped from the none too clean mug as I tried to warn McAllister of the consequences of downing the contents in a single gulp. I didn't get the message across and McAllister's eyes bulged after his first taste of country booze. Sarzonov allowed himself a fleeting smile as he watched McAllister's reaction.

"I am Mitia Sarzonov." He said in heavily accented English. "You must know that you have placed me in a very dangerous position." It seemed a common theme. "If I talk with you, I risk serious trouble with the authorities. If I refuse to talk with you, I risk the displeasure of Comrade Roskovin and her many friends." He sighed helplessly. "All because, in a moment of weakness, I spoke to a stranger over a glass of vodka." He looked at the drink in front of him. "I have lived in this village all of my entire life. You would think that I would know better than to talk to strangers in a country where secrets are held almost as sacred as my icons."

Mitia Sarzonov could have been an orthodox priest. His beard was long and unkempt and, sitting in the dimly lighted room, his dark peasant clothing could have been robes. Only his eyes gave any hint that he might be younger than his stooped shoulders and deep voice would have indicated. He appraised each of us carefully and, even on an occasion that must have been stressful for him, noticed that McAllister was watching the lad who had originally admitted us to the modest hut as he, in turn, watched us from his place in the corner.

"The boy does not speak English." Sarzonov told McAllister. I am showing him that Americans are not the devils that his friends say they are. I know without asking that he has a difficult time believing this when he sees that one of our guests carries a weapon."

He was very observant. McAllister stirred uncomfortably, his hand moving automatically to the small of his back where his jacket covered the gun.

"We have already lost three friends on this trip." McAllister explained, self-consciously. "We feel it is necessary to protect ourselves and any new friends we make along the way."

Sarzonov looked sadly at Sanya. "You have not told our friend of the uselessness of such a gesture?" He asked.

Sanya shrugged.

McAllister frowned.

"We need information." I said desperately. "We will do everything we can to protect you from coming to harm."

Sarzonov poured himself and McAllister another drink but when he spoke, he addressed me. "Your friend carries a gun and you are the one who is going to protect me and my son." He shook his head. "It is clear to me that there is much difference between our cultures."

He stood and walked to the shrine in the corner. "In Russia, if one wants to commit suicide, he does something you, as an American, take for granted. You fight your government. As Russians, we learn early to avoid talking with anyone about anything other than the weather and the next three-day horse fair. A man's home is his refuge only until the door is broken down by hoodlums or agents of the people. People disappear and not one of their friends can remember their names. The village just closes around itself like water in a bucket.

"The fault is mine. I have lived a life in this country and not learned the lessons it has to teach. My only concern is the boy. I must ask for your assurance that when I am taken away, you will provide for his welfare." He looked to Sanya but was talking to me.

I looked at McAllister who nodded as if to say, why not. He didn't believe the gravity with which Sarzonov was speaking.

"Mister Sarzonov, my name is. . ."

"Your name is no importance." Sarzonov interrupted. "Nor is that of your friends. I may not know your names but I do know who you are and what you represent. Ever since the night I spoke in that accursed traktir, I have known this day was coming. I am only thankful that it is you who have come first so that I may trade what little knowledge I have for a legacy for my son."

It was an unspoken question so I nodded my head in understanding and acknowledgement.

His relief was apparent. He sighed as if a great load had been removed from his shoulders and he ran his hand over the surface of the icons before he returned to his seat at the table. He looked to the roughhewn timbers over his head, deciding where to begin his story.

"My great-grandfather, my mother's grandfather, was a jeweler before the Great Revolution. He worked as an apprentice for Faberge in the Master's shop on Morskaya in St. Petersburg. He was happy at his work and was proud that he was destined to become a member of the merchant class, something his father before him had failed to do.

"Then came the seeds of revolt, the fall of the Imperial Family, and the Bolsheviks, who took over everything from farming to factories."

He rested his arms on the table and leaned closer to me.

"My beloved ancestor believed he had found a way to insure his family's future. Faberge and his trusted ministers had fled to Switzerland, the country was losing a war, and the Social Democrats were fueling the flames of revolution from their places in exile. Alone and faced with conscription or a return to serfdom under Lenin and his new Communistic reforms, he decided to loot the remains of the Faberge salon and flee to a new and better life. He was able to secure two crates of Faberge products and hide them somewhere, but there his plan fell on frozen ground.

"Being an honest man all of his life, he had no idea how to take advantage of his windfall, so he sought the counsel of a friend who was familiar with such situations. However, when he returned to the place he had hid his newly found merchandise, the goods were no longer where he had left them."

He seemed to remember something and stood suddenly, causing McAllister and I to start. He held up an arm to calm us as he knelt to reach under a small wooden box which he placed on the table before us.

"Still believing that the revolution was only a temporary state of affairs, he taught his trade to his children, who passed them to their children until I came to learn the craft from my father."

The box was the size of a shoebox and the hinges squealed like an old oak door. He removed several pieces of cheap glass jewelry mounted in oven baked clay on frames of birch and elm. They were cleverly designed and unique, but seriously prehistoric. Nevertheless, Sarzonov displayed them as if they were worth their weight in gold. McAllister began rummaging through the box as if it were a bargain table at Macy's.

"My great-grandfather's tutelage if not his optimism for the return of the czarist regime paid off. About four years before young Alexander was born, a group of men came to this village in search of members of the Denikin clan. Since my mother was the last of her family, they found their way to our humble home.

"Their only concern was if any remaining Denikin people knew of gem cutting or enameling. Sensing opportunity rather than danger, my mother called me in from the fields to meet with these men. I showed them those very same trinkets." He pointed to the box that was occupying McAllister.

"Before I could say anything, I found myself in a basement room of the Zimmy Dvoryets, the Winter Palace. These men asked if I could copy some of the things they had. Things like buttons and combs that were luxuries rather than necessities. I worked for weeks on little things; cuff links, push bells, pens and desk sets. I worked ten, sometimes twelve hours a day. My overseers were patient but persistent. They took each finished piece and examined it for correctness of detail. Many men came and went from this room, but only a few stayed as the projects they gave us became more complicated and challenging."

"What was your purpose?" McAllister interrupted.

"We were given two different explanations for these exercises." Sarzonov answered. "At first we were told that the smaller items were to be sold in the In-tourist and duty free shops as trinkets for tourists or gifts for foreign dignitaries. When we progressed to larger pieces, we were told that they were to replace museum and exhibit articles for security reasons."

"Security?"

"It was explained that both foreign and internal hooligans could not be trusted with genuine Russian treasures." He looked to Sanya to see if he had insulted his guests. Sanya let the remark pass without concern. "We were told that we would be creating substitutes for our country's greatest treasures while the authentic articles were held in a secure place. It would be much like the rich dowager who wears imitation jewels to a function while the real ones are at her home in her safe."

"When did you find out it was more than that?" I asked.

"One day I was working on a copy of a Royal Bulgarian Presentation Cigarette Case. It was made of gold, diamonds, rubies, emeralds, silk cord, and wood. The original was presented by King Ferdinand I of Bulgaria to General Baron de Reutern, Aide-de-Camp to Czars Alexander II, Alexander III, and Nicholas II. I was working from a photograph and having a difficult time when three men stopped at my workbench.

"These men look and act like KGB and it is not long until I hear who I later learn is Rastov, call the man in charge Major Kalinishkov."

We were hearing what McAllister wanted to hear and I could sense his pulse quickening as he temporarily abandoned the contents of the box and leaned toward Sarzonov across the table. He was about to interrupt again but a sharp glance from me held him in check. At least for the time being.

"They tell me they are very happy with my work." Sarzonov continued. "They ask if I can work with another man, Mossolov, on reproducing Imperial Eggs. I wonder why the KGB is interested in art, but I say yes. The pay is good and I am treated well, so why not? The next morning Rastov takes me to another room where I begin my work with Miska Mossolov.

"The swine Rastov is a man feared by everyone and Miska is quick to give me a lesson about the KGB. No longer is the pace of work relaxed or casual. We are forced into longer days and times between projects are shorter. The only times we can be truly at ease is when Rastov is someplace on an errand for KGB Major."

Sarzonov bowed his head. "Two years ago my wife died. Rastov does not tell me this until a week after she is buried. He looked toward the boy in the corner. "The boy was only nine."

We let him fight his ghosts in silence for a full two minutes. There was nothing we could have said and we all knew that words of sympathy would have rung hollow.

"It is only after that when Miska tells me what he expects is our true purpose in the secret room in the palace. We are making forgeries for art pieces stolen by KGB."

"I knew it!" McAllister slammed his palm on the table. He stood up and began pacing, a feat that held him to three short steps in each direction because of the cramped quarters. "The first thing we have to do is get him back to the States." He stopped to wave an inclusive hand. "The boy too, of course. That the old man speaks almost perfect English is a bonus. We can get him on 60 Minutes, Larry King, hell, maybe even on Letterman or Leno.

"We'll get him a great PR man, an agent, the whole works. This is great."

I had nothing to say.

"You did well, Grange." McAllister said reluctantly. I felt like I was in the driver's seat and said smugly. "As usual, you're off and running before the gun has sounded." I said. "You have nothing more than a poor collaboration of a theory plagued with holes."

McAllister didn't like my attitude.

"Grange." McAllister snapped. "Spare me with your negativity. I think you should quit while you're still in the race."

"Bobby, I. . ."

"Let me tell you something, Grange." His tone was milder but sincere. "You've argued with me and questioned my methods from the very first day we met. Even after I rubbed your nose in the biggest hoard of treasure ever found by modern man. When are you going to learn?"

"Learn what?"

"I don't know." McAllister clutched for a logical answer.

"Your damned lessons, Grange."

I guess that made sense.

"You wanted proof. Here it is." He pointed to Sarzonov. "This man has been in the thick of things. He is an eye witness to everything we started out to prove. What more could you ask for."

"First of all, hard evidence." I answered. "What you have is a common peasant," I turned to Sarzonov, "no offense, Mitia, who has a story, no physical evidence, no official standing in the government, and has yet expressed any desire to defect.

"This man is not a general or a politician. The United States might not even let him in. While he is certainly socially depressed," I waved an illustrative arm around the crude cabin, "we have nothing to prove political oppression. Just because he says he is being forced to participate in a conspiracy doesn't mean the immigration service is going to believe him."

"Your friend is right, Comrade." Sanya said. "I can tell you of many cases when a man has risked his life in more ways than one to escape the borders of Russia only to be returned by a country who did not want more poor people in their society. I believe your country has done that exact same thing with people from Mexico, Cuba, and the island of Haiti."

Sarzonov looked around as if confused by the conversation. "Leave Russia?" He asked as if it were the furthest thing from his mind.

"Well, yes." McAllister couldn't believe that anyone outside the contiguous forty-eight would not be itching to get in.

"Why?" Sarzonov asked simply.

"Well. . ." McAllister looked as confused as the poor peasant, "for movie stars, swimming pools, that sort of thing."

I looked at McAllister. "The Beverly Hillbillies?" I mouthed, only slightly astonished. McAllister shrugged.

"Everyone in America has these things?" Sarzonov asked.

"Sure." McAllister answered off-handedly. "Well, almost everyone." He changed his mind again. "Well, many do anyway."

"And you know movie stars?" Sarzonov persisted.

"Well, no." McAllister admitted. "One, maybe. But he hasn't done much since that cowgirl movie." He smiled. I don't think it was a big hit here in Russia."

We were getting sidetracked.

"In order to have any credibility, we have to have some hard evidence." I said. "We are not going to get that from a man who is frightened for his life and is not impressed with winning a trip to America."

"Leave Mitia alone, will you, Grange?"

"What?"

"I have the information that confirms my hunch. That's all I need." He turned to Sarzonov. "I'll have Sanya set up some sort of trust for your son, Mitia. Neither one of you will have to worry about money anymore." McAllister looked toward the boy. "You and your son are welcome to come with us to America without being obligated to put on a Dog and Pony show, either way, I want to express my appreciation and concern that I may have placed you and your son in jeopardy."

Sarzonov looked confused. "What is this Dog and Pony?"

McAllister smiled. "A figure of speech, Mitia. You can come to America without having to tell your story."

"You do, not owe me, Comrade." He looked at his son in the corner. "I only ask that should anything happen to me that you take care of my son. I thought this talk would be the help I could offer." He continued. "I do not know what I have done to warrant your kind generosity."

"Trust me, you have been helpful." McAllister thought for a second. "But, maybe it would help if I let you finish your story."

"Yes, of course." Sarzonov began. "You already know what happened to poor Miska. He was a talented man who, in spite of the reason for his work, was very dedicated and honest. He often smuggled pieces out of our workshop, not because he was trying to profit, but because he would work on detail in his own home. That he was robbed by someone is what led to his painful demise."

"You said three men." I reminded him. "Who else besides the major and his KGB hit man?"

Sarzonov waved a dismissing hand. "That would be Patek." He said offhandedly. "He is the least of my problems. Or yours for that matter. He is a bumbling sort of man. Polish, I believe. He often acts without thinking and Major Kalinishkov and Rastov must keep a constant watch on him. He is often disciplined by the major for his interpretation of how the department is to function. Rastov is his watchdog but even he is not always around to keep him in check."

Could this be the man who was haunting my dreams? I felt my pulse quicken and my breathing stop. "What does this Patek look like?" I asked.

"Like the village butcher." Sarzonov answered. "Well fed, but still a peasant. He wears clothes like a farm animal but he is strong and eager to please the major and Rastov. I doubt he has had a clear thought since he was born."

My mind was at a crossroads. I was trying to match an incompetent oaf with the accurate description of some unknown petty criminal acting on orders of his government against the memory of a man in Paris who had completed the electronic circuit that had brought me to Russia. While I could see similarities, the words of this brave but frightened conscript farmer was not quite enough to convince me to begin a manhunt for an inept agent who was probably following orders. If Patek was the man I sought, I wanted to extend my desire for revenge to his partners and employers. I took a deep breath and leaned back while trying to assess this information.

"Would Patek murder someone if his boss ordered it?" I asked.

Sarzonov considered my question carefully. "He would be more likely to kill as a mistake and suffer the wrath he would bring upon himself."

His answer made a vague impression more confused. If I was going to take my position of an avenging angel to its natural conclusion, I did not want to act in an inappropriate and pointless manner in which my suspicions overruled absolute confirmation.

"Patek," I persisted. "Where would he . . ."

"What the hell is this?"

I turned to McAllister who had gone back to exploring the contents of Sarzonov's box of trinkets. He was holding something between his thumb and index finger. Sarzonov identified it immediately.

"When my great-grandfather returned to the spot where he had hidden the looted contents of the Faberge shop, that was all he found." He said. "How strange it is that, after finding a Czar's fortune, he should be left with only a worthless button." It must have been brass because it didn't appear tarnished, but it was as light as plastic. It was made in two pieces; a bowl shaped backing with a domed cap that appeared as though it snapped into place. The contradiction was that the front piece did not seem to be a cheap knockout. Instead, I would have guessed that it was custom made and part of a uniform. It had a carved border made to look like rope and, in the center, an anchor crossed with a design that resembled a medical insignia. Below the anchor was a series of curves that probably was meant to represent water because a fish with angel shaped wings leaped above the waves. I remember thinking that it needed closer examination.

"It is much like an omen." Sarzonov continued. "When the Czars died, their fortunes disappeared also. Instead of a privileged class and a land of happy workers, we all became menial bondservants of communism." He smiled, not with humor. "It is a very Russian thing to think in this manner."

There was no way to respond to a comment like that, so I returned to the subject of the three KGB agents.

"This major," I asked, trying to connect Kalinishkov to Cramer or Kleinfeld, "a dark man? Crescent scar on his chin? Maybe conversant in several languages?"

"Dark, yes." Sarzonov confirmed. "But I have never seen him without a beard. He speaks Russian diplomat's phrasing but when he is angry, he sounds like old Siberian Army. He may speak English, but I have never heard."

"Could he be Jewish?" I asked.

Sarzonov snorted. "A Jew and a KGB?" He asked. "You know even less than you think."

"Could he speak in Hebrew tongue?" I rephrased.

"If he were from Moscow, surely." He answered. "But it would be Russian Yiddish, not something that could be spoken in the new Jewish homeland or one of their temples."

I looked to McAllister who was looking bored. He had a verbal confirmation of his theory and could not have cared less if Kalinishkov spoke Hawaiian.

"How can we help you?" McAllister asked, hoping there was something specific we could do besides furnish father and son with money that we could provide and protection that we couldn't promise to deliver as long as they remained in Russia.

"Do not return to my village." He said simply. "My dearest Sanya will know if something happens to me. My son is a good boy. See that he is taken care of."

"Would you like for us to take him with us now?" Asked McAllister who was already on his feet and looking anxiously at the door. Sarzonov slowly shook his head.

I reached across the table to shake hands with Sarzonov but he was staring at his hands as if he were alone in prayer. I wondered if I were looking at a dead man while wishing he would have jumped at McAllister's offer to help him defect or take custody of his son. I would have much preferred seeing him give himself a fighting chance than to sit in his poor surroundings waiting and fully expecting his door to be broken down on some dark, moonless night.

We left the cabin with mixed emotions but a common bond. Frustration.

As we followed Sanya back to the village, McAllister grabbed my sleeve to hold me back out of Sanya's earshot.

"I want you to give Sanya the equivalent of one hundred thousand US dollars in rubles to set up some kind of trust or just open an account for the boy. Give her the equivalent of twenty thousand U.S. dollars for herself for her trouble. You understand?"

"I understand." I said like a child would say to an adult. "But I don't think it can be done legally here."

"Legally or otherwise, I want it done." McAllister said finally.

I was going to ask him where he got a gun, but I was distracted by his instructions.

"Are we being covered by any of our people right now?"

McAllister looked perplexed. "I don't know." He looked around. "Why?"

"Because we must look like a scene out of 'The Russians Are Coming.'" I smiled but he couldn't see my face. "Except in reverse. We're putting them all in jeopardy."

"Whose fucking idea was it to come to Russia, Grange?" McAllister asked, stopping in his tracks while glaring at me.

Sanya stopped and turned.

"Let's save this for tomorrow." McAllister said before I could answer him. "We must keep walking." Sanya admonished. "It would not be good to draw attention." She looked impatient. "Nor will it be wise to be found away from your lodging."

McAllister placed a hand on my shoulder and pointed to the village. "Let's go."

We continued to walk silently but I could tell that McAllister's mind was working at Mach speed.

When we were a good distance from Sarzonov's cabin, McAllister broke his silence. "Listen, Grange. Our purpose here is to gather information and attract attention. The Russian Government is not going to risk doing anything as long as we act within certain bounds. What we have to do is make them nervous enough to follow us when we leave. When that happens, I figure one of two things is going to take place. Either they are going to sink the Second Prize on the open sea or they are going to wait until they have a chance to steal my eggs. I'm gambling that it's going to be the latter."

"Gambling?"

"Yeah, well, what we have to do is walk a fine line so we don't get them pissed off enough to blow us out of the water. We can handle them if they make a run at us back home. We would not stand a chance in the middle of the Atlantic Ocean against something like a sub."

As I was staring at him, I think my mouth must have been gaping.

"Hell. Don't looked so surprised, Grange. It was your idea to begin with, remember?" He continued. "And . . . you were right, incidentally. Did you know we have been followed since we got here?"

"They don't have to follow us." I reminded him. "We have our faithful little In-tourist guide with us every step of the way."

"Not when you make unauthorized trips to the local gin mill."

If McAllister had someone watching us, it stood to reason that they could have observed someone following Sanya and I to the traktir. I had a very sick feeling in the pit of my stomach.

"Then both Byachev and Sarzonov could be in real trouble. Sanya too."

"Not if, instead of being followed, you were being led."

My head snapped in Sanya's direction. She was about ten yards in front of us as we passed back through the closed market-place and I doubted she could hear us.

"You've been acting stupid on purpose."

McAllister smiled. "Everything I do is on purpose, Grange." He said smugly. "Pretty good, huh?"

"Don't flatter yourself." I said. "It's not that much of a stretch."

McAllister looked at me tolerantly. "That's not the point and you know it. All you have to know is my two most important rules in dealing with people when it comes to business."

"And what are they?" He was expecting me to ask.

"First," he said, holding up an index finger, "never tell anyone everything you know. Any more questions?"

"Cute." I said. "Very cute."

We were approaching the parking lot of the Moskva Hotel's Motel, so Sanya stopped to allow us to catch up.

"This is where I must leave you." She said, none too apologetically. "Is there any more you wish of me?" It was clear she hoped we would say no.

McAllister stared at me long enough to realize it was a cue for me to speak with Sanya in private. Realizing that I had read him loud and clear, he thanked Sanya for her help and walked away leaving me to make the financial arrangements with her. There was no doubt that McAllister was practicing the first rule of his credo.

I made arrangements to meet Sanya the following morning and caught up with McAllister.

"I hope we can trust her, Bobby." I said. "I wish there was a way to check her out."

"I already have, Grange." McAllister replied in a tone of finality.

That was good enough for me.

"So what do we do now?" I asked, doing some fishing of my own.

McAllister scratched his chin. "I think we have been doing what they expect of us so far. If we automatically suspect everything we are told, I think we might learn more than what they want us to know."

"That's double talk." I said. "And according to you, I've already had my fill of all that. I think it's about time we got some real answers."

"I spent a lot of years looking for the Hacha and the Prize, he said, exhibiting more patience than I thought he possessed. "Sometimes you never learn the whole truth.

"The fact of the matter is that my theory has been proven. That's all I'm concerned with at the moment." He paused as if in deep thought. "The old man gave you a name tonight. Patek, wasn't it?"

I knew McAllister had been listening while he seemed to be preoccupied as he had rummaged through the old man's mystery box earlier.

I nodded.

"I think we should operate on the assumption that the man in Paris is known around here in St. Petersburg. Therefore, it follows that we are both closer to our goals.

"We still have a few days left. I think we need to see if any more information will turn in our favor."

"So you think we should wait things out." I summarized.

"Yeah." He said thoughtfully. "I have a feeling we are not finished meeting people in dark places."

It was a prophesy that was not long in becoming reality.

When I opened the door to my room, I belatedly remembered that I had left the room in darkness, so the first thing I noticed was that the bedside light was on. On the opposite side of the room, looking stern and betrayed, sat an angry Irina Denikoff.

* * * * *

"This is bullshit, Comrade. The Americans are all in one place. We could take care of them all at once and plunder that pompous capitalist's gaudy boat at our leisure."

"Use your head, my friend. A dozen Americans at the hotel and at least three more on the boat. All with families, loved ones, and friends. Our tiny section could not bear the strain of such close scrutiny by at least three governments. Remember, the woman's father is an influential politician in his country."

"They are getting closer to us."

"So what? They are totally impotent. We could bump into them on the Nevsky Prospekt and they could do nothing. The best thing we can do is to allow them to gather all the information they want. As long as all they do is listen to the talk of a few dissatisfied peasants, they will have little or nothing to take home. This is not an invasion. It is a handful of Americans who, in a very few days, will return to their own borders to do nothing but talk about a Russian conspiracy, something that has been going on, in one form or another, since 1906."

"Still, I would handle things differently."

"That is why I am in charge, and you are under my authority."

"What will they attempt next?"

"I do not know. But rest assured, our friend on the inside will tell us before they have the chance to act."

"I hope you are right, Comrade. I would hate to see you proved wrong."

The last statement was not true.

* * *

CHAPTER SEVEN

"Can you tell me why I should not report you to my superiors and have your visa revoked?" She asked.

For a normally attractive woman, Irina Denikoff looked cruel and unusually harsh. The friendly In-tourist guide was replaced with a stern and unforgiving mistress.

"I am an American. I'm used to being able to take a walk when I feel like it."

"You're not in America at this time." She reminded me unnecessarily. "Would you walk through your neighbor's property without permission on one of your late night airings?"

"No more than I would enter his bedroom without assent." I said pointedly.

She used her arms to propel herself out of the chair. "You do not understand." Her tone was a mixture of accusatory and pleading. "In Russia, you, as anyone else, are tolerated by the generosity of the state. You have betrayed the trust of your written promise to respect the rules of your host government."

"For Christ's sake, Irina." I said, trying to sound casual. "I went out for a breath of fresh air. If I were some kind of a spy, I certainly wouldn't have entered the country through a major port just to be assigned an In-tourist guide. You're making a mountain out of a molehill."

"Your behavior is my responsibility." Some of the bitterness was going out of her voice. "You have compromised my position."

"I think you have compromised your own position." I said, looking at my watch. "What would your boss say about you coming to the room of one of your charges well after midnight? How long have you been sitting here waiting for me?"

She looked around uncertainly, as if there were someone else in the room who could have answered for her. "You're trying to trick me." She said, on the verge of tears.

Although I didn't want to lose my psychological advantage, I softened nonetheless. I tried to keep the upper hand by establishing my territory. I flung my jacket on the bed, kicked off my shoes, and emptied my pockets on the nightstand. It was probably like a dog pissing on the couch, but it did help me feel in control.

"I'm not trying anything." I said, gently enough to stem the sniveling. "How could anything as innocent as a late night stroll insult your government?"

"Where did you go?" She asked, regaining control of herself, if not the circumstances.

"Nowhere." I said, flapping my arms in a helpless gesture. "I just walked around town a little bit. Saw the market-place. Even had a drink in one of those backyard bars. That bathtub stuff is terrible." I made a face. But the people were nice."

"You should have called me." She said, not yet sure if she should believe me. "I would have been happy to show you the approved areas." She stressed the word approved. It was an empty invitation.

"Then your boss would have thought we were out on a date." I smiled at the irony.

"Mister Lawton." She said. "That is the second time you referenced my boss. The state is my boss." She hesitated. "And I do not date."

"So that's your problem." I said it louder than I intended.

"Your problem, Mister Lawton, is that you have no tact."

I did not understand that remark.

"Also, you did not let me finish." She said defensively. I do not date within my professional capacity."

"Yeah," I said, suddenly having a flashback. "I used to be the same way. That was, until I met one particular lady."

I must have projected more than I meant because Irina looked touched by what I had said or the way I had said it. Of all things, she went over and sat on the bed. "Is it something you would like to talk about?"

Of all the things in the world that had happened to me, this was setting itself up to be the dumbest. There I was, about as far away from home as I could get without being shot into outer space, and a Russian tour guide, politically connected to social idealism to which I was fanatically opposed, was the first person to show concern about my feelings about Sally's death. I don't know if it was the potent Russian vodka, the presence of a beautiful woman in my hotel room, or just a vulnerable moment in my life. I was forming a touching and heartfelt monologue when she spoke first.

"What is this?"

"Huh?"

"This!" She said, holding up something she had picked up from my nightstand. "Where did you get this?"

She was holding the brass button I had seen at Sarzonov's. She had acquired it from the pocket holdings I had dumped on the nightstand and I had no idea how it had gotten there.

"I . . . uh,"

"Mister Lawton, I must insist. Where did you get this button?"

"I have no idea how that got there." I said honestly.

She turned it over in her hand. "I have to know where you got this."

"I must have picked it up in the market-place." I said, regaining a bit of composure. "What's the big deal?"

"The big deal," she shot back, "is very personal." She stood up abruptly. "You will wait here." She commanded, heading for the door. "I will return within the hour." She marched out of the room as if she were heading a regiment in a May Day Parade.

I did what every red—blooded American would have done in my shoes. I panicked.

I paced the room long enough to give Irina a good head start and picked up the phone in a flurry of hysteria. It was dead. It took a moment of terror to realize that phones were turned off at night. I bolted out the door and ran down the path toward McAllister's room, fully expecting to hear the Russian command for halt! Followed by the sound of a thirty-three caliber report.

When I made it to McAllister's door uninvited, I pounded the door with my palms until a bleary eyed McAllister angrily yanked it open.

"The shit has hit the fan." I said as I barged past him into the room. "We gotta' get outta here."

Larkin came out of the bathroom in a floor length furry robe but McAllister was standing next to the door in his BVD's.

"What the hell are you talking about, Grange?" He asked, none too politely.

"Irina was waiting for me when we got back." I answered. "She knew I was out of the room."

"Let me guess." McAllister said caustically. "She's wearing black leather and wants to punish you for being a bad boy."

"Worse!" I said, ignoring the crack. "She found that brass thing-a-ma-jig we saw at Sarzanov's tonight and it tripped some sort of trigger. She went out of the room like someone on a mission and told me not to move until she got back."

McAllister was shaking his head like one of those springy dogs in the back window of a car while suppressing a laugh. I'm sure he was trying to think of another smart remark. "So?" Was the best he could muster?

"Whatever it was," I said, grabbing his shoulders and shaking him, "it got her attention in a hurry. She saw that Goddamn button and took off like a house on fire."

"So what do you want to do, Grange?" He wasn't being serious. "Hide under the bed?"

"Bobby! Will you please be serious?"

"What do you want to do?" He repeated his question.

"I want to get the hell out of here. Right now. Before she comes back."

"Where you gonna go?"

"Me? Where?" He certainly wasn't helping my mental state. "Outta here! All of us. Let's go get packed. Better yet, leave everything. Let's get the hell gone."

"I don't know, Grange. I was kinda' looking forward to another Russian Puppet Show or something like that." He smiled. "I'm having too much fun to leave right now."

Luckily, Larkin spoke up, preventing me from losing my temper with McAllister. "Where are we going to go, Grange?"

"I don't care!" I said, very near the end of my rope.

She came across the room to take my hand and guide me to a chair.

"We can't go anyplace, Grange." She said gently, as if talking to a child. "We don't have any transportation and, even if we did, the Second Prize is docked next to a naval yard. How far do you think we would get?"

"We gotta try." I insisted. "What choice do we have?"

"You're the one who got caught out of bounds." McAllister said with feigned sternness. "Looks like you're going to be shipped off to Siberia or someplace like that." He flashed his trademark smile. "I told you that you should have been a little friendlier with our tourist guide."

Larkin studied her husband for a second before dismissing his remark.

"Me?" My voice had gotten a full octave higher. "You want me to go to a Russian jail for your scheme?"

McAllister pretended to think about my question. "Sure. Why not?"

"Bobby!" I shouted. "I'm supposed to be along for the ride. Where does it say that the scribe goes to the slammer for tagging along with the rich master?"

"It's chiseled in stone, Grange. When the scribe thinks he's smarter than his master, then he has to pay the price. It's that simple."

McAllister was having fun at my expense. Lots of fun.

I pleaded with my eyes for the return of his senses.

"Will you please take it easy?" McAllister sat on the edge of the bed and ran his fingers through his hair. "What's the worst case scenario? They kick you out of their country after giving you a flogging and a stern lecture. We can handle that."

"That's a pretty optimistic worst case." I argued. "The worst case I see is me in a Siberian gulag watching my toes turn black from frostbite."

"Hmm, we never had to worry about that when I was in the slammer in Arizona." McAllister smirked.

"Be serious!"

"Look, Grange. All you've done is talk to a couple of people." McAllister finally reasoned. "They can't prove anything."

"They don't have to prove anything." I think I was whining. I'm not sure. "This is their country and they can do anything they want."

McAllister shook his head, appearing to be annoyed.

"I think you're overreacting." Larkin said calmly. "If you were really in some kind of trouble, you would probably already be under arrest, don't you think?"

I stopped for a second to try to reason things through. In spite of the reassurance I was getting, at least from Larkin, it didn't look good.

"No." I said. "I think she found out that I was out of the room and was originally going to give me a lecture about midnight constitutionals. But then she found that button and something snapped. I'm in deep shit here, folks."

"Irina is benign, Grange." McAllister said with confidence. "Besides, if worse comes to worse, we have one of the best lawyers in the country. We can have him here in a matter of a few days."

"You're talking about that overgrown Maynard G. Krebbs in shorts?" I asked incredulously. "They won't even let that sixties reincarnate in the country! Suddenly your worst case scenario has turned from getting kicked out of the country into a few days in the local hoosegow."

"Actually, it would probably be a little bit longer than that." McAllister admitted. "It would take a couple of days to get here, but it might take longer to sober Ned up."

That damned McAllister!

". . . And they'd probably want to interrogate you. You know how thorough the KGB can be."

"Holy shit!" I couldn't believe McAllister's display of careless indifference to the seriousness of the situation. "I'm outta' here. I can walk to the boat. Hell, I can swim to Finland. All I need is a head start."

McAllister couldn't suppress his laughter any longer. He roared. He was enjoying himself immensely at my cowardice.

Larkin looked confused.

The knock at the door dashed the last of my hopes. Although it didn't sound like a detachment of storm troopers ready to break down all barriers in order to apprehend a dangerous enemy of the state, each rap still sounded like a step closer to doom. McAllister regained his composure and the three of us spent a full thirty seconds looking back and forth between each other. The hammering sounded more insistent the second time.

"I better answer that." McAllister said needlessly.

I nodded frantically.

Irina Denikoff stood in the doorway clutching a package wrapped with string. She looked at me, switched to Larkin, then to McAllister, still dressed only in his shorts. "Here you are." She said, returning her attention to me. "I told you to wait for me."

I shrugged innocently. I was surprised that she was alone.

"I haven't gone anywhere." I said.

"I must speak with you." She demanded, looking with undisguised discomfort toward McAllister who stood there shamelessly and unconsciously posed in his BVDs with a smirk planted all over his mug.

As the McAllisters began distancing themselves by moving discreetly to a corner of the room, Irina said firmly, "Alone."

I was beginning to believe that my position was improving. Irina had yet to enter the room and, unless she had a company of armed soldiers hiding in the bushes ready to kidnap me, all she really wanted to do was talk. I'm not really proud of the fact that I felt it necessary to insure myself against being snatched by persons unknown, still an option in my mind, by not crossing the threshold.

"The McAllisters are involved in this as well." If I was going to take a dive, those two smug chicken-shits on the other side of the room could damn well join me. "I told them everything so far and they want to be a part of this. Whatever this is." McAllister shook his head from side to side marveling at my shame while Larkin merely looked disappointed.

Irina looked at the couple and made an instantaneous decision. She stepped into the room and closed the door.

"You have the button?" She asked me.

I nodded. "But don't you think we should talk someplace else?" I don't know what made me think of the microphones in the parent hotel, especially after I had just incriminated myself with a half hour of my whimpering.

"No." She said flatly. "I think I should be speaking with Mister McAllister."

The McAllisters looked at each other with a mixture of mild surprise and amusement.

"Please, Irina. Do talk to me in the future." McAllister said with sudden impatience. "Mister Lawton is only my scribe."

Irina looked confused and Larkin smiled.

"Give her the damned button, Grange." McAllister ordered.

Irina placed her package on the table and held out her hand. I handed it over to her.

"I am risking much by talking so freely, Mister McAllister." She began with the anxiety that linked all Russian people. "But this is personal and I must have answers."

"Personal?" McAllister asked with incredulity.

I couldn't help but think of the possible consequences of our refusal to answer. Larkin, however, recognized something in her tone and immediately tried to form a sisterly bond. "This has nothing to do with Granger violating your tourist curfew, does it?" She asked.

"Only that he has found this." She said, displaying the button. "In fact, I must ask for your confidence in discussing this matter. I could invite much trouble for myself if certain people found out I was breaking rules."

McAllister slipped into a robe and sauntered over to Irina. "Are you familiar with the term, quid pro quo?"

"Yes, I am, Mister McAllister."

"Great." He said. "That's the name of the game we will now play." He said, and then raised a finger. "But . . . This is the last game we will play. Okay Irina?"

She nodded in agreement.

"Tell her what she wants to know, Grange." He said, and then he added. "Excluding specific names, answer her truthfully."

Although McAllister didn't say as much, I'm sure that he would not exclude the possibility of using any confidentiality shared as a future leverage if needed. To me, the thought had definite appeal.

"My grandfather was only a boy when he went into service for Czar Nicholas II. He started as a cabin boy on the Imperial yacht, Standart.

"The Standart was built in Denmark and, fitted with every comfort and luxury known to modern science of the time, and was considered the most perfect boat afloat. It was sleek black, with gilded bowsprit and stern.

"I know that your boat is very extravagant, but the staterooms aboard the Standart were nearly as large as the personal apartments in the summer villa at Peterhof. It was also the scene of a huge State dinner for Romanian royalty and officials on the occasion when a wedding was proposed between Grand Duchess Olga and Prince Caroll of Romania.

"My grandfather was very close to Derevanko who was the sailor who was a personal aide to Alexis and was even the man who taught the Czarevich to walk."

McAllister sensed the beginning of a long story so he signaled Larkin for drinks. When she handed Irina neat vodka, the In-tourist guide's hands were shaking. She took a long drink.

"In August of 1914, the Standart returned to St. Petersburg and became permanently docked away from her port in Yalta. It was during this time that my grandfather met the woman who was to become his wife. When his duties allowed, he spent all his time with my grandmother in a small apartment in the city's newer district. In three years they had three children; two boys and a girl, my mother.

"In July of 1917, almost a year to the day before the Imperial Family was murdered; there was a massive demonstration in St. Petersburg and my grandfather was called to return to the docks to help see to the security of the Standart.

"At this point you must understand that emotions were running high against the Czar. Although he and, in turn, his brother Michael had abdicated only a few months earlier, the Revolution was in full force and anything to do with the dynasty of the Romanovs was in danger of being ravaged by unruly mobs. They had already burned many of the homes of those of the ruling class who were unfortunate enough to live in isolated areas and the only deterrent to the violence was a show of force including superior fire power. My grandfather, newly promoted to steward, proudly wore his uniform, but wisely resorted to the back streets on his way to assume his station aboard the Imperial Yacht.

"On his way to the docks, he passed through the downtown district, staying in the alleys, when he saw a man who was apparently hiding something in a dead-end passageway. Thinking it was worth investigating, he waited until the stranger left and slipped into the alley to see what he had been concealing. He found two heavy crates amongst the rubble and, assuming the boxes to contain something of value.

"He enlisted the help of a shipmate and together they returned to the alley and retrieved the cases, re-secreting them somewhere on the docks near the Standart. Because of the insurrection, they had no time to open the crates."

She stopped long enough to finish her drink and Larkin immediately refilled her glass. The three of us refrained from making any verbal interruption, afraid to break the spell she was weaving. McAllister was listening and studying her intently as if he were mesmerized. With a fresh drink in her hand, Irina continued.

"Fortunately, the demonstration that day ended with little or no bloodshed and my grandfather was able to return home safely. Tensions, however, still ran high and, since my grandfather was known to be in the employ of the Czar, he rarely left the sanctuary of his apartment in the weeks that followed.

"Then came word that Nicholas and his family had been detained by forces loyal to the Duma and the final thrust of the revolution began in earnest. The Bolsheviks organized a demonstration against the provisional government and the streets turned bloody. The army was fraternizing with the mobs and even the Volhynian regiment of the guard mutinied, killing its officers and marching through the streets inciting the people to join the revolt.

"Remarkably, through all of this, diplomats and delegates were left to conduct business as usual and discuss the course of the war. They were entertained lavishly and Princess Leon Radziwill continued to throw elaborate parties with exceptional dining, music, and dancing. While queues formed outside the butcher and baker's shops, champagne flowed freely in dining rooms and clubs.

"Meanwhile, the man who helped my grandfather pirate the two crates was found murdered on the Kirovskij Most."

She finished the second drink and looked around. "Am I the only one drinking?" None of us had touched ours, so we all self-consciously took a drink.

"Still loyal to the Czar, now an absolute concept, my grandfather feared for his life. He began making arrangements to leave Russia, planning to send for his family after he found a safe haven.

"Now, we must back up in time for a moment. In January of 1917, an Italian delegation had arrived in St. Petersburg, then called Petrograd, to discuss the course of the war. The ministers were so unnerved by the civil unrest that, in spite of their luxurious treatment, they sought the protection of the British for safe passage home, leaving their ship, the Phantome, in the harbor next to the Standart.

"When the captain of the Standart asked for volunteers to help him sail the Phantome back to Italy, my grandfather jumped at the opportunity. Under the cover of darkness, he smuggled the two crates aboard the Phantome and the next day, sailed for the Mediterranean.

"While he was in Italy, the war ended and Lenin returned to Russia to lead the Council of Working Men and Soldier Deputies, the Soviet, and my grandfather became a refugee, afraid to return to Russia because of his loyalty to the Czar.

"It was not until he arrived in Italy that he was able to inspect the contents of the boxes that he literally risked his life to smuggle out of Russia."

"I hope it was worth the gamble." McAllister thought aloud.

Irina looked to McAllister. "You decide." She said simply. "There were over thirty Faberge eggs ranging from half completed product to fully finished pieces. In addition to the eggs were trays of diamonds, rubies, emeralds, sapphires, amethyst, opal, and topaz, the lightest tray weighing almost four kilograms."

It didn't take long for McAllister to decide. I could see him mentally converting kilograms to pounds, multiplying pounds by the number of trays, applying the ball park figure into karats, and stopping only when he realized that the loose stones alone had to be worth well over a hundred million dollars. I could see the light behind his eyes and I could visualize the wheels as they spun at the speed of sparkling light.

Something, however, didn't sound right. How could a man with a bizillion dollars, comfortably situated thousands of miles from a disorganized and unsuspecting government, still leave his wife and three children in the middle of a volatile political environment that could be extremely dangerous for former supporters of the Czar. Since, at that time, McAllister was capable of thinking only in numbers, I asked what happened next.

"I cannot speak for my grandfather." She said. "After all, he died long before I was born. I can tell you however, that he sent a message to my grandmother with one of the returning crewmen who had helped return the Phantome. He said he was going to America to arrange for her and the children to follow him later to a new and better life."

"He told a friend he had a fortune in precious stones and jewelry and the friend says something like 'wonderful, Sergi. I'll tell your wife you're going to be millionaires in America'?" I asked skeptically.

"His name was not Sergi."

"It was an example."

"He told his friend nothing." She continued. "He wrote to my grandmother and entrusted the letter to a man with whom he had sailed. That is all."

"Okay." McAllister must have bored himself with his mental calculations, and finally spoke. "How did he plan on getting to America and what did he do with his sudden windfall?"

"He booked passage on a ship, the Cassandra, and took the cache with him." She answered.

"How do you know this?" Asked McAllister.

"He kept a diary." She said a little testily, sensing McAllister's cynicism. "I will explain.

"During the passage, my grandfather became very ill. He believed it was acute appendicitis. It kept him below decks in a cramped berth for most of the voyage in much pain. When the ship finally approached the United States, he enlisted the help of a couple of fellow travelers to carry him up on deck.

“After the ship docked, he somehow managed to disembark under his own power, apparently taking his treasure with him. He was never heard from again.”

“You have a way to tie all of this to a button Grange found in a gypsy market-place in Russia?” McAllister asked.

“My grandfather left some personal things, including the journal he kept aboard the ship. It was found by an Italian steward who had befriended my grandfather and, finding my grandmother’s address on the inside cover of the diary, he returned the personal effects to her. The only clues we have as to what happened to my grandfather are contained within those pages.” She reached under the string of the package she had brought and produced an old, bound booklet, its imitation leather cover cracked and flaking, the edges of the pages dirty and worn with age. She held it out to McAllister with both hands.

If it was meant to prove something, it was beyond me. The less than paperback sized volume contained about a hundred pages, eighty of which were blank. The remaining sheets were written in hand written cryllic, block letters printed with a fountain pen that left numerous blotches of leaking ink on almost every line of text. The stiffness of the brittle paper certified that it was old, but other than that, it was all meaningless to me, although McAllister made a show of examining it carefully before handing it back.

“Since you do not read the language, I will be happy to translate.” She said, opening to a page halfway into the part of the volume that was covered with the neat scrawl.

> “Although the passage goes well, I am ill beyond the point of tolerance. My fever has been running high and the pain in my side is intense. I have not been able to eat and find myself almost too weak to hold this pen. Everyone has been most kind and although I do not understand the words, I have the feeling that they are offering me reassurance that a comfortable hospital bed awaits my arrival in America.”

She skipped a couple of pages and continued.

> “I made my way down to the hold earlier this morning to check on our precious cargo. It is safe and I can only imagine the shock it would cause among the crew and passengers if they knew what was packed in those two plain and simple boxes. I am told that

customs will inspect all freight upon arrival in America so I must find a way to circumvent this process.

"Health wise, however, I have paid dearly for my secretive trip to the hold. I can only hope I have the strength to carry out my mission."

She turned another page. "And this is the final entry." She took a deep breath.

"We are within sight of land. Against the protestations of those who have been so kind to me in the last few days, I have insisted on being assisted to the main deck for my first view of what is to become our new home. "It is difficult to describe the beauty I see. Shore birds sweep across the deep blue waters to greet us and, in the distance, the lady stands tall and proud, her arm held high, welcoming us to this wonderful land. The sun is setting behind her and forms of a halo of light around her that makes her presence seem mystical and almost heavenly. "I know how I will hide her riches until the doctors can remove this terrible pain in my side. If anything happens and I am unable to fulfill our dreams, you must look to the lady. She will point the way. "I must go now to prepare the way for our future. Know in your heart that I love you and our three darling children with all my soul. May God and the saints of our parents watch over me in this accursed pain."

She gently, almost reverently, closed the book. "That was all that was written."

I thought she was going to add something, but she carefully laid the book aside and slowly began unwrapping the rest of the package. When the thick brown paper was folded back, she produced a uniform jacket and a cap. The jacket was flap fronted with a row of buttons on each side of the chest. Probably pure white at one time, it was dull with age but immaculately pressed and folded. The hat was a round rim with a dish-like topping with a satin ribbon hanging from the back. Irina unfolded the jacket.

"This was among the personal effects that the Italian steward returned to my grandmother. It was my grandfather's uniform. He was wearing this jacket when he found the crates of Faberge in the downtown alley." She pointed to the left side of the tunic. "The button you found belongs here."

I blinked. McAllister smiled. Larkin looked puzzled.

"That's it?" I asked. "You went ballistic over a missing button from a World War I era sailor suit?"

"You don't understand. . ."

"You're right. I. . ."

"Shut up, Grange. You've said enough already for one evening, or morning, or whatever the hell it is. Let her talk." McAllister said.

Irina smiled at the McAllisters and continued. "Uniforms in the service of the Czars were as distinctive as the titles of the royal family. My grandfather was attached to the Naval Department because of his service on the Standart, but had no official standing in the service. He was, perhaps, one of only five men who could have worn a uniform of that style with those particular buttons.

"He told my grandmother that, after finding those boxes on the day of the demonstration, he was reprimanded by his superior because of the missing button. And, because of the insurrection, materials were in short supply and he was unable to have the uniform restored to regulation."

"It was your grandfather's. Wasn't it, Irina?" McAllister was tuned into her orbital parity or something. He sounded very melodramatic.

Irina looked at McAllister for a few seconds. Larkin had noticed the strange exchange between them, but they were oblivious of time and space.

Here we go again. I thought.

McAllister knew that the cheap knick-knack was, indeed, from the tunic that Irina was treating like the Shroud Of Turin.

"Yes." Irina finally said. "It is, Mister McAllister."

"I agree." McAllister said solemnly. "Now what?"

"If we can backtrack where this button came from," Irina answered. "I can validate what my grandmother has told us all these years." Irina lowered her head. "I would like to tell my mother that the stories her mother told her were true. That her father did not desert her family like so many people of the time had said."

McAllister shook his head sadly. "I can understand your excitement at finding a connection to your family history, I really can, Irina. But I don't want your enthusiasm to cloud your judgment. "

Irina cocked her head.

"Granger found a doo-dad." McAllister continued, "it may probably well tie in somehow with your grandfather. But to what extent?"

Irina just stood there in silence.

"Okay." McAllister threw up his hands in a gesture of helplessness. "Let's suppose that your grandfather sails into what is apparently New York

Harbor and sees the Statue of Liberty. Someone reads him the inscription; 'you're tired, you're poor, the wretched refuse and huddling masses'. I'm paraphrasing, but you get the idea. "Grandpa says, 'hey, wait a minute, I'm not poor. I'm a very rich man!'

"So he lands in New York City, a virtual mecca compared to a Russia defeated in war and without definitive leadership, and decides to build a new life.

"Other than his immediate health problem, his financial backing is, basically, stolen treasure. So, he does what almost anybody would do in that situation. He hides the loot, builds a new life, and in order to hide his past, he changes his name, manufactures a fictional past, and enters the business world in some very prosperous times. He becomes a citizen, finds a new wife, starts another family and, in very short time, is unable to revert to his old way of life without jeopardizing his new position."

Irina began shaking her head.

"Do you have another scenario?" She asked, hoping that he did.

"There are hundreds of scenarios, Irina." McAllister said gently. "I'm just showing you what is most likely.

"Remember, as you said, Grandpa was a very sick man in a time when even a simple appendectomy was a major operation. I'm not a doctor, but I do know that a high fever and anesthetic is a very dangerous combination. Suppose his mind was affected by the surgery? Maybe he didn't survive. Even if he did, he could have suffered serious brain damage. Memory loss. He would have become just another immigrant absorbed by the biggest city in America, wandering the streets not knowing his past or future."

I don't think I ever heard McAllister using genuine logic. Definitely, never did I witness him playing the role of a Devil's Advocate.

"Either way," Irina said, clutching her grandfather's old tunic, "my mother is entitled to a legacy."

"A legacy?" McAllister asked with a surprised look on his face.

Irina faltered. She actually hung her head in embarrassment.

McAllister offered a pitying smile. "Are you prepared to roll the dice, Irina?"

Irina looked confused.

"Are you prepared to follow your dream and find your legacy?"

"I don't know."

Larkin approached Irina, placing a comforting hand on her shoulder. "My husband is a dreamer, Irina. He has followed his dreams to the ends of the world." She glanced at her husband. "And found them."

Yeah, I followed McAllister's dreams too. I thought.

"But. . ." She began before Larkin continued.

"I think you should listen to him." Larkin said. Glancing toward her husband.

"If my grandfather lost his money or died, his fortune is yet to be found. Is this not so?" Irina asked McAllister.

"What did he say?" McAllister asked, pointing to the diary. "Something about 'look to the lady. She will point the way'? The Statue of Liberty doesn't point. She holds a torch. 'A lamp beside the golden door.'" He quoted again. He then turned to me, "Grange. Do you think Ned could get us a permit to walk around Manhattan with a pick and shovel, or maybe salvage rights to the Statue of Liberty?"

He was joking . . . I think.

"Take the button, Irina." I said gently. "Sew it back on your grandfather's uniform and show it proudly every time you have the chance. Believe me, it is only an heirloom, not an endowment."

McAllister glared at me. "I told you to keep your big mouth shut, Grange. That means the rest of the time we're in Russia!"

Irina was already re-wrapping the old tunic. It was obvious that I had broken the spell of the evening that had begun with great excitement and expectation for her and had ended in disappointment and despair.

"Irina. . ." McAllister began.

"It is very late." She might have been stifling tears. "We have a busy day ahead of us." She turned to me. "I will not report your infraction, Mister Lawton." She said, resuming her officious demeanor as our In-tourist guide. "But I must warn you that such breach of conduct will not be tolerated again. Please see to it that you adhere to the rules of my country."

Larkin again placed a gentle hand on her forearm. "Are you going to be alright, Irina?"

She shifted her head a couple of inches and thrust out her chin defiantly. "I am Russian," she said, challenging contradiction. And with that, she made a dignified and exaggerated exit.

I remained silent.

McAllister shook his head as if forcing himself back from someplace far away. "Too much coincidence." He said to no one in particular. His brow still furrowed in thought. "They either think we are dumber than a lobster or we have stumbled into an amazing set of circumstances. What do you think . . .?" I started to reply, but he ignored me. ". . . Larkin?"

"You don't believe in coincidences, Bobby." Larkin said. "For some reason, I believe that you are no longer interested in cracking a KGB conspiracy plot." She smiled and shook her head.

"How did you guess?" McAllister asked with feigned surprise.

I raised my hand.

"What?" Asked McAllister.

"Things are happening quickly." I said meekly. "And from apparently different quarters. It does seem strange that, after only a few days, we have gathered a great deal of information concerning exactly the things that we initially came here to piece together." I looked at the table in the corner. "And here is another interesting development."

"What?" Asked McAllister.

I picked up Irina's grandfather's journal. "She left this."

McAllister waved it off. "You succeeded in getting the poor girl upset! Has anyone ever told you that you have no tact whatsoever?"

If he only knew. I thought, but did not say.

"She was on the verge of tears! She barely made it out of here without having a nervous breakdown."

"Or. . ."

"I don't want to hear you say, or even try to convince me that she left it on purpose, Grange." McAllister said evenly.

So much for that thought.

Larkin spoke up. "Bobby, maybe, just maybe she left it here in case we wanted to have it authenticated."

"Which we, of course, will, Larkin." He took the book from me and tossed it to Larkin. "Give this to Artur." He directed her. "See what he thinks." He said, then added, "Very good thinking, Larkin."

"What are the chances her story is true, Grange?"

I should have figured it would come back to that. But still, I was content at having been included back into the picture.

"Off the top of my head?" I said, more to myself than out loud. "Not entirely unlikely, but definitely questionable."

"Well, I'm glad that we don't have to argue that point." McAllister said.

"Bobby, it's quite possible that, fearing for his life, Faberge might have left behind a fortune in gems. After all, he was the Imperial Jeweler and, as such, was probably subsidized by the Czar. It was probably the Czar's money and he didn't lose anything by leaving it behind. That a common apprentice looted a fortune and hid it in the alley to be found by a merchant seaman who, in turn, robbed the thief is another story.

"I suppose stranger things have happened, but I can't think of anything like it offhand." I said facetiously.

"Not even something like a curious vacuum cleaner salesman finding the Lost Dutchman Gold Mine?" He asked, a twinkle coming to his eye.

He was referring to my first book, a fictional murder mystery/ adventure that enjoyed moderate success as a paperback.

"We're not going to go through that again, are we?" I asked. McAllister had constantly made mention of that novel as if it were a true story during his search for the Prize and Larkin.

"It's just proof that fact can be stranger than fiction." He replied, his grin attesting to the fact that McAllister the dreamer was thinking of making an encore. "Do you want to know what I think?"

I almost said no; definitely not. "Sure." I said, knowing I was going to hear it anyway.

"The treasure, in some form or another, exists, Grange. It may not be fifty pounds of precious stones in neat little pieces, but I truly believe there is some validity to Irina's story."

He wanted me to ask why, but I wasn't about to give him the satisfaction.

"Why?" Asked Larkin.

"The St. Petersburg salon was the flagship of Faberge's operation." He began eagerly. "At any given time, dozens of people, probably well over a hundred, worked in that single shop. The inventory of that one outlet must have been incredible and, even though they were in the middle of a revolution, the aristocracy wanted to create the impression of business as usual. Toward the end, however, there was no one willing to venture out to go shopping, so the stock kept piling up as the workers kept producing goods.

"Faberge didn't take anything with him when he left. He probably worked right up to the very end, always hoping his friend, the Czar, would pull things out and he barely got to Lucerne with his own skin, let alone a fortune in gems. We have already seen that he didn't bequeath a fortune to his survivors, Theodore lives comfortably, but certainly not like he inherited riches beyond belief."

"I think it's possible that a fortune exists and, however much it was, someone managed to get it out of the country." McAllister said.

At a point like this I normally would have argued with McAllister, but it was late, even by my standards, and I was getting tired.

"Look at it from two directions." He reasoned. "If we are being led around by some complicated KGB plot, we're being fed information at a carefully calculated rate. The Russians have had over three quarters of a century to find this treasure and now they have decided they need help. And, of course, being familiar with my talents , or luck as you may call it, they may be hoping we get lucky again and lead them to what they consider is rightfully theirs. It's a no lose situation for them. If we don't find anything, no harm, no foul. If we should stumble onto something, they learn what we learn. If we actually find these two crates, they simply cause harm to us and simply take them away, one way or another."

I didn't bother to remark that it was "the other" that had me worried.

"On the other hand," he continued, "my subliminal orbital parity must be in perfect alignment and brought us here. We could have been the factor that brought all the pieces of the puzzle together, and that is probably what happened, you know, why we're attracting so much covert attention."

"Let's see." I said, scratching my head in feigned wonder. "Now where have I heard this kind of talk before, Bobby?" I asked as I looked toward Larkin to see her reactions.

She smiled, knowingly.

"Like I once told you, Grange. You don't have a decent belief system." McAllister said, also smiling.

"Yeah, well I do recall that astounding revelation. And, like I thought before, I didn't believe there was such as system."

"Well there is."

"Back to covert attention," I changed the subject. "If Irina is a KGB actress as well as an In-tourist guide, we are probably being monitored right now." I waved my arm around the room to help make my point.

"You didn't seem to be concerned with that possibility when you were sniveling like a baby tonight."

I had that coming.

"Irina discounted the fact that the room might be bugged, but she might have been both showing her bosses what a good performance she could give while, at the same time, putting our fears of being overheard to rest. At this moment, we could be having more than six ears in this room listening to our plans."

"We aren't making any plans, Grange." McAllister said, laughing at the thought of Irina being a KGB agent or the KGB eavesdropping on us. "All we're doing is covering ground that they have probably gone over a hundred times."

I couldn't help wondering how he could have assumed that as a fact.

"Anyway," he continued, undaunted by anything as intelligent as logic, "I'm convinced that the treasure exists, and, is hidden someplace, waiting for us to find it." He smiled and began counting off on his fingers. "It didn't stay in Russia, because the Russians don't have it. It didn't go to Switzerland. No one in the United States has it. It just seems natural. . ."

"Hold it!" I had to interrupt. "Back up a minute here. How can you say that nobody in the States ever had it?"

He looked at me like I was a moron. "Grange, do you have any idea how much money that was by today's standards?" He asked, knowing neither of us could even guess the exact figure. "That kind of money had to make somebody's 'most wealthy' list. It wasn't Getty. He was in oil. It didn't involve sex or booze, so it wasn't the Kennedys. The Rockefellers were industry. The Carnegies were steel. The DuPonts were chemicals. The Vanderbilts. . ."

"I'm sure you could go on and on," I said, stopping him again, "but right now, you're as full of stuffing as a Christmas goose. The last time the

Arizona Republic ran a list of the fifty richest men in America, I didn't recognize thirty-eight of the names.

"A thousand things could explain why that kind of money doesn't show. Not everybody lives like Donald Trump. Meyer Lansky lived in a three bedroom house in a modest section of Miami even though he had enough mob money to buy the entire town. There was that television actor who lived in a tepee in South Dakota.

"The loot might not even exist anymore. That stuff dates back to the nineteen-teens, for Christ's sake. Say the poor schmuck who found the bounty put it all in the stock market and along comes October twenty-nine, 1929. Suppose he actually invests in one of those time-share things and it turned out to be in the Everglades. He could have lost it all at the tables in Vegas."

"There was no Vegas in 1918."

"That's an example, Bobby, not Gospel."

"If it were Gospel, I definitely wouldn't believe it." He smiled again, almost benevolently. "Once in a while, Grange, you have to have a dream . . . and follow it."

If I had a dollar for each time I heard that speech before, I wouldn't have any place to put any more money.

"The fact is, Grange, I believe that the Faberge treasure is out there, waiting to be found. And you know what, Grange?"

I was afraid to ask.

"Irina will have her legacy."

"Oh?"

"The lady is going to show us where to find it."

"Irina?"

"No, Grange." McAllister smiled. "The lady with the torch."

Damn!

* * * * *

I was far too tired to do anything as futile as argue with McAllister, so I called it a night. Fortunately, I was used to McAllister's dramatic pronouncements so I didn't waste any time losing sleep over his sudden shift in priorities. I knew he would be making plans, some outrageous, some necessary, and the only way I could deal with him was react to what he said or did with common sense, something he considered a waste of his time and mental exertion. The only reason I didn't bother telling him that scouring the streets of New York City would be the biggest expenditure of time and money without the prospect of measurable success was because, if we were right about our unseen escort, we would probably be followed every step of the way by someone with whom I had some unfinished business. If we were not on the KGB's list of ten most followed American tourists, I could always return to Russia on my own and try to pick up where I had left off. I was used to McAllister and his loaded gun approach and was resigned to playing the Devil's Advocate to his oftentimes irresponsible ways. . . and the only reason I objected to being awakened by the incessant knocking later that same morning was that the pounding roused me just as my sleep-refreshed mind was about to settle on some significant fact. I was still trying to figure out what I had barely missed when I opened the door to Artur.

"Mister McAllister asked me to go over this with you." He said, holding up Irina's grandfather's journal. "I just spent the last half hour reading it for him."

"What did he say after you read it to him?" I asked, still trying to figure out what it was that my mind had tried to bring into focus.

"Not much. He just nodded like he had heard it all before."

"What was your impression?" I asked. "Not about what was said, but how it was written."

Artur looked confused by the question.

"Is it believable as a document that was written in 1917 or 18?" I clarified, "Phrasing, handwriting style, that sort of thing."

It was clear that I was asking our translator to go a step further than his job description called for. He shrugged, almost indifferently. "I guess so." He said. "The handwriting seems to deteriorate as if the guy was really sick and getting worse. It was written with an old fashioned fountain pen and I don't think anyone uses those anymore. Yeah, I would say it's authentic. At least as far as the writing goes. I can't comment on what the guy was saying, though. What was he talking about?"

"Dreams," I answered. "At least that's what Mister McAllister would say."

"You mean you think he was delirious?" Artur asked.

"No." I answered. "But some other people might be suffering from that disorder."

It was obvious that I had confused Artur further, but then why should McAllister be the only one who practiced rules in business dealings.

McAllister returned the diary to Irina at breakfast. She glanced around as if she was afraid of being seen, and launched immediately into a dissertation of our scheduled plans for the day.

She kept up the monologue stoically and without alluding to our earlier conversation, throughout the day. As we passed through cast iron gates and over a wooden bridge into the fifteen hundred acre park that surrounded Pavlovsk, Irina kept up the In-tourist patter about how Catherine

II gave the land and the palace to her son, Paul, in 1777. We hardly noticed the most beautifully restored palace in all of Russia as McAllister, Larkin, and I walked the grand halls, each absorbed in thoughts of our own. The day went faster than I would have thought and we were back at the Evropeiskaya in time for dinner. Without so much as a hint of things to come, Irina left us as soon as the cars stopped in front of the hotel.

After dinner, I took my usual stool at the late night bar and was well into my third, what the Russians call rum and an American Coke when Irina silently took the seat next to me, holding up a finger to the bored bartender, signaling for a drink.

"We have to stop meeting like this." I said in acknowledgement.

She looked around as if I might have been talking to someone else. "Like what?" She asked when she realized we were the only two in the room.

"Never mind." I answered. I guess American humor wasn't part of glasnost.

"We have spent the entire day together and you have not mentioned our conversation of last night." She said, matter-of-factly. It was not a question but she clearly expected a response.

"What did you expect, Irina?" I asked, truly not knowing what she wanted to hear. "There is not much we can do about something that happened as long ago as your grandfather's," I struggled for a word, "acquisition."

"Mister McAllister has found gold from treasures that have sat on the ocean floor for many centuries." She reasoned. "Is this not the same?"

"Of course not." I was getting tired of the strictly materialistic motives of others when my only incentive for being involved was not for profit. "Even if Mister McAllister did find the Faberge fortune, what makes you think you are going to benefit in any way?"

"You do not think these things belong to me and my family?" She asked, shocked.

"No." I answered frankly. "I don't. I have no idea of how things work in Russia, but if you think you have a legitimate claim to any of this, I think you are sadly mistaken, Irina.

"First of all," I began, making my points before she could interrupt, "there are International laws of salvage. If that treasure is intact today, it belongs to the person who finds it. I can't say for certain exactly how those things work, but there comes a time when untouched or unclaimed valuables constitutes abandonment.

"Secondly, and again I'm speaking from a laymen's perspective, even if your grandfather left you this stuff in some kind of will, it would not be valid. I know that someone cannot bestow something to someone who hasn't even been born.

"Third," I was on a roll, making things up as I went along, "your grandfather stole this stuff from someone who was apparently stealing it himself. If someone robs a bank and hides the money before he goes to jail, he is not entitled to keep the money when he gets out just because he served the time. A person cannot profit from his or her crime.

"And finally," I wondered how my final point could have ever escaped her, "you live in Russia. Do you think that the government is going to allow you to keep even one lousy little gemstone? Not in your little closed society where the ruling class makes all the rules."

"But I would not stay in Russia." She protested. "I would move to someplace where I could live without the fear of reprisals from those who would try to deprive me."

"Deprive you of what?" The bartender turned around and looked at me from his place at the end of the bar. I lowered my voice instinctively. "Haven't you been listening to me?"

It was at that very moment that I realized it was I who had not been listening to her. The thought that had eluded me earlier had suddenly hit me like a mild thunderbolt.

She was saying something about the worker's paradise not being all it was cracked up to be, but I was only hearing bits and pieces. Something was wrong and I wanted to get to someone I could trust to talk it out before I inadvertently let something slip in front of our not-so-innocent and naive guide.

"Listen, Irina," I interrupted, "what is on the program for tomorrow?"

"The Grand Palace. Why?"

"I just thought of something." That much was true. "Let me have some time to go over a few things with Mr. McAllister before I raise your hopes over anything. I may be on to something."

Apparently I didn't pull it off as casually as I had intended because Irina looked both suspicious and disappointed. "Really," I said, nodding like a cast member of Chicago's Second City Comedy Improv Group. "Trust me."

"We will talk tomorrow?" She insisted on being reassured.

"Promise." I answered, holding up three fingers as I slid off the barstool. I felt her eyes on my back as I headed for the elevator.

In his usual fashion, our floor porter watched me carefully as I walked down the hallway paying special attention as I passed my door and continued to McAllister's room. When he answered, I tried to convey urgency without anxiety as I told him I wanted to talk.

"Is that Sadko place next door open at this time of night?" I asked.

He caught my drift immediately. "I think so." He answered. "Are you having one of your cravings for caviar blinis?"

"Sure am." He knew I didn't eat caviar. "Wanna' get some?"

"I'll get my jacket."

We had no sooner cleared the front door of the hotel when McAllister was on my case. "This had better be good, Grange. I didn't get much sleep last night."

It was only a matter of steps to the entrance of Sadko and I had my hand on the door when I gave him the news. "I think we have proof we are being set up." I said.

"So you think you have all this figured out, do you?" The small orchestra was playing a discordant ballad that necessitated him speaking directly into my ear. I pointed to a table in the corner.

"Irina's story is bullshit." I said as we sat down. "When I realized that, everything points to the fact that we are being led around by the nose. She talks about never seeing or hearing from her grandfather because he supposedly died before she was born."

"So?"

"How would she know?"

"This is your startling discovery?" He asked. "You find one little inconsistency in Irina's story and you approach panic at the speed of light? Why didn't you notice that relatively minor fact last night? Larkin did."

"Listen," I was surprised he wasn't taking me more seriously. "I never put that button in my pocket at Sarzanov's place. It is not the kind of thing I would have done, even without thinking. Irina never had a grandfather that smuggled Faberge stuff out of Russia. Sanya Roskovin makes me nervous, and I'm afraid that I might be looking for the wrong man if everything else we've been told is a lie. I think it's about time to exercise the option to abandon this project while we still have our asses in one piece."

"We are not in danger, Grange." He said, holding up a hand to stop me from saying anything as the waitress approached to take our order.

"I'll agree to some extent that we have been listening to a story, but that just proves a point I have already made." He continued after we had ordered. "In the last thirty-six hours, you have stumbled onto more information than coincidence would allow in a lifetime. If you were sleeping with Carl Faberge and the Director of the KGB at the same time, you wouldn't have learned this much in years.

As long as they are feeding us information, we can count on the fact that we will not be harmed. They want us to have this information for one of two reasons. First, they might be trying to distract us from our original mission. They send us home with some story about Faberge, we tear up New York City trying to find it, we look stupid doing that, and when we bring up another story about art forgery, we look even dumber. Not only do we look like idiots, we get caught trying to promote another story that sounds like sour grapes on our part.

"Second possibility; the story is true. The only exception is that we are getting facts from actors playing a part. Hell, the Russians have had over three quarters of a century to find the stuff and, so far, they have come up empty. They probably figure that they have nothing to lose by telling us what they already know and, if we get lucky, they simply take it away from us."

The waitress returned with our order, caviar blinis for McAllister and shish kebob appetizers for me.

"How do we know which option is more likely?" I asked, after she had left again.

"It doesn't matter."

"What?!"

"Well, look at it this way, Grange. . ."

Here he goes again, I thought.

". . . If the grandfather story has any validity, they will want to be sending someone with us to monitor our progress."

"And?" I asked anxiously.

"It doesn't really matter who sent Irina, Grange. I feel that there is supreme reason for us finding her or her finding us."

"This wouldn't happen to be connected to your orbital parity theory, would it, Bobby?"

"Something like that." He smiled.

I chose not to get into that subject. "Irina made overtures along those lines just a few minutes ago."

"Orbital parity?"

"Bobby!"

McAllister grinned broadly at my impatience. "Oh, you mean her going with us. Good!" He rubbed his hands together. "Let's keep throwing the ball back in their court. Tell her we are not going to go off halfcocked, looking for some vague treasure that can't be verified."

"And then?"

"Then, the orbital parity theory will be consistent with my conclusion."

"Humor me, Bobby. Make sense, will you?"

"Have I ever been wrong, Grange? I mean in the long run?"

"If you mean that the end justifies the means. . ."

"Yeah, that."

"Not that I can recall. But. . ."

He held up a hand. "I am right. And, she and whoever her backup is, will want to make some kind of a deal."

"Who the hell is her backup?" I said, wondering where he had come up with that idea.

"I don't know," he answered as if it was irrelevant, "a brother, a cousin, maybe an uncle, the KGB. Who knows? She has to have someone. After all, she's just a girl."

For someone who had been speaking fairly intelligently, disregarding his pie in the sky theory, for the last few minutes, he was following up with some pretty chauvinistic shit. I told him as much.

"C'mon, Grange," he said, trying to coax me into his way of thinking, "there is no way they are going to let this little wisp of a girl alone on something like this."

"So it follows that she needs reinforcements every step of the way?" "Of course." "Maybe you never heard of liberated, capable, and intelligent women?"

"Oxymoron." He answered simply. "Words that don't go together in the same sentence."

"Two words," I said, "Mata Hari."

"Two more," he replied, "military intelligence."

"Eleanor Roosevelt."

"Jumbo shrimp."

"Golda Meir."

"Smart jock."

"Larkin McAllister." I thought I had him.

"Civil war." He didn't bite.

"Roseanne." I stopped myself. "Never mind. I just helped you make your point."

"My point," McAllister continued, "is that we will be watched very carefully every step of the way. One person can't do it alone. What did you tell her tonight?"

"I told her I had to talk to you about something unspecific. I'm supposed to talk to her again tomorrow."

"Good." He finished off the last of his snack. "String her along. Tell her we came to Russia just as common tourists. Don't commit to anything. If you have to, tell her you need to clear everything with me. Let's find how much more information we can assimilate by appearing to be reluctant to go along with everything they hand us."

I had to agree with him. Even though it appeared that our Russian hosts had partially dissuaded McAllister from his initial quest, I was still on a mission that required more than just a name to fit the face of a fleeing assassin in Paris. Now that I had that name, I was more determined to stay in Russia until my pursuit came to a satisfactory end. If stringing Irina along is what it would take to come face-to-face with Sally's murderer, I was capable of giving a performance worthy of an Oscar nomination.

McAllister clapped his hand on my shoulder as we exited Sadko on the way back to the hotel. "I know what you are thinking, Grange. Try to relax."

"You don't know what I'm thinking, Bobby."

"Hey." He smiled. "Remember? I was born in the City Of Dreams!" His smile turned into a smirk as he winked.

"Yeah, and you're dreaming now." I said.

"I can say it with one word, Grange." He looked serious.

I was silent.

"Revenge."

* * * * *

"My plan is working." The caller's voice exuded confidence. "They are following my program as if I have been guiding them by the hand."

"I still do not believe this is our best course of action. In fact, I think you have acted in an irresponsible manner. Who gave the authorization to act in this way?"

The caller's voice hardened noticeably. "I need no authorization to act in a manner consistent to secure my own future. This is not a matter of who is in charge. It is a matter of who retains control of the situation. Had it been up to you, these fools would still be walking around in museums listening to the same canned drivel afforded all tourists. If this pompous American happens to get lucky with a mystery that has plagued my country since the days of the Czars, I intend to profit. You are the one who is motivated by artistic purity. I cannot live on prized possessions hidden in my basement, nor can I continue to depend on your generosity."

"Your greed will be your downfall."

"As long as your objectives are met, you should be satisfied. If my plans work, you would more than triple your present status. You would have the world's largest collection of truly authentic Faberge eggs and I could live comfortably in a country more suitable to my tastes."

"This started out to be a simple theft, but you are tempting fate by making things complicated. You are escalating at a dangerous rate. "

"And how much has all this cost you?" The caller asked. "We have managed nicely these many years without varying from our original agenda. We have committed the perfect crime not once, but several times. The Americans have a saying: 'if it is not broken, do not repair it'. Surely you see the wisdom in this kind of thinking."

"I see the odds against us mounting at an incredible rate. How long do you think we can continue to defraud not only individual collectors, but entire governments as well?"

"Your actions continue to be rash and unnecessary. We would have been done with this man by now had it not been for your many failures."

"Failures that took place because your American connection is a fool. I cannot believe he came so highly recommended." The caller's tone was pure contempt. "It is the last time I will employ anyone who is attempting to satisfy a personal grudge while doing a job."

"Speaking of grudges, what happens if we are unable to dissuade the author from his desire to find that idiot Patek?"

"Then I will have to pay him a personal visit." The caller replied thoughtfully. "To convince him the error of his ways."

*   *   *

CHAPTER EIGHT

We took the hydrofoil down the Neva into the gulf southwest for the twenty mile trip to Petrodvorets. Peter the Great personally designed and supervised the building of the three hundred acre park and the palace that he hoped would rival Versailles. Fountains cascade through the park and gardens, the most impressive being the Sampson Fountain portraying the strongman prying open the jaws of a lion as a spray of water gushes sixty-five feet into the air from the lion's mouth. The hundred twenty nine fountains pump nearly seventy-five hundred gallons of water a minute and cover almost thirteen miles as they converge on the Grand Palace.

The buildings were heavily damaged during World War II, but using the original plans, careful restoration continues on a daily basis. St. Petersburg is an exceptionally clean city, a product of great pride among the residents, and the grounds of the Grand Palace hardly show any of the debris associated with the extensive reconditioning that is constantly in progress.

Irina and I had stopped in front of the man and the beast spewing water, the fine mist lowering the air temperature a good ten degrees.

"Irina," I began hesitantly, "I don't think you understand why we came to Russia. What I'm trying to say is: I don't believe there is anything that the McAllisters and I can do for you."

"I . . . I do not understand." She looked more frightened than disappointed.

"Mister McAllister has a small collection of Faberge eggs." I explained. "He became interested in the history of the eggs and wanted to see first-hand their country of origin.

"Bobby McAllister is a rich man who can indulge himself in almost any manner he chooses, but he is also a very careful man. For him to risk his fortune and family in something as flimsy as what you have told us the other night is a chance he does not want to take and, quite frankly, I agree with him wholeheartedly."

"No." Her worst fears confirmed, she was very near panic. "This cannot be true. I was led to believe that you and your friend, Mister McAllister were brave men who fought odds to obtain your goals. This talk makes you sound like old women, the babushkas who sweep the streets with their twig brooms each morning. Surely such courageous men would not fear the ghosts who guard my grandfather's treasure."

Why is it that women always attack a man's virility when they think they can't get what they want through reasonable arguments?

"Believe me," I said, smiling with what I thought was the proper amount of sympathy, "Bobby McAllister is the last person in the mortal world to be afraid of ghosts. As a matter of fact, he has two personal ghosts he has known on a first-name-basis since he was ten years old, not to mention the ones he briefly met.

"The fact remains that all you have given us is a story, a uniform, and a diary supposedly written by a sick and probably delusional man. Although Bobby is a sucker for ghost stories, that is not the kind of evidence you need to begin a search of this magnitude."

It was clear that Irina had been expecting a much different response. She stuttered without saying anything intelligible for a few seconds before she resorted to the second womanly trick in as many minutes.

"I do not know what I can do." She sniffed, tears forcing their way to the corners of her eyes. "I had very much counted on your help. What can I do now?"

If I was buying her story, I might have been touched. Instead, it was difficult to not tell her to knock it off. I stiffened my imaginary resolve and twisted the knife.

"Frankly, Bobby doesn't think there is a treasure and I agree. If all that treasure actually made it to New York, it is probably spread so thin by now that the biggest share left is part of the cocktail ring someone's Aunt Bessie got from the Home Shopping Network. We both think you need to put this thing to rest and get on with your life."

"My life is nothing without my dreams." She swiped at a tear that had made its way down her cheek. If she started telling me about dreams I was going to send her to the expert himself. Then I remembered that she had read about McAllister and his dreams in something I had written in the novel, Fool's Paradise, hoping it was a tidbit she could use to impress me. Little did she know.

"I'm sorry, Irina." I wasn't less apologetic for anything in my life. "I can talk to Bobby again, but I honestly don't believe it will do any good."

"Then maybe I could talk to him." She said hopefully.

I felt like agreeing with her, but I knew better. I sadly shook my head.

I saw more than disappointment in her eyes. I saw failure. It was the same look that I had seen in McAllister's eyes on a few occasions. I honestly felt that McAllister was being convinced by this unassuming Russian girl. And, I knew I had to shield him from her. I also saw a determined squaring of her shoulders and a purposeful step as if she had reached a new and sudden decision. I wondered what was coming next.

* * * * *

It was after I had spent a couple of hours waiting for her at the bar when I decided she was going to wait until the next day to seduce me, the only avenue I felt she would think she had left for a trip to the States in search of her own legacy.

When I nodded to the porter and approached my room to see light seeping from beneath the door, I couldn't help but wonder two things. The second was if anybody in Russia knocked, and finding no one in, actually waited someplace other than in the personal quarters of whom they intended to visit. I was wondering how far I would allow Irina to go before I pretended to agree to her appeal.

Until the second I opened the door, I guess I had secretly hoped that Irina was going to be waiting for me, provocatively draped atop a Russian sable, naked on my bed except for the satin ribbon around her delicate neck. Most of all, however, I wondered if I would have the resolve to rise to the ranks of gentleman pirate and, in my best imitation of Clark Gable, deliver the "Frankly my dear, I don't give a damn." line.

Then I toyed with the idea of a little harmless recreational sex. Irina was not some Russian shot putter with bulging muscles and her hair in two severe buns at the sides of her head. She was petite with long dark hair that framed an attractive face with a pixie nose and bright green eyes, the type of girl a man would be proud to take home to meet his mother. She had a school girl figure and wore western style clothes from a carefully selected wardrobe that highlighted her slender legs and perfect proportioning. Not quite in Larkin's league, but she had a subtle femininity that I was reminded of every time she walked ahead of us to point out yet another attraction.

Still undecided as to how I was going to be the master of my own seduction scene, I opened the door.

The man sitting on the edge of my bed stood up quickly, holding a finger to his lips and showing his palms in a gesture meant to assure me his intentions were friendly.

"We have only a short time." He said, waving at me to shut the door. "The device I have placed on the microphones causes heavy static interrupted by neutral sounds like running water and bed springs, but it only lasts about five minutes."

"Who the hell are you?" I asked. I don't know if I was more disappointed or surprised.

"My name is Sargo Roskovin. I have been told by a mutual friend from your Chicago that you might require my assistance. I would have contacted you sooner, but I was in Yalta on business and only returned this afternoon. I am now in your service for as long as you need me." He bowed from the waist as if he had just asked me to dance.

I tried not to let my confusion show, but it was a difficult and perplexing moment for me. If the man in front of me was, indeed, who he claimed, then I wondered who had been leading me around for the last few days. If he were an imposter, he had an incredible amount of nerve showing up this late in the game. This version, for one thing, was a male. He was tall and broad shouldered with a single thick eyebrow shadowing both dark eyes that showed little emotion other than slight amusement. He was much less appealing to look at than his similarly named counterpart. He wore workmen's clothes, dark cotton slacks and a loose fitting shirt with long sleeves and a nineteenth century collar. He had a Roman looking nose, probably owing to the fact that it had been broken several times, and thick, stubby fingers but well-manicured nails. I decided to question him.

"You said I had a friend in Chicago." I said. "Actually I have many friends in that part of the country. Which one sent you?"

Knowing he was being tested, he smiled showing crooked but clean teeth. He nodded slightly as if approving of my cautionary tactic. "I do not like to use his name." He answered cryptically. "Would it be enough to say that I received the electronic apparatus I used to confuse those who listen to you from him? He acquired that particular instrument from his favorite uncle. I think his name began with a 'J.'"

"The uncle's name begins with a 'J'?" I asked.

"The uncle's name begins with a 'G.'" He answered evenly.

Jeff Camper. There was no doubt now.

"Have you ever heard of a man named Serge Byachev?" I asked, suddenly changing the direction and pace of my questioning to see if I could catch him off guard.

He cocked his head an inch to the right. "No."

"Mitia Sarzonov?" I persisted.

"No."

"How about Irina Denikoff."

"Your pretty In-tourist guide." He answered, smiling again.

"A man in my profession must make it his business to know who deals with those who visit my country."

"Why?" I asked, honestly curious.

"Not all visitors are tourists, he replied, "as I suspect you may know from your own motives for coming to Russia."

"Do you know a man named Patek?" I asked. "I'm not certain of his first name."

"Not an uncommon name." The less appealing version of Sanya observed. "Do you know what he does or where he lives?"

"He may work for the government."

"That does not tell me much."

"Possibly KGB?" I ventured.

The single eyebrow went up a half inch. "I know of no man named Patek," he said carefully, "but where the KGB is concerned, names mean very little."

I was becoming surprised that he was not as apprehensive about time as I was. I looked at my watch. "We need to talk more." I said. "Can you check on those people I mentioned and find out what you can about them?"

"This is all you require?" He asked, somewhat surprised. "Information about these people?"

"That's it for now." I answered. "When can you get back to me?"

"I will examine your schedule." He went to the microphone in the headboard. "If I am unable to speak with you outside of the hotel, I will return tomorrow night. I must ask you to keep my involvement confidential. Remember, I must live and work in this country."

After I nodded, he held his finger to his lips again and removed an alligator clip from behind the headboard. He went to the other listening device and repeated the procedure and raised a two fingered salute as he silently slipped out the door.

I was left alone with the thousands of questions running through my overworked and now overwrought brain.

* * * * *

Most pre-planned tours include a day of free-time for shopping or returning to an attraction of special interest and Russia has no exception to that rule. The difference is that the fashionable shops along the Nevski have little selection and even less clientele walking the aisles or standing in line at the cash registers. Irina escorted Larkin through the boutiques while, in typical masculine fashion, McAllister and I affected bored but tolerable expressions as we moved from bench to park bench outside the stores as we talked in low tones.

"So you decided to listen to the Campers after I forbade you. That's in the past. I know you thought that they could be of more help in finding Sally's and Antonio's murderer than me." McAllister summarized. "And now you're in a spot because you didn't listen to me and you can't distinguish the players without a scorecard. Does that pretty much cover it, Grange?"

I had it coming. The best things for me to do at this time was remaining silent and swallow the bitter medicine.

"As usual, you have managed to sum up a complicated situation in your folksy and charming southern manner." I said. "And equally as usual, you placed warranted blame on someone else for something that probably taught you quite a bit but is deemed unsatisfactory because it was not obtained on your infallible imitative."

So much for remaining humble.

McAllister smiled. "I seem to remember an idealistic young author who once criticized me for my association with Donald Ducetti, the 'Duck', a mobster who moved to New Orleans from that toddlin' town." He wasn't angry or upset; he was simply reminding me that I wasn't any better than him.

I didn't want to get McAllister all wound up, so I tried to keep quiet.

"Well?" Was all he said.

"Okay, Bobby." I sighed. "Do you want to get into a debate about motives, virtues, and methods, or do you want to figure out how we should be reacting to the present situation?"

"All right." McAllister still could not suppress a rueful smile. "Who do you think is the real 'Chicago-connection'?"

"Too close to call." I said, giving him the conclusion it had taken me most of the night to reach. If the first Roskovin is legitimate, the second is unaware of the first or he is a complete idiot. If the male Roskovin is authentic, the pretty one played things too close and wound up getting caught.

"The problem is, how do we go about finding out which is which? Do we ask them for two pieces of I.D.? Check fingerprints? Run their credit? And what about the gender difference?"

"I don't think it matters." McAllister said thoughtfully. "They've simply underestimated me."

"It seems to me that, either way you look at it, this proves my point about being led around."

As if on cue, the ladies came out of one store, ignoring us completely, and entered its next door neighbor. We moved down a bench.

"If our female version of Roskovin is an imposter, she has already done her job by leading us where we were supposed to go. The appearance of the second Roskovin was 'allowed' to convince us that the first one was a phony. Therefore, we divert our trust to someone like Irina thinking that, while she is a mere wisp of a woman, we can certainly handle her.

"If Roskovin the Second is the pretender, he casts doubt on the credentials of the first and, again, we turn to the neutral corner represented by Irina.

"Just out of curiosity, which is your gut choice for the real Roskovin?"

I shook my head. "It's still a toss-up. Obviously, I'd like it to be the pretty one, Sanya, who supplied us with what we wanted to know in an unbelievably quick fashion. Almost too quick if you ask me. She hung around every step of the way as if she was there to make sure everything went as planned.

"Number Two has more polish and sophistication. He had all the right answers and showed no recognition when I began mentioning the KGB. He has the ability to act like a good spy and seems better educated than someone you would associate with the black market."

McAllister stroked his chin and stared off at the golden spire of the cathedral. "I want to meet this second guy."

"Here's your chance." I pointed with my chin. "Here he comes now."

The man who called himself Sargo Roskovin was walking idly in front of the shops, casually inspecting the wares on display as he slowly made his way toward us. In front of the store that Larkin and Irina had recently abandoned, he pulled out a pack of American cigarettes and began patting his pockets as if looking for a match. Finding none, he appeared to notice us for the first time, approached us, and said something in Russian.

McAllister looked at me as if to ask if this was part of the game.

"We don't speak Russian." I said. I thought it would be the response he expected.

"Americans!" He said, with a much thicker accent than he had used the previous night. He smiled broadly as if he had made a great discovery. "You have a match? A light?"

I handed him my Bic. "Relax, Sargo." I said. "Mister McAllister already knows who you are."

Sargo eyed McAllister suspiciously but spoke to me in a lower, less accented voice. "Pleased to meet you, Comrade McAllister," he made that bowing motion again.

I decided to exercise some of the authority I thought I carried. "Our mutual friend whose name begins with a 'J' has led me to believe that I could expect cooperation from anyone with whom he put me in contact."

There was a flash of defiance in his eyes, but it died quickly. "As you wish." He said, his smile returning. "I only hope my interests are being kept from those who have no business in my affairs."

McAllister spoke up. "You have our assurances and our mutual friend's protection. Is that enough?"

The single eyebrow went up. "I hope you are as correct as you are confident, Comrade McAllister."

McAllister and I both nodded.

Sargo looked at McAllister again over the flame of the lighter, mentally shrugged, and pocketed my Bic.

"The names you gave me," I nodded again, prompting him to continue, "Serge Baychev is a caretaker at the Winter Palace. He changes light bulbs for dead Czars.

"Mitia Sarzonov lives on a collective farm south of the city. He is well known around his village because he does not often work on the farm. He must leave his son with one of the village grandmothers while he goes wherever it is he goes. He lives like a peasant but always has rubles to meet his needs and pay his debts.

"You know your In-tourist guide. She lives in a small apartment in the Debrolyubova District and stays much to herself. She has no known lovers or male visitors. No one seems to know of her family or where she is from, but it is known that she speaks many languages and works for many hours at her job.

"I have found nothing of this Patek you spoke of. If he does work for State Security as you suggest, this would not be unusual. Many agents of the KGB work under one name and live under another to keep their neighbors from knowing who they are. It is most common."

McAllister suddenly stared at me ruefully and suspiciously, shaking his head.

"Do you know anyone who might want to impersonate you?" McAllister asked, barging into the conversation as if it were his natural right.

If Sargo was surprised by the question, it did not show. "No, I do not." His tone indicated he didn't appreciate McAllister's abruptness. "Everyone in Russia wants me or wants what I can supply, but no one would wish to be me. I make enough money to live better than a common peasant, but I am not in the same class as the man from Chicago. Why do you ask? How many Sargo Roskovins would an American know?"

"Obviously more than you." McAllister muttered.

The single eyebrow knotted in the middle, but before Sargo could formulate another question, I held up a hand.

"I want you to find Patek." I said. "'J' told me he could find almost anyone in a day's time. I would expect no less from any of his associates."

"You think things are so simple?" The wry twist of his mouth matched the eyebrow. "My organization is small. I have limited resources."

"Then I will call Chicago and ask for additional help."

That got more reaction, and McAllister's renewed interest.

It also got Sargo's attention.

"I will do my best." Sargo said quickly. I would not wish to disappoint a colleague."

Larkin and Irina stepped out of the shop at that moment and Sargo saw us look in their direction. Without turning around, he stood a little taller and the thicker accent returned. "Enjoy St. Petersburg, American Comrades." He said, louder than necessary.

"You will find much to experience during your stay."

Although I couldn't say for certain, I thought that Irina watched him walk away for longer than necessary.

* * * * *

We actually did get around to having our pictures taken in front of the former location of the Faberge Salon. Although the building front probably closely resembled the shop as it appeared at the turn of the century, the interior favored a 1960's unemployment office that I used to frequent in East Mesa, Arizona before I got my first book published. Laden with Larkin's shopping bags full of everything from furs and jewelry for her, to hand carved wooden toys for the twins, we made our last stop at Dom Knigi, the largest bookstore in the city, where Larkin bought books on everything we had seen during the last few days. The building itself was once the headquarters of the St. Petersburg branch of the Singer Sewing Machine Company and, as I wandered about the distinctive structure, I couldn't help but wonder what happened to the company that had flourished in that location almost a century ago. We had dinner across the street at Kavkazky and were back at the hotel before seven. Larkin was talking about the opera again, so I quietly deserted McAllister and, after a quick shower, once again went to keep the lonely bartender at the late night bar company.

When Irina joined me in her usual quiet fashion, I suppressed the urge to comment about her making the hat trick of overtime meetings. Even though the Russians were great hockey fans, I doubted the American triple play expression had crossed the North Atlantic.

"You take your work entirely too seriously." She said. "Who was that man you spoke with in front of the silver Beriozka this afternoon?"

"What the heck is a Beriozka?"

"It is the name of all government-run shops." She answered. "It means 'little birch tree', and before you ask, I do not know where the name originated."

"Seems funny." I said. "We don't call our supermarkets 'Douglas Firs'. It must lose something in the translation."

"You are changing the subject." She was losing her tour guide patience. "Who was that man?"

"Relax." I said, a bit surprised at her borderline rudeness. "He was just some guy that needed a match and when he found out we were Americans, insisted on practicing his English. What's the big deal?"

"It is not wise to speak so casually with strangers in Russia." She admonished sternly. "You never know to who you are talking."

"Whom." I could lecture too.

"Whom?"

"To whom you are talking." I said, "And it's not wise to have eye contact with people in New York City, but sometimes it can't be avoided."

"You are mocking me." She accused.

"And you are acting as if you have some kind of authority over me." I didn't think I had spoken sharply but she went through about three different expressions before she settled on a combination of despair and disappointment. Tears again formed in the corners of her eyes. This time the tears did not seem to be forced.

"I have made you angry." She whimpered. "This means you and your friends will not help me?"

"It means you're pushing too hard, Irina." I corrected. "I told you once that people on vacation don't want to hear about your personal problems. On one hand, you warn us about getting involved with unfamiliar situations and strangers while, at the same time, you try to convince us to assist you in pissing off your government while breaking God knows how many laws in the process. That's what I would call having your cake and eating it in Siberia."

"I will be honest." She announced, stiffening her shoulders and her resolve. "My government has known about your interests in Faberge products since even before you and your friends applied for your visas. I worked very hard to arrange to be assigned as your guide, calling in many favors.

"Two days before you arrived, I was called before my supervisors and two other men who were introduced to me as 'government officials'. I suspect they were agents of the KGB. They told me that you had visited a Faberge expert in France as well as an aborted attempt to speak with Theodore Faberge. While they say they do not believe you and your friends are subversives, they consider your behavior curious and suspect. I was told to watch you carefully and report any doubtful conduct on the part of any members of your group.

"In spite of the questionable actions of the last few days, I have reported nothing that would cause alarm among these paranoid and overcautious bureaucrats. This is contrary to any job security I might expect if you were to leave Russia without taking me with you. On blind faith I have protected you and your friends and you return this favor with indifference."

"What happens to your family if you leave Russia suddenly?"

"Stories about retaliation against a defector's family are mostly Western propaganda." She said. "The economy here is such that one less mouth to feed is a blessing and the government turns a blind eye to anyone who wishes to leave as long as they do not take any precious military secrets with them. I know of no secrets that I could offer a foreign government."

"So you think you can just walk away?" I asked.

"It is, of course, not that simple." She replied. "I am saying that, after I am gone, I will be neither missed nor sought, yet I can be of great value to you and your friend Mister McAllister."

I failed to see how she could help find treasures when she had supposedly already told us everything she knew.

"I can't promise anything." I said, "but I will tell Bobby what you have told me."

* * * * *

Had I not been so immersed in thought, I would have noticed that my hallway watchdog was absent from his perch as I made my way to my room. Although Irina did not exactly promise anything other than moral support for McAllister, her lingering touch on my hand, the veiled look in her eyes, and the provocative way she leaned toward me every time she spoke promised volumes that would exceed my greatest expectations. The Sanya-slash-Sargo mystery forgotten for awhile, McAllister's quest for greater riches ignored, I fantasized about Irina and what we might be able to be together if she once and for all renounced her past and obsessions and returned with me to the mountains of Arizona. The only emotion I had been feeling recently was lust and I was well ready to act on that sensation without guilt or second thought.

Until I opened the door.

He was standing in front of the window where I could see him as soon as I entered the room. Although the suit was different, it still looked like he was wearing someone else's clothes that had been slept in for the last week. He looked more confident than he did the last time I had seen him, perhaps because of the gun he held loosely. However, even with the unpointed pistol hanging at his side, he appeared to be nothing more than a bully and a coward. He moved sideways and back when I came into the room, the same motion he used when he ran like the gutless bastard he was, after he had pushed the button that took an innocent young life. My muscles tensed and my legs felt weak, not because of fear, but because I was undecided as to how to charge him and shove that gun up his ass without getting myself shot. I would have really hated to do something foolish before I had a chance to rumple that suit even further as I rearranged his limbs.

"Do not think of doing something foolish, American." Apparently I wasn't very good at hiding my emotions or intentions.

"Patek." I said, trying to make it sound obscene.

"Yes, you know my name." His accent was very thick and hesitant, as if he were still learning the language and was very unsure of himself. "I would be most interested to hear how you acquired this information."

"Your English is only fair." I said from behind clenched teeth. "Do you understand the meaning of 'fuck you'?" Patek bobbed his head in cynical amusement. It was clear that he would not be intimidated by me and his casual handling of the gun, still hanging idly at his side, showed his lack of annoyance. "You talk as if you are in charge of your own destiny at a time when you should be cautious. My superiors lecture me often about defiance in the face of a predicament. They say a reckless attitude can jeopardize an otherwise successful operation. In an organized society it is necessary to observe strict rules of conduct."

"Does your organized society allow for the senseless slaughter of innocent people?" I asked.

Patek didn't mind spouting asinine rhetoric. "Sometimes it is mandatory to make sacrifices to insure a positive outcome."

I snorted at his stupidity. "There is no possible way you can justify murdering three people, at least to those who did not give a royal shit about your organized society."

"That act has brought you to Russia." He answered. "It is much easier to find someone when someone else is being sought. In this case, you have sought me until I have found you."

"I thought you guys always worked in pairs." I said. "Doesn't it make it easier to rough up old women or jaywalkers? Or can't you find anyone who wants to work with a piece of low life pond scum like you?"

The word "jaywalkers" confused him but he tried to bluff his way through.

"This has become a problem I feel I must give my personal attention." He said. "I must make amends for a slight error I made in Paris. But first I must know how you came to know my name."

"You were on America's Most Wanted, ass hole."

That confused him even further. I could see him trying to make sense out of my remark, but a knock at the door startled both of us.

"You will not answer." Patek ordered, raising the gun for the first time.

The knock sounded again, louder and more insistent. "Grange! Open up! I need to talk with you!" It was McAllister.

"No answer." Patek repeated.

"C'mon, Grange, open up." The knocking continued.

"He knows that if I'm not in the bar, this is the only other place I could be." I wanted McAllister in the room to better my odds. I wasn't thinking of the danger he might have to face.

Patek waved the gun for me to move and we circled each other as he worked his way to the door. It was clear he didn't appreciate or anticipate the interruption and was perturbed by the unexpected change in his plans. He took up a position next to the door and, in a move that had to be taught in some KGB academy, swung the door and yanked McAllister into the room in one smooth motion. As McAllister made a vaudevillian stumble into and over the bed, Patek shut the door quickly and took a stance with the gun pointed halfway between us. McAllister struggled to his feet, ready to be indignant, but when he saw the pistol he stopped, arms across the bed, his knees still on the floor.

"Your friend has made things difficult." Patek said, frowning. "Difficult, but not impossible."

"What the fuck is going on here?" McAllister kept looking back and forth between Patek and me until it dawned on him who was standing over him. "You!" He said, his eyes narrowing. He turned to me. "This is him, isn't it?"

I nodded. McAllister got to his feet slowly, not taking his eyes off of Patek. "Why is this ass hole still alive, Grange?"

"Brave words." Patek smiled wickedly. But you seem to have confusion. I am the one who asks questions and when I am satisfied with the answers, you are the ones who will die."

"Are you nuts?" McAllister glared at Patek. "We happen to be American citizens. You can't afford to murder two Americans and expect to get away with it."

Patek almost laughed. "You think your country of origin makes a difference to what happens to you at my hands in my country?"

He asked. "Did it help your friends in France?" His expression changed to serious distaste. "You are in Russia now," he banged a fist against his chest as if the country belonged to him personally, "and you will die by my rules.

"Russia will not kill you," he spat at McAllister, "your friend who comes to know so much will do that for me. Then, in a fit of belated remorse, he will jump to his death from this very window." He moved closer to the window. "So now you will tell me what you know of me or your tragic fates will be far more painful and lingering."

"We know your name is Patek." McAllister said without hesitation. "We know your partner is a guy named Rastov who is supposed to be even more ill-tempered than you."

I couldn't believe my ears. "What the hell are you doing, Bobby?"

"Shut up, Grange." McAllister was talking to me but he was staring intently at Patek. "I can take a bullet. Larkin wouldn't like me to be mutilated. Too messy."

"Your friend is wise." Patek's evil grin returned. "You would do well to learn from him, Scribe. In Russia we have far worse fates than a fall from an open window for those who write books."

"You can't be serious." I was talking to McAllister. "He can't get away with this. I can't believe you're knuckling under to this piece of dog shit in a bad suit."

"Back up, Grange. I can't live forever. I've had a good run at life. We all have to go when it's time to go." He turned back to Patek. "If I tell you everything you want to know, you have to promise not to harm my wife. She doesn't know anything about this. She thinks we're here on vacation."

Patek didn't answer. "Who told you my name?" He asked. How did you know where to find me? What do you know of my business?"

"My brother-in-law thought you were Russian from the way you talked. He remembered you just before he died. We found you here because one of your fellow agents, a beautiful one at that, named Sanya Roskovin or something like that, gave us your name. Seems that your own people wanted your identity to be known to us."

I couldn't believe McAllister said all that with a straight face.

"I know of no such person!" He spat.

"Well, she knew of you, a beautiful red head.

"Balderdash!" He replied.

"I haven't tried that dish. Is it Russian cuisine?" McAllister smiled. "We know you're KGB in charge of a forgery mill dealing in stolen Faberge products and your boss is a guy named Kalashnikov, or something like that. We have no proof of anything and we probably know less than you thought. We don't even know your first name."

"Grigori." Patek said, without thinking.

"Listen, Grigori." McAllister spread his hands in a pleading gesture. "Maybe we can make a deal.

"Since we have been here, we have learned something that could make you a very rich man."

Patek waved the gun for him to continue.

"We have heard about a stolen Faberge treasure that we think we know how to find. It's in America and both Grange and I have the connections and resources to be able to find it. We can cut you in on the deal."

Patek laughed a short barking sound. "You speak of fairy tales." He said. "Russian children hear these stories from their grandmothers from the time they are old enough to listen. Many people have searched for this treasure and found nothing. Why do you think you can succeed where others have failed?"

"I have a history of succeeding where others have fallen short." McAllister allowed the hint of a smile creep to the corners of his mouth.

Patek thought for a moment, but shook his head. "I must know everything you know." He said. "Then I will decide."

"Don't tell him shit, Bobby." I said. "It won't make a damned bit of difference!"

"Cool it, Grange." McAllister said without taking his eyes of Patek.

Patek suddenly pointed the gun toward me. "I don't need you now my writer friend. . ."

"Patek." McAllister said calmly. "I was talking to you," not unlike a school teacher taking control of her class.

Patek returned his attention to McAllister. I was grateful.

"Please excuse Grange, Mister Patek. He's still a little upset over the loss of his girlfriend. Certainly you can understand that." But before Patek could reply, McAllister continued. "It's a show of good faith, Grange. We'll tell Mister Patek everything we know and when he sees that we are being straight-up with him, he will know he can trust us.

"We know you are a part of a counterfeit ring who substitutes art pieces with expensive fakes. We know you tried to steal Antonio's Spaskoie egg in Monaco and might have stolen it from his cottage in France after he was killed. We wanted to expose your operation and, at the same time, boost my reputation as a serious collector of Faberge art.

"Instead, we found out about the stolen treasure and decided that we probably should concentrate our efforts in that direction."

I decided to keep quiet.

Patek looked baffled.

"You join us, Grigori and you have a choice." He told him. "If we find the treasure, you can be a hero in your own country or you can take your share and start a new life someplace else. What do you think?"

"You have learned a great deal, Comrade McAllister. I must say that I am impressed. But I think you are trying to confuse my loyalty with a promise that you cannot keep." Patek moved closer to the window, a response to McAllister's nonchalant move to his left. "You are a very rich man, yet you offer me none of your wealth, only a chance at finding something that probably does not exist. In the meantime, you will scheme to do away with me at your first opportunity. I am not a fool, American!"

"Then tell me what you want." McAllister insisted, taking yet another casual step to his left. "There has to be some arrangement we can make."

"The only arrangement I seek is for my own security. I know of no such girl with red hair! You are a liar, American. You and your friends have failed, and the penalty you and your traveling companions must pay for failure is with your lives."

"Are you sure we can't work a deal?" McAllister sounded more annoyed than afraid.

"Certainly." Patek answered, smiling broadly and turning the gun on McAllister. "The deal is; I live and you die."

McAllister made a couple of slow but delicate moves that made him look like a third base baseball coach. He wiped his forehead, patted his right shoulder, and crossed his arms, all the time smiling ruefully at Patek.

The tinkle of the glass distracted me for a millisecond but my attention was immediately returned to Patek who grunted and, wide eyed and opened mouthed, vaulted forward, tripping over the chair as he fell. It wasn't until he sat up that I saw the hole, both in the window and in Patek's body, a neat little puncture where his right arm met his shoulder, a hole that was already leaking a steady stream of blood. When I finally got around to looking at McAllister, he was sticking the gun that, only a second ago was pointed at him, into Patek's neck. "Not a sound." He warned him.

I looked back at the hole in the window, craning my neck, hesitant to step into the frame for fear of becoming another target.

"How did you do that?" I asked, astonished.

"Later." McAllister answered.

"You will pay dearly for this, American." Patek growled.

"A minute ago you were prepared to shoot me and throw Grange out the window." McAllister said. "I don't see many things worse than that, Comrade."

I peeked out the window to see if I could tell from where the shot had come.

"You won't see anything, Grange." McAllister said as if reading my mind.

McAllister motioned me to join him at the far end of the room out of Patek's earshot.

Before I could ask any questions, McAllister held a finger to his mouth and began. "It was Mark."

"Mark?"

"Mark is a former Navy Seal and he really knows his stuff, don't you think? You saw him when he left the boat before we landed and he has been covering us ever since. We keep in contact with him through a radio that's about as big as a cigarette. It's disguised as one of Larkin's tubes of lipstick." McAllister smiled. "Clever, huh?"

I was amazed.

McAllister then went to the window to make another curious signal after motioning me to remain where I was.

I had a sudden flash of realization. "Jesus, Bobby. This room is wired. They're listening to us right now!"

"Relax, Grange. This is the listener right here." He waved the pistol at Patek. "And quit calling me Jesus, will you, Grange?"

"Now how the hell would you know that?" I asked.

"Because you just called me. . ."

"Be serious! If you possibly can for Christ's sake."

"There you go again." He said with an overabundance of confidence exuding from his aura. But before he gave me a chance to really lose my remaining composure, he continued. "I saw him in the lobby." McAllister flashed his famous Georgia shit eating smile. "When it dawned on me who he was, I decided to check out where he had come from so I knocked on the door he had just exited. There was no answer, so I sneaked a look. A stairway led to a basement room that looked like a control center at NASA, but no one was there.

"When I caught up to him again, he was flashing an I.D. at the hall porter who took one look and took off like a greyhound out of a starting box. When he went into your room, I hid in the stairwell until you showed up. I had my ear to the door almost as soon as you shut it. Pretty neat, huh? If timing is the secret to good comedy, it looks like the joke is on him."

"And now the joke is on us." I said. "Here we are with a wounded KGB agent and no place to go. What the hell are we going to do now?"

Patek smiled through his pain. "Your friend is right, American." He said rather harshly. "Give yourself up now and I will see that things go easier on all of you. Try to escape now and everyone will suffer."

"I don't think so, my dear comrade, Patek." McAllister taunted his quarry. You have lost." McAllister assumed his comfortable theatrical pose. "You sound like you took a cheap correspondence course from the Gestapo School of Snoops and Intimidation. I haven't heard such pathetic drivel since I last saw my departed friend, David R. Banning!" McAllister folded his hands in front of him. "Oh. Excuse me. You don't know Mister Banning. Too bad, you two would have made a great pair." McAllister looked at me to see if I was enjoying his state of recurring madness masked as humor.

I chose not to encourage him.

"I haven't quite come across a predicament like this before. Close, yes. But never a real KGB agent. However, I did see a scene similar to this in an old 'B' movie on the Turner Late Show on channel seventeen one time." McAllister feigned exasperation, but mine was real. "Damn! I can't remember how it ended."

I was getting bored.

McAllister must have noticed my frustration as he again joined me at the far corner of the room where I waited like some Pekingese mutt."

"What are we going to do now, Bobby?" I had to ask.

"You once said to me that you didn't want to be Don Quixote's Sancho. Now you expect me to be Sir Quixote?" McAllister relished victorious moments like this. After all, he did have a few notches on his pirate's sword. "What would the Gallant Knight do in a situation like this, Grange?"

"P u l e e e s e!" I couldn't take it anymore.

Patek couldn't hear us but he could not help but notice McAllister's strange demeanor. He simply remained quiet.

"Did you think that I would not be fully prepared for a situation of this magnitude?"

"I didn't expect anything, Bobby. Just cut the crap, will you?"

"I have it all planned out, don't you worry." McAllister leaned closer and whispered. "We're doing the only logical thing to do, Grange."

"Which is?" I whispered back.

"We're getting the hell out of here!"

Patek heard that reply loud and clear and he was as unimpressed as I was. "How will you do this, American?" He asked, gently probing his wound as he spoke. "You cannot leave by airplane and our patrol boats will overtake your pretty yacht before you can lift your anchor."

McAllister ignored Patek. He straightened and whispered to me. "Go tell Larkin that everything went according to plan. Then come right back."

"Reluctantly, I left the room and hurried down the hall. I rapped lightly on the door of McAllister's room and before I could lower my hand, Larkin threw open the door. Behind her, sitting on the edge of the bed, Irina sat with both hands covering her mouth.

Both women looked relieved to see me.

"Bobby said to tell you that everything is going according to plan." I said. "He said you would know what to do from here on.

She nodded; relieved that her husband said things were going well, but anxious about whatever it was she had to do next.

"He told me to come right back." I pointed, still waiting for a response.

She nodded again and shut the door in my face.

I hurried back to the room.

"I need to know what you have in mind, Bobby." I said after I had closed the door. "This whole thing is making me very nervous."

"We have an emergency evacuation plan." He pulled me back to his favorite corner and again lowered his voice so Patek could not hear. "One by one, everyone makes their way to the Second Prize. If anybody gets stopped, they are to use the excuse of taking dirty clothes to be laundered or to exchange items. When everyone reaches the boat, we sail for Helsinki as fast as we can."

"You call that a plan?" I asked, skeptical and disappointed. "Have you forgotten that we have to sail a two hundred foot yacht past half the Russian Navy? What do you expect them to do when they see us idly cruising out to sea? "

"Wave good-bye."

"Get real, Bobby!"

McAllister looked exasperated. "I told you before, Grange, he said, "they want us to leave. It's all part of the game. Everything that has happened in the last week has been carefully choreographed to make us believe we can find Faberge treasure. Until we find it, or until they lose all patience, we are safe as if we were still in mother's womb. All we have to do is play by their rules and make it look as if we don't know we are being manipulated."

"What about him?" I pointed to Patek.

"I think he's acting on his own without any official authorization." He answered. "After all, he deserted his post."

"What if you're wrong?" I asked. "One little flaw in your great plan and we go to the bottom of the Baltic in a ball of flames."

"Wrong again." He said. "We would never make it that far." He shook his head. "But what would you have us do?" He asked, using the gun to point at Patek. "Wait around until his buddies find out he's not sitting in the basement with his earphones in place? We have a simple choice right now. Stay here and answer for shooting an officer of the KGB," he paused significantly, "or head for open sea. Do you want to die in a cold Russian prison cell or take charge of your own destiny?"

I looked at Patek. He was still leaning against the bed, holding his wounded shoulder, his expression remarkably bland. McAllister was undeniably right and I was more than mildly disturbed that our options were so limited. When I looked back to McAllister he was studying his watch.

"Ten forty-five." He said. "By eleven-thirty, anyone not aboard will be left behind. That will put us in Helsinki by dawn." He turned the pistol around, holding it by the barrel as he held it out to me. "He's your trophy, Grange. Do whatever you deem fit to make sure he doesn't bother us before we can get to the American embassy in Finland." He placed a hand on my shoulder. "It's your call, my friend."

Before I could take my eyes off the gun, now inexplicably in my hand, McAllister was about to close the door behind him. He paused and said, "Don't miss the boat, Grange."

Had Patek chosen that opportunity to rush me, he might have been able to regain the upper hand. Instead, he elected to talk.

"It is not too late, American." It was clear he was still trying to run bravado and arrogance to his advantage. "Tie me up and you will have time to make it to your embassy. Your friends will never make it to sanctuary in Finland. Our Navy boats and the planes of our Air Force will have them surrounded before they are out of sight of the fortress."

For months I had fantasized about what I would do if I had Patek within my reach. He had haunted my dreams, ruined my digestion, and brought out a darker, far less pleasant side of me that I had not known existed. Sweat mingled with the gun in my hand and the room began to swim as imaginary, oppressive heat made my throat constrict painfully. My hearing failed and my sight blurred as I fought with demons and angels alike and silently cursed McAllister for leaving me to make this decision by myself. If I had been able to hear some input from my friend McAllister, I could react to suggestions or argue with him in a sane and rational manner. Left alone, I could only wonder how I would be regarded by my fellow man if I took this scumbag's life. What would Sally want me to do? How about Antonio? McAllister's driver? My God! All I knew was how I would be judged by a higher authority at the appropriate time.

Although I am not predisposed to committing cold blooded murder in fashion, and I do not know if it was my religious upbringing, but I knew what I wanted to do to Patek right there at that very moment with that very pistol. But maybe it was just simple cowardice that kept me from pulling the trigger. It wasn't the first time.

Instead, I transferred the gun to my left hand and began tearing the bedclothes into narrow strips. In spite of his limited mental capacity, Patek knew I had reached a decision and he breathed a long sigh of relief.

"It takes a special kind of person to kill in cold blood." He said in a voice that knew his personal crisis was over. "I knew that your American sense of fair play would prevail. Had you been Russian, you would not have been so tentative."

"Shut up, borscht breath." I said, taking out two different kinds of aggression on the sheets. "It's enough for me to know that your superiors are going to do a much more painful and impressionable number on you when they find you trussed up like an Egyptian mummy."

His laugh was like a short bark. "Painful, yes." He winced. The ironic snort of laughter had aggravated his wound. "But only for the stern lecture I will receive. My punishment will be to seek revenge for this failure so we will meet again, American, and perhaps next time you will not have a hidden assassin to do your dirty work for you."

"You're in a pretty precarious position to be threatening me with another meeting between us." I said. "In fact, you're trying to agitate a very unstable man right now. I want to kill you."

"But you won't."

"How do you know I won't finish you off right now, just to prevent another undesirable meeting with you?"

"You have already demonstrated that you have no stomach for killing in anything but self-defense." He smiled a demonic expression that telegraphed his delighted anticipation. "Maybe next time I will use that knowledge to my advantage. Perhaps, instead of coming after you, I will shoot the little In-tourist defecting whore. However, in the future, I will not act in haste as I did with your girlfriend in Paris. Next time, I will be sure to take my personal pleasure first."

The bullet hit him a fraction of an inch above his sneeringly curled upper lip. In a split second, he knew he was dead as his eyes widened in shock and his head jerked violently against the bed. A fine spray of grey tinted blood erupted from the back of his head, turning into a thick, spreading stain on the mattress behind him. Not knowing that the rest of him was already dead, his left leg jerked convulsively, his heel beating an uneven staccato on the hardwood floor. Oddly enough, the noise of the post traumatic knocking sounded much louder than the sound of the shot. I looked unbelievably at the gun and dully wondered why it wasn't smoking.

I had fired left handed, a circumstance that normally would not have allowed me to hit a wall in a four-by-four room. As the leg finally stopped its useless drumming and the final tension released its grip on the lifeless body, I let the gun slip from my fingers and clatter to the floor. I looked at my watch. Time of death, I thought, eleven-oh-five.

* * * * *

I have no vivid recollections of the next half hour of my life. McAllister told me I looked like one of his many friends who had just returned from a dangerous mission in Viet Nam. Sort of like one of the pod people when I boarded the Second Prize, but my only memory of that time is vague images; a blurred mental picture of a surprised hall porter pointing me out to no one in particular as I exited the lobby of the Evropeskaya, cloudy impressions of back streets and alleys as I made my way to the docks, somehow remembering to keep the fortress on my right to keep from getting lost, a hazy concept of Irina calling to me from the deck of the Second Prize as I staggered blindly up the pier.

My next clear awareness was watching the lights of St. Petersburg recede and people waving good-bye as I stood at the stern rail, wondering if I was just imagining things, and if I had lost my hearing. Puzzled, I turned around to see McAllister standing about five feet behind me, a concerned and anxious look on his face.

"I can't hear the engines, Bobby." Even my own voice sounded far away and childlike.

"We're running on the auxiliary electrical propulsion system." His voice sounded normal, but uncertain. "It's quiet, but we can only make three knots. Are you okay, my friend?"

"I'm fine." I answered automatically. "Won't it take a long time to get to Helsinki at three knots?"

"We plan to use the regular engines as soon as we clear the harbor." He was talking to me as if I were a child, someone to be pitied. "Are you sure you're all right?"

"Sure." I smiled weakly, without feeling. "You know me. Kill a guy and bounce right back. You of all people should know how easy that is."

McAllister shook his head. "This was something you had to find out for yourself, Grange." He was speaking frankly, but not without sympathy. "I could have told you how you were going to feel this very moment, but you would not have believed. The truth of the matter is, you have only hastened what would have happened sooner or later. You may not agree, but the world is a better place because this happened sooner.

"Patek's death at your hands is something you wanted since that day in Paris. If you had not gotten him tonight, you would still be burning. Revenge is a powerful emotion and second guessing yourself now is only part of the aftershock.

"If you think that Sally is going to get justice any other way, you are sadly mistaken. If you thought that Sally could come back by anything you did, you are even more in error."

"I killed a man tonight." I said, without feeling. "More than anyone, I should know that two wrongs don't make a right. I have preached to you about violence and tonight I shot a defenseless man."

"You saved France the cost of a trial."

I didn't like the thought of a man dying at my hands to be justification for the overworked criminal system of Paris. "So you suggest we base justice on economics?" I asked rhetorically.

"Nothing I could say right now would be right, Grange." It was almost as if he regretted leaving me in that hotel room. "But someday, you will see the wisdom in what you did tonight."

"Thanks, Bobby." He was right; nothing he could tell me would ease my tortured mind. "I'll be sure to mention your name on judgment day."

"As an example," he warned, "not as a reference."

I almost smiled.

*

Over the years, I have had occasion to interview several war veterans from various conflicts, a suspected mafia hit man, and even a woman convicted of murdering over twenty terminally ill patients left in her care. Each of them had their own rationalization for killing; the soldiers eliminating a nameless and faceless enemy for God, country, and apple pie. The contract killer for removing those even too dangerous or traitorous for the mob. And, the nurse who portrayed herself as an angel of mercy. Their common bond was a sense of duty and a job well done that I could not force my troubled mind to recognize no matter how hard I tried. I knew I had rid the world of a cold and ruthless killer, saved the country of France the cost of a trial and subsequent incarceration, and avenged Sally's untimely and cruel death, but I questioned my right to act as judge and executioner upon another human being no matter how despicable that person had been. But instead of feeling pride and honor at ridding the world of a self-confessed vermin, I felt hollow and guilty at second guessing God and his purpose for creating such an abomination. McAllister, having been in several confrontations in which he took part in life and death situations, offered only silent sympathy as I stood looking at the city I would never forget, not because of its beauty and history, but because of the flight of a few ounces of lead and the destruction that resulted from that seemingly insignificant distance from barrel to brain.

A low rumble signaled the starting of the engines and the Second Prize picked up speed quickly causing white foam to cap the wake on an otherwise calm and black sea. Above and behind the bridge, a scoop shaped dish began to rotate, searching the darkness for any sign of pursuit. I waved again to my imaginary farewell wishers. McAllister watched me from a distance then took me by the arm and steered me toward the lounge.

"If anybody ever needed a drink," he began, "I think it might be you."

I agreed.

McAllister had apparently chased everyone from the lounge area because we were undisturbed as we sat in near darkness and McAllister watched me drink, making sure the booze was not as free flowing as it would have been during a celebratory occasion. Minutes stretched into hours as McAllister's prediction gained credibility as we closed the distance between us and the relative safety of Finnish waters.

Somewhere around two-thirty, or what must have been the halfway point, I broke my silence.

"I don't hear the twenty inch guns of a Russian destroyer behind us."

"And you won't." McAllister was not sure of how much the rum was affecting me. He looked at his watch. "Right about now Captain Olsen is contacting the Finns to tell them we are fearing pursuit by the Russians. I personally don't care for the wording of that message, but he said it is the proper thing to do and he is the captain. We should have an escort in no time.

"As soon as we land in Helsinki, we will have to go to the American embassy."

I looked at him through a haze. "To turn myself in?" I asked skeptically.

"The very last thing we do is say anything about Patek." He answered. "Chances are, they know nothing about what happened last night."

"So why go to the embassy? Why don't we keep going until we're back in the States?"

"We don't have any passports." He explained patiently. "They are still sitting in a drawer somewhere near the front desk of the Evropeiskaya. The law says we have to stop at the nearest American embassy to report the loss."

"Aren't they going to ask why we didn't go to the embassy in St. Petersburg?"

"We're supposedly fleeing St. Petersburg." He reminded me. "Besides, there is no embassy in St. Petersburg. Only Moscow."

I thought back to Patek who had told me I had enough time to make it to the embassy before an alarm was sounded. A clever lie. I caught myself halfway through a thought about what I would say to him when I saw him again.

"What do I say if I'm accused of murder?" I asked instead.

"By the Americans or the Finns?"

"Either." I answered, frowning at yet another complication.

"If it's the Finnish police, you won't leave the embassy until we can get you out of the country. If it's our people, you still have your Constitutional rights. You don't say anything until we can get you legal representation."

"Ned Hoffman?" I asked.

"Who else?" Was the reply.

I was too tired to respond. "I think I want to lie down for a while."

"Are you going to be okay?"

"Yeah, fine." Again, an automatic response. "Maybe I'll go downstairs and watch Gilligan's Island on your entertainment system. Maybe I can find the episode when they nearly got off the island."

"You're trying to be funny."

"No, I'm trying to be sarcastic." I said uncertainly. "This isn't the proper time for humor." To myself, I sounded rational and glib; he would have been in for an argument. Instead, he nodded and pointed toward the door.

"Still remember which room is yours?" He asked.

"Of course." I answered, wondering why he had asked.

Unable to sleep, I stared at the cabin ceiling for an undetermined amount of time until I heard the higher pitched hum of a smaller boat's engine running alongside the Second Prize. I looked out a porthole to see a twenty foot gun boat with Finnish markings. Even with its fifty caliber gun mounted on the front deck, I was not reassured by their presence. Knowing the Finn's history of neutrality, I was certain they would stand without firing a shot should the Russians elect to blow us out of the water. Although I was certain that Captain Olsen was in radio contact with our escort, the distance they kept from the Second Prize only bolstered my impression that they had no intention of being anything other than witnesses to our destruction.

It was a surprise, therefore, when, as the sun was just beginning to cut into the darkness behind us, the laboring engines slowed and we joined the maritime traffic surrounding Helsinki's busy harbor.

At first, the physical and cultural closeness between Helsinki and St. Petersburg made me nervous. Much like St. Petersburg, Helsinki had been once ravaged, not by a World War siege, but by an 1808 fire that burned the city to the ground. John Ehrenstrom rebuilt the city, carefully charting and restoring the city with wide streets, plenty of parks, and buildings designed by distinguished architects like Carl Ludvig Engel. We docked at a crowded marina and McAllister delegated a landing party in two shifts to make the trip to the embassy. It was decided that Irina would go in the second wave, the better for us to prepare the folks at the consulate with her decision to leave Russia with us. During the short drive to the American compound, McAllister must have asked me three times if I was all right as I silently watched the city as we headed east on Mannersheimintie, past the Parliament House and the National Museum.

McAllister fumed at our treatment when we arrived at the embassy; that of a security risk as opposed to citizens seeking aid. We were cleared through no less than half a dozen check points, each requiring positive identification, inane questioning, and long and boring waiting on furniture designed for utility and not for comfort. It was almost noon before the five of us, McAllister, Larkin, Mark, one of Mark's peers, and I, were ushered into the office of a bored and self-important attaché named James Hayes who pointedly did not introduce us to the other embassy staffer who sat silently in a corner smoking an unlighted pipe.

"So you fled St. Petersburg without your passports," Hayes was saying, "because you wanted to help your guide defect to the United States. How did you manage to sail a ship the size of most American destroyers past the bulk of the Russian Navy?"

McAllister smiled as if daring Hayes to call him a liar. "Just lucky, I guess. The point is, we acted in good faith and reported to the nearest United States Embassy as required by law. Do you have a problem with that?"

"My 'problem', Mister McAllister, is why didn't you just wait until your visas had expired to leave?" Hayes sounded more like a police officer than a diplomat.

"Because we would have been subject to an exit search that would have turned up our stowaway." McAllister answered with exaggerated patience. "What is the matter with you? We are no illegal immigrants trying to make a run for the American borders. We are citizens attempting to go home with as little trouble as possible. What is that going to take?"

"At this point, we are not yet certain, Mister McAllister." Hayes was using the "we" term to avoid being blamed personally for any difficulties. Not trusting McAllister's normally short fuse, I decided to try my diplomatic skills.

"Mister Hayes," my voice was squeaky from lack of use. I cleared my throat and began again. "Mister Hayes, Mister McAllister is financially and politically connected to two Western powers that are not what you would call sympathetic to Soviet ideals." McAllister looked at me in surprise. "Because of these affiliations, Mister McAllister did not wish to create an International incident simply because he wanted to help a repressed individual seek freedom. We all agreed to act a little impulsively to avoid embarrassment."

"I'm afraid it's a little too late for that, Mister Lawton." The man with the pipe spoke for the first time. While McAllister was annoyed by the interruption, I was nervously suspicious. I didn't remember my name being mentioned in front of the previously silent observer.

"Last night," he continued when he was certain he had everyone's attention, "we monitored an unusual amount of radio traffic emanating from the St. Petersburg area. Although we don't pretend to understand all of it, we do know that Navy and Air Force units were put on full alert and then, sometime around two-thirty, mysteriously ordered to stand down."

"Who the hell are you?" McAllister asked, leaning forward on the arms of his chair.

"My name is Russ Miller." He answered. "I'm the agriculture liaison officer connected with the embassy."

"Well, we're not hauling any produce. What the hell. . ."

Miller interrupted. "If you will allow me, Mister McAllister."

Miller got our attention.

"Such behavior by the Russians is highly unusual," he continued without waiting to be acknowledged, "and we were curious, to say the least, until we heard from the Russian ambassador at nine o'clock this morning."

McAllister's eyes narrowed suspiciously.

"It seems the Russians are missing some valuable works of art." Miller tapped the tobacco in his pipe. "National treasures at that. They have asked us to investigate as they believe someone in your party might be responsible."

"Absurd!" McAllister blurted. I wondered if anyone had noticed that I had been holding my breath.

"Nevertheless," Miller was saying, "we are obligated to investigate these charges and I might add, Mister McAllister, things do not look good at this point."

"What the hell is that supposed to mean?" McAllister was dangerously closer to an outright explosion.

"In addition to notifying us of their complaint," Miller went on, unperturbed, "our Soviet friends have filed a formal complaint with our host country. That means the Finns will not allow your ship to depart their waters until our investigation is complete. Adding to that is a report we received just minutes ago from the States." Miller reached into his pocket and withdrew a single sheet of paper, folded lengthwise. "It seems that a certain police inspector from Florida has information that implicates you, Mister McAllister, in just about every crime known to man." He consulted the paper. "Petty theft, fraud, larceny, extortion, murder, and." He paused, "failure to pay Florida taxes."

"Frank Kipper." McAllister said under his breath, seething.

"Mister Miller," Larkin spoke for the first time, "my husband has repeatedly successfully defended himself against these ludicrous charges invented by a spiteful and vengeful man. Why do you give any credence to what this man says?"

Miller stopped tamping his pipe. "Because he is a police officer." He said simply.

McAllister snorted. Larkin threw up her hands in a hopeless gesture.

"What exactly is Mister McAllister accused of?" I asked.

"Nothing." Hayes admitted. "We are acting on a complaint and conducting an investigation."

"What am I supposed to have stolen?" McAllister demanded.

"Unspecified art treasures." Hayes responded, his face a blank. "We expect more information this afternoon."

"What about Miss Denikoff?" I asked.

"Who?" Hayes was caught off guard. "Oh, the In-tourist guide." He shuffled some papers on his desk. "Have her come by this afternoon. We will process her case on an independent basis. We have no argument with her decision to defect, only her choice of avenues."

McAllister was on his feet. "Listen you little toad." He leaned over the desk that separated him from Hayes. "I don't have to take this shit from you!"

Miller hadn't moved, but his tone took on a more commanding presence. "You don't have a choice, Mister McAllister. Any attempt by you to undermine this investigation or leave Helsinki without this embassy's approval will be dealt with in accordance with International Law. You will find that being forcibly detained under those conditions can be most uncomfortable."

Larkin had her hands on her husband's arm, encouraging him to retake his seat. "How long can we expect to be detained?" She asked Hayes.

"Not long." He answered, regaining his composure quickly. "I would say three days at the outside."

McAllister reacted as if he had been kicked. Quite frankly, I would have expected a much longer delay. At Miller's mention of McAllister's checkered past, the two employees that had accompanied us in the first wave both raised their eyebrows but remained silent while McAllister groused and Larkin tried to calm him and I tried to remain invisible. Fortunately, it didn't take long for McAllister to accept our temporary inconvenience and we were out of the compound far quicker than we had entered.

"What do you make of that?" I asked after looking out the rear window of the limo for the third time.

"I wish I knew." McAllister was still grumbling. "The only thing I can figure is it was some kind of a stall."

"A what?"

"Something went wrong someplace." McAllister said thoughtfully.

"They needed more time for something."

"Patek!" I said. "Somehow he was an integral part of this and without him, they needed time to recruit and train a replacement. You said yourself that he probably acted on his own when he confronted me. We probably put a damper on some grand design when I shot him."

"It's more than that." McAllister replied. He turned to Larkin.

"When is the last time you heard about an agriculture consultant monitoring Russian radio traffic? That guy Miller is CIA. I'm sure of it."

"Why would the CIA be involved in this?" Larkin asked.

"Because they are the only agency in the world that we haven't dealt with so far." McAllister smiled. "Why else?"

"Be serious." Larkin admonished.

"They aren't." McAllister was verbalizing as fast as he was thinking. "Patek may have been a stumbling block, but I don't think his death was all that important. If it was, Grange would probably be looking out through barred windows by now.

"Look at it this way. The Russians know damned well we didn't steal any of their so called art treasures. You and I know we didn't steal anything. But our own American friends don't know that. Just the fact that we are probably going to have to produce the eggs we have on board the Second Prize is going to cause an air of confusion even though we can secure legitimate receipts and documentation proving they belong to us. This complaint is going to be investigated and the authorities are going to tell the Russians that they could find no evidence to support their claim knowing that the Russians are not going to be happy with that kind of response.

"Essentially, the Americans – specifically the CIA – are going to know that the Russians are going to watch us carefully, hoping for a chance to recover their supposedly stolen artwork. That means that if some CIA operative happens to see a Russian counterpart from the KGB snooping around us, they might be inclined to turn a blind eye to their activities."

"So the Russians accuse you of stealing something so they have an excuse to follow you in case you find something?" I summarized. "If we do manage to pull off a miracle and locate any part of the Faberge treasure, it's going to be better covered than a football player's murder trial. Why not invite the press along? Larkin can make sandwiches, you could sell gold coins, and I could autograph dust covers."

"It would have taken us five days to get back to the States," McAllister said to no one in particular, "plus another half day to take on fuel somewhere along the way. They had to stall us for another couple of days. Why?"

Nobody answered.

* * * * *

Wanting to keep a low profile, I spent as much time away from the Second Prize as reasonably possible. Our second wave of temporarily displaced refugees had obtained the necessary paperwork to apply for limited visas and I was the first to go through the unpleasant experience of dealing with apathetic immigration officials who only grudgingly accepted my application for a seventy-two hour stay in their country. Shortly after four in the afternoon of our arrival in Finland, I returned to the ship and slept through the night.

Sensing that my best opportunity to remain out of sight and out of mind was to stay as far away from McAllister as possible, I made arrangements for a tour of Helsinki's islands south of the city. My motives were not entirely selfish. Since the brunt of the embassy's investigation centered on McAllister, I was making myself unavailable to inadvertently contradicting anything he might tell the authorities; and if the Russians did decide to discover their murdered KGB agent, I was distancing myself from my friends and even drawing attention away from Irina, should I be arrested. I thought I was being remarkably considerate.

I had planned to see the eighteenth century fortification of Suomenlinna Sveaborg, reputed to be the largest sea fortress in the world. Often called the Gibraltar of the North, it was built in 1748 when Finland was part of Sweden and Marshal Augustin Ehrensvard was its architect and first commander. The fortress had fallen to the Russians in 1808 but defended itself successfully against an Anglo-French fleet during the Crimean War in 1855.

Instead, I wound up on the nearby island of Susisaari. Shrugging mentally, I made the best of the mix-up, visiting the museum and the nearby island of Kustaanmiekka with its depiction of the lives of the nineteenth century Finnish gentry as well as the Coast Guard Defense Artillery Museum and the tour of the submarine Vesikka.

When I returned to Market Square on the mainland, I sought out the kiosk where I had purchased my tour ticket to see why I had wound up on the wrong island. Closer examination of the departure schedule showed my mistake almost immediately. In the crowded confusion of the hectic square, where most every sightseeing tour both began and ended, I had simply misread the roster of the boat names and departure times and boarded the right boat at the wrong time. The man in the booth noticed my confused expression change to realization and embarrassment.

"You are having difficulties?" He asked in an accent that sounded both Swedish and Russian.

I explained what happened. He smiled.

"It is most common." He said. "In the busy square it is easy to become confused. One minute you think you are going to Susisari, and the next you find yourself on Kustaanmiekka. Embarrassing, yes. But unless you persist in going to the same place time after time, no harm is done."

"Do I owe you any money?" I asked, not wanting to cheat the system.

"No." He waved me off. "What is it you Americans say? 'No harm, no foul.'"

I thanked him and wandered off, suddenly wondering what it was that was trying to make its way through the overflowing electrical impulses in my gray matter. I strolled along the brightly colored stalls that sold everything – flowers, fruits and vegetables; trinkets, fresh fish, – until long past the time when the shop keepers closed their booths; and walked casually back to the Second Prize. Mark met me at the gangplank.

"Mister McAllister is having dinner at the American Steakhouse at the Hesperia Hotel. He asked if you would join him there."

"Yeah, thanks." His presence made me nervous. I looked at the "Taksi" stand and the idle cabs.

"Are you all right, Mister Lawton?"

"Yeah." I said, I was sick of people asking me that question. I ran my fingers through my hair. "Listen, Mark. . ."

"Forget it, Mister Lawton." He knew what I was going to try to say. "Mister McAllister told me that you wanted that guy. That's why I only tagged him in the shoulder. If you hadn't finished the job, I would have. Buster was a friend of mine for almost fifteen years."

"Buster?"

"He was Mister McAllister's driver in Paris." He replied. "We had more than one score to settle back there, Mister Lawton. I know you don't feel good about it, but if it wasn't meant to be, it wouldn't have happened. You have to develop a soldier's way of thinking about these things."

I looked at the dock at my feet trying to think of something to say anyway. "Thanks," was all I could manage.

* * * * *

McAllister and Larkin were sitting at a window table overlooking Hesperia Park. Larkin saw me first and waved, using her other hand to tap her husband who was engrossed in a thick pile of papers, scattered on his half of the table.

"This is a sack of shit." He said when I reached the table. "That ass hole Miller and two other guys showed up on the docks at ten this morning asking for our cooperation. Can you imagine that? Like we had some kind of choice in the matter."

"Good evening." I smiled as I pulled up a chair.

"The hell it is." McAllister grumbled. "I have to get a proper bill of sale for every one of those damned eggs, including the fakes. And you know something else? The bill of sale isn't enough! I need statements from any importer or exporter who ever handled them as well as any documentation on provenance.

"I've already been told that I'm in violation of half a dozen laws for carrying them around with me. Can you beat that? I can't take my own property with me. These guys are even telling me I have to get some forms filled out because, supposedly, I can't even move them from Venezuela to Savannah without both governments knowing.

"We had to rent a room here at the hotel so I could send and receive all this crap by fax. I've seen less tape at a 3M factory!"

"Are you feeling better today, Grange?" Larkin asked. I felt sorry for her having to listen to at least twelve straight hours of McAllister's griping.

"Much, thank you." I replied. "How are things going with Irina?"

"Apparently very well." Larkin answered. "It seems that there is no opposition to her unannounced departure and Mister Hayes said she will most probably be allowed to leave with us and apply for immigrant status when she reaches the States."

"How long is this stuff going to take?" I pointed to McAllister.

"Forever." McAllister answered, throwing up his hands. "Tomorrow Miller and his cronies plan to search my boat, the bastards. They have some embassy Marine posted down at the docks right now to make sure we don't try to smuggle anything off without their knowing."

"Do we have anything that needs to be smuggled?" I asked.

McAllister looked around and lowered his voice. "Guns." He said, looking around guiltily after he said it. "But Mark is going to take care of that tonight."

"So our only problems are a couple pounds of paperwork and a funeral at sea for some illegal weapons?" I asked hopefully.

McAllister finally realized that I wasn't really all that concerned about his problems. "I think you're in the clear, old buddy." He smiled as he leaned forward. "I don't think you have a thing to worry about."

"Why the hotel room?" I asked, relieved but trying to act cool. "I thought that the Second Prize had all the bells and whistles you might need."

"Not a fax machine." He shook his head and waved a hand to correct himself. "Yeah, I got a fax, but no way to hook it up. At least not the way I'd like to get it hooked up." He winked as if I was supposed to know what he meant.

"Something is bothering me." I said, hoping that talking would improve my mental processes.

"I told you that time is the only healer." He said it kindly, but it was obvious he was distracted by his mound of papers.

"No, it's something else." I said.

"Well, don't bother me with it right now." McAllister said, all traces of sensitivity gone. "I have enough to worry about right now."

"Well, far be it from me to add to your confusion." I wasn't insulted or put out. I was familiar with McAllister's moods and knew enough not to bother him when he was suffering from tunnel vision. "I think I'll head back to the boat." Larkin smiled and wished me good night. McAllister lifted a hand a few inches off the stack of papers he was studying and wiggled his fingers.

* * * * *

"What in the name of hell's half angels was that brilliant tactic all about?"

"I did not expect that idiot Grigori to take matters into his own hands." The caller said, knowing he was going to have to listen to a verbal censure. "I knew they would run to Helsinki so I wanted to cause them delay to give me time to take care of some business."

"What kind of business?"

"The American author." The caller said simply. "He has to be eliminated."

"Why? Won't that make his friend more wary? He might even give up and go home. That would ruin everything." The caller chuckled. "Then you do not know much about the treasure hunter's mentality. He will only stiffen his resolve, thinking and saying that he is fulfilling his objective to honor his friend's memory."

"That still seems rather drastic."

"The author has acted drastically and without sensible reason." The caller said without logical authority. "The organization I work for frowns when one of their own is needlessly murdered. They would not tolerate allowing him to live. Retaliation is a matter of honor among us."

"So you have the blessing of your superiors in this situation?"

"I do not need my superior's permission for such a sanction." The caller said testily. "It will be done as a matter of policy."

"I simply wish you could handle things differently." The man sighed. "This is far more than I bargained for."

"So are the rewards, my friend." The caller reminded him. "So are the rewards."

* * *

CHAPTER NINE

By five-thirty the next afternoon, Miller and Hayes had finished their investigation and told us all to report to the embassy the following morning. They pointedly avoided telling us the results of their probe, but from McAllister's pompous and pleased mood, I assumed we were in the clear.

I had spent the day between the National Museum with its archaeological displays from Stone, Bronze, and Iron Ages and the Linnanmaki, Helsinki's answer to Copenhagen's Tivoli. Refusing to meet McAllister in the Russian Restaurant of the Hesperia – I had enough things Russian to last a lifetime – I snacked at the lobby buffet and played twenty-five cent Roulette, the country's legal betting limit, until McAllister and Larkin joined me after their evening meal.

"You haven't been spending much time with Irina." McAllister said suggestively. "I would have thought that you would be playing the part of the comforting and reassuring hero to our frightened and confused refugee."

"Why?" I asked. I placed a chip on thirty-two. "Has she been asking for me?"

"Only eight or nine times a day." He answered. "What's the matter? Have you lost all taste for Russian spies, pretty ones or otherwise, since you had to shoot one?"

I squeezed the chips I was holding. The little steel ball landed on nine. "That's not cute, Bobby." I put a chip on twenty-seven.

McAllister assumed his professorial pose. "Like it or not, she is still very much a part of the KGB, Grange. Are you going to be able to handle her?" The wheel came up on eighteen.

"If she is only along to observe and report, why do I have to, as you say, 'handle her?'" I put a chip on number four.

"So you can keep her busy while I try to figure out who her accomplice is and where he might be coming from." Number thirty-one popped up.

"I thought you wanted me for my mind. Now I find all you really want is my body." I stretched to place a chip on a zero.

"We all have to make sacrifices, Grange."

Twelve.

I tossed my remaining chips on the table, letting them land on about fifteen different random numbers. "I'm not cut out for this, Bobby." I said in a more serious tone. I waved at the table. "After all, James Bond always wins and I haven't come close yet." As if to prove my point, the ball dropped into number three, the only number on the entire table not covered by one of my plastic markers.

"Never give up hope." McAllister said, placing a shiny American quarter on number eleven. "Don't be afraid to dream." "Now where have I heard that before?" I mumbled. "I'm going back to the boat." I said, wanting to leave before gravity forced the little ball to fall out of its counter clockwise orbit. I was almost out the door when I heard the croupier.

"Red. Eleven!"

Go figure.

* * * * *

McAllister's banter had been light and only half serious, but it caused me to think about Irina's continued attention towards me. It did seem fairly obvious that she had selected me to plead her case and seek out when she wanted to talk. But while Irina fervently believed in her grandfather's legacy, her suspected partner at the local branch of the KGB dismissed the story, almost with his dying breath. It was a problem I had tried not to think about for two days but was surprised it had not disappeared. I was, however, amazed that, even in my distracted state, I discovered I was being followed.

It was a cool evening, almost chilly, and still sunny at eight-thirty, so the mile and a half walk back to the docks seemed an excellent idea. Less than halfway to the harbor I stopped to look at a store display when a furtive movement caught my eye. In the reflection of the window, I saw someone, a man, duck into a doorway. Ordinarily I wouldn't have noticed a fourteen wheeled garbage truck behind me even if it had had its exhaust pipe stuck up my . . . nose, but the move that my newly acquired tail made was so Keystone Kop-ish, it was almost hard not to distinguish. It only took me two more blocks and three glances to identify my shadow. Sargo Roskovin. Sargo the Second.

At the intersection of Mannerheiminite and Simonkatu is the Forum, the closest thing in Helsinki to resemble an American Mall. I made sure that Sargo saw me enter the low rise plaza and I dawdled among the boutiques and shops that displayed mostly novelty items, slowly making my way to the fourth floor restaurants. I found one I liked, asked for a table by the window, and waited.

Separated by less than three feet and a pane of glass, Sargo stopped to look around, confused and frustrated. He appeared so baffled and inept, I considered following him for a while to see what he might be up to. Instead, I tapped on the window with a fork. Sargo jumped as if he had been shot. When he calmed down enough to see me through the glass, I pointed to the door and the empty seat at my table. He looked around as if afraid of being seen and reluctantly headed for the door.

"Looking for someone?" I asked as he squeamishly approached the table.

"You are the man who shoots an agent of the KGB, yet you walk around as if nothing has happened." He sat down across from me but his eyes continued to dart around the room. "Do you have one of your friend's sharpshooting bodyguards watching you right now?"

In a statement and a question, he had said two very disturbing things. I put on a more serious expression. "You're talking about things you can't possibly know anything about. Would you care to explain why you would make such comments?"

He leaned closer and lowered his voice. "In my business, information is as valuable as product," he said, "and when the KGB is involved, the stakes become doubled. Word of your ambush on the KGB pig, Patek, has spread very quickly. The details of your deed are the basis for legend in my country. In spite of a society of limited freedoms, we have an information network that rivals your famed computer highways."

"Okay," I conceded, "you have a grapevine that is competent. Now suppose you tell me why you were following me like a bad imitation of Inspector Cluseau."

"Who?"

I simplified the question. "Why were you following me?"

"Aha!" Sargo raised a finger. "Several reasons, really. The first is to warn you. The KGB does not react lightly when one of their agents meets with violence. It is an unwritten rule of the agency that states that all acts perpetrated against the agency will meet with retaliation, regardless of the circumstances.

"Secondly, I have some disturbing news. It appears as though you have been deceived. I have discovered that during my absence from St. Petersburg, someone was representing himself or herself to be me in dealings with you." He turned his head slightly and regarded me suspiciously. "But of course you know this. Why did you not tell me?"

"I had to be careful." I said with as little reaction as possible. "After all, how would I know who the real Roskovin is?"

"Your silence nearly cost me my life." He said sternly but without rancor. "I was forced to flee for my own safety. I was hoping you would sponsor me to America. Once I am there, I am certain to be able to work for our mutual friend in the city of Chicago."

"So you decided to follow me like some kind of a cheap dime novel private detective?" I questioned.

"I had to make sure you yourself were not being followed." He said. "It would not do either one of us good to have the KGB kill two birds with one stick."

I wasn't fond of his analogy. "We're almost ready to leave Helsinki." I said. "I'm not sure Mister McAllister would be willing to wait around while you get your papers processed."

Sargo shook his head. "I do not wish to make my movements known. I want to enter your country without the authorities knowing from where I came."

"You mean illegally?"

It was a stupid question that Sargo was kind enough not to ridicule. "I am a black marketeer." He said simply. "It is the only trade I know. Should I be fortunate enough to reach Chicago alive, I will seek employment with Geoff Camper." He studied me for my reactions for a couple of seconds. "A real American Gangster, no?"

"I thought you didn't want to mention any names." I said suspiciously.

"I don't, but I must reassure you of my legitimacy."

"That's a funny word to use."

He looked puzzled.

"So, you wouldn't want to make yourself known to the police." That was a statement which I intended to be a question.

He shrugged.

"Do you have a place to stay until I can talk to Mister McAllister?"

"No." He shook his head again. "In my position, it is best to keep moving."

"I'll talk to Mister McAllister," I said, "but I won't be seeing him again until morning. Can you meet me some place tomorrow morning after ten?"

"Of course." He looked around again. "Where?"

"I'll be somewhere around the booth that sells the trinkets for the boats. Watch for me there."

"You will not regret this, Comrade Lawton." He said, getting up to leave. "You will find that people in my business have long memories."

I nodded.

"One more thing." He smiled. "Beware of red headed strangers. Especially the female kind."

* * * * *

"Well, that certainly makes things easier."

We were on our way to the embassy to hear Miller and Hayes's pronouncement on our case when I told McAllister about Sargo. He seemed pleased and I wondered why.

"This means we don't have to rack our brains trying to guess who Irina's accomplice is." He continued. "Here I've been worrying about how I was going to figure out who he was, and he walks right up and makes himself available."

"How do you know this is the guy?" I asked.

He looked at me with mock scorn. "You can't honestly believe this guy is for real, Grange. Who the hell else would he be?"

"Why not exactly who he says he is?" I asked.

"Look," McAllister was not in a mood to be contradicted, "a successful black marketeer is used to running and hiding from the cops. An operation big enough to attract the attention of the mob in the States doesn't simply shut its doors because of a little trouble caused by outsiders. All he would have to do to survive in Russia is to lay low for a while. All we have to do is leave him standing on the docks and we never have to worry about him again."

"What if this particular Roskovin is just an expendable part of a bigger organization?" I asked. "Besides, I'm not an advocate of either Roskovins. No matter who they claim to represent, both of them are used to lying and cheating as a way of everyday life. Don't you think it would be better to have him where we can see him instead of worrying about what's behind every bush and tree?"

"You might be right." McAllister said thoughtfully. "We will probably never know who is pulling the strings in this little drama, so you may be right to have as many of the players together as possible." He leaned back in the seat.

"All right." He continued as the car entered the embassy compound. "We take Sargo with us, but we don't let him out of our sight." He turned to me again. "By the time we're finished in here, I'll have a plan."

I could hardly wait.

Although our entry into the building went much faster, it was no less complicated than the first visit. After clearing all the checkpoints, the metal detectors, and the scrutiny of stone faced security guards, we were ushered into the same office that Hayes had occupied during our previous meeting. This time, Miller was standing in front of the window behind Hayes, his arms crossed and his face blank. Hayes did not stand as we filed into the room. McAllister held one of the wooden chairs facing the desk for Larkin and remained standing next to her.

"Are we here to get replacement passports or to listen to more of your redundant pencil pushing bull shit?" If there was a fight to be had, McAllister was not about to back down.

Hayes sighed heavily before answering. "There is no cause for acrimony, Mister McAllister." He said patiently. "We are simply government officials trying to do our jobs."

"Including the farm boy over there?" McAllister nodded toward Miller. "Since when does an agriculture specialist have a license to act like an inquisitor from the middle ages?"

Miller frowned distastefully but Hayes appeared remarkably unperturbed.

"Government cutbacks have caused all our embassies to be very short-handed." Hayes answered as if he had rehearsed the response. "Many of us find ourselves doing double and sometimes triple duty. I apologize for any inconvenience you have experienced and only hope you understand that we are merely doing our jobs."

"Isn't that what the Nazi war criminals said?"

Hayes tried to ignore the comparison but Miller's eyes narrowed at the insult. I would have preferred that McAllister just shut up and allow us to be on our way, but his belligerent barometer was set on low and this was a permanent part of his personality, so he would not be denied having his say.

Hayes passed a stack of cardboard covered papers across the desk. "Your actual passports will have to be replaced when you arrive back in the States." He said. "These temporary papers will allow you to travel until such a time as replacements can be issued. I have taken the liberty of having the South American authorities validate Mrs. McAllister's papers until such a time as she can obtain the documents required by her home country."

Larkin thanked him as McAllister thumbed through the papers.

"The man serving as your interpreter," Hayes continued, "this Ladvick fellow. His story is different. He is a citizen of the former U.S.S.R. with visiting student status in The Hague. In essence, he is a displaced person. A man without a country. We have issued you a temporary travel permit on his behalf. He has one week to decide how he wishes to handle his own affairs. I would suggest that he retain an attorney as he will only be allowed to return to The Hague after a great deal of legal dealings and a mountain of paperwork.

Miss Denikoff has the permission of the State Department to apply for immigration status upon her arrival in America. I would suggest that this be of the highest priority. The Department does not look kindly upon waffling on a matter such as this.

"You are cleared to depart Helsinki at your convenience, a course of action I would recommend to be taken as soon as reasonably possible. The Finnish do not take kindly to diplomatic differences between the U.S. and Russia and consider their policy of neutrality to be the perfect solution to a problem of this sort. They have not expelled you, but you are an embarrassment to them. Any questions?"

"This appears to be a reversal of attitudes of just forty-eight hours ago." McAllister noted. "Why the sudden change of heart?"

Hayes looked to Miller whose expression of distaste had not changed. Getting no help from that sector, he returned his attention to McAllister. "As a matter of fact," he began, "the Russians have withdrawn their complaint without explanation as of late yesterday afternoon. This information was delivered by messenger and I have not been able to obtain a satisfactory reason for this sudden reversal."

"So instead of informing me, you let me sweat things out through the night."

Hayes cleared his throat uncomfortably. "In view of your past associations with law enforcement agencies, we felt it in the best interest of diplomatic relations to authenticate the message through channels."

"What the hell is that supposed to mean?" McAllister was starting a slow burn.

Larkin was tugging on her husband's sleeve, but Miller was already answering.

"It means we know you're dirty, McAllister." His tone was much less diplomatic than Hayes. "Our only bright spot in this whole matter is that we think the Russians dropped their complaint because they wanted to take matters into their own hands. You had better hope that you're clean on this one because if you aren't, you're going to find an American prison a cakewalk compared to what you have in mind." He smirked. "Like for instance, Arizona, wasn't that where. . ."

McAllister cut him off. "That sounds like a pretty empty threat coming from someone who is supposed to be a clod-kicker." McAllister sneered back at Miller.

McAllister was a well known individual when it came to law enforcement agencies throughout the world, for everything from spitting on the sidewalks to reluctant capital murder. Even though he was either innocent or justified in each and every case, his arrogance, attitude and knowledge of the law of most lands won him no friends in the legal or law enforcement community. Standing toe-to-toe with a probable agent of the CIA would only broaden his antagonistic reputation and I couldn't help but wonder how many files were in existence listing me as guilty by my association with the present day pirate. I cleared my throat.

"Things have been kind of tense these last few days." I said, trying my own hand at diplomacy. "I'm sure all of us have been affected one way or another, and everyone's nerves are a bit on edge. Now that everything is settled, I would hope that everyone can return to their respective jobs and responsibilities without holding a grudge."

A half dozen pairs of eyes turned to me with expressions ranging from bored to indifference No one bothered to verbalize the fact that I sounded like a bad playground monitor, but the distraction was enough to dampen the sour mood, and with little more than minimal conversation. The meeting was over. We filed out of the Embassy office, at least happy with the prospect of being allowed to return home.

"What's your plan?" I asked McAllister as the car cleared the front gate.

"I don't think we have to make this complicated." He knew what I was talking about. "It seems that we can board our friend from the opposite side of the boat as soon as we are cleared by customs. If he is halfway as resourceful as he would have us to believe, all you should have to do is tell him what time to paddle up to the side."

"And what time should that be?"

"I'll check with Captain Olsen and the Port Authority." He answered. "I would like to leave as soon as possible. I hope he's not real disappointed about my promise to visit his homeland on our return journey."

* * * * *

I strolled amongst the usual crowd in the vicinity of the ticket kiosk, trying to appear casual and unconcerned. It didn't take Sargo long to find me, walking back and forth in front of the ticket booth, still wondering how I could have made the error of boarding the wrong tour boat and still perturbed at why it bothered me so much when the ticket seller had assured me it was a common, everyday mistake. When Sargo sided up to me it was a bit of a shock, surprising me because I had not seen him approach in the clumsy fashion he had exhibited the day before.

"You have good news for me, Comrade?" He was looking at something or nothing out in the harbor and immediately admonished me for turning to face him "Act as if we were strangers," he said, hardly moving his lips. "One never knows who may be watching."

I thought his caution was a little bit melodramatic. The connection between us was probably already known and if we were, indeed, being observed, it was only because the Russians did not wish to create an International incident that we were not already dead. I don't know why I was unconcerned about that fact.

"We sail at nine-thirty tonight." I said from behind clenched teeth, mocking him rather than mimicking him. "Mister McAllister wants you to board from the port side as soon as the customs officials have left."

Sargo nodded without turning his head. "Your friend thinks this will work easily?" He asked skeptically.

"My friend thinks that you are resourceful." I answered, a bit impatiently. "He may be trying to cover his own ass by making you responsible for your own actions. I don't believe he wants to have any more to do with the civil servants of either Finland or America. He could have told you to go to hell."

"Be calm, my friend." Recognizing my tone, he immediately turned conciliatory. "This will take some doing on my part. After all, I am no match for your Mark Shaefer. It will be difficult for me to make necessary arrangements on such short notice."

"Desperate times call for desperate measures." I said, wondering how he knew about Mark, especially his name, and how Sargo had made it out of Russia if surreptitiously boarding a ship was a challenge. "Don't be late or you'll miss the boat. We will not be delaying our departure."

"I will manage." Sargo said determinedly. He turned to leave. "Until tonight, my friend."

When I looked in his direction, he had already disappeared into the milling crowd. I shrugged and headed back to the transient marina.

McAllister was sitting in the outdoor lounge when I returned to the Second Prize, and I helped myself to a drink before taking a seat across from him. He was idly polishing some sort of undetermined spear gun and didn't even bother to look up when I told him about my most recent meeting with one of the Sarzanovs.

"He will be here." He assured me confidently. "He has the entire Russian station in Helsinki to help make certain he makes it by the time we sail."

"Then you're sure that this is a bogus Sarzanov." I speculated.

"And our friendly little In-tourist guide's back-up." He answered nonchalantly. "We are going to have to be very careful when we get back to the States."

"Not before then?" I questioned.

"I certainly hope not. Nor do I see any danger before then." He laid the spear gun on his lap long enough to take a sip of his drink.

"Remember, they want to see if we can solve a mystery that has eluded them for almost a hundred years. If that were not the case, we would have been sunk well before we were ten miles from St. Petersburg." He picked up the spear gun. "Otherwise, I wouldn't have felt comfortable about getting rid of all our armament except for this."

"Including the. . ." I still couldn't bring myself to identify with the weapon I had so recently used.

"Everything." McAllister answered with exaggerated patience. "That's the best part about shipboard living. When you want to get rid of something, you can be pretty certain it won't ever be found."

As long as he was in a question answering mood, I decided to press him about a few things that had been bothering me. "The night before we landed in St. Petersburg, I saw Mark in a wet suit." I said. "Surely he didn't swim the last fifty miles to be able to sneak into Russia."

McAllister smiled. "Of course not." He was proud of all his toys, but he guarded his secrets like Gollum guarded his 'Precious' ring in the Hobbit story. I was somewhat surprised when he continued. "The Second Prize is fitted with an old magician's trick called a wedge. Basically it's a hiding place that is much larger than it appears, designed to look like something other than what it is. In this case, it's part of the hull configuration."

"Why don't you hide the guns in there?" I asked.

"Alas," McAllister sighed. "It's not waterproof. That's why Mark had to wear a wet suit and scuba gear for the trip into St. Petersburg's harbor. Besides, I got the idea from a couple of Columbian drug smugglers I used to know in Key West. It stands to reason that if they were willing to tell me how they operated, their method might not be all that effective. I decided not to press our luck."

I didn't bother to ask how well he knew, or how he came about knowing a couple of drug smugglers in Key West, but knowing McAllister as I did, I wasn't really surprised. "Has anyone found it yet?"

"Not so far." He didn't sound very certain of his answer. "It served its purpose for this trip so the loss of a few easily replaceable guns doesn't seem important." He looked at his watch. "In a few hours, we will be underway and I can't see why we would need handguns on the open sea." McAllister smiled. "Besides, Grange. I like throwing guns in the ocean."

How well did I remember.

I also didn't bother to remind him that we were not supposed to have any need for armament from the beginning of the venture. "So you're convinced that there is no validity to Irina's story about her grandfather smuggling Faberge jewels to New York?"

"I didn't say that."

"Well, what do you mean?"

"I'm certain that the Russians believe the treasure went to America. And I believe that Irina is convinced that her dearly departed grandfather smuggled it there. However, I'm not satisfied that they wound up in New York, or N'ork, as another pretty little redhead once reminded me."

I remembered his story of how Leo Troutman's daughter once rebuked him for not pronouncing New Orleans the correct way, N'orlens, and how she had used N'ork as an analogy. But something else that had been bothering me for the last couple of days was suddenly fighting to make itself known because of McAllister's cryptic remark. I must have looked as though a great revelation was trying to surface because McAllister stopped polishing his speargun and eyed me carefully.

"What?" He asked.

I shook my head. "I don't know." I said, breaking my train of unconnected thoughts. "Something jogged my mind. Keep talking. Maybe it will surface."

McAllister laid the speargun on the table next to him and leaned forward, intent on helping me come to some sort of realization. "Okay, what was I saying?" He didn't take his eyes off of me. "Oh yeah, N'ork."

"Not that!"

"Oh yeah. Maybe Irina's grandfather, or whoever found the Faberge spoils, didn't even go to New York. After all, the east coast of America is almost three thousand miles long. He could have landed anywhere from Bangor to Miami."

"You're not making a good case." I observed. "You just expanded the focus of our search into an impossibly huge area. Besides, according to that diary, Irina's grandfather described the Statue Of Liberty. How many harbors on the east coast have something like a fifteen story statue in the middle of the bay?"

"He didn't describe the Statue Of Liberty." McAllister countered. "He said something about a lady welcoming them."

"A lady he saw from the deck of a ship." I reminded him. "Somehow I don't think he would have spotted the Welcome Wagon Woman standing on Pier 57 pointing to the perfect place to hide a fortune in jewels."

McAllister smiled his tolerant but-I-know-something-you-don't-know smile and stood up. "Come with me." He said as he ducked into the companionway.

We went down to the lounge where he took his place behind his desk and immediately began rummaging through one of the file cabinet sized drawers. With a mumbled exclamation of discovery, he produced a thick folder. Halfway through the stack, he extracted a smaller pile of papers and handed them to me. "Read this." He commanded.

The packet was a pre-printed folder entitled "Historic Savannah" and was a typical compilation of advertisements, travel information, and visitor's guides issued by Convention and Visitors Bureaus of most every city throughout the United States. McAllister's finger, however, rested on the inside flap of photo-copied materials concerning Florence Martus, the so-called "Waving Girl" of Savannah. Supposedly a legend throughout the sailing world. I had only heard of her through my association with McAllister and a chance sighting of a statue of her during a whirlwind tour of Savannah. Had it not been for those accidental circumstances, I would not have known Florence Martus from Florence Nightingale, an item I attributed to the fact that there are not too many salt water ports in the vicinity of my home in Payson, Arizona.

According to the article, Florence was born in 1868 on Cockspur Island in an undistinguished frame house in the shadow of Fort Pulaski. Her father, a German immigrant, served forty years in the U.S. Army, most of which was spent as an Ordinance Sergeant at the fort.

In 1877, Florence's brother, older by seven years, joined the lighthouse service and in 1887, took his mother and younger sister to live in a lighthouse keeper's cottage on Elba Island. The mother died in 1909, and brother and sister remained on Elba until 1931 when brother George retired and they moved to Savannah.

Beginning at the age of nineteen, Florence consistently waved at every single vessel – – liners, tramps, tankers, and pleasure craft – - entering or leaving the Port Of Savannah. According to legend, in forty-four years – – a white handkerchief by day and a lantern by night – – she did not miss acknowledging a single incoming or departing vessel.

Rumor had it that Florence was once engaged to a sailor with a wedding date planned on his next shore leave but the prospective bridegroom was lost in a hurricane, never to return to Savannah. Florence took up her welcoming vigil either as a tribute to him or a hope against hope that, someday, he would miraculously return and the first thing he would see would be her cheery greeting.

Another rumor said that a young Florence almost froze to death on a journey from Savannah to her home and developed severe diphtheria. The attack deprived her of speech and hearing and she took to waving at passing ships as some kind of self-proclaimed therapy. The children of the time probably called her "crazy old lady Martus" while the adults either pitied her or chuckled at her eccentricity, but her tenacious devotion to her self – appointed task gained her notoriety so that, even today, arriving and departing ships salute her with a blast of ships' horns as they pass the bronze statue erected in 1972 in her honor.

When she died in 1943, the flags of ships of all nations flew at half-mast and she is buried under a lighthouse tombstone in Savannah's Laurel Grove Cemetery.

Among the papers was a copy of a faded newspaper clipping dated 1893 documenting Florence's and George's heroic effort that saved the lives of thirty-one men. A dredge had caught on fire and the two used a small boat to ferry the men to safety. Lacking twentieth century reporting skills, the article was woefully short and lacking in detail.

Florence raised collies and cultivated a garden of exotic plants, but her love affair with ships afforded her greatest pleasure. She was quoted as saying: ". . . My love for the ships has never abided, and I shall always love them. The Captains and the crews are good to me too. I know it must be troublesome for them to speak to me as they do, far across the water, but I am also sure that they do not begrudge me the favor, for they must know how I love the ships and how it cheers me in my loneliness to have them acknowledge my salutes."

Her obituary photo showed a skinny, frail woman with short white hair, a long narrow face and a rather hawkish nose. It did not show a shy and starry-eyed girl who never dreamed that her simple gesture might mean happiness and a sense of tradition long after her passing for those who sailed up and down the river of dreams. . .

During her lifetime, she received thousands of letters, hundreds of gifts, and was the subject of countless newspaper articles. In death she was honored by friends, politicians, civic leaders, industrialists, and crews of ships from around the world, and finally, by the statue of her and one of her handsome dogs in Morrell Park, facing the river she loved.

The final page of McAllister's biography on Florence Margaret Martus contained the words of inscription on her monument.

"Her immortality stems from her friendly greeting to
the passing ships, a welcome to strangers entering the
port and a farewell to wave them safely onward."

I closed the folder and looked across the desk at McAllister. "The romantic side of me would like to believe that Irina's grandfather was talking about Florence." He said. "But in 1917, every immigrant coming to the United States was processed through Ellis Island. If I could justify the old man picking Savannah as his port of entry and getting away with it, I would bet he landed in Georgia with the Czar's treasure. That would be my link to destiny. My purpose for being here on this very quest." McAllister looked saddened. "But, I guess I want it to be. . ."

I interrupted. "He got on the wrong boat, Bobby." I said, almost as if I were in a trance.

"What?"

"That's what has been bothering me for the last couple of days." I said, coming out of my trance-like state. "The other day, I went to take a tour of the Suomenlinna Sveaborg Island. I thought I was going to the fortress, but I wound up on some other, less popular, island. The market was very crowded and confusing and I simply boarded the wrong boat. The ticket seller said it was a common occurrence.

McAllister was nodding, encouraging me to continue.

"Look," I said, thinking faster than I could talk, "commercial trade wasn't routed through New York. What if Irina's grandfather, alone in a busy Italian port, makes a simple mistake and boards the wrong ship. He's in a foreign country, doesn't speak the language, might not be able to read, it's busy, confusing, people all around pushing and shoving. Before you know it, he's out to sea in a ship headed for Georgia rather than the Big Apple. What would you do if you were the captain? He paid his fare, now he's sick; it's far too costly to turn back over one misguided passenger. If you were in charge, you would continue on your way, planning to rectify the situation from the destination end."

"You're right!" McAllister slapped the desk. "How do we prove it?"

"You know better than I." I said. He was probably too excited to think straight. "We already know the name of the boat. All we have to do is verify the destination, check the passenger manifest, and perhaps get a copy of the captain's log."

"Sir Godfrey!" We both said it at the same time.

"I'm going to talk to Irina." I said, gaining some enthusiasm for McAllister's orbital parity, destiny theory. "Maybe she can shed some light on this new idea."

"I'll get a telex off to Sir Godfrey." McAllister said, stuffing the papers back into the drawer. "What was the name of that ship?"

"The Cassandra, I think." I said from the door. Promise me two things."

"Sure." I knew if he started to pick up momentum; there would be no stopping him. "What?"

"Promise you won't send Sir Godfrey to that musty old library in Seville." I said. Then I took a deep breath. "And promise me you won't try to dig up poor old Florence Martus."

He laughed. He didn't, however, promise me a thing.

* * * * *

My parting remark was not frivolous or without concern. Sir Godfrey Stewart was a prominent marine archaeologist and scientist who has assisted McAllister during the "Hacha" project, but McAllister was not beyond asking a Knight of the Realm to trot off to Spain to do something that could just as easily be accomplished with a telephone call.

In the past, Seville played an important role in the discovery and colonization of the New World as a seaport connected to the Atlantic by the Rio Guadalquivir. Today, that same port city contains an archive second to none in maritime history including the manifests, passenger lists, captain's logs, sailing dates, and routes, and probably the menus of every ship, regardless of the nationality or purpose, that ever sailed. If Michael did, indeed, "row the boat ashore", you can bet that fact is recorded somewhere in that old, dusty, and boring building. Since the information we needed dated only back to 1917, I doubted that the type of research McAllister had expended during the "Hacha" project was required in the present situation.

Secondly, it would not be beyond McAllister's gall to try to exhume the mortal remains of poor old Florence Martus simply to see if she was pointing in some vague direction. McAllister's rationale would be that cemeteries have proved to be an excellent source of information, but since Florence apparently outlived Irina's grandfather by more than a quarter of a century, it would be rather unlikely that she would still be pointing to any treasure that he had hidden.

I tried to put these thoughts behind me as I went looking for Irina, and when I asked one of the crew members where she was, he told me he thought he had seen her in the galley.

When I entered the stainless steel and tiled room, spotlessly clean and big enough to rival the kitchen of a fine restaurant, she was standing at a counter, elbows deep in some sort of recipe. When she glanced up and noticed me, she looked away quickly as if hoping I would not notice her presence.

"What ya' doing?" I asked nonchalantly and conversationally. "You're a guest here. You don't have to worry about the boring cooking duties."

"I am making caviar blinis." She didn't look up. "I thought it would be a nice surprise for you."

I looked at the array of ingredients on the counter and wondered how, in this enlightened day and age, anyone could still believe that the way to a man's heart was through his stomach.

"You're barely started." I said. "Why don't we go out for dinner instead?"

She almost looked relieved. She started to make the obligatory protest, but I cut her short with my equally expected insistence. Within minutes, we were being seated in one of the many drinking rooms of Keppeli, just off Market Square. In a bandstand across the adjoining park, a lively concert accompanied us as we ordered. After our waiter left, I leaned forward.

"You said your grandfather was befriended by a steward aboard the Cassandra." I said. "Do you know who he might have been?"

She looked at me with a combination of curiosity and confusion. "An Italian man." She confirmed. "Other than that I do not know."

"This Italian," I persisted, trying to get my own thoughts in order, "he's the one who returned your grandfather's personal effects to your grandmother?"

She nodded.

"How did he do that?"

"Why, he shipped them, or course." She had no idea where the conversation was going.

"Yes," I said impatiently, "but how? Parcel Post? Fed Ex?"

"Fed Ex?"

"Never mind." I waved her off. "Just how did your grandmother receive them? In the mail?"

"I have no idea." She replied. "This is important?"

"It may be." I kept pressing. "Tell me what you know about this Italian."

She turned her head thoughtfully. "Grandfather spoke of him only once in his diary," she said, straining her memory, "and then not by name. Apparently this man, a steward, took a liking to my grandfather and brought him food as he was far too ill to dine with the rest of the passengers."

"Did he say anything about the ship? The Cassandra?"

I was reaching – – free associating – – for any seemingly irrelevant fact and it was confusing her further. She wrinkled her brow, mentally reviewing everything she had ever read in that journal.

"I'm not sure I understand what you mean." She said slowly.

"Your grandfather was a sailor." I said, still not knowing what I was looking for. "Did he describe the ship? Mention any ports between Italy and the United States? Did he describe any landmarks? Mention any names?"

"No." She answered, still deep in thought. "Just the reference to the statue that I read to you. I do not believe the ship stopped at any ports. Otherwise he might have left the boat to seek medical attention."

We were interrupted by the waiter bringing our salads and I couldn't help showing my disappointment and frustration. Irina picked at the food with her fork and suddenly stopped toying and adopted a thoughtful expression.

"There was one thing." She said, completely unsure of how I would interpret what she was about to say. "It may mean nothing. Grandfather wrote something I thought was odd. It is hard to explain without the exact words, but it was something about coming full circle. As close as I can remember, it was 'to come so far from home only to be reminded of the place of my birth'. He wrote that when the Cassandra was three days out of port and probably in the middle of the ocean, so I took it to mean that his illness had somehow caused him to reflect on his life."

She was right. It didn't mean anything. To me . . .

* * * * *

"She wasn't able to help." I said, taking my drink and dropping into one of the more comfortable lounge chairs. "I suppose it's way too early to expect that you heard something from Sir Godfrey."

McAllister, Larkin, and I were the only three persons in the spacious lounge, sitting very close together like co-conspirators trying not to be overheard by those who would disrupt our grand scheme. Everyone else on board were busying themselves for our departure and about the only thing left for us to do was wait for Customs and Immigration to clear our passage and see to the boarding of our illegal stowaway.

"We can consider ourselves lucky if my telex reached him within the next forty-eight hours." McAllister said, running his fingers through his hair, a sure sign of his impatience and annoyance. "A man like Sir Godfrey could be most anyplace on the globe at any given time. Did she remember anything that might help us?"

"No," I answered hopelessly. "Just some rambling about his childhood. Probably the delusions of a man with a high fever recognizing the fact that he was a very sick man and probably afraid to die."

"Delusions usually have a basis in fact." Larkin commented. "Do you remember exactly what it was that she said?"

"I don't know." I said, not really paying attention to what I was saying. "Something about being miles from home and recognizing his birthplace. He was in the middle of the Atlantic Ocean when he wrote it, so it makes no sense at all."

Larkin thought about it for a moment as we each sat there in silence. When I looked at her again, a slow, sly smile was spreading across her face.

"It doesn't make sense unless he knew where he was going." She said.

I didn't have to ask if McAllister had filled her in on our conversation of just a few hours earlier. The fact that she thought she had an answer for us was written all over her face. In a fashion learned from her husband, she allowed the suspense to build.

"Georgia!" She said at last. "If he knew he was going to Georgia, he might very well have been from Georgia."

"Of course! McAllister said. I must have looked as confused as I felt. "Georgia is part of what used to be the USSR. I don't know what the map looks like today – – it seems to change on a weekly basis – – but Georgia was a pretty good sized chunk of the former Soviet Union. If I'm not mistaken, part of Georgia is on the Black Sea where Irina's Grandfather might have been influenced to become a sailor."

It felt like a bomb had exploded in my head. I just stared at McAllister without saying a word.

"Go ask her, Grange." He ordered.

And I would have, but the Immigration people took that moment to board, Customs agent in tow, and asked Captain Olsen to assemble everyone on the afterdeck. Because we were departing, the formalities were cursory and less formal and only lasted as long as they did because the customs man used his position to tour the Second Prize, clearly envious of the luxury he was seeing. The crew members were excused one at a time and silently returned to their duties. When Irina and I finally had the necessary stamps on our temporary passports, I guided her to a quiet spot near the starboard rail.

"Where was your grandfather born?" I asked, trying to sound casual.

"Near Batumi." She answered. I had never heard of Batumi.

"Why?"

"It's an American policeman's trick." I said, thinking fast. Mister McAllister and I are trying to build a psychological profile of your grandfather. That way, we can learn more about the way he was inclined to think."

"And knowing where he was born will help you know what he was thinking?" She asked skeptically.

"It's more than that." I said, realizing how lame I sounded, "but every little bit helps. His birthplace is part of his cultural background." I added, just as unconvincingly.

I edged my way backwards as Irina watched me, obviously wondering how an obscure village in Soviet Europe could be of any importance to vacationing Americans. Let her wonder, I thought. In a civilization where doing something as simple as getting directions to the nearest restroom constituted compromising a state secret, it was high time she got a taste of her own inbred tendency to shadow and distort the truth.

"Batumi." I said to Larkin when I found her and McAllister back in the lounge. Since McAllister didn't know exactly where Soviet Georgia was, it was unlikely that he knew the location of one of its cities. "Do you know where it is?"

Instead of answering, she turned to the shelves behind her and pulled down a five year old Atlas. Without any trouble, we located Batumi as a port city on the Black Sea, very close to the Turkish border. It was described as being one of the best bays of the Black Sea and the capital of the Ajar – Atchar – Autonomous Republic of Georgia. We grinned at each other as if we had struck oil. "It's the Waving Girl, all right! Right there in Savannah!"

* * * * *

McAllister shouted. He reminded me of the time he announced his theory of where the Prize was located.

"This still doesn't prove anything." I said, attempting to bring McAllister back to reality, and doing my best Devil's advocate routine. "We still have to wait for a response to our query to Sir Godfrey"

"Take my word for it, Grange." McAllister said confidently. "I knew it all along." He flashed one of his famous Georgia smiles. "The lady. Florence Martus. Right there on the River of Dreams." He turned serious instantly and scribbled something on a pad, tore it off, and thrust it in my direction. "Do me a favor, Grange." It was more like a command. "Take this to Captain Olsen."

Since the Second Prize was equipped with state of the art onboard communications, I knew I was being excluded from something between McAllister and his wife. I wondered why, but didn't voice disapproval or a challenge. McAllister often kept me in the dark, and sometimes I had to curse the darkness instead of turning on the light. He often had his mind made up which precluded me from bringing up anything that would have been considered speculative, hoping that when I listened to his fully formulated opinion. I could maybe offer an objective assessment. It was part of his personality that I had accepted long ago, so I merely acquiesced and left the McAllisters for a trip to the bridge.

My path to the upper levels of the ship took me past Mark Schaefer, standing at the port rail with a rope ladder at his feet. He was, no doubt, waiting to take on our Russian black marketeer when he arrived and Mark was carefully scanning the shore, watching for the expatriated man to make his approach. He nodded politely as I passed, and for no apparent reason, a chill went up my spine. I guessed that he made me nervous because of our complicity in the murder of Grigori Patek and quickly dismissed my uncomfortable feeling as an aftershock to our crime. I wondered how long it would be before my uneasiness and guilt would take to wear off and finally decided it was something I would have to live with for the rest of my life just as I reached the door to the bridge. Still, it was funny, in a strange sort of way that Mark would cause such troublesome feelings in me and I went to my cabin after delivering McAllister's note to Captain Olsen. I was pouring my third drink when the vibrations of the deck signaled the starting of the engines and our departure from Finland. I would have one more drink and retire early, I thought. It had been a long day.

* * * * *

If it is true that the mind works better at rest, then I should have spent more time sleeping. When my head came off the pillow with sudden realization, I was acutely aware of three things. The first was the bedside clock, its red digital lights informing me that it was four-thirty and still pitch dark. The second was a consciousness of why the picture of Mark Schaefer, standing at the rail awaiting Sargo's arrival had caused me a pang of apprehension. The third was that I was not alone.

It was one of McAllister's hard and fast rules that, with the exception of the lounge, there was to be no smoking below decks. I smelled the fumes of tobacco. Cheap tobacco. I searched the darkness for the telltale glow of a lighted cigarette, saw none, and fumbled for the bedside lamp.

"Good evening." Sargo said when the light came on. "Or more accurately, good morning."

"What are you doing here?" I guessed I was not fully awake.

"I guess you would say I was tying up a few loose ends." He was sitting in one of the armchairs just inside the cabin door with a good view of the entire stateroom.

"This couldn't wait until a decent hour?" I asked, trying to keep the fear out of my voice.

"I am afraid not." He answered in an accent still Russian but extremely precise. "I have already set plans into motion and am now committed to a course of action that is irreversible. I have only a few simple questions before I continue."

"I have a few of my own." I said, reaching for a robe. He watched me move carefully, his single eyebrow dipping in the middle.

"Most likely." He said, self-assured. "Perhaps a friendly exchange of information would be a more civilized way to do business. That is the gentlemen's way. Even for black marketeers."

"You're not who you represented yourself to be." I said bluntly.

"And how did you arrive at that conclusion?" He was enjoying this part of his little game. There was a twinkle of amusement in his eyes.

"It just occurred to me that Mark Schaeffer was not a visible part of our group when we landed in Russia. There was no way you could have known his name unless you were more than a simple street criminal. I don't believe I even knew his last name until you mentioned it in the Market Square this afternoon – – yesterday afternoon."

"Aah." He looked at the ceiling. "An uncharacteristic error on my part. I will have to be more careful in the future."

"You're KGB." I accused, already reaching that conclusion.

"Of course." He was surprised he was confronted with such an obvious point. "Who else would be able to identify a former Naval Seal from the fingerprints on the rifle he left behind? We knew who he was almost before you left the harbor that night."

"I don't believe that." I said. "Otherwise you wouldn't have needed extra time to decide what to do. That is why we had to spend the last few days in Helsinki, isn't it?"

He didn't like being contradicted. "A formal complaint had to be lodged against you and your friends so the authorities would respect our legitimate claim on anything you might uncover in the future." He said, making it sound like a threat. "It was only a last minute decision to have me use my cover as your friend Comrade Roskovin to stage my defection. That way we could keep a closer watch on your future activities."

"So, who are you?" I asked, already knowing the answer.

"Rastov." He said it as if he only had one name. "You have perhaps heard of me?" He took my non-answer for affirmation. "Then you know that poor Grigori was my partner."

"I didn't know that snakes worked in pairs." I said caustically. Rastov smiled with genuine amusement.

"That means you were also part of a cruel and senseless murder in Paris." I continued. "Where I come from, people don't readily admit to associations like that." Rastov sighed heavily "An unfortunate incident." He said as if he truly regretted the event. "And I must agree with you, totally unnecessary."

"Sadly, Grigori was as short on common sense as he was long on impulse. With your friend Antonio Tumbas out of that farmhouse he had made his personal fortress, it would have been easy for men of our talents to recover the Spaskoi Egg. Had we known that your friend McAllister possessed it, we would not even had occasion to be in Paris."

"So you're saying that Patek acted on his own? Without orders?"

As soon as I had said it, I didn't see how it made any difference.

"Your friend McAllister has been at the center of several major failures of my organization and therefore, a source of great frustration for both Grigori and I, even though it was in no way his fault." Rastov tried to rationalize. "If he had not been so concerned about things that did not affect him personally, none of this would have happened."

"That's horseshit!" I said, showing disgust and contempt. "You beat Antonio Tumbas half to death trying to steal the Spaskoie Egg, you, or your friend, Alexander Malik, tried to burglarize McAllister's home in Venezuela, Patek murders three people in Paris, one of you is most likely responsible for Luigi Paretti's death, and you think McAllister was wrong to show concern? That's like saying Lincoln had nothing to fear from an out of work actor."

Rastov didn't understand the reference to Lincoln, but he did know what I was talking about and hastened to correct me.

"It is true we attempted to relieve the drunk, Tumbas, of an item of our National heritage." He confessed. "But from that point on, you are mistaken about our motives. Our problems stemmed from a complication of internal security, not overt action.

"You understand what it is my department wishes to accomplish?"

"Sure." I said. "Monopoly of a specific area of the art world. You counterfeit Faberge Eggs while stockpiling the originals."

"While at the same time increasing the value of the product." He added. "In this way, Russia will someday hold all or most of the world's most exclusive and expensive art treasure in a narrow and discriminating field."

"Big deal." I said, unimpressed.

"Oh, but it is. Rastov insisted. "You see, our attention to Faberge Eggs is only a pilot program. If it in any way proves to be successful, the program will be expanded to other areas of art as well. And when we have a firm stranglehold on the cultural pulse of the world, the political lackeys will become our puppets."

"I think you're exaggerating the importance of art." I said. "What makes you think that entire governments will fall because less than one percent of the population is deprived of works of art?"

"Because that same percentage are the people who control the governments." He said simply. "Art has been the collateral of industry and business for centuries. If someday your capitalistic giants find that their investments are worthless, think of the confusion and financial loss that will be certain to follow."

"I think you have an overstated opinion about the importance of a lousy Easter Egg." I countered. "Or for that matter, any form of art. What makes you think that entire governments will roll over because they own a forged painting or a bogus egg?"

"It is a theory based on the domino principle." He continued. "If a small nation, its resource that of cultural or collected art, were to suddenly discover that their greatest asset is worthless, they would be financially dependent on other, wealthier nations. Do you think that Egypt would have a tourist economy if the pyramids had been built ten years ago instead of in the time of the Pharaohs? Of course not. If, then, the country lacked those precious tourist dollars, they would be forced to seek aid from other countries better able to support those underprivileged nations. The shift of spreading unsecured money over the world would greatly alter the economy as we know it today."

It seemed a bit farfetched to me. "You can't move the pyramids to Russia," I reminded him, "or move the Vatican to Moscow."

"Of course not." He replied. "But for years the British government raped the antiquities of many nations to stock their highly touted museums. In addition to the intrinsic value of those items, how many Englanders will never leave home to visit these foreign places simply because the art that is representative of those very same places is only a few blocks away from their flats on a permanent exhibit?"

The conversation was going nowhere. I was arguing world politics and economy with a man who had been brainwashed by a lunatic with a craving for art. "Why not try the same thing with something quicker and more common?" I asked. "Like oil or wheat?"

"Too well regulated." He answered with a wave of dismissal. "We are a patient people, willing to wait for the proper time to take our place in history."

To me he sounded more like a Nazi general than a KGB flunky. I wasn't getting anywhere discussing reality, so I changed course slightly. "So your problems were internal?" I asked. "How?"

"We found we had a criminal within our organization." The remark was so absurd, a short bark of a laugh escaped from somewhere within me.

"Very well," Rastov was untroubled by my skepticism, "for purposes of our discussion, there was a traitor within our ranks.

"We recruited only the finest craftsmen for replication of our masterpieces. Of course, in order to do this, we tested a great many men. As you might say, we had to kiss a great many frogs to find our princes. Although we thought our methods and background investigations were unparalleled, we made an unfortunate error. We employed our men in pairs to compartmentalize our operation as well as to allow the teams the opportunity to critique each other's performance, so our 'traitor' was not difficult to find.

"At this point, I must digress. About ten years ago, we had planned an attempt at the Forbes Collection. Our purpose was not to steal, but to substitute. We felt that the Forbes Collection was such a permanent exhibit; the likelihood of a successfully planted forgery being discovered was highly improbable. To this purpose, we manufactured a duplicate Resurrection Egg. When further research proved that such an operation was not feasible, we temporarily abandoned the project and placed the replacement egg in storage in the basement of the Winter Palace. This storeroom also contained many of the failures of our experiment, including the products that were not up to the standards of our goals. One of our forgers found a chink in our armor, so to speak, and found a way to smuggle the Resurrection egg and another inferior piece out of the warehouse."

"Miska Mossolov." I said, more to myself than out loud.

"Exactly." He didn't bother to ask how I knew the name.

"Mossolov made contact with Luigi Paretti, a known Faberge collector, while the late Italian was visiting St. Petersburg on a trade mission, and offered to sell him the two eggs he had stolen from our facilities. His second mistake was when he deferred payment until he could flee Russia and contact Paretti after his escape. Paretti, already exhibiting the early signs of impending bankruptcy, took the eggs, sight unseen, and left Russia.

"Unfortunately for Mossolov, Paretti was somewhat of an expert on Faberge art, and as soon as he got home and unwrapped his treasures, he knew he had a very good copy of an original that was on display in New York, as well as a piece of junk. It did not take long for Paretti to put two and two together and make the assumption that the Russian art community was somehow trying to undermine the Forbes Collection, as well as the collection of whoever owned the Lily Egg, was someone he apparently knew.

Through a complicated process that has no bearing on this story other than the fact it happened, Paretti contacted my superior and offered to sell the forgeries back to our government for a half million American dollars. He made it very plain that we would also be purchasing his silence.

"This is the point where your Mister McAllister entered the picture. Quite by accident, Parretti found out that McAllister was unschooled in this endeavor. He sold his entire collection to your Mister McAllister and to blackmail our government against any form of retaliation, he somehow switched pedestals during the Euro bank exchange, thinking to use them in some undisclosed manner of which I have no knowledge. A short time later he was dead with no way of finding out what his motives actually were. In the meantime, Miska Mossolov saw the error of his ways and saw fit to confess his sins and face the appropriate punishment."

I couldn't help wincing at such a casual description of torture and execution. "Why did you come after McAllister?"

"An unfortunate decision of my own." He shook his head sadly. "While in France, I came into possession of the authentic Lily Egg. It was my thinking that the egg that Mister McAllister had purchased was one of such poor quality, that it was bound to be uncovered as a forgery. My excursion to his estate was to serve two purposes. First, I would switch the real egg for the imitation, and second, I would steal the Resurrection Egg."

"Why?" I couldn't follow his logic.

"As an amateur collector, I felt certain that your friend would not know of the Forbes Collection and if he did, would not be familiar with the contents. If at some time in the future he was to find that the Resurrection Egg was in a New York museum, he might conclude that either the agents of the museum were responsible for the robbery or that the piece was purchased through intermediaries I believe you call a 'fence'. If that were the case, his actions, legal or otherwise, would be directed toward the Forbes people and away from our operation."

"But why replace the Lily Egg?" I asked. "Why not leave the forgery in place or steal it too?"

"If I were to steal the Lily Egg, and that information somehow became public, it might alert the owner of the 'authentic' Lily Egg that he possessed a forgery. On the other hand, if the forgery was allowed to stand in your friend's collection and he was to make an insurance claim for the Resurrection Egg, it is possible that the insurance company would bring an expert to evaluate the entire collection and the Lily Egg would be declared a fraud."

"What would be wrong with sticking McAllister with a fraud?" I asked.

"Bad news travels quickly in the art world." He explained. "If it were discovered that Mister McAllister possessed a counterfeit egg, it might prompt other egg owners to authenticate their collections. We could not afford to take that risk."

"Your conspiracy is developed to that extent?" I asked in awe.

Rastov smiled the embarrassed pride of accomplishment.

"That still doesn't explain the fact that you overtly sought to obtain the Spaskoie Egg, beating a man half to death one time, and killing him the second time along with two innocent people."

"Most of our mission concerning the Spaskoie Egg was accomplished at the auction in Monte Carlo." He replied. "The value of the egg was established, albeit at an inflated worth, and would bring even more at subsequent offerings. There was no need to allow it to sit in a private collection gathering dust while, in circulation, it could appreciate each time it changed hands. It is the bidding mentality that makes one piece more, for lack of a better word, intriguing; more desirable.

"As to the beating, Antonio Tumbas invited it upon himself by electing to resist in a misguided attempt to protect his property. Do not the police of your country advise to yield to armed robbers and thieves to avoid the possibility of violence? If he had simply turned over the case to Grigori as demanded, he would have suffered no physical harm."

"So you decided the next time you met, to preempt the possibility of getting kicked in the balls by murdering him?"

"I decided nothing." He repeated. "I was being regrettably detained by the Paris Police on a misdemeanor charge which left Grigori alone to lament our first and only failure. It is sad that he was not the brightest of operatives and elected to act on his own to atone for our error. I can assure you he was severely reprimanded by our superior when he returned home."

"Oh," I said, unable to hide the sarcasm. "As long as he got a good chewing out, I guess that makes everything okay. We wouldn't want a miscarriage of justice, would we?"

"You are oversimplifying a complicated matter." Rastov's tone was neither commanding nor apologetic; merely practical. "I am certain that none of the events that have taken place since your unfortunate visit to Paris would have happened had Mister McAllister not been so tenacious in discovering the nature of our work. After all, he was not an injured party. From what I understood, Senor Tumbas was somewhat estranged from the rest of his family. McAllister need not have become involved. Had my mission to South America been successful, it would have served both of us quite nicely."

"If!" I was wide awake, and losing my patience. But I didn't want to turn off the faucet of enlightenment I was receiving. "If my aunt had balls, she'd be my uncle!" I added.

"What are you saying? He looked confused. "Your aunt has testicles?"

"Never mind." My mind was racing. "How the hell do you figure that both parties would benefit if Mister McAllister had simply allowed himself to be ripped off?" I was having a hard time following Rastov's logic. In fact, McAllister's psycho-logic made better sense, a concession I thought I would never stipulate to.

"Quite simple." He answered with a smug expression plastered all over his face. "Mister McAllister would have eight authentic eggs instead of seven, and his insurance company would have reimbursed him for the loss of the ninth. At the same time, I would have broached his security and been aware of the pitfalls surrounding his fortress when it was time to return to relieve him of the balance of his collection."

"You don't know McAllister very well, do you?" It was rhetorical. I didn't expect an answer.

"That is not my position or purpose." He replied offhandedly. "In fact, after my aborted attempt at the substitution in Venezuela, I was directly ordered to forget about Mister McAllister and Senor Tumbas. I neglected to tell Grigori of that fact and his precipitous action in Paris was the result."

"A result that also netted you the Spaskoie Egg." I interjected.

"Alas, that is not true, comrade Lawton." He sighed. "Oh, we did search the house outside of Chartres, but it was too late. Someone had already been there and it was fairly obvious that their only objective was the egg.

Since it was the only thing that seemed to have been taken in the burglary, we naturally thought Mister McAllister was responsible. Since we had been ordered to forget about him and his now late brother-in-law, we took no further action."

"I guess that explains why you're here now." I had not lost my sarcastic edge, but it didn't seem to bother Rastov.

Perhaps I knew all along that I was in deep shit, but when I stood up to fix myself something to drink, Rastov confirmed the ultimate motive for his untimely visit. For the first time since I had awakened; he reached into his lap and produced a pistol, the ugly cylinder of a silencer fastened to the barrel. The gun looked like an automatic, and for some reason I assumed that the noise suppressing attachment must have been of custom design to be able to fit the irregular shape of the discharge end of the weapon. However, his casual handling of the gun made me think that he was not yet prepared to use it, he was just reminding me who was in charge.

"I was getting myself a drink." I said, pausing in mid-stride. The single eyebrow went up a half an inch. "You have vodka?" He asked hopefully.

I shook my head. "Just rum."

"Very well," he said, the eyebrow returning to its normal scowl, "but just a small one."

I hadn't remembered making an offer.

Just the same. I handed him a glass and poured from the bottle until he waved the gun for me to stop, and when I sat on the bed with my own hefty measure, he returned the pistol to the folds of his lap.

"So you were ordered to forget about McAllister" I prompted. "What changed your mind?"

"Ironically, the same man who issued those very same orders." He shrugged as if to suggest it was a common occurrence.

"My major was shocked to find that you and Mister McAllister returned to Europe and the very first person you visited was the forger, Kublec. Although it had been many years since he had been utilized outside, your subsequent visit to the newspaper and Scotland Yard established that you would have been able to identify two of his alter eggs. He had gone to much trouble establishing his identity as a respected Jewish businessman and was distressed to find you had made that connection."

"So Kleinfeld is really a KGB major." I deduced. "I assume your boss is the infamous Kalishnikov?"

"Kalinishkov." Rastov corrected. "Or Cramer, or Kopov, or a couple of other clever pseudonyms even I am not privileged to know. You must know that the major was involved in this project far longer that I have been. Even I do not know the extent of our department's work.

"When you left England after a failed attempt to interview Theodore Faberge and sailed up the coast toward Russia, Major Kalinishkov made plans to have you sunk to the bottom of the Baltic Sea. He sent two patrol boats to intercept you for that purpose and it was only last minute intervention by Moscow that prevented that from happening. It was decided that between Mister McAllister's notoriety and Mrs. McAllister's political connections, extreme prejudice was not a viable option."

"Not to mention a famous American author." I added.

"To the best of my knowledge, your name did not enter the discussion."

So much for my apparently over-inflated ego.

"Instead." he continued, "the major was told to initiate a program of disinformation, but before a plan could be initiated, fate intervened on our behalf.

"Comrade Denikoff, whose grandfather was long suspected to be an accomplice in the disappearance of certain materials belonging to Czarist Russia, was appointed as your In-tourist guide. On the spur of the moment, it was decided that, instead of disinformation, we would sidetrack your investigation with the evidence we possessed on an unsolved part of Russian history."

"So Irina's story is true." I said, amazed.

"Whether her story is true or not, I cannot say." He said, waving a hand as if the facts were unimportant. "The circumstances, however, are a matter of record. Alexander Nuchek was a steward for the Czar who defected and disappeared sometime during the Great Revolution. He bragged to a friend and in letters to his wife that he was going to live in America on an unspecified fortune he claimed to have found. He vanished sometime in late 1917 or early 1918 from a shipping port in Italy and was never heard from again. Our problem was how to encourage you to drop your investigation of your present day activities and become more interested in chasing ghosts from the past.

"We did not count on the cooperation you received from Sanya Roskovin. All of our information suggested you came to St. Petersburg on a whim and were without contacts that could have aided in your search. Since espionage is not a game for amateurs, we could not depend on Comrade Denikoff's help, other than to keep track of your activities, so we recruited one of your group members to help us facilitate our goals."

That got my attention. Who, in our small party, could have been enlisted as a spy for the KGB, and for what reason? What could they possibly gain that McAllister was not already providing them? Someplace in the back of my mind, I started going over the possibilities.

"We were dismayed to find that you had found Serge Byachev and Mitia Sarzanov until our informer told us that something had happened after your first visit to our master forger. Out of nowhere, it seemed, you were suddenly coming into the very information that we were desperately trying to force upon you. We had originally hoped that by exaggerating Mister McAllister's talents as a treasure hunter, Comrade Denikoff would seek his counsel at her very first opportunity."

"Exaggerate!?" I was appalled. "The man found over nine hundred million dollars in gold!" I was surprised at my spontaneous reaction to defend McAllister's worth. "Do you call that an exaggeration?"

Rastov dismissed my interruption with a look designed to say that McAllister's worth was of no importance to him. "Still, her hesitation to interest Mister McAllister may have cost my department the services of a skilled counterfeiter." He shrugged. "Regrettable, but necessary."

I wondered what fate poor Mitia Sarzanov had suffered and how McAllister would be able to keep his promise about seeing to the welfare of the sad eyed and shy boy.

"The only thing left for us to do was to pick up the pretty, young Sanya Roskovin and question her as to exactly what you had discovered through her untimely intervention." Rastov smiled. "I never thought of it before, but I was actually impersonating a woman." He shook his head at the thought; then continued, "In fact, all I had was a name; Roskovin, initially. I wasn't aware of a difference in gender."

"That's odd." I began, but he ignored me and continued.

"So you see, my friend, your inappropriate and intrusive meddling have not only caused three deaths in Paris, but several lamentable casualties in my country, bringing the total to a staggering dozen." He shook his head as if he were disappointed with something I had done.

"Twelve?" My brow knitted as I mentally counted bodies. "You're exaggerating again."

"Hardly." He said with mock grief. "Three in Paris, Sarzanov, the drunken janitor, Byachev, your pretty red haired black marketeer friend, Roskovon, the old man Kublec and his meddlesome wife, ..."

I closed my eyes and moaned.

". . . the thief, Mossolov, ..."

"He was your 'internal problem.'" I reminded him, irrationally trying to lower the body count.

". . . poor old Grigori," he continued, ignoring my objection, "our operative within your midst . . ."

A chill went up my spine as I realized he had killed one of our group in the short time since he had been on board.

". . . and," he paused significantly, "of course, you."

Ever since some sixth sense had awakened me I had assumed that this was his ultimate plan, and although I should have been terrified, all I could think of at that time was; yep, that's twelve all right.

Which is not to say I was going to my own death willingly; far from it? I guess I was in a state of shock. It would have been obvious to an idiot that, after telling me the details of a scheme that had left another eleven people dead, that he couldn't allow me to live, but I clung to the fact that I wasn't dead yet, and maybe there was something I could do to mess up his projected count by staying alive. My second thought was to stall for as long as I could.

"You've told me everything else," I said, "can I at least know who was the traitor amongst us?"

"I don't see how it can help you now."

"You haven't dampened my curiosity by announcing my impending doom." I reasoned.

"Artur Ladvick, of course." He said as if I should have known. "You honestly did not know?"

My money would have been on one of the security guards, other than Mark, or course. It only seemed natural that, as a mercenary of sorts, someone in that position would, by definition, be loyal to the highest bidder. I said as much.

"That young Artur was from an area that is no longer part of the Soviet Union did not mean that certain members of his family were beyond our reach." Rastov smiled. "Besides;" he had already been of service to us during the Kushman trial. He was most anxious to be of assistance again."

"Then why eliminate an asset?" I asked.

"Because when you were killed, it might have frightened him into seeking protection from your Mister McAllister." He answered. "Also, he could identify me. As it is, he is a perfect scapegoat. I have arranged for evidence to be placed among his effects that implicates him in your sudden demise so that I may continue our journey to the United States."

"Why the need to kill me? You could have maintained your pretense of being Roskovin and still travelled with us. We had no proof of who you were or were not."

"You killed my partner." He held up a hand to forestall any objection from me. "Granted, he was an insufferable oaf, and granted, he disobeyed a direct order by abandoning his listening post and going to your room. You might even say it was the major's fault for not allowing him to know the details of our operation. But the fact of the matter is that you murdered an agent of the KGB. We, as an organization with a reputation as ruthless as it is decisive, cannot allow such an act to go unpunished."

It was an argument that had no convincing rebuttal so I switched gears. As long as he was talking, I wasn't dead.

"Why haven't you dealt with Anthony Wilson?" I asked. "He was the one that got McAllister interested in your little scheme in the first place."

"Anthony Wilson is an aging fool who has been crying wolf for a great many years. As long as we ignore his rantings, he is impotent. Like the people who keep harping the word conspiracy in regard to the Kennedy assassination. The longer they talk, the crazier they sound. To eliminate such a person would be to lend credence to their stories."

"You said you wanted to exchange information." I said, still stalling. "What is it you want to know?"

"I am only somewhat intrigued by Mister McAllister's interest in the so-called Faberge treasure. Does he really believe he can locate the things of myth and legend?"

"You mentioned ghosts earlier" I reminded him. "McAllister not only believes in ghosts, he talks to them on a regular basis." Now I was exaggerating – – or was I? I really didn't care at that moment. "He has an uncanny way of asking members of the spirit world to help him separate myths from facts and then acting on that information."

"Do you believe he can find the Faberge jewels in such a manner?" Rastov seemed not only surprised by my accounting of McAllister's methods, but also by my apparent belief in his supernatural ability.

"I know for sure that it has worked in the past. In fact, I believe that the ghost of a lady has lead him here on this mission."

"What lady?" He asked.

I had to change the subject "He prefers lady ghosts."

While he was pondering my answer I reached for my drink. He reached for his gun.

"No fair." I said. "A gun against a drink?" I tried to lighten the mood like a condemned man telling a joke just before the gallows trap opened.

He relaxed his hold on the gun and said. "I would truly like to see this amazing ability for myself." He genuinely looked impressed. "To return to Russia such an incredible find would indeed make me a hero of extraordinary proportion."

"You're forgetting one thing."

"Oh?" He asked, focusing again on the present.

"If you kill me. I am going to use all my afterlife strength to contact McAllister to have him avenge my death."

Instead of giving him pause to think, he scoffed. "I think our conversation is about over. Comrade Lawton." He picked the gun from the folds of his lap. "And now it is time to go our separate ways."

When he stood up, I braced myself for the bullet and almost barfed up my previous night's dinner. Too bad I didn't eat the caviar blinis because I know I would have lost it all over his lap, gun and all. Weird things were going through my mind. . . The irony of being saved by fish eggs, and the fact that I hate seafood. When I returned to what was left of my senses. Rastov went to the door and opened it cautiously. For a split second I thought I was going to live, but after checking the hallway, he waved the gun toward the darkened corridor. "Be very quiet Mister Lawton." He warned. If you make a sound or try to run, you will only endanger the lives of others while getting a large bloody stain on your friend's expensive carpet."

He stood well back as I passed him, but as we walked up the companionway, the gun nudged my back, reminding me that he was right behind me. I had read somewhere that when an aimed pistol is within close range, it is possible to slap the gun out of the line of fire before an assailant can react and discharge the weapon. My arms, however, felt like rubber and my heart was beating so fast I was mollified by the fact that I would probably suffer a massive myocardial infarction long before Rastov could pull the trigger. We emerged on deck next to the afterdeck bar and Rastov motioned me close to the stern rail.

"Jump." He commanded.

"What?"

"Look at it this way." His smile and the single eyebrow made him look devilish in the dark shadows. "I am giving you a chance to survive. If you jump now, you might have the stamina to persevere. I am certain, however, that your ability to swim would be greatly hampered by an extra ounce or two of lead."

I hesitated, weighing the odds. I had just about decided to take my chances in the water when I realized that was exactly what he wanted me to do. I doubted anyone could swim the width of the Baltic Sea before dying of exhaustion or exposure, so the only purpose of this "sporting chance" was to make me suffer. Although it had to be impossible, I pictured myself lasting long enough to bump into the floating, bloated body of Artur Ladvick. I turned away from the rail.

"I'm not going to do your dirty work for you." I said, almost praying for a heart attack. "You're going to have to use one of those bullets."

"As you wish." He said, raising the gun slowly. "Da Sve. . ."

He never finished the parting words. A sound like a shaken bottle of soda pop being opened came from about twenty feet away and Rastov was suddenly staring at a barbed projectile sticking out of the front of his chest. I recognized the spear from the underwater weapon McAllister had been polishing the day before, its inch round shaft having gone almost completely through from back to front. Blood was spurting from the three wider gashes caused by the flanges of the spiked tip and Rastov stared unbelievingly at the sticky point. He started to turn around to see where the lethal shot had come from, but somehow must have known he wasn't going to make it. His eyes narrowed in a final gesture of contempt and the gun, still pointed in my direction, wavered slightly. As if he had known exactly how much strength and time he had left, he grinned evilly with the satisfaction of someone who was going to have the last word, and squeezed the trigger.

The gun fired.

I saw the light from the thrusters of a space shuttle launch, heard the roar of the rocket lifting and then . . .nothing.

* * *

CHAPTER TEN

I saw the traditional tunnels of white light, except that it did not seem as pure a white as I had expected, and every time I turned my head, the light became less bright, more of a pale yellow. Sounds came to me in the form of mumblings or droning, and the occasional voice that was directed to me had the deep bass inflection of a tape recorder in slow motion. At times I felt that I was either swimming or floating while at other times I felt pain, a perception rather than a true feeling. I saw images of my life as well as visions of things long forgotten or something that had nothing to do with me. It was like God was trying to figure out where I should be going, but I wasn't worried. Even Moses had killed a man and I couldn't picture him stoking ovens for the devil.

When I was able to comprehend three of four spoken words in a row, I decided to risk opening my eyes. The result was dizziness and a whirling sensation that was not altogether unpleasant, but mildly nauseating. It was during those times that my throat felt massaged and cooler and I began to look forward to the opportunity to experience those feelings. There was constant motion around me, but every time I attempted to direct my attention toward one particular thing, it slipped out of detail like a poorly focused slide on a projection screen. At one point, I experimented with speech and was rewarded with sound of a rusty hinge and several concerned murmurs. When it became apparent that any cohesive verbalization on my part was not being taken seriously, I surrendered myself to the comfort and peace of total darkness.

It was difficult to think, and at times I could remember with startling clarity how I came to be in the condition I was in, but I could not recall simple things like my name or age. At other times, a kaleidoscope of fantasy images pranced before my closed eyes, treating me with scenes of pleasant creativity or horrific nightmares.

Finally, my mind seemed to grasp on the idea that I was still alive, but since I could not get an accurate assessment of by what margin, I decided to fight for consciousness. One of the first things I saw when I opened my eyes were several men standing above me, all holding an outstretched arm in my direction.

"How many fingers am I holding up?" He asked. He was speaking slow and loud as if English was a language foreign to me.

I concentrated on the digits that were thrust in my face. Fifteen, I counted. Three on each hand.

"Who . . . is . . . the . . . pres. . . si. . .dent. . .of. . . the. . .U. . .ni. . .ted. . .States?"

Although I knew it wasn't true, the only name I could think of was George Washington.

"Maybe he needs more time, Bobby." A feminine voice came from out of my range of vision.

"The doctor said he should be coming around about now." The man insisted.

"He also said that there might be memory loss or some other type of brain damage." The unseen voice cautioned. "He said that we would have to take things slow and easy."

The man put his face close to mine. "Do you know who I am?" Determined to prove that my brain was functioning as well as anybody else in the room, I mustered all my strength and blurted out the word "three", answering his first question rather than the last. I fell back asleep, exhausted.

The next time I registered any impression was again of the white light shining into my eyes. As I watched, the tunnel of light took on more and more definition until I saw that a brass circle surrounded the passage. At regular intervals, five Phillips-head screws were imbedded in the brass.

A porthole!

I congratulated myself with a chuckle.

"Grange?" A female voice again. "Are you awake?"

Who the hell was Grange, I wondered.

I felt long fingers at the back of my head and a straw was thrust into my mouth. I wondered what that little contraption was for and got a feeling of inner joy as I realized I could use it to blow bubbles in some kind of receptacle somewhere below my chin.

"Don't blow." The voice said. "Suck."

I giggled to myself at the imagined double entendre.

Nevertheless, I closed my lips and drew on the straw.

Heaven! I thought as the cold, bubbly liquid filled my mouth and trickled down my throat. I'm in heaven! I sucked harder.

"Easy." The disembodied voice said as the straw was pulled from my mouth. "Easy does it. Too much right now might be bad for you."

How anything so ambrosial could be bad for me, I wondered as the room grew darker again.

When I opened my eyes, artificial but muted light filled the room. The man who had quizzed me about fingers and presidents was sitting in a chair next to my bed, reading some papers. I struggled to remember a name.

"Bobby." I said. To my ears it sounded like "Broogruph."

"Grange?" He said, dropping the papers and changing his seat to the edge of the bed. "How'ya doin', buddy?"

"Thirsty." I said. That time it sounded like a real word.

He reached for something out of my vision and I felt the straw being inserted into my mouth. I got its use right on the first try and recognized the taste of ice cold ginger ale.

"What happened?" I asked, almost out of breath from trying to rehydrate myself in a single gulp.

"You got shot." He answered. "You were lucky."

As I tried to reconcile the two separate sentences into one thought that was not an oxymoron, I wrinkled my brow and felt the tape of a fairly large bandage over my right eye. Visualizing a four-by-four bandage as the only thing holding my brains in place, I was afraid to ask how badly I was wounded.

"Why aren't I dead?" I asked instead.

"He must have gotten the gun wet as he was coming aboard." McAllister answered. "Either that or the silly silencer he had on the end of that thing slowed the bullet down enough so that, by the time it hit you, it didn't pack a full punch."

"I'm. . ." I swallowed hard. "I'm not gonna' die?"

"Not unless you drown yourself." McAllister looked at the large plastic tumbler I had emptied and began refilling it from a two liter bottle. "Still, you got a hell of a dent in that thick skull of yours. The doctor said you're going to have to take it easy for a while."

"Doctor?" I didn't remember having a doctor onboard.

"We stopped in Copenhagen." He answered. "We were about halfway between Stockholm and Copenhagen when you got nailed and we decided to make a run to Denmark because it was about twenty miles closer. We were on the radio all the way, trying to get a helicopter out to pick you up, but apparently the Danish Coast Guard never heard of air/sea rescue. We thought it was rather ironic that you survived getting shot in the head but then faced bleeding to death. God! What a mess you were."

"The police?" I was having a hard time picturing myself bleeding into the scuppers of the fantail and wanted to break away from that mental depiction.

"We told them it was an accident. A shark rifle that went off accidentally in rough waters."

"And they bought that?" I asked, clearly surprised.

"They didn't have a choice." He smiled. "Half a dozen witnesses swore to it and you certainly weren't in any condition to contradict anybody."

"Where are we now?"

"About a hundred and fifty miles east of Savannah." He broadened his smile. "We'll be home sometime tomorrow."

I didn't bother to point out the fact that Savannah was twenty five hundred miles away from my home in Payson, Arizona.

"How long was I out?"

"Almost six days." He held the straw to my lips again. "You really gave us a scare. Larkin was saying Hail Marys' at the speed of light, I was yelling at everyone from Captain Olsen to the cook, Irina couldn't stop crying, Mark was. . ."

"Irina?" I interrupted. "What happened to Irina? Where is she?"

"Take it easy." McAllister laid a palm on my chest. "You don't think I was going to let her get within a New York mile of you until I got your story, do you? She is being kept in good company by one of Mark's friends. Incidentally, Mark has been standing outside your door since we got you out of the hospital. Won't leave. Blames himself for what happened to you. Says he should have searched Sargo more carefully when he came on board."

"It wasn't his fault." I said, suddenly remembering my final cognizant thoughts from almost a week ago. "Sargo was really Rastov. The real Roskovin was Sanya. She's dead."

"I figured it was something like that." McAllister replaced his smile with a sad frown. "Listen, why don't you get some more rest and we can talk about it in the morning?"

At first I thought that McAllister was making, what for him would be a concession of gigantic proportions by not grilling me for every bit of information he could glean. Then, from the sudden after taste I was getting from the ginger ale, I knew why he wasn't being persistent. The drink was obviously laced with some drug, no doubt something prescribed by the Copenhagen Hospital that was making my eyes droop uncontrollably.

"My left leg and arm feel tingly." I said with effort. "Almost as though they aren't there."

“They’re there,” McAllister smiled, using his best bedside manners. “Don’t worry, you’ll be fine.” We’ll talk about it in the morning.” McAllister repeated. “Get some rest now.”

I don’t know if it was my lights or the cabin lights that went out.

* * * * *

When I woke up it was daylight again and although I had aches and pains in places I had previously taken for granted, I had a measure of satisfaction in knowing I was still alive. One of the aches was more familiar than the others and when I tried to get out of bed to make my way to the head, it seemed as though part of my body was lagging behind in some way. I attributed the sluggishness as some form of atrophy, and was more concerned by the renewed dizziness I was experiencing as I sat on the edge of the bed. After a moment, the ache in my bladder turned into pain, reminding me through my light-headedness of the primary reason I had attempted ambulatory activity. McAllister came through the door just in time to see me fall flat on my face. He dropped the papers he was carrying and rushed to help me to my feet.

“Bathroom.” I said through parched lips.

He lifted my arms around his shoulders and dragged me to the head. I glared all the way, not at McAllister, but at the fact that I had little or no feeling in my left side. I balanced myself on the sink until he shut the door then turned myself clumsily into position.

It seemed that every time a book is published or a movie hits the theaters, people have normal lives except when it comes to using the toilet. You read about, or see them shower and bathe, shave their face or legs, depending on gender, brush their teeth, and even clip their toenails. However, when it comes to using the oversized dog’s water bowl that, in reality, gets used more than anything in that cramped room, accurate depictions are lacking. Not wanting to be a pioneer in this field, I’ll spare the graphic details simply by saying that the everyday function that I had come to take for granted became a traumatic experience. By the time I was finished, I didn’t know whether to laugh or cry. On the other hand, I had survived a professional assassin’s carefully aimed bullet to the head, but the price of remaining alive might mean that I would have to spend the rest of my life having someone assisting me in a very personal and necessary objective. When I opened the door, still in shock over the time and effort I had just expended, McAllister was there to help me back to the bed.

“The doctor said the paralysis might take some time to go away.” McAllister said as he lowered me back on the sheets. “We have all the medication you need. It's just a matter of getting the proper exercise when you're feeling better."

The relief of not being permanently paralyzed was like a grand piano being lifted off my chest. When McAllister said those few words, I think I did cry.

"We can talk more after you rest a bit." He said.

"Now." I said with more resolve than ability.

"But. . ."

"Now." I repeated, and McAllister pulled up a chair to the side of the bed and I began telling him how I had figured Sargo/Rastov to be something other than what he represented only to awaken and find him sitting in my room. I had got to the part where Rastov was telling me about substituting the Lilly Egg when I realized I had not said anything for a long time. I opened my eyes to an otherwise empty room, and from the position of the sun shining through the porthole, knew I had slipped off to sleep in the middle of my narrative.

I was only re-awakened for minutes when McAllister and Larkin came in, peeking first to check on my welfare. Larkin was carrying a glass of ginger ale and when I expressed reservations about drinking, McAllister assured me that the soft drink was unadulterated. I took a healthy swallow and continued my chronicle before they even sat down. It was almost dark when I finished.

"Any questions?"

McAllister shook his head. "You couldn't have been more concise if you were preparing a manuscript for publication."

"Good." I said. "I have a few."

McAllister grunted as if I had made a colossal understatement.

"Where are we?"

"Fifteen miles off the coast of Savannah. We got here late this morning and we're anchored near the same spot we were when you came out for the party.

"Speaking of 'full circle'"

"Funny, huh?" McAllister smiled with an 'I-told-you-so' expression on his face.

Suddenly tired of being cooped up in the cabin, I insisted we continue our talk on deck. McAllister enlisted Mark to help and together they managed to get me to the afterdeck lounge without dropping me. On the trip up, my leg seemed to be working from the hip to a spot just above the knee and my arm had feeling, but it was the numb-stiff-tingly feel as if I had fallen asleep in the wrong position. When I was settled into a deck chair and Mark had retreated a reasonable distance, I turned to McAllister.

"Who shot Rastov?" I asked.

"I did." He said it without hesitation, but he lowered his eyes when he spoke. "Mark was making his rounds and when he noticed that Sar . . ., Rastov was not where he was told to stay, Mark came for me and we went looking. We were right above you when the two of you came out from below decks." He pointed.

"You cut it a little close, don't you think?"

"The son-of-a-bitch had the only gun on boat. We didn't dare rush him."

I raised my good hand and let it drop. "I'm just glad you thought of the spear gun."

"A friend of mine used one quite effectively too." He said lowering his head.

I remembered. I think his name was Ben Driscoll.

"Anyway, I don't think Rastov will be washing up on any beaches. Do they have sharks in the Baltic Sea? I hope so."

"So where do we go from here?"

McAllister opened his mouth but Larkin spoke first. "A follow-up medical check for you, Grange." She said. "You have an appointment with Doctor Charles Harris at the Candler Memorial in the morning. He's a neurologist and tops in his field."

"It may make you feel good about going to that hospital because that's where I was born." McAllister smiled. "Well, actually it was the Warren A. Candler Hospital back then."

"A long time ago." I shook my head in mock amazement.

"Well, not that long ago." McAllister corrected.

I nodded politely to Larkin and ignored McAllister's defensive stance about his age. "What else?" I asked no one in particular.

"We got a response from Sir Godfrey." He said, knowing what I wanted to know. "The Cassandra did leave Italy, bound for Savannah, on the same day her sister ship, the Cassiopeia, left for New York. The captain's log doesn't mention anything about anyone who could be Irina's grandfather, but he might have been covering his ass by not documenting the fact that he had an illegal Russian immigrant on board. We have a passenger list, but it wasn't much help because we didn't know his name. We didn't want to ask Irina because we didn't know how she fitted into the situation with Rastov. You might say we kept her under house arrest. We haven't let her out of her cabin since your, . . . ah, accident."

"It looks like she's legitimate." I said. "And in competition with you."

McAllister smiled. "Legitimate maybe." He said. "Competition, I doubt it." His smile turned mischievous. "Maybe I should keep her in her cabin indefinitely."

I watched his eyes to check for sincerity. He laughed.

"Just joking, Grange." He conceded.

"Yeah, I bet, Bobby." I began. "What's the matter, too much like looking in a mirror?"

"What do you mean by that?"

"She's the same as you." I explained. "Ever since she was a little girl, she's had a dream, and, except for her social circumstances, grew up just like you, hoping someday to find the treasure that her family ghosts told her was there for the taking. The Faberge jewels represent her version of a pirate ship called the Prize,. . ." I looked at Larkin.

". . . And a beautiful golden hair apparition, excuse me, goddess, in the form of a wooden carved figurehead of the same ship."

Larkin crossed her arms. "Apparition?" She asked.

"Well, you know what I mean, Larkin." I bowed my head humbly. "All that surreal and spooky stuff is way over my head, and defies comprehension on my part."

Larkin unfolded her arms in a manner of acknowledgment of my analogy.

McAllister was observing the exchange between Larkin and me, and as I was taking my foot out of my mouth, he said, "So, what are you suggesting, Grange?"

"First of all, I think we can stop treating her like a hostage." I answered. "She has left her homeland in search of her dreams and since she was the one who, directly or indirectly, caused you to be at this very spot at this very time." I paused, unable to believe my verbal endorsement of McAllister's 'pie-in-the-sky' theory. "She is the one who convinced you to abandon whatever quest you were on in Russia to come back to your hometown and look for the lost Faberge treasure. I think she should share in any recovery."

"You're absolutely right." He said magnanimously. I'll reward her monetarily."

"That's not what I had in mind, Bobby."

"What did you have in mind, Grange?"

"I think she should have the pick of the litter of her grandfather's treasure."

"I said I'll give her a generous amount of money." McAllister reiterated.

"Treasure, Bobby. Not money." I countered.

"Can you be more specific?"

"Twenty-five percent of her pick of the treasure."

"Okay, whatever." He said. "I'll see what Irina wants." He conceded. "I guess it is her dream too." He added.

"Good."

McAllister was still silently grumbling about the arrangement that he had more or less agreed to. There was no sense in reminding him that twenty-five percent of nothing was still nothing. He would never think in terms of failure.

"Captain Jim is bringing Excalibur up from Florida." He said. "He should be here by tomorrow night."

"Why do we need Excalibur?" Even though it was my boat, I wouldn't have objected to anything McAllister required of her. In a moment I was certain he secretly regretted, he had given me the stately yacht and in six years I had used her twice, each time for less than forty-eight hours, and I didn't even leave the dock. He had simply to ask for its return and I would happily hand it over, saving me a small fortune in insurance, docking, and licensing. While it was true that Captain Jim Feathers made a living with her, paying all these fees, there was not much to be gained by absentee ownership and Jim could go on making a living with McAllister as the owner just as well as having me retain title.

"Excalibur has the equipment we need." He said. "I figure old grandpa knew there was no way he could get two crate loads of jewels past customs, so he dumped them overboard before the Cassandra docked. Since he was unable to identify landmarks, he used Florence Martus as a point of reference, and when he was sure he could estimate the distance he was from her, kerplash."

I looked at him, truly amazed. When I found my voice again, I said the first thing that came into my head.

"That's nuts."

"No it isn't." He argued. "The old man was a sailor. He might have known it would take time and effort to make a recovery, but he also knew it was probably his only chance to get his treasure into the country."

"He could have seen Florence Martus anywhere in a hundred eighty degree arc." I reasoned. "You're talking about hundreds of miles of ocean floor to find two crates that have probably long since succumbed to the elements. You certainly can't use the blasters. You would blow the loose gems all the way back to Russia."

'Blasters' were elbow shaped contraptions fitted on the rear of salvage vessels that redirected the prop wash to blow accumulated layers of sand off the ocean floor. They were used primarily for uncovering large wrecks and were capable of digging a trench twelve feet wide and as deep as the prop pressure would reach in the sandy bottom. Excalibur had two such devices.

"You're right about the blaster," he conceded, "but you know as well as I do that there are other ways to uncover sunken treasure. We even have a good reference point for beginning. Irina's grandfather said something about the sun setting directly behind Florence. Shipping lanes on this side of the coast are pretty well defined. That narrows our search area considerably."

"And it makes it far more dangerous." I added. "You can't be working underneath the water when some supertanker comes cruising into port. You're talking about a pursuit that could take years."

McAllister smiled again. "It took two hundred and fifty years to find the 'Hacha' and the 'Prize'." He said, a twinkle in his eye.

Underneath the bandage on my forehead, a dull but stabbing pain had begun. "I don't think I'll be sticking around that long, Bobby." I said.

McAllister stared off toward the shores of his beloved Savannah.

"You never can tell, Grange." He said. "You never can tell."

* * * * *

She came in shortly after I had settled into bed. Before I had the opportunity to turn the light back on or even speak a word of greeting. She was sitting on the edge of the bed, two fingers pressed to my lips to keep me from talking. For a long time, she just sat there, studying my face in the available light of the full moon streaming through the portholes. Her face was in shadow but I could see a flicker of phosphorescence in her eyes as she ran her fingers lightly over my features and through the hair on the side of my head. Several times I started to say something, but each time she silenced me with a single stroke of her hand and barely audible hushing sounds.

After an interval that was deliberately prolonged and extraordinarily sensuous, she stood up and removed the garment she was wearing with a grace that was stimulating both visually and audibly. She raised the corner of the sheet and slid into the bed so smoothly and effortlessly that I was not certain she had joined me until I felt the satin touch of her skin against mine. I wrapped my good arm around her shoulders and she laid her head on my chest, her velvet hair covering me like the wings of a thousand butterflies. Her lips caressed my ribs as she pressed herself closer and her hands continued an endearment of physical communication that aroused every nerve end, every pore of my skin, every essential part of life.

When her tender caress became even more personal and her own needs surfaced in the form of kittenish whimpering and increased body heat, I gently whispered that my physical limitations might keep me from performing in a way that would be satisfactory.

I was wrong. . .

* * * * *

Some of the sting of having to spend the next few days in medical care was erased from my mind as the launch took me to Savannah the following morning. I was so distracted that Larkin felt it appropriate to make several comments, all designed to alleviate the apprehension I had about follow-up care. I smiled each time she made a reassuring remark and immediately drifted back into memories only a few hours old.

I was met in the reception area of the Candler Memorial Hospital by a nurse with a wheelchair, and before I could thank Larkin for the kind words and the ride, I was whisked off to a series of examination rooms. As the day dragged on, I was punctured, and electronically photographed by doctors, nurses and mechanics until I was certain that I was more of an experiment than a patient.

Doctor Harris finally saw me for the first time a little after three o'clock and after introducing himself, told me he was recommending that I be admitted for a few days of observation. Although I could feel the strength returning to my left side throughout the day, I reluctantly agreed, wanting to be as certain of my physical future as much as to avoid the possibility of a malpractice suit. I was wheeled off to a private room on an upper floor, given unspecified medication, and was sound asleep before I finished reading an article in a Reader's Digest I had found somewhere along the way.

As a result of retiring early, I awoke with the first gray light of dawn, feeling stronger and more alert than I had in over a week. When the nurse responded to my call for something cold to drink, I inquired about the day's agenda.

"Some more tests and x-rays this afternoon." She said, consulting a chart at the foot of my bed. "Then an appointment with Doctor Harris."

"I sure could use a cigarette." I hinted.

"Sorry, Mister Lawton," she said, shaking her head. "Candler Hospital is a smoke-free environment."

"Any objections if I wheel myself outside for a breath of forbidden carcinogens?" I asked, pointing to the electric wheel – chair next to my bed.

"Not from me. I'm a smoker myself." She confided. "Just try not to be conspicuous."

I finished a carton of cold orange juice and managed to get myself into the wheelchair without adding to my physical injuries. I was in remarkably good spirits. My left arm seemed to be working again, even if it was a little sluggish responding to my telepathic signals, and my left foot had the same sensations that had been in my arm only a few days ago. At my insistence, I was wearing a sweat suit I had brought with me anticipating an overnight stay, a far more comfortable and stylish alternative to hospital gowns, and it only took a couple of minutes to learn acceptable skills as to the use of the motorized chair. I took my wallet out of the bedside table, hoping the gift shop at least sold cigarettes, and headed for the elevators.

At a picnic table a short distance away from the front door, I smoked two cigarettes, drank a can of Tab, and flipped through one of the magazines I had purchased at the gift shop. After a half an hour of fresh air and first hand smoke, I headed back toward my room, hoping the continued observation I was experiencing might be moved to an earlier time.

While waiting for an elevator, I glanced idly around, taking in my surroundings, when I was seized by an idea prompted by a sign on one of the first floor office doors. I guided my electric transporter to the open door of the Medical Records Department and politely waited until someone noticed me. It didn't take long.

"May I help you?" He was a young man, probably in his early thirties, wearing a tie but no coat and obviously more interested in the papers in his hands than me.

"I was wondering how long Candler Hospital has been around."

He looked up from a sheaf of notes. "You mean the Candler Memorial Medical Center, or the old Warren Candler Hospital downtown?"

"I didn't know there was an old one downtown."

"Where are you from?"

"Arizona."

"No wonder." He replied.

I scooted my chair further into the room. "Actually, I'm a writer."

I added. "Just looking for a little background information."

"That's a first." He sat the papers down. "I've never been interviewed for 'background information' before. You going to use my name?"

"Not unless you want me to." I had learned to hedge on that often asked question.

He considered for a moment. "Naw," he said, "you don't have to if you don't want. You probably have to change all the names anyway."

"How old is 'the old' Candler Hospital." He continued, thinking out loud. "Must be pretty old. At least before the turn of the century."

"Really?"

"Well," he clarified, "it wasn't at this location, like I said, but it was next to the 'Big Park' downtown. It was called the Warren A. Candler Hospital then."

"Do you have medical records that go back that far?" I asked.

"Some." He said, shrugging as if the system back then was not under his control so he couldn't say for sure. "Records of any significance weren't documented until after the turn of the century. Today, everything is on computer of course."

"Then you might have files from 1917?" I asked hopefully.

"Possibly."

"Chronical or Alpha?"

"Cross referenced." He patted a computer monitor.

"You can check on a name for me?" I asked, trying to sound casual.

"I don't know about that." He said hesitantly. "Medical Records are supposed to be confidential."

"C'mon," I cajoled. "We're talking about a patient from 1917, who has long gone to the promised land, not Mrs. Ferdenmucker's gall bladder operation that took place last week."

"I don't know." He said, still not convinced. "They can be pretty fussy about things like that around here.

I decided to try something McAllister would do. Taking a pencil and a piece of scrap paper from his desk, I wrote down my name and number and Irina's grandfather's name. From my wallet, I took a one hundred dollar bill and tore it in half.

"I'll tell you what," I said, returning the pencil and note with the half bill to the corner of the desk, "you think it over and give me whatever information your conscience will allow. I promise if I ever put anything into a book, I won't use your real name."

I gave him my most sincere smile as I wheeled out of the office.

I didn't see him again until after I had been re-probed, re-tested, x-rayed until my only medical problem was radiation poisoning, and fed the blandest meal since the discovery of fire. He didn't know it, but he could have had the other half of the bill if he had only brought me a Big Mac.

"Good news and bad news. Mister Lawton." My eyes went to the computer printout in his hands. "Which do you want first?"

I was never good at making decisions in the little game he was playing and I told him so.

"Then you must not write mysteries." He said. "You have no flair for the dramatic."

I reached into the bedside cabinet and took the half a hundred and set it on the over-bed table, deliberately covering it with a glass of water. Half of Ben Franklin smiled up at him through the liquid magnification. He got the point.

"I couldn't find anything under 'Alexander Nucheck.'" He said, pulling a chair around to face me.

"I hope that's the bad news." I remarked drily.

"It may be." He started shuffling the bi-folded paper. "I expanded my search by looking for variations and came up with a guy named 'A. Newcheck.'"

I sat up more fully. "And?"

There is very little information, really." He consulted the printout. "He was admitted and died two days later. No first name, no date of birth, no medical history, no family."

"What caused his death?"

"Peritonitis."

"Which is?"

"An inflammation of the serous membrane lining of the abdominal cavity."

"And what would cause peritonitis?" I persisted.

He shrugged. "Lots of things. Infection mostly. Could have been cancer, ulcers, appendicitis."

"Appendicitis?"

"Sure." He said offhandedly. "If it was acute, it could have caused an infection. Remember, we're not talking about modern medicine here. Although I don't doubt the dedication of the doctors of the time, medicine, and especially surgery, was very primitive back then."

"What happened to the body?" I asked. "Did anybody ever claim it?"

"No, but here's the real strange part. According to this, he laid around for about a week before he was finally buried in some Potter's Field."

"Why would that be so strange?" I asked. "Wouldn't they refrain from burying him in hopes of locating some family or maybe even some friends?"

"That's not the strange part." He answered. "I thought it was unusual that he was buried in a pauper's grave in some cemetery that probably doesn't exist anymore. According to this," he tapped the papers he was holding, "he wasn't exactly destitute. The nurse that admitted him and inventoried his belongings listed a small leather pouch containing, and I'm quoting, sixteen gemstones; eight diamonds and eight emeralds."

* * * * *

"Yo. The Reef."

"The Wretched Reef?"

"Yeah."

"Is Ned Hoffman there?"

"Who wants to know?"

"A friend of Bobby McAllister."

"Just a sec."

It was more like a full two minutes. In the background, a Jukebox, clinking glasses, and raucous laughter.

"Hello." It was dragged out but not slurred; just carefree and friendly.

"Ned Hoffman?"

"At your service."

"My name is Granger Lawton. I'm a friend of Bobby McAllister."

"Hey, hey! The guy who wrote Fool's Paradise." He put mock displeasure in his voice. "I hear you don't like the way I dress."

"My words." I answered defensively. "Somebody else's description."

"Just kidding." His tone was back to normal. "What can I do for you? Is Bobby in trouble again?"

"Not at the moment." I answered, hoping I wasn't lying. "I need a legal slant on something I heard."

"Do I bill you or Bobby for this, ah, consultation?" He asked. He was kidding again.

"Bobby, of course."

"Bobby won't pay, but fire away."

"A man enters a hospital," I began, trying to make it sound hypothetical, "and two days later he dies. He has no friends or family. The hospital doesn't even know who he is for certain. However, he has fifty thousand dollars cash in his pocket. Oh, did I mention? This all happens in 1917 or '18. What happens?"

"Some overworked orderly steals the money?" He wasn't sure what kind of answer I was looking for.

"No," I clarified, "everything is done aboveboard."

"The late case becomes a case for the Public Administrator." He answered, turning very professional sounding. "His assets are liquidated, but in this case it sounds as if that has already happened, his bills are paid, and a mortuary is assigned to make a proper disposal. The balance of his assets goes to the state or local governing authority."

"Would he be buried in a Potter's Field?"

"Probably. Who would care?"

"Accountability?" I asked.

"As far back as 1917?" He scoffed. "C'mon. I couldn't even begin to guess. But you can bet it wasn't buried with him." He changed tracks. "Does this have anything to do with some telephone calls I got from London?"

"Yeah." I admitted. "Sorta.""

"This gonna' be another book?"

"Not yet."

"Well, if it turns into one, try to be a little nicer about me, will ya'? I have a reputation to uphold." He burped. I'm sure he did it on purpose.

"I'll keep that in mind."

* * * * *

Doctor Harris saw me for the final time the next morning and, pleased with my physical progress, pronounced me fit enough to be discharged. I could walk with a cane and I trusted my left arm enough to use it for minor tasks, but I was still required by hospital regulations to ride in a wheelchair to the point where a taxi met me at the front door.

Dennis Feathers was waiting for me at the docks, and although he greeted me enthusiastically, he was obviously told to downplay my temporary handicap. He never said a word about my condition, but his furtive glances at my hand and leg spoke volumes of his barely contained curiosity. We sailed down the Savannah River, and had barely cleared the mainland by about a mile when I saw Excalibur on the horizon. When he didn't turn in that direction, I tapped him on the shoulder.

"Isn't everyone on the Excalibur?" I asked.

"Well, yeah." He answered. "But Bobby said you'd be more comfortable on the Second Prize."

"Take me to Excalibur." I ordered. He reluctantly changed course.

When we arrived, Captain Jim met us at the top of the boarding ladder. After we exchanged pleasantries, I pointed to the depths.

"What's going on?" I asked.

"Bunch 'a damned nonsense if ya' ask me." He replied, shaking his head in bewilderment. "Russian spies 'an chasin' all over foreign countries, 'an sumptin' 'bout Easter Eggs. Nuttin' makes much sense, lookin' for two boxes sunk in these waters. Like lookin' for some rich dame's wedding ring on board the Titanic."

"There's one difference." I pointed out. "We know where to find the Titanic."

"Ain't much difference." He looked out over the ocean. "Water ain't clear like down Florida way. We ain't got no claim. We got traffic comin' and goin' like we was waitin' in line at one 'a them Disneyworld rides, 'an all on the word of some Russian woman who ain't never left Russia or even met her own grandpa."

"You don't believe any of this?" I asked.

Captain Jim shook his head again, searching for the right words. "I know if there is sumptin' out there, the one man who has any chance of findin' it is doin' his damdest to find it right now."

"He's diving right now?"

"Him and the missus." Jim nodded, looking toward the water. "And this afternoon it's gonna' be him and that Navy diver. I'm cancelling all my stuff back home for the next six months." He shook his head as he turned toward the bridge. "It's gonna take him that long to find the bottom 'round here."

He was exaggerating of course, but I couldn't help but share his pessimism. In searching for sunken treasure, a number of factors go into making a recovery. McAllister's only hope of finding Alexander Nucheck's treasure was pinpoint accuracy, something that was next to impossible considering that the evidence we had already didn't amount to squat.

Since there was nothing for me to do aboard Excalibur and McAllister knew I wouldn't strap on a tank and jump over the side even if the boat were on fire, I asked Dennis to take me back to the Second Prize. Thirty days, I said to myself. If McAllister didn't turn up anything in one month, I was headed back to Payson. Period.

* * * * *

"Let me see if I understand everything I think I know about all of this." McAllister said as he paced back and forth on the afterdeck of the Second Prize.

There were eight of us altogether; McAllister, Larkin, Irina, Mark and two other divers McAllister hired on Mark's recommendation. I looked for Gary Caldwell to be there upon our return, but I figured he was 'invisible'.

Mark had been going almost non-stop for eleven days, and having found nothing worth more than scrap metal and other equally worthless forms of garbage, McAllister had called a meeting to look for new ideas and solutions.

"We have the finest and most sophisticated equipment money can buy, the right people manning the tools, the most modern backup systems, the most comprehensive charts and graphs, and it's all backed up by state of the art computer software back at the plantation that we have linked up with us here on the Second Prize. We're even hooked up to satellite intelligence. What more do we need?"

"More patience and an army." Jim grumbled under his breath. McAllister spun around and glared at him.

"More information." I said quickly, hoping to keep McAllister from saying something to Jim he might later regret. "Precise information."

"Like what?" McAllister asked. "We know that Irina's grandfather came over on the Cassandra. As soon as we found out what his name was, it took us only seconds to find him on the passenger list. We know the Cassandra came to Savannah. We're pretty sure the old man was talking about Florence Martus instead of the Statue of Liberty. We're also fairly certain he died two days after he landed. And, from his last entry in that diary, we can assume he hid the treasure, expecting to recover it when he got out of the hospital."

"Wait a second." I said, thinking about the diary. "He expected the worst. His final written words to his wife were in the form of a clue as to where he hid the stuff in case something happened to him. Would this man expect his wife to go scuba diving off the coast of Georgia, USA if he wasn't able to make the recovery himself?"

In almost two weeks, it was the most convincing argument I had been able to raise, but it was one that finally got McAllister to pause. "Where do you suggest we get more information?" He asked me. "We have everything on the Cassandra from the archives in Seville. We have the hospital records and his death certificate. We have the diary. What else can we possibly find, and where?"

"I don't know," I said, "but there has to be something. Maybe tracking down the Public Administrator that Ned told me about would help. Newspaper records might tell us something. Maybe he confided in someone who wrote about it somewhere. It could be in some long buried source of rumors that didn't get attention because pirate stories were far more glamorous. You're the expert. You tell me."

"Then that's a good job for you, Grange." He said, pointing to me. "But until you come up with something new and informative, I take it everyone is in agreement that we keep diving, right?" He didn't wait for an answer. "Good."

The meeting ended, everyone went their separate ways but McAllister side tracked me into the lounge and poured me a drink. He looked frustrated and troubled, but managed a knowing smile as he settled behind his desk with a larger than average drink of his own.

"So how are you two getting along?" He asked.

I knew what he meant and resented the question. Although we had made it no secret, Irina's visits to my cabin had, at least, been discreet; not every night and supposedly after everyone else had retired. I knew better than to ask him how he knew, but I objected to the fact that someone felt he should know.

I expressed my feeling by cocking an eyebrow and making a careful study of the liquid in my glass.

"I'm not asking out of some perverted sense of voyeuristic curiosity." He said, carefully rearranging his face to delete the wry grin. "I have a reason."

"Then maybe you better rephrase the question." I suggested.

"Very well," he said, taking the hint, "has she said anything that might be useful?"

"I'm not sure I like that question either." I said testily.

McAllister sighed. "Look, Grange." He began, making an effort to refrain from saying anything insulting. "You know as well as I do that she wants those jewels as much as me. You also know that people sometimes say or do things that might trigger a different kind of response when they are relaxed or unsuspecting. Deep in their subconscious they have important facts that may be trivial to them but taken in a different context, place a completely new slant on things. I just wonder if you have picked up on something."

Even though I knew we had not discussed the methods McAllister was employing, I began to experience doubts caused by one of my own submerged thoughts. Something was again nagging at a piece of gray matter behind the dent in my forehead that had been trying to surface for the past few days. I ignored it for a moment.

"You don't sound like your usual confident self." I said instead.

"Damn it, Grange! I'm not." He stood up and started pacing again. "I hate to admit it, but I'm just not getting the right mind set here. It's like some instinct, some sixth sense, is telling me I'm wasting my time."

That was unlike the normal unflappable and sure footed McAllister. I told him as much.

"Maybe it's because I haven't had much encouragement." I started to object by reminding him that it was his notion that Alexander Nuchek committed his two crates to the deep but waved it off and continued. "If only I had some kind of sign. Something that would show me I'm on the right track."

"Like a message from the spirit world?" I asked skeptically.

"Call it what you want." He said, noting my cynicism. "The fact remains that something I'm doing has some form of merit."

"Why do you say that?"

"Because somebody has been going to unusual lengths to keep tabs on us."

I knew better than to question him on matters of security, but I wanted to know what he thought he knew. I fixed myself a refill while I waited for an answer to my unasked question.

"For the last week now, someone has been watching our every move." He said. "They have the resources to use a different boat almost every time, but it's always the same two guys. Even with telescopic lenses, I haven't got a clear enough picture to identify them, but I don't believe its coincidence or paranoia."

"Is there any way we can find out who they are?"

"Nothing short of an overt act approaching piracy." He answered. "We did manage to get the numbers off two of the boats, and when Mark traced them down, found one of them to be from a charter service out of Harbour Town Marina in Hilton Head. When we called the service, we were told the charter was arranged by a 'Mister Smith'. We haven't been able to find out who the other boat belongs to, and that in itself seems strange."

"Hilton Head?" I didn't know where that was.

"Hilton Head, South Carolina. Across the river and up the road a ways."

"Oh."

McAllister stared silently out toward the eastern horizon.

"Cops?" I suggested. "Drug Enforcement? You have to admit that conducting dives along commercial shipping lanes is suspicious at best."

"Since I'm not doing anything illegal, I'm not going to worry about that aspect." He said. "I sure would like to know who they are though."

"Give them something to be even more curious about." I advised.

"How?"

"Bring up something while they're watching you." He smiled, liking the idea, so I continued. "Then break up your schedule. Tomorrow afternoon, as soon as you think you have them sighted, have Excalibur winch something up from below. Then, the next day, don't dive. We can go into town, have lunch, and make some sham telephone calls from public phones, generally act as if we have something to hide. If they are following us, they will probably trip over their own dicks to get closer to see what we have. Even if they turn out to be cops, we haven't done anything illegal."

"Great idea, Grange." He toasted me by holding up his glass." "Tomorrow we start 'Operation Identify.'"

When I got back to my cabin, Irina was waiting. She ran to me when I entered the room, throwing her arms around me and nearly knocking me down.

"Where were you?" She asked, almost scolding. "I was worried."

"Bobby and I were talking." I laughed at her concerns. "There's nothing to worry about."

I told her about the meeting and what we were going to be doing for the next few days. Her eyes narrowed as if she were wary and concerned. "We are not giving up?" It was a cross between a question and a positive statement.

"No," I smiled gently, trying to relieve her apprehension, "just trying to protect our interests."

"You are not worried that these men might be policemen?" She asked.

"Believe me," I said, expressing amusement at her concern, "those guys being cops would be the least of our problems."

She shook her head in wonderment. "In my country, the police are feared for their tactics as much as the KGB."

"It's not quite like that in the United States." I assured her, thinking that McAllister would definitely disagree with me, but then again, he no longer considered Arizona as part of his country. I also failed to mention people like 'Officer' Frank Kipper who thought the Constitution was a morning walk to the outhouse. "At least it's not supposed to be like that." I amended.

Irina sighed as she sat on the corner of the bed. "I will be much happier when all this is over." She said. "Then I will go to your home in Arizona and I could cook caviar blinis for you and we could make love every day of the week."

"That sounds great." At least part of it did. "But, please let me show you some great western American recipes that I know. . ."

She interrupted me with a kiss.

I looked into her beautiful and innocent eyes and said, "Well, maybe we don't have to wait until we get to Payson, Arizona to make love." I reminded her.

We didn't.

* * * * *

Armed with the information sent by Sir Godfrey, the computer file supplied by my friend in the medical records division of the hospital, and a copy of Alexander Nuchek's diary, I decided to begin my paper chase at the public library on Bull Street below the 'Big Park'. My other two choices were the Bureau of Vital Statistics and the Savannah Morning News office, but I felt I should have all my facts in order before I visited those offices and that left the library as the logical place to start. I found a table in the corner next to a window and spread my papers across the top to dissuade anyone from joining me. My first job was to find a Russian/English dictionary and translate Irina's grandfather's journal from the beginning to end. It proved to be a larger task than I had anticipated. Although I was lucky enough to find a translation text that worked both ways, the interpretation went slowly. Irina's grandfather was apparently less educated than I had originally thought and deciphering his handwriting into something that resembled Cyrillic alphabet was difficult at best.

After three hours, I finally got in to a natural rhythm and the last part of the text seemed to come out more easily. I could have asked Irina for a word by word translation, of course, but something McAllister had said the night before prompted me to do the job myself, looking for a contradiction, a nuance, or something that might lose or gain substance in the translation.

I did have trouble with one particular phrase. It seems that Alexander, in spite of his sickness, went to the cargo hold of the Cassandra once a day to check on his precious freight. At one point he wrote a passage that literally translated to; "I look at our many boxes of jewels". Thinking that the phrase had lost something in the nether world between Russian and English, I wrote it down the way it came across and underneath wrote; "I look at our boxes of many [much] jewels. (?)".

When I finished, I had a fairly reasonable piece of copy with only a very few words I could not define. From what I could tell, Irina had given us a fairly accurate rendering of the passage she had read to us and the rest of the subject matter was unrelated to our objective.

By the time two-thirty rolled around, I had only uncovered one point of interest and was about to leave for the newspaper office when McAllister walked through the front door, looked around, and walked over.

"Mission accomplished." He said, his expression was somewhere between arrogant and matter-of-fact, "The bait was taken with the proverbial hook, line, and sinker."

"Tell me about it over lunch." I said. "I'm starving."

Since my leg occasionally showed grudging ability to function properly and I was still using the cane, we took a taxi to the restaurant at the 17Hundred76 Inn on President Street which was one of McAllister's old haunts. He couldn't wait for our drinks to arrive to tell me about his little ruse.

"We saw them on their way out," he began, pausing to accept a complimentary pitcher of Chatham Artillery Punch, "the same two guys in yet another boat, acting like they were fishing or sightseeing the way they had been doing for over a week now.

"One of Mark's men took up a lookout and when he saw them coming back, nice and slow like they always do, we were ready. We had a net hooked up to the winch, filled with junk, just dangling in about thirty feet of water. Larkin and I waved to everyone aboard Excalibur while the net was being hoisted and everyone on board made a big deal about swinging the net on board without doing any damage to what was in it. The charter swung around and started playacting as if something had fallen overboard. When we pulled up anchor and headed for the Second Prize, they took off full throttle for shore."

"It sounds like we got a reaction from somebody." I commented.

"What do you think we should do now?" He asked, almost gleefully.

"The ball is in their court now." I said, "But I don't think you should do any more diving for the next couple of days. Let's wait and see what happens."

He nodded his head in vigorous agreement. "And in the meantime, I'll have Mark prepare a reception for them in case they decide to come calling."

"Tell him not to get too overanxious." I cautioned. "They still might turn out to be cops."

"That doesn't matter, Grange." McAllister shot back. "The Second Prize and Excalibur are now both anchored in International waters." He reminded me.

I hoped I hadn't created a monster.

"You said that you had some information." He prompted, changing the subject. "What did you come across that's going to help us?"

"I don't know if it's going to help." I qualified. "I just found something noteworthy." I opened my folder of papers and withdrew a sheet from the information sent to us by Sir Godfrey. "According to this," I handed him the flimsy across the table, "the Cassandra docked shortly after noon on the seventeenth." I withdrew the computer printout from Candler Memorial Hospital and passed it over. "But correspondingly, the records from the hospital state that "A. Newcheck' wasn't admitted until the morning of the eighteenth."

"So?"

"So, doesn't it seem odd that a man who has been complaining of acute illness and pain would wait almost twenty-four hours before seeking medical attention?"

"Maybe he had trouble clearing immigration." McAllister reasoned.

"I doubt that, even way back in 1917, a man would be denied lifesaving medical attention simply because he didn't have a turn of the century green card." I replied. "My bet is that he managed to debark and find a place to hide his jewels."

"Yeah?" McAllister was skeptical as well as sarcastic. "Where?"

"Somewhere he could find them after he got out of the hospital." I said in the same tone of voice.

McAllister recognized that he had been rude and backed off a bit. "Sorry, Grange." He said, as the waiter placed our sandwiches in front of us. "I guess I've been kind of hard to live with lately. The point I was trying to make is that the guy had nowhere to go. He sure as hell wasn't familiar with Savannah, he didn't know anybody, and he was sick as a plow horse with a hernia. Maybe the hospital records were wrong. Maybe somebody just got the dates mixed up."

"Or maybe he thought he had found a friend." I suggested.

"You mean Florence?"

"Why not?" I answered his question with one of my own.

McAllister took his time chewing a bite of food to consider. When he swallowed, he made a comment, but he did not sound at all sure of himself. "It's a long way out to Elba Island and back."

"He had twenty-four hours." I reminded him.

"There were no bridges back then." He continued as if I hadn't spoken. "No paved roads, no guideposts. Do you think he really might have gone out there just because some old lady waved at his boat?"

"You were the one who suggested that he dumped over a hundred million dollars into the ocean because of Florence Martus." I said. "Besides, in 1917, Florence was not an old lady. She would have been somewhere in her forties and very well might have been quite beautiful; even angelic looking."

"He still would have needed help." McAllister's arguments were growing weak, almost as if he wanted to be proven wrong . . . or, be convinced.

"When his belongings were catalogued at the hospital he had sixteen gems; eight diamonds and eight emeralds. Doesn't 'eight' seem like an unusual number to you? Why not ten? Or even a dozen? Why eight?"

"He was Russian." It was the type of answer McAllister would give when he often stepped out of the bounds of logic. "Maybe they count differently in Russia."

"I think he met Florence." I said.

McAllister used the excuse of a mouth full of food to abstain from commenting.

"I think she helped him." I continued.

McAllister remained quiet and thoughtful for a full minute before he gave in. He shook his head in wonderment and said. "God! I wish that were true. It's such a beautiful story for old Florence, who loved her River of Dreams."

"You're a hopeless romantic, Bobby." I meant it.

His mind was working at warp speed. He said nothing.

"What's out there on that island, Bobby?" I asked.

"Elba?" He shrugged offhandedly. "I don't know. The old lighthouse, I guess. Not much else."

"Did Florence and her brother live in the lighthouse?"

"No. They had a separate two bedroom cottage. I don't think it's even there anymore."

"Why don't we take a look?" I suggested.

"When?"

I looked at his empty plate. "No time like the present."

* * * * *

Elba Island marks the south channel of the Savannah River and the lighthouse is only a few short miles from Fort Pulaski and the birthplace of Florence Martus. I couldn't help but think that this lonely old woman had attained almost world-wide attention and probably never traveled more than a few miles from home. It was said that she had never missed greeting a ship in forty-four years, so most of her adult life had to have been spent on that little spit of sand and vegetation that stood in the face of hurricanes and existed in a solitude that is difficult to imagine.

The lighthouse was, indeed, still standing and untended, a product, I imagined, of modern technology once again replacing the human held torch. Although I didn't ask, I assumed that the light was operated by a photo sensitive device, a timer, or a switch at some central location, getting individual attention only when something needed replacement or repair.

The island itself was untended and overgrown with thick vegetation that stretched into the shallow water of its source. There were a few trees, but those that had survived the unpredictable weather and other hostile elements were permanently bent and misshapen. Even the shore birds made Elba only a temporary stop, a place to rest before finding more suitable feeding grounds or better protected nesting areas.

As McAllister beached the boat on the muddy, reed infested shore and tied a line to a nearby scrub bush, I tried to make myself believe that Alexander Nuchek, desperate and ill, had made his way through this same thick undergrowth over seventy-five years ago with only one thought in his fever ravaged mind; to find a safe place to hide his riches.

When he finally got a close look at Elba Island, he must have been disappointed.

"Well, where do we go from here?" McAllister was still not convinced that Irina's grandfather had options other than throwing two crates of precious gemstones into the drink. "How many paces from the old Live Oak that looks like skull and crossbones?"

"You're the pirate," I said as I used my cane to vault onto shore, "isn't there a fixed formula for that sort of thing?"

It was lighthearted banter to cover the feeling that we were surreptitiously trespassing like two adolescent boys on a dare or planning some juvenile prank. The growth was thick enough to resemble a tropical jungle but not dense enough to require hacking our way through like the machete bearing explorers of the Amazon and in a few minutes, we stood at the base of the lighthouse.

"Couldn't be here." McAllister stood looking up, his legs apart, fists on hips, in a pose I'm certain made him feel like a swashbuckling buccaneer. "Too obvious."

"What's in there?" I asked, making a note of the old fashioned, overhand swing padlock that secured the weather-beaten door.

"A spiral staircase and a very big light bulb." At least his tone was more jocular than sarcastic.

The structure was, indeed, a step below distinguished. Its familiar shape rose less than three stories with an extra room attached to its base, just large enough to be a storeroom for spare equipment and tools. I knew McAllister's crack about the bulb was facetious; that it was the design of the glass around the lamp that magnified a light that could be seen for miles. However, it was that thought that reminded me of a book I had read, or perhaps it was a movie, wherein the multi-faceted glass that surrounded the source of illumination was made from precious jewels. I shook my head to relieve myself of the fantasy. Irina's grandfather might have had the strength and resolve to hide his fortune, but he never would have been able to muster the time or talent to design and build a complicated lens from a bucket full of gems. I went to the door and rattled the knob. In spite of its shabby and neglected appearance, the closure was firm and solid. I walked around the base, looking for inspiration rather than anything physical, and finding neither, returned to McAllister's side.

"Satisfied?" He asked in the tone of an indulgent parent.

"Not entirely." I said, forcing my mind to function. "What kind of floor do you think is inside?"

"You mean possibly a dirt floor?" He was anticipating my thoughts. "One where he might have dug a hole and buried something?"

I nodded.

"That won't wash, Grange." He said in a tone I had often used on him. "First, you have to remember that George and Florence lived out here, isolated and alone, their one and only responsibility being that lighthouse. Don't you think that either of them would have noticed something as obvious as a freshly dug hole? Secondly, I seem to remember that the WPA did extensive renovations on all government owned lighthouses whenever that program was instituted and thirdly, even if it were buried under a more recently laid concrete floor, getting permission to dig it up would cost more and take more time than what we are doing now and after all, the government would claim any treasure as their own."

He was probably right, at least about the last part.

"What about the house?" I asked. "Where was that?"

"Right over there." He pointed. "But it stands to reason that, if he couldn't bury it in the lighthouse, he sure as hell couldn't bury anything under the cottage."

I nodded agreement as we walked to an area that seemed more recalcitrant to support the growing of natural vegetation. In the difference in growth, we could see the outline of the small home shared by brother and sister for almost a century. Further evidence of past habitation was the occasional brick or piece of rotted lumber but, other than that, all traces of the house were gone, the forces of nature working hard to reclaim its former territory.

My leg was causing me a bit of discomfort so I found a small patch of bare sand and used the cane to lower myself to the ground. I was sitting in a spot very close to where I figured the front porch of the humble cottage had been staring east toward where Excalibur had been anchored only that morning. Florence Martus had stood on or near that very spot waving her white handkerchief at passing ships, and I tried to picture what it was that made Alexander think she was "pointing the way" toward something.

In my very early youth I remembered my grandparent's farm near Chicago, and how my grandmother stood on the porch and waved when my parents and I arrived from the city. Not long after my father died an untimely death at forty-nine, I remember telling my grandmother that my earliest memories were of her standing at the top of the steps waving as we approached the old family home. When I told her of that pleasant memory, she snickered.

"I wasn't waving." She said, recalling times even then long past. "Your father, he drove like a madman. I was always telling him to slow down."

Down, I thought. Slow down.

Down. Downtown. Downfall. Downplay. Downstream. Down-to-Earth. Sit down. Weigh down. Point down. . .

"What's that?" I asked McAllister. McAllister had taken a seat next to me.

"What?"

"That over there. That pile of rocks."

"Oh, that." He answered disinterestedly. "I don't know. Probably what's left of the old well?"

It took a full five seconds to register. At the same time, we looked at each other in amazement.

* * *

CHAPTER ELEVEN

Picks, shovels, more flashlights, preferably the lantern type, a winch capable of hauling at least five-hundred pounds, a tri-pod, buckets, plenty of rope, both packing rope, and rope for the winch, quick assembly scaffolding, enough to stand, say, fifty feet, and pry bars. Can anyone think of anything else?"

With the exception of Captain Olsen and his crew, and the kitchen staff, we were all gathered in the lounge of the Second Prize, where McAllister was giving instructions as he paced back and forth like a football coach at half-time.

"Divide up that list", he continued, "and make your purchases at different stores around town. We don't want to make ourselves conspicuous or tip anyone off to what we are doing here. Our little game this afternoon hasn't yet caused much of a reaction, so I'm assuming that our friends who like to fish from a different boat everyday are not law enforcement types. If you think you're being followed, break off and return here immediately.

"We go to Elba Island as soon as it's dark tomorrow evening. We're only going to have one chance at this thing, so, we want to do it right. Mark, you go in tomorrow morning and approach the island from the other side. Decide how you're going to set up your security perimeter. You and your men should be in place no later than six o'clock. Are you sure that you can manage without Gary, I kinda' promised him that he could participate in the actual 'recovery' when the time came."

"No problem, I only hope that Gary won't be disappointed." "Okay, Gary and Steve." McAllister turned to address Gary, his life-long friend, and Steve who had recently been hired by Mark for his expertise in the 'lay-of-the-land'. "We need to take diving equipment for the three of us. We don't know how much water is down there so we better take two extra tanks each. Grange and Larkin will remain at the well head to shuttle supplies and equipment. Irina is in charge of coffee and drinks and act as a utility hand." He was giving her a job out of courtesy, not because he expected her to act like a waitress.

"Right after dark we take Excalibur as close to shore as possible and shuttle in from there. We don't know if we're going to find anything, of course, and if we don't, we still have our original options, don't get your hopes up to high. Everyone still gets their after-expenses percentage, and for those who think that one percent doesn't amount to much, just remember, that if Grange is anywhere near correct, that one percent may amount to over a million bucks each. Any questions?"

There were none.

"Good. Everyone get a decent night's sleep. We're going to have a big day tomorrow."

McAllister held me back as everyone filed out of the lounge, eagerly discussing among themselves how they were going to spend their share of their fortune. Irina looked back with a question in her eyes, and I made some signal designed to indicate we would meet later. She apparently understood because she nodded before she turned away.

"Sit down, Grange." The seriousness in his voice put me immediately on guard. "We have to talk."

I fixed myself a drink and limped to a chair.

"What would you say if I told you that Irina Denikoff was not what she appeared to be?" He asked, watching me carefully for my reaction.

"I'd say you were being paranoid," I answered levelly.

"Just because I'm paranoid doesn't necessarily mean that someone isn't out to get me."

"Rastov gave her a clean bill of health," I reminded him.

"Maybe he didn't know." McAllister had anticipated my response. "Maybe his department works on a need-to-know basis and he was out of that particular loop. Besides, you know as well as I do that Rastov was the type of person who would have enjoyed sending someone to their grave believing a lie. After all, he told you that Misha Mossolov was a thief, while Sarzanov insisted that the pieces Mossolov smuggled out were stolen from him. I think it's a fair assumption that we can't rely on anything Rastov might have told you, regardless of the circumstances."

"Do you have any evidence that Irina might be involved in some complicity?" I asked.

"Not a shred," he answered honestly. "Just call it a gut feeling. I have a couple of seemingly unrelated incidents that are bothering me, but nothing chiseled in stone. I just want you to keep an open mind when you're around her, that's all."

"Well, I think you're way off base on this one," I said. As far as I can tell, she has done nothing to warrant this mood of yours, in fact, she has gone out of her way to be helpful and has unquestioningly agreed to everything we have asked of her, including agreeing to the percentage she should take on her recovery. "

"That's just it," McAllister contended. "Maybe she's been a little too over compliant."

"Bobby," I began. "She comes from a country where nothing comes easy; any windfall is gladly taken when experience has proven that common things that you and I take for granted, might be the ultimate luxury for someone less fortunate."

"I hope you're right. Grange, I really do," he said, shaking his head. "Just don't take any unnecessary chances."

"Is there something else on your mind?" I asked, sensing he wasn't finished.

He hesitated, obviously more concerned than he first appeared.

"Rastov told you that the KGB always retaliated when one of their own was killed," he said, choosing his words carefully. "That means both of us have to be very careful. Since nothing else has come of our little charade with the bogus recovery this afternoon, we have to consider all the possibilities. Since Rastov hasn't reported to his superiors, it becomes very likely that those guys on the boat are associates of his. When they saw us bring something up this afternoon, they may have decided that now is the time to act."

I nodded my head in understanding. For a few short days I had been under the illusion that, since I was back in the land-of-the-brave, and the home-of-the-free, I was immune from any further secret police-type, and the cloak-and-dagger routine. McAllister's warning had brought me back to reality.

As I made my way back to my cabin, I was haunted by McAllister's twin exhortations. I had long ago, learned that he had an uncanny ability boarding on extra-sensory perception, that was not to be ignored, and that his hunches always had an underlying vein of fact. That his intuition overlapped into concerns about Irina especially bothered me because of my own anxiety and unfounded uncertainty. I wished I could put my finger on exactly what it was that was causing my reservations, but the harder I tried, the more obscure my reasons became. It didn't help that, when we were alone, Irina did everything in her power to make me forget about everything except the pleasure we shared.

In that respect, that night was no different.

* * * * *

With Excalibur anchored less than sixty yards from shore, it took us only minutes to shuttle equipment and personnel onto the dark and almost mysterious island. Gary and Steve did most of the carrying while McAllister led the way to the well with Larkin, Irina, and me bringing up the rear. Even though I knew that Mark and his men had already been in place for hours, the island still felt eerie and spectral, the reeds and high grass swaying, the moon casting darker shadows into the night, and the breeze sounding almost like a mournful moan as it rustled across the sand.

The rotating beam of the lighthouse afforded us very little light; its powerful signal designed to alert things distant rather than provide illumination for the island. If anything, the revolving beacon only emphasized the darkness and lightened the shadows.

Very little time was wasted talking as Larkin and I began the assembly of the tripod and rigging of the hand-winch as McAllister, Gary, and Steve began clearing the rocks from the wellhead. At first I thought that the entire pit had been filled with rocks which would have made our job far more difficult. I was therefore surprised as anyone when the rocks were cleared away to reveal a thick wooden panel covering the hole. The overlay had apparently once been a door to a barn-like structure or an old door, and gave us more trouble than the rocks because the corners and edges were partially buried in the heavy dirt and covered the thick growth that resembled Bermuda grass. Steve suggested simply breaking through, but McAllister insisted it to be removed to better define the edges of the shaft.

It took all six of us to make the final lift, standing on the wide side of the board and heaving together. Skirting the edges, Gary and McAllister got the door vertical while Steve and I pushed it past the point of balance with the pry bars. It crashed down in a cloud of dust and sand as it hit, a loud and unnatural noise, excessively clamorous in the otherwise quiet night. I shined a flashlight into the hole.

My first impression was that it was not nearly as deep as I would have expected; perhaps sixteen to eighteen feet. The walls were lined with the same smooth river rock that had covered the opening and it was dusty dry; the bottom clay-like dirt that looked impossibly hard packed. We all looked at each other, each waiting for someone else to make a remark but, since nothing seemed appropriate, we went to work picking up tools and stacking the underwater gear as if each of us knew what we were doing and why.

The opening was about five feet in diameter and the tri-pod fit across as if it had been custom designed for the job. With the winch attached, it was well enough to one side so that five of us could peer over the edge and watch Gary as he lowered himself effortlessly to the bottom. He probed the dry dirt with the tip of a shovel and looked up.

"It's packed pretty solid," he said, his voice sounding hollow but muted. "It might be a bit hard at first but it should go easier once we get started."

"Does it look like it was filled in?" McAllister asked.

"No." Gary answered, stomping a foot as if to determine the firmness of the ground. "I think it just dried up or the water table dropped from beneath it. There isn't much room, though. Only one of us at a time down here for the digging."

In answer, McAllister lowered a bucket. "We can take shifts," he said. "Ten minutes apiece until the going gets easier, then we can increase to twenty minutes."

Steve took the hint and began digging, replacing Gary.

It took six to eight scoops to fill a bucket and we raised and dumped each bucket about ten feet from the opening. By always having two extra buckets standing by, the person digging never had to wait, so we progressed at a rate of about a foot deeper every half hour. I even took a shift myself, but my physical inability slowed me to such a pace as McAllister soon became impatient and told me to get out of the way to allow him to dig. After McAllister dug three feet, the hard-packed dirt turned into a softer, sandier type of filling and the excavation stepped up its pace considerably. McAllister continued digging until he was again replaced by Gary.

We were all filthy. Covered with dust, we all began sweating in the humid night and the perspiration trickled off our faces and arms causing streaks of mud that made each of us look like painted warriors in the dark. It's odd that I remember how beautiful Larkin was; her golden hair drenched in dust and sweat mingled with the ever-present swarm of gnats and mosquitos, created an angelic-glow that caused me once again to wish I were Bobby McAllister.

Of course, the assortment of winged insects attracted to the light and the odor of stale perspiration and fresh blood was very annoying to everyone except Larkin, who seemed to be oblivious to the elements. Flying bugs that I had never seen before were buzzing in front of open eyes, fouling our mouths and nostrils with their bold and persistent presence, even flying bugs that glowed in the night.

We had one false alarm when Gary hit something solid, but it turned out to be one of the large, smooth rocks that lined the sides of the shaft and was heavy enough to strain the winch as we lifted it out.

"How far do you think we should go?" I asked McAllister at one point.

"As far down as it takes," he answered as he watched Gary fill yet another bucket. "Or until we reach China."

"Can you be serious, just for a moment, Bobby?" I asked, totally miserable from the effects of the elements.

"My mother told me to always be serious and sincere, whether I meant it or not." Replied McAllister who was attempting to inject humor where humor was not appropriate.

"How about we dig until we hit water." I suggested.

"Okay. Whatever." McAllister answered. Did I ever mention how McAllister could be so annoying at times?

I thought of how much heavier the buckets would be, filled with water-laden mud, and groaned. Larkin and Irina never complained, however, so I tried to keep my aches and pains to myself as I hauled another pail of dirt to the spreading dump. For the record, the ladies not only refrained from differing or dissent, they kept up a steady stream of cold drinks from an Igloo cooler we had brought and, together, even hauled the occasional bucket of dirt to the discard pile. At one time, Irina had been fiddling with the stack of scuba gear and when McAllister asked her what she was doing, she answered that she wanted to take the accessories back to the two shuttle launches to save us a trip later. McAllister told her not to bother, that if we struck water, the well might fill up and the assorted paraphernalia might be needed. McAllister stared at her for a good minute before he resumed what he was doing.

Along the sides of the well were water marks where, throughout the years, the stain of the wall indicated the various levels of the water. I asked McAllister what caused the variation and why we had not, now almost eight feet further down, re-struck water.

"A great many things affect the water table," he explained. "Annual rainfall, the seasons, dredging the river, even the amounts of other wells dug in the area. Most likely, somebody has tapped into this water supply at a different location and depleted it below where this well was originally sunk."

Thus far educated, I returned to hauling dirt while McAllister traded places with Gary.

The only light we were using was focused into the well causing a funnel of pale yellow to radiate from the hole. The vertical shaft of light intersected with the horizontal beam from the lighthouse every fifteen seconds, a strobe that marked time with the regularity of a fine watch.

Inside the well, the shaft was bright as day except for the dust which still almost obscured the bottom and whoever was shoveling at that time. We looked like a band of grave robbers; our dirty, sweat-stained features made somewhat grotesque in the available light. And like common thieves, we worked mostly in silence, each carrying out our duties with a patient, mechanical perspective. McAllister soon tired and traded places with Steve.

Somewhere around two-thirty, we heard the unmistakable sound of a shovel blade striking something solid. Five of us dropped what we were doing and rushed to the well-head. Steve was barely visible through the gray haze, on his hands and knees, using gloved hands to dig around his latest find.

"What have you got, Steve?" McAllister asked, trying not to show his anxiety.

"It looks like an ammo box," Steve said, waving the dust from in front of him to keep from choking. "It has some writing on the lid."

"Ammo box," McAllister repeated. "What the hell?"

"Hey!" Steve called from the bottom of the hole. "It's got some sort of chain through the eye-bolt that holds down the lid. Wait a second. I think the chain is attached to something else."

"What does the writing say?" McAllister and I shouted down into the hole, almost in perfect harmony.

"I can't," Steve answered. "It's written in some foreign language like Greek or Italian."

Latin or Greek, I thought.

"Italian!" I blurted out. "Many boxes."

"What the hell are you talking about, Grange?" McAllister looked at me as if I had slipped a cog.

"In his journal," I said, talking about Alexander Nuchek, "he mentioned going down to the Cassandra's hold to check on his 'many boxes' of treasure. I thought I had made a mistake in the translation. This box here," I pointed down, "has Italian lettering on it. He repacked the boxes while he was in Italy!"

McAllister studied me for only a second. "I'm going down," he said, and grabbing the rope, began a hand over hand descent.

In the cramped quarters, McAllister and Steve dug with their hands with renewed purpose. It took them fifteen minutes to uncover three more boxes, all hooked together by the same length of chain. McAllister called for a rope from the winch and, once attached to one of the links of chain, Gary and I began cranking the handle. It was like trying to pull a weed with an intricate and complex root system. As we held the tension from above, McAllister and Steve attacked the dirt below with shovels, picks, and pry bars. The legs of the tri-pod groaned and bent in protest, not from the weight of the boxes, but from the resistance of the ground that was holding whatever was still below the packed dirt at the bottom of the well. McAllister grunted in pleasure each time another box was freed and kept a running count on the number of exposed cases that dangled on the chain halfway between the bottom of the well and the surface like some giant charm bracelet. When the count reached fourteen, the winch began to have a different feel and two more boxes literally popped out of the ground as a result of our labored cranking. McAllister took the time to come up to ground level using the boxes strung on the chain as stepping stones and giving Steve more room to hack at the ground below. With a final drawn-out effort from the three of us manning the winch, the dirt below cracked and parted, and four more boxes burst through the dry clay. The chain with twenty boxes, each a little smaller than a bread-box, bounced wildly with the release of tension and we all looked anxiously into the hole to see if Steve had been hurt by the swinging and jerking of the train of chain and containers that had hung in the hole. He was already halfway out, climbing up one of the ropes, a wide grin on his face.

When we had the entire cable out of the shaft, we spread it on the ground next to the opening to examine our find.

Altogether, twenty boxes, some hopelessly rusted, some remarkably preserved. All twenty were identical, made of a light metal, not aluminum, but thick tin or thin sheet metal. The tops were held in place by a levered clamp, very much like my grandmother's mason jar lids, except that each clamp had an eye-bolt, instead of padlocks, the links of the chain drawn taut against the lids. Larkin shined a flashlight across the boxes, reading what printing was still legible.

"What does it say?" She asked no one in particular.

"Sewing machine parts," answered Irina, toeing one of the boxes. "And this one says, 'screws', and this one says, 'bolts'." She bent down and used her hand to brush off one of the boxes that was less rusty. "They are consigned to the 'Imperial Sewing Machine Company' in New York."

"Wouldn't it be the shits if we spent the last six hours digging up sewing machine parts?" Gary asked, his tone indicating a wish to be contradicted.

McAllister shook his head. "Where have you ever seen a box of bolts?" McAllister asked, picking up one of the boxes. "That weighs as little as this?" Discounting the weight of the chain, the boxes were fairly light. The heaviest part of the bizarre string of boxes was the chain that held them together. Had the boxes, indeed, held what they were labeled to contain, our winch would never have had the capacity to extract them from the well.

"Besides," McAllister continued, "what would a shipment of Italian sewing machine parts being shipped to New York be doing in Savannah? It was Irina's grandfather that hopped the wrong boat, not unconsigned cargo."

"I don't think I've ever heard of the Imperial Sewing Machine Company," Larkin added. "But I have heard Russian Czars referred to as the Imperial Family."

We all smiled at the obvious reference.

"Larkin, what would I ever do without you?" McAllister said in admiration of his wife.

"I don't think you have to worry about that, Bobby." She smiled. "Well, we aren't going to get these boxes open here," McAllister said, looking at his watch. It was almost three-thirty. "I suggest we clean up here and get back to Excalibur to examine what we have here." He started assigning us specific clean-up duties, but Irina was already amongst the diving equipment.

"We can leave that stuff until later," McAllister told her. She, however, continued to busy herself with her back turned toward us as if she had not heard a word McAllister had said. When she finally turned around, she held a familiar object.

"Do not move," she said in a voice almost caustic with menace. "And do not try to call out to your friends who are out there." She flipped her head in a non-direction. We all stood perfectly still.

If it wasn't the gun that Rastov had possessed, it was its identical, right down to the cumbersome silencer. To be face-to-face with the weapon that had already caused me great pain and unpleasant memories, especially in Irina's hands, was too much. I groaned almost pitifully as I sat down in the sand, holding my cane as if it were a staff with a white flag fluttering from the handle.

"We thought that Rastov had dropped that overboard when he fell."

McAllister, standing next to me, sounded unsurprised and calm. "We searched your cabin twice and couldn't come up with it."

"You miserable Americans," she said contemptuously, almost as if the word was an obscenity, "with your superior attitudes and your silly sense of fair-play. Did you really believe I would meekly accept your pitiful offer of twenty percent, and that by giving me that, you would earn my eternal gratitude? You have many freedoms in this country that has affected your mind."

"What are you going to do, Irina?" McAllister asked, still unruffled. "Even if you leave here with those boxes, you have no place to go. No one knows these waters better than I. It would only be a matter of time before we tracked you down."

"Then I guess I will have to kill you all." She said.

McAllister actually laughed. "You don't have enough bullets to kill us all." McAllister said half-heartedly, seeming to be amused.

Now was not the time for McAllister to be amused, I thought; but then again, I have seen him talk his way out of the Grim Reaper's grasp many times.

Irina seemed to be considering what McAllister had just said, as she stood in front of us in silent defiance.

McAllister seemed oblivious to Irina's threat. In fact, he actually laughed out loud. "Besides, who are you going to kill with a gun that, even at point blank range, did nothing more than give Grange a headache?" He chuckled again.

Irina stepped forward. She kept her stance wide, but the way she shifted from foot to foot, and the way her eyes darted around at the five of us betrayed her amateur status at handling guns.

"We will just have to see who wakes up with a headache and who does not wake up," she said, though her bearing made known her unprofessional status as a gunman, the cruelty in her eyes and voice left me no doubt that she would pull the trigger if she felt she must. I looked up at McAllister and begged him with ray eyes not to antagonize her further.

"You and you," she pointed the muzzle briefly at Steve and Gary, "gather up those boxes. When we reach the boats, you will place them in the blue one." She kept her eyes on McAllister as she skirted the well and moved closer. "You will all walk in front of me until we reach the shore. I will then decide if you are to live or die. If one of you makes an error between now and then, we will see how effective the gun of my late comrade really is."

"Look, Irina," McAllister tried to sound reasonable, "before you make a mistake that can't be corrected, think about what you are doing. You're alone in a country that is unfamiliar to you. You don't have any contacts. You don't know anyone. You don't have any money."

"You fool!" She shouted derisively, waiving the gun. "I have all the money I need." She pointed to the boxes.

"That's not money," McAllister said frankly. "You can't go into a Piggly Wiggly or Winn Dixie Market and buy a Moon Pie, and a 'Nee-High' cola. That treasure has to be converted into cash through proper channels. I have the resources to do that. Twenty percent of what I could get you would probably be more than what you could get for the lot."

"Another of your capitalistic fabrications," she sneered. "You believe that because I come from a communistic society that I know nothing of free enterprise or economics. Or is it because I am a woman? Either way, you are mistaken. You know nothing of the Russian mentality. We are far more proud and determined than your bourgeois conceit allows you to believe. We have survived since the beginning of time. What is America compared to the four thousand years of Russian history?"

"Listen to yourself, Irina." McAllister actually sounded as if he were pleading for her to understand, not because he was afraid of what she may do, but for her own good. "You sound like a tape recording of your own government's propaganda. This is not a matter of ideals or pride. This is common sense; a matter of practicality. If you shoot us, you tilt the odds against yourself. You become a hunted criminal by your own country, my country, and even Larkin's country. Larkin's father, Roberto Tumbas, is worth five times what is in those boxes. He would spend every dime to see you brought to justice for the murder, or even harm to his daughter, you can count on that, Irina."

McAllister might have been exaggerating since it was Bobby's wealth that had helped Senor Tumbas elevate himself to the position he maintains today. However, since revenge was one of those Russian traits that Irina had just been thumping her chest about, she hesitated ever so slightly.

"You're also forgetting one important factor, Irina." McAllister pressed his advantage. "Mark Shaefer already knows that I have never trusted you completely. He is paid a great deal of money to protect me from those who would cause me, my family, and friends any harm. I would lay odds that, right now, he has you in his sights, waiting for a signal from me to drop you like a bad habit."

The threat didn't work. If anything, it strengthened Irina's intentions the way a playground dare instills false courage. She stepped around the well-head so that her back was to the now empty hole and she adjusted her stance, like a power hitter expecting a fastball right down the middle of the plate.

"I have waited too long for this moment," she said, calling McAllister's bluff. "I have come too far. If I am to die on this wretched, bug infested island, then my fate is sealed. But I promise you one thing. No matter how mortally wounded, I will not be the only one who spills blood into this disgusting dirt you call part of your great nation."

In spite of the venom of which she spoke, I was not afraid of dying. I was having a difficult time comparing the bitter but determined figure in front of us with that warm and tender young woman who had slept peacefully in my arms only twenty-four hours ago, but that was not my reason for my dispassionate feelings. McAllister was trying far too hard to dissuade Irina from her course of action. Normally, in a situation of confrontation or disadvantage, McAllister became overly sarcastic or caustic. He had to have some pre-arranged protection for a contingency such as this, or he would not have been acting so cavalier.

"It won't work, Irina." McAllister said, softly and gently, almost with a touch of regret. "Give me the gun now and we can forget this little incident ever happened."

Irina was losing her demeaning stance. I could tell that she was touched by McAllister's gentle and genuine attempt to dissuade her from following through with her threats to us, and sealing her own doomed fate. It was obvious that McAllister was trying to appeal to Irina, the bright and kind young woman that every one of us adored. McAllister was trying to appeal to Irina as a distinct entity, separate from the young Russian, In-Tourist guide, who had been brainwashed by the Russian Propaganda machine.

As if Irina was reading mine and McAllister's mind, "you must think of me as very foolish." Her initial nervousness gone. She extended her arm full length and pointed the gun at McAllister's nose. "Now, pick up those boxes and do as I say, or be the first to test the capabilities of this weapon."

Larkin broke her silence, "Do you realize what you're doing, Irina?" Larkin asked, as if they were the best of friends. "You're turning against your only true friends. If it wasn't for Bobby, you would have never known the truth about your grandfather's disappearance, nor would you have ever seen any of his looted treasure." Larkin continued in a soft imploring voice. "Don't do this, Irina. Toss that ugly weapon in the well and let's all of us get back to accomplishing what we came here to do. I give you my word that none of us will hold this incident against you if you will only listen to "your heart, not your Russian up-bringing. Please, Irina, cross back over to our side, you will never regret it."

Irina was touched by Larkin's words. Irina's eyes began to swell with tears as she lowered her hand which held the gun, to her side as she bowed her head and stared down to the ground.

Seconds later, Irina dropped the weapon and Larkin began to move toward Irina to console her. Larkin looked at McAllister for some sign of approval. McAllister shrugged his head non-committedly, almost sadly.

Irina raised her head when Larkin reached for Irina's hand, but she ignored Larkin and began to sob. "Irina, all the treasure and wealth in the world will never bring you happiness. Only love and true friends are cherished beyond monetary value." Larkin's hand was reaching out to Irina. Irina hesitated, and then reached out to Larkin, visually searching the darkness for me. Our eyes met for a fleeting second as she accepted Larkin's hand. It was the last thing Irina did in her present life-time.

"Comrade Denikoff!" The sound of gunfire burst from the darkness. We all turned our heads, searching the night for the un-seen gunman. "Irina!" screamed Larkin. "Bobby! Oh my God!"

The bullets struck Irina in her chest. In one quick motion, McAllister shoved Larkin to the ground. "Stay down!" McAllister commanded his wife. But before he could reach Irina, the force of the gunshot's blow staggered her backwards. Her feet, out of position, causing her to lose her footing and balance, got tangled beneath her and she began to topple. For an impossibly long moment, she seemed to remain suspended over the open mouth of the well. Twice she made an ineffective grab at one of the tri-pod legs before gravity finally asserted itself and she dropped out of sight. There was a one-second pause and then a sickening thud. I scrambled on hands and knees to the lip of the opening. In a cloud of re-settling dust, Irina laid on her back, a trickle of blood coming from her mouth and nose. With a surprised look in her eyes, Irina stared without seeing at the inner depth of the well. McAllister and Larkin came to stand above me looking down at the dead woman, their expressions cheerless, but more than that, disappointed. As I turned for one last look at the second woman in my life that I was going to bury, McAllister spoke.

"Who the hell shot her!?" He was livid. He looked out into the darkness, "Goddamitt, Mark!" McAllister shouted, obviously thinking that it was Mark or one of his men who shot Irina. There was no reply.

McAllister turned toward Larkin and me and said, "I didn't want it to happen this way," he lowered his voice and continued quietly. "This was not called for." Larkin placed both of her hands on her husband's arm, comforting him. "Honest, I tried. . ."

There was nothing else to say. McAllister seemed oblivious to the fact that there was a gunman amongst us. But I was thankful that McAllister did not attempt to say anything more about Irina, and seemed to focus more on the hidden threat.

I lifted my head and visually combed the shadows from where I thought the distracting shout and gunfire had come. Everything had happened so quickly that I had also assumed that Mark had been the one who had called out her name, and fired the lethal shots, but then I remembered that the voice had called her "Comrade". Would Mark do that, I wondered?

The same thought must have occurred to McAllister because when I looked up at him, he was also staring into the darkness with a puzzled expression. When I looked back to the spot he was watching doubtfully, three dark figures slowly emerged from the shadows. Invisible from fifteen yards away, they moved closer to the light, almost cautiously, not as an ally, but as suspicious strangers.

From five yards away I could tell that at least two of them were not unknown to three of us. Frank Kipper was on the left, smiling gleefully when he saw that he was recognized by McAllister and me. At first, I thought that the siege was arranged by him, but when they stopped about three feet short of the other side of the well, I recognized the man in the middle. McAllister still had not made the connection, so he addressed himself to Kipper.

"Hello, Frank." As surprised as I was, McAllister seemed to accept the presence of his old nemesis. "Is this little party your idea?"

All three men were, quite naturally, armed; Kipper and the man in the middle with silenced pistols, and the third member of their little surprise party, with one of those compact machine pistols with the square grip. I think it was an Uzi, but since my knowledge of guns is limited, I can't say for sure. Confronting unarmed men and a semi-defenseless woman, they held their guns at their sides casually. They had nothing to fear. They were all professionals, and a five-second burst from that menacing Uzi would have meant five more occupied drawers at the morgue.

Without taking my eyes off of the three men in front of us, I reached up a hand so McAllister could help me to my feet. As I struggled to a standing position, I spoke directly to McAllister, but loud enough for everyone's benefit.

"This is the man we were destined to meet," I said, not happily. "If you look closely enough, you can see the crescent-shaped birthmark just above the jaw on his right cheek."

Steve and Gary looked at each other questioningly, but McAllister and Larkin knew immediately who our latest intruder was.

"Major Kaliniskov," McAllister acknowledged politely, but genuinely surprised, "I can't say that it's a pleasure to meet you, but I am surprised."

"And why is that, Mister McAllister?" he asked, his voice was deep and rich, almost accent free.

"I would have figured the KGB to be much smarter than to be in league with the likes of Frank Kipper."

Kipper started to object but Kaliniskov held out a hand to stop him.

"Gee, Frank," McAllister continued, "how low can you actually go? Cop, con-man, pimp, hustler, now you're in bed with the KGB. Was your name Judas Iscariot in a different life?"

"Fuck you McAllister!"

"Good, Frank," McAllister teased. "Clever retort."

Kipper seethed but it was Kaliniskov who spoke.

"Is she dead?" He pointed with his chin to the well.

McAllister nodded.

I couldn't believe that the two men were discussing Irina's death as if she were a wild game trophy.

"You're goddamned right she's dead!" I shouted. "You fucking blew her away, you cowards! She was one of your own 'Comrades', ass hole." I started toward Kaliniskov, but McAllister grabbed me so hard that I fell back down on the ground, just as the man with the Uzi raised his lethal weapon aiming it in my direction.

"Pity," he said, without emotion. "Another example of a talented amateur who attempted to beat the system." He sighed theatrically. "Also a sad waste of a marginally capable and sometimes inventive seductress." He turned to me. "But you would be the one to be the judge of that, Mister Lawton."

"She was working for you?" I asked. I wasn't particularly surprised, just a bit numb.

"It started out that way," he answered, sighing again, but as evidenced by tonight's turn of events, it seemed she had other designs. I believe my business associates told her far too much when she was recruited. Good help, as the British so often complain, is so very hard to find."

"What's his part in all of this?" McAllister asked, pointing to Kipper as if he were a worm infested slab of meat.

"We often make use of our local law enforcement officials in our forays into foreign countries. It paves the way for a smoother operation." Kaliniskov glanced sideways at Kipper. "We often find that the local police are most helpful in providing information and profiles on subjects that interest us." He smiled at McAllister. "I must say, however, you have been most successful in thwarting our Lieutenant Kipper's efforts at most every juncture."

"I told you this bastard was tricky," Kipper interrupted. "Besides, it was Rastov who failed at the house in South America after I told him I already lost two teams down there. How was I to know that Rastov wasn't operating under your orders? You two don't exactly...." He shut up, realizing that he had already said more than what Kaliniskov wanted to divulge.

"Speaking of Comrade Rastov," Kaliniskov continued as if Kipper had not interrupted. "I must assume that the poor man has not made the crossing with you as planned."

"Not unless he has amazing powers of resurrection and is capable of swimming really fast." McAllister answered.

Kaliniskov nodded his understanding. "I thought as much when I saw Mister Lawton still alive."

"And Artur Ladvick?"

"Rastov got him before he went after Mister Lawton." He feigned a sigh. "At least I have one less loose end to tie up. And what have we here?" He pointed to the chain of boxes.

"Just what it says," McAllister answered seriously, "sewing machine parts. Somebody must have thrown them in the well to displace the water to a higher level."

Kaliniskov looked at McAllister reproachfully. "Come now, Mister McAllister," he said, "we have been so refreshingly candid up to this point. Why must you embarrass yourself with such a clumsy lie?

I'll tell you what, he continued, as if the idea had just occurred to him. "I will demonstrate my sincerity in dealing with you honestly, in exchange for like treatment by telling you first exactly where we stand at the present time."

"You mean quid pro quo"?

"Exactly, Mister McAllister."

"How about this idea. Let my wife, Lawton and my two hired helpers leave unharmed and I will stay here and tell you everything I know."

"Nice try Mister McAllister. Let's be real. I'll tell you what, I'll go first, Okay?"

McAllister nodded his head.

"You have a total of four men guarding your little force here. None of those four will be coming to your assistance. Fortunately, for Lieutenant Kipper, he is aware of your penchant for having someone watch your back at all times, and since their attention was divided by watching you, we caught them off-guard, and it was not difficult to neutralize them.

"We have no more secrets. There are only the three of us standing before the five of you. Since we have weapons, and, therefore, the advantage, we can take what we want, when we want, and depart at our convenience. To employ a metaphor, you are out of trump and my hand is trump tight."

"So we tell you what you want to know and then you kill us." I couldn't help but notice that some of the swagger had gone out of McAllister's voice.

"We could have done that ten minutes ago," Kaliniskov pointed out. No, in spite of your fears, I bear you no malice. As far as I am concerned, this weapon is nothing more than a deterrent." He half raised the gun and let it drop back to his side.

"Grange killed one of your men." I wanted to slap McAllister for reminding the KGB major of that bit of information. "So did I. We were led to believe that your organization always retaliates for something like that."

"Alas," Kaliniskov shrugged, "I no longer consider myself to be part of that august organization. Like the late Comrade Denikoff, I now consider myself to be a gentleman and a business man much like my associate. I have, so to speak, retired from the cloak and dagger profession for the genteel life of a respected citizen of a country I am certain you will understand if I do not name."

"You expect us to believe that?"

"On the souls of my blessed parents," he raised his right hand as if taking an oath, "I will walk away from here without firing another shot from this cursed weapon."

From a quick look around, it was clear to me that nobody believed him. Gary and Steve were wary, Larkin was hopeful, McAllister was frowning distrustfully, and I was praying for a miracle.

"I guess it doesn't make much difference," McAllister said after a lengthy pause. "It would be just as easy for you to kill us either way. What do you want to know?"

"I assume you believe those metal boxes to contain the looted Faberge jewels", Kaliniskov said. "To satisfy the curiosity of my former profession, I would like very much to know how you came to discover them at the bottom of a well in this wholly insignificant southern state."

McAllister cocked an eyebrow at the slight of his beloved Georgia, but he summarized the story, nicely and told the whole tale from the day Irina showed us the diary, right up to the time when McAllister and I sat staring at each other over the capped well. It took about five minutes, and while Frank Kipper fidgeted, and the other man maintained a neutral expression, Kaliniskov listened, hanging on every word. When McAllister finished, Kaliniskov was actually grinning about what he must have considered our ability, luck, and sheer audacity.

"What a marvelous story," he said happily. "It is one I will tell my children if I am ever fortunate enough to start a family." He winked at McAllister. "Of course, I will have to change a few things to take credit for myself, but that will not be a problem."

"Since you're being so honest and forthright," I interjected, "Would you be kind enough to tell me how you kept tabs on Irina?" After I had asked, I wondered why he had been so polite and civilized. I must have been thinking that he had promised to set us free and that it would be best not to antagonize him. "And what her specific duties included?"

"A betrayed lover seeking rationalization?" he asked, almost as if he pitied me. "I am afraid I can offer no solace.

"Comrade Denikoff's orders were to gain the confidence of any key member of your party by whatever means she felt appropriate. In the short time we had before you arrived in St. Petersburg, we taught her a simple, yet comprehensive method of delivering coded messages. Every night that you were not in a location of our choosing, she was to update us on your activities by shining a flashlight message from and to a predetermined point on a compass.

"Since you people have spent the last few weeks on your prized yacht, no pun intended, I deemed it prudent not to acknowledge her messages for fear of someone on your boat intercepting my response. I fear that her feeling of being neglected gave her the false impression that we had abandoned our pursuit and prompted her to go freelance. Most unfortunate, I agree. But the one good thing about employing amateurs is that they are readily expendable.

"In the event of Comrade Denikoff's duplicity was discovered by you, a small, self-contained transmitting computer chip was sewn into her handbag and several items of her clothing without her knowledge. We knew within thirty feet your exact whereabouts since you left St. Petersburg."

With un-disguised admiration, he turned again to McAllister. "Imagine the surprise and confusion you caused when we found your destination to be Georgia instead of New York. We feared that you had given up and were returning home. It was only because of Comrade Denikoff's continuing diligence to duty that first convinced us or your diving incident ruse of the other day and then brought us here this morning."

"You must be very proud," McAllister said icily.

"Not as proud as I am pleased," Kaliniskov admitted. "But now that everyone's curiosity has been satisfied, it is time for me to gather that which now belongs to me and make good my departure." He took a step forward. "And to prove to you that I am a man of my word," he extended his hand, his pistol resting on his upturned palm, "I offer this as proof that I am no longer a threat to you." He turned his hand over and the gun fell into the well.

"Now, if you will follow Lieutenant Kipper's instructions, we can load one of your boats – the blue one I believe Comrade Denikoff suggested – and I will take leave from this bug infested out door steam bath for a more suitable clime."

Gary and Steve sighed in relief, but both McAllister and I knew we were a long way from being out of the woods. There were still two armed men watching our every move and we both had learned long ago that two men with guns against five unarmed people still meant that the guys with the guns were the ones in control. Kipper immediately began giving orders to the hired hands but never took his eyes from McAllister. He just kept staring the same way a cat watches an aquarium.

"You two guys grab those boxes and load 'em into the boat," he ordered. "With that chain on there, that stuff has to weigh close to four-hundred pounds, Steve complained.

"Then get the writer to help you," Kipper replied, pointing to me. "If he isn't enough, get the broad to help. I want to keep this sneaky bastard McAllister right where I can keep an eye on him. "

McAllister stiffened at the crude remark about his wife but didn't otherwise move or say anything.

We managed to drag and hoist the unwieldy burden across the thirty yards to the Second Prize's shuttle without Larkin's help and when it was spread in the bottom of the boat, we stepped back on shore. The five of us stood together in a little group, prepared to watch Kaliniskov shove off with his stolen-again fortune when he turned to us a final time.

"I may have neglected to mention one final thing," he said, smiling sadistically. "Lieutenant Kipper is now discharged from my employ. I have paid him handsomely for his services, he has performed satisfactorily, and now our association is terminated. Therefore, I can no longer be held responsible for any endeavor that he and his associates," he turned to the third man who had yet to utter a single word, "may endeavor to undertake. Isn't that right, Mister Coolidge?"

"Coolidge?" McAllister looked momentarily confused. "That's right, ass hole." Kipper stepped forward. "Jack Coolidge, you may remember his brother, Web. Some people called him Tank."

Oh shit. I thought. McAllister looked at Coolidge. "That was your piece o' shit brother who tried to rob me in my own home last year?"

Talk about stress... I really thought McAllister had sealed what was left of our last chance for an optimistic and positive outcome of our doomed fate. I couldn't believe what I was hearing, even from McAllister!

Larkin and I exchanged doubtful glances, and instead of Coolidge answering, he raised the gun for the first time.

Oh shit! I repeated, except this time I said it out loud.

McAllister had to know something that Larkin and I were not privy to. It happened so fast, it is difficult to put in proper order. To the best of my ability, it started with a flat cracking sound like two boards being slammed together, followed immediately by an automatic weapon being fired. Kipper went down as if he had been swept off his feet by a well-placed kick. Coolidge did a three second jig and fell flat on his face, and Kaliniskov dropped to his knees bleeding from no less than a half dozen holes in his torso. By the time I looked at McAllister, he had tackled Larkin and smothered her head with arms, protecting her with his entire body. I stood frozen in place, wondering why I wasn't feeling any pain. After checking myself and finding no puncture wounds, I looked up to see Kaliniskov, still on his knees, reaching for the boat as if pleading for help from some invisible source. I was thinking that, to survive such an onslaught, maybe being Russian did have some mystical significance when the slap sound repeated itself and a large section of Kaliniskov's scalp disappeared in a frothy spray. He toppled over in slow motion.

Before Kaliniskov's body finished twitching, two men ran from the brush not ten yards away. One of them ran to Kipper who was in a sitting position holding his leg and screaming. The guy butt-stroked Kipper in the chest with a hunting rifle, stepped on his wrist to keep him from reaching for his dropped gun and aimed the barrel at the middle of his forehead. Kipper shut up and stared at the muzzle. The other man casually inspected the bodies of Coolidge and Kaliniskov, prodding them with the barrel of a smoking machine gun of a type I couldn't even begin to identify and, satisfied that neither man would be bothering anybody soon, looked over at me.

"Mister Lawton?"

My voice didn't work, nor did my ability to nod or shake my head.

"That's him." I heard the voice from behind me. I think it was Steve. The man with the machine gun stepped forward, casually swinging the gun to be partially covered by his body, a gesture designed to be non-threatening to me.

"Mister Lawton," he repeated. "I'm a friend. Are you all right?" I still had not regained any physical ability, so I concentrated on mental images. The two strangers were dressed similar but not identical. Both wore jogging suits, but not the loose or baggy kind. They were custom fit and probably very expensive. The taller of the two was well over six feet, medium length dark hair, muscular, but not beefed-up. The one standing on, and over Kipper was more my height, with lighter hair and the beginning of a bald spot. Both looked like they were in their mid to late thirties. Someone's husband and father as opposed to men who had just fired weapons in a lethal manner. They didn't have the air or mannerisms of cops, but they did have a certain aura of confidence.

"Are you all right?" he asked again. He had a non-descript accent and a smooth, quiet voice like that of a minister or a physician.

"Who are you?" I managed to ask. I looked toward McAllister and Larkin who were beginning to sit up.

Rather than answering my question, he turned to McAllister and Larkin. "And you must be the famous Bobby McAllister?" He hesitated as if he had forgotten something. "And of course, Larkin?" Larking smiled, and McAllister replied "yes".

"Excuse my manners, Mr. and Mrs. McAllister, we are your friends."

"I figured as much." McAllister said with a smile.

"Of course, if you need a name, you can call your friend in Chicago." He said, still using his gentle, almost hypnotic voice.

"That's not necessary, I read you loud and clear." McAllister said, still smiling. "But how. . ."

The man raised a hand as if to silence McAllister as politely as he could.

"Please let me explain." The man continued. "When we found out that our mutual Russian friend was dead and you and your friends had left St. Petersburg ahead of schedule, my employer, ah . . . your friend in Chicago became concerned for your safety. We spent the better part of a week trying to track you down, and when we got the word that your yacht was spotted off the coast of Georgia, Harry and I were sent down here to check on your welfare."

"You're the guys on the other boat. . . I mean, 'boats'" I said.

The man nodded his head as if I had just told him that two plus two equaled four. "We thought your behavior was rather strange so, not knowing the situation, we kept our distance. After all, you were anchored outside the limit; people were coming and going to the other boat that showed up, there were blinking lights coming from below decks at night. We just didn't know what to make of it. We didn't want to barge in and introduce ourselves since we couldn't get a firm grip on what your situation was.

"We called up to Chicago a number of times and we were told to keep a low profile and to watch your backs. Unfortunately, we didn't know that there was somebody else interested in you and your expedition until tonight. We got here shortly after these three fellas', but not in time to keep them from killing three of your men, and badly wounding a fourth."

"Wounded?" McAllister asked with a trace of hope in his voice.

"Tall guy," he summarized. "Dark complexion, big hard-type, probably ex-military."

"Mark!'" I interrupted. "Is he hurt bad?"

The man shook his head. "He can make it if you get him to a doctor in time. We treated him with the First-Aid kit he had on his belt, and left him about a hundred yards on the other side of the lighthouse. We would have acted sooner, but we had to sort out the good guys from the bad guys and make sure they didn't have backup. Then we had to get into position for a clear field of fire."

"What happens now?" I asked. McAllister seemed to be making consoling and comforting gestures to Gary with his hand on Gary's shoulder. I imagine that Gary felt guilty by having been replaced by John, who was not trained in security matters, and died rather than Gary.

"It's almost daylight," the man said, looking to the east. "There are half a dozen dead bodies on this island, so you and Mr. McAllister and company better get the hell out of here so we can clean things up a bit. That is, if you, and your friends are safe for now."

There was nothing I wanted more than to be far away from Elba Island. McAllister was holding Larkin close to him in a protective manner, deferring his questioning to me.

"There is just one more problem." For the first time, the man exhibited hesitancy.

"What?" I asked.

"What do you want done with him?" He pointed to Kipper. "I'm sure Mister McAllister will want him to join his friends." He asked, this time directing his question to McAllister. "I'll get the pistol; you can do the honors, or I will if you want."

The Man from Chicago and I were staring at McAllister, waiting for his reply. The man had a quizzical expression on his face; Larkin whispered something in her husband's ear.

"Kipper's already been taken out of action. We're not going to kill him."

"Don't you think that this situation calls for Kipper's neutralization?" I asked. Surprising myself that I took that position.

"For all practical purposes, Grange, Kipper has already been neutralized." McAllister smiled. "And maybe, neutered." McAllister liked saying that.

"Besides, if I know Kipper like I'm sure I do, he will run, or crawl, in this instance, back to Florida with his tail between his legs, which I might add, is probably the only thing between his legs, and he will take an early retirement from the Florida Department of Justice, and join his old buddy, Matt Hoover, giving boat rides in the Everglades on one of those flat-bottomed boats with the big fans."

"But, Bobby. . ." McAllister cut me off.

"Listen to me very carefully, Grange." McAllister began in a scolding manner. "We're not cold blooded murderers like that bunch of bastards! Kipper's already dead as far as I'm concerned. Just leave him alone; he can explain why there are so many dead bodies lying around, and how he managed not to be one of them. He can also explain why he was consorting with the KGB; you know that whoever investigates this battleground, even the Chatham County Police, for Christ's sake!" McAllister started counting bodies for effect, but then stopped, and continued his admonition. . . "will learn that the fucking KGB's involved, and simple ballistics will show that at least one of the bullets fired around here came from Kipper's "Police Special" issued to him by the great State of Florida!"

"Yeah, but. . ."

"Yeah, but – hell!" I should have quit before I got McAllister all wound-up, but knowing Kipper, he would find a way to put this all on McAllister.

"God dammit, Grange!" I knew I wasn't about to hear the end of McAllister's tirades any time soon. McAllister moved away from Larkin, walked over to me and put his face to within inches of mine. He began, however, with a slow, southern monotone. "Grange, if I went around killing people just because I didn't like them, I'd run out of bullets way before I ran out of victims." He began to smile as he backed off a few inches.

"Look, Grange." He pointed to the man from Chicago. "He has already offered to provide us with a pistol. If you're so god damned adamant about killing Kipper, go ahead, shoot him dead, if that will make you feel better." McAllister said in a feigned mocking tone.

Kipper was watching our exchange with his head moving from me to McAllister like he was watching a tennis match. If he hadn't crapped his pants already, I'm sure he would before it was over. His emotions changed from hopeful to doom faster than a tennis ball could be served.

"Not me!" I said. "Nope, no way!" Realizing I had once again been snared in McAllister's mental trap.

"That's what I thought." McAllister said in a tone of finality.

I think Kipper actually smiled. . . Or finished crapping in his pants. I couldn't really tell.

McAllister wasn't finished yet. "I'm sure that our friends from Chicago will agree that killing cops even dirty cops like Kipper, is not good for business. Just let our friends here, do their jobs, clean things up a bit, and sit Kipper's ass somewhere out on Victory Drive. I don't care what they do with him. But I will tell you one thing." McAllister looked smug.

"Kipper's days are numbered. You want to know why?

No, not really. I thought.

"Because," McAllister's tone became sullen. "Kipper has some very bad Karma."

* * *

CHAPTER TWELVE

The sun had fully risen by the time we reached the Second Prize. Gary and Steve had taken Mark in Excalibur's shuttle and raced up-river in search of medical attention. Mark had been conscious when we loaded him in the little speedboat, but even in the gray of early dawn, he looked pale and fatigued. Larkin, McAllister, and I had unloaded the supplies and boxes onto the Second Prize but, too exhausted and emotionally drained, didn't even bother opening any of the suspected loot. We agreed to transfer the entire find, intact, to the plantation where we would examine our previous night's haul in detail after we had got some well-deserved rest.

We trudged into the Second Prize's lounge looking like modern day survivors of the Donner Party and collapsed into chairs. McAllister rested only seconds before standing up to go to the bar.

"Who want's drinks?"

Both Larkin and I raised a limp hand. McAllister handed us each a bottle and glass.

"If you want ice or mixer," he said, returning wearily to his chair. "You can get it yourself."

We each concentrated on pouring our own drinks.

"So tell me," I said, making a face after taking a slug of straight, tepid liquor, "Why didn't you take care of Frank Kipper once and for all?"

"I thought I made myself clear, Grange." McAllister said impatiently.

Personally, I was getting tired of the rising body count our expedition had accumulated, but I doubt that I would have objected if McAllister had decided to permanently terminate his relationship with the crooked cop.

"Did you see where that guy shot him?" he continued. "Right through the kneecap. Frank will never walk in a normal way again and I have to believe that this will end his career. He will have to leave the department, and that will give him a few years to think about how healthy I am and how crippled he is. For someone like Frank, there are things worse than death."

"What about Irina?" I asked after a prolonged silence. "How did you trip to what she had planned?"

"I never had an inkling as to what she had planned," he admitted. "Just a few things that, without definite proof, didn't mean anything.

"First, there was the gun. When Rastov finally went down, he still had a breath or two left in him. I couldn't imagine that a man as determined as he was to take a few other people with him, would relax his grip enough to drop his gun overboard. As both of you had collapsed on deck, Irina was the first to rush to your side. Either Rastov gave her the gun with his dying breath hoping she would finish his work, or she decided to sneak the gun into her possession for use at a later date.

"Second, was something you said. Do you remember telling me that, back in Helsinki, you found her making caviar blinis for you?" I remembered the incident, but I didn't remember telling him. "You hate caviar. You know it and I know it, but Irina thought you would like it."

I had a sudden flash of realization. "At the hotel in St. Petersburg!" I said. "When I got you out of your room to go someplace to talk, you jokingly suggested we go someplace to get caviar blinis."

McAllister nodded wisely. "The only way she could have known that fact was to be sitting next to Patek in that basement sound studio when I said it. Of Course, the other explanation could be that everyone in Russia is absolutely crazy about caviar blinis, and for you not to like them as much as everyone else would be unthinkable. As I said, suspicion, but very little fact."

That was very slim, I thought. I would have been hesitant to hang my doubts on those circumstances.

"There was one more thing." He took a drink straight from the bottle. "Your medicine seemed to be disappearing fast. I have no way of knowing how many pain killers and sedatives were originally prescribed to you, but it did seem like the supply went down rather quickly. We figured she was putting them in a nightcap for you so she could send her flashlight messages from your cabin. Of course, we didn't know that she was sending messages, so we had even less reason to think she was not boinking and zoinking you every night.

"In the end, Larkin and I decided to keep a close watch on her. We talked it over and established that if she were working for the other side; we would do everything possible to convert her, cajole her, and convince her that we were her real friends. Lacking success, we told Mark to watch her while we were on the island and if she displayed a weapon, he was to shoot it out of her hand. You already know that Mark is a helluva' marksman – no pun intended.

"When Mark didn't shoot, the only thing I could figure was that he couldn't get the proper angle to fire without endangering someone else." McAllister was lost in thought and sadly shook his head. . . ."I never would have been able to trust her again." McAllister continued. Then he just looked at me for a few seconds. "Grange, I'm really sorry. I never expected this to happen."

I understood what McAllister was saying. After all, I wasn't doing so well in my development of long lasting meaningful relationships with women who had departed at a high mortality rate. But I was touched nonetheless by his concern.

"It's okay, Bobby." I said. "I'll be alright. I just wonder what our friends from Chicago would be doing with her bo. . ."

"Stop it, Grange!" McAllister stopped me from asking how the mob would go about getting rid of the dead bodies. McAllister didn't know the answers himself and I'm sure he didn't want us to speculate. Besides, there are some things better left unsaid, so I shakily got to my feet and headed for the door.

"I'm going to bed," I said. "Wake me up in time for Christmas."

* * * * *

Actually, I didn't expect or need the time until Christmas to feel better. I awoke thinking we had only to open the twenty boxes to bring our saga to a close but, as usual, McAllister had other plans.

"I want you to write a synopsis of everything that has happened since we began this little enterprise," McAllister told me. "Not a book. Just an accurate outline in chronological order. Try to keep it to something like twenty pages, and leave out anything that happens from now on."

The "anything" he was talking about was the opening of the boxes, an event made almost ceremonial by McAllister.

In the gallery of the plantation, McAllister had removed all his art-work and installed three long workbenches on which the boxes were placed. Captain Jim had been treating the lids and latches with some kind of penetrating and lubricating oil to un-inhibit the rust and years of neglect, and on a beautiful fall afternoon, three days after our nightmare on Elba Island, a dozen of us descended into the gallery-turned-workroom to cut off the chains. In a fashion typical of McAllister, he would not allow a single box to be opened until all forty latches had been freed from its bonds and each box was lined up neatly on the table.

The group was suitably rewarded when McAllister stepped forward and flipped the latches on the first box. The lid contained a rubber gasket that had inhibited the penetration of moisture and other corroding elements and the interior was as dry and as unaffected as the day it had been packed. Nestled in coarse straw and wrapped in jeweler's cloths were two magnificent Faberge eggs. One depicted Jesus praying in the Garden of Gethsemane and the other was a miniature portrayal of a zoo or menagerie of tiny animals.

Altogether there were thirty-eight eggs, eleven of which were in various stages of completion when work on them had been suspended. We oohed and aahed and marveled as each was removed from its packing and crowded around the table for closer inspection when McAllister, with great care and reverence, placed each item next to the box he had just emptied. Sixteen boxes contained eggs packed two or three to a box, attesting to the fact that Easter of 1918 was intended to be the most extravagant gift-giving season the Imperial Family had ever experienced. The subjects ranged from deeply religious to frivolous with history and practicality represented in the mix.

Box number seventeen yielded about two hundred miniature items – probably destined to become part of future eggs – including animals, flowers, carriages, ships, and precious metals and gem-stones. As in all the Faberge works, the detail and craftsmanship was incredible and the pieces had a life of their own.

The final three boxes were literally crammed with lose precious stones. Hundreds of diamonds and rubies in one, emeralds and sapphires in another, and amethyst, opal, and topaz in the third. Each stone competed for attention with its own brilliance and clarity as McAllister poured them out in separate piles that must have contained close to eight hundred gems in each category. I freely admit to knowing next to nothing about the value of exquisite jewels, but looking at the seven small mountains of glittering gems made me feel that my ballpark figure of a hundred million had to be on the low side by a considerable amount. As magnificent as the creative artwork was, no one could resist the allure of closer examination of the piles of loose stones.

We had a celebration dinner in the dining room upstairs and everyone got slightly tipsy from the continuous rounds of toasts extolling our successes and memorializing our losses.

The following morning McAllister flew in an expert on Eastern European art from Columbia University and another friend who owned an upscale jewelry store at the Oglethorpe Mall. The two men spent three entire days cataloging and appraising the collection while McAllister and Larkin discussed renovation of the gallery with an architect and a contractor. I spent the time in the library, studying up on Faberge art and the Romanov Dynasty. Something I should have done before I ever left Payson, and composing the review of our campaign that McAllister had requested. I came across one interesting item that aroused my natural inquisitiveness enough for me to send off a fax for further information and clarification and was waiting for an answer when McAllister told me we were leaving for Venezuela in the morning. Knowing I wouldn't get a straight answer if I asked why, I asked for how long. Just a day, I was told. Perhaps not even overnight.

Larkin, McAllister and I flew to Atlanta and from there to Caracas where we were met at the airport by Larkin's father and the twins. That Senor Tumbas was in the capital city came as no surprise, but dropping Larkin and the children at a hotel was, and the three of us drove on to an area of stately mansions. From the different flags flying from rooftops and gatepost of the dignified mansions, I figured us to be on Embassy Row and when the limo turned into a driveway flanked by the hammer and sickle flags of Russia, my anxiety increased dramatically. Deep in thought, McAllister did nothing to reassure me.

Our appointment was with the ambassador, Vladimir Bulganon, and he greeted Senor Tumbas warmly, coming around the desk to shake hands and showing concern that Senor Tumbas' wheelchair was comfortably positioned. After introductions and pleasantries were exchanged and refreshments politely declined, McAllister took control of the conversation.

"First of all, Mister Ambassador." McAllister began, "I would like to impress upon you the fact that, although this meeting is informal and off the record, the interests of Venezuelan citizens is being represented by my father-in-law and the concerns of Americans are represented by Mister Lawton and myself. The reason we are pursuing our business here in Caracas instead of Washington, D.C. is because Senor Tumbas has your friendship and vouches for your discretion in a delicate matter and assures me that you are a man with whom we can place our trust."

Bulganon nodded solemnly, accepting what I am sure he considered to be a compliment.

"Recently," McAllister continued, "in a non-political capacity, my wife and I entertained several guests and employees in France, England, Scandinavia, and Russia on holiday. This leisure time was marred by the deaths of three of our party in Paris by a man we later identified as Gregori Patek, an agent of your government's KGB."

Bulganon sat forward in his chair and started to interrupt.

"Please, Mister Ambassador," McAllister held up a hand to avoid any intrusion in his monologue, "we are convinced that the information we have in this matter is irrefutable and we will not be dissuaded from our beliefs no matter how strongly you might attempt to change our minds." Bulganon didn't like being pre-empted, but he remained silent.

"My interest in Faberge was the common factor that prompted our trip to the various countries of Europe and, although I admit this reluctantly and sadly, also the component of a serious conflict of interest.

"It seems there is a Russian government agency that is determined to corner the market on certain specific areas of art. The authors of this conspiracy were of the mistaken opinion that the best way to propagate their scheme was through fraud, thievery, intimidation, and even murder. As a result of that perverted delusion, my brother-in-law, a close friend, and a valued employee died violently.

"The man responsible for this atrocity was the KGB agent, Patek, who also threatened my friend, Mister Lawton in his hotel room in St. Petersburg. When Mr. Lawton eliminated that threat in an action that can only be termed self-defense, we felt it prudent to protect our personal interests by leaving Russia.

"Unfortunately, two Soviet citizens used this untimely departure to seek our assistance, not for purposes of defection as they told us, but for ulterior motives. One was planning retribution — remember that word; retribution - - for the demise of the KGB agent, Patek, the other for the prospect of personal gain. Both died under circumstances that, only peripherally, have any bearing on my conversation with you. Continuing in this disastrous vein, and also seeking personal gain, a high ranking KGB officer continued where the other agent left off and also paid for his indiscretion with his life.

"I asked you to remember the word retribution because all of these events were originally instituted by a bumbling incompetent who was hardly missed by an organization as usually efficient as the KGB. There is no reason for compelling revenge for the balancing of the scales of justice in this case; simply illogical retribution.

"To date, at least eighteen people have died as a result of my involvement with Faberge art; six Americans, eight Russians, at least three by the hands of their own people — two British subjects, one Venezuelan, and one of undetermined nationality. Eighteen human beings, Mister Ambassador, died as a result of a domino principle that was of your fellow countryman's design."

Bulganon sat with a blank expression, one hand on the edge of his desk, the other beneath his chin. "Mister McAllister, I am certain you do not expect me to justify these unfounded allegations with comment regardless of the fact that we are speaking off record."

"As a matter of fact, I do not." McAllister opened his briefcase and withdrew the report he had asked me to type. He placed the papers on the corner of the desk. Bulganon made no move to pick them up.

"My purpose here today is to convince you of my sincerity on two fronts concerning the subject I have already described to you. First, I think this needless violence should cease. Here. Now. Forever. It's over, Mister Ambassador. Finished.

"Secondly, should someone take it upon themselves to continue this discord, I will fight them on three different levels. I will take my case to the International Courts, the media, and I will repay every act of aggression with swift and decisive vengeance. I will pursue this attitude until I run out of financial artillery or until the annihilation of this planet, two things that will probably not take place in my lifetime."

Bulganon cocked an eyebrow. "That sounds very much like a threat, Mister McAllister."

"It is." McAllister said firmly.

"I still do not understand why you have approached me with this distasteful message," he replied. "Surely you do not believe me to be part of your problem."

"Not a part of the problem," McAllister answered, a solution."

Bulganon remained silent.

"With utmost respect for your position and abilities, Mister Ambassador, my father-in-law and I have come to beseech you to use your persuasive powers to convince members of your government that there is nothing to be gained by further overt action. In less than a week, my collection will be a matter of public record, all aboveboard and detailed to the last piece of colored glass. My personal records and collaborative evidence of what I have told you here today are in the hands of people who are consigned by me to make public all my information should I meet with untimely or suspicious harm. There is no reason for subterfuge or bloodshed. I don't even want an apology. Just assurance."

"Surely, Mister McAllister, you do not expect my government to insure the safety of your collection or to guarantee your personal protection," Bulganon snorted sarcastically.

"All I want is the confirmation that the violence is over," McAllister said, displaying more patience than he knew he possessed. "Put it in any form you want, just let me know somehow that your government also feels that additional bloodshed and retribution has ceased. In spite of what you may have heard about me, I am not a difficult man to get along with. I am a gentleman but, more importantly, I am a man of my word."

Bulganon looked decidedly uncomfortable. "Then as a gentleman," he began uncertainly, "You will understand that my only participation in this matter will be to relay your comments and concerns to Moscow."

"I would ask for nothing more," McAllister responded.

Five minutes later we were back in the limo and out of the compound.

"You really think something like that is going to work?" I asked.

"Allow me to answer your question, Senor Lawton." Roberto Tumbas was the consummate diplomat who could grasp almost any situation and cut to the quick with a minimum of effort. "In politics, it is often the unspoken word that is heard more clearly than the audible comment. Ambassador Bulganon knows that I will undoubtedly be elected to the Senate next year. He knows that my ranch, El Empleado, supplies Russia with over seven million pounds of beef per year. He knows that Venezuela is a member of OPEC. But most of all, he knows that by my presence in his office today, that I will give my full support to my son-in-law, both politically and personally.

"The Russians will back off," he said confidently. "Or they will face economic difficulties exceeding those which they are trying to create through this attempted manipulation of the art world. I doubt they will abandon the entire project, but I can almost promise you that the focus of their purpose will shift to a different venue. By way of confirmation, Robert will receive some kind of gesture of goodwill. When he receives that hidden message, he will know he is safe. His conversation and allegations of today will never be mentioned again."

We picked up Larkin and the twins at the hotel and fought rush hour traffic on our way back to the airport. By midnight, we were back in Savannah.

* * * * *

The response to my faxed query was in an envelope that had been slid under the door of my guest room at the plantation. I read through the three pages carefully before dressing and going downstairs for an early lunch. McAllister was in his study pouring over pages, calculators, and a check book and appeared far too engrossed to be disturbed, so I checked out a car from his small fleet and drove to the library on Bull Street south of the Big Park — it was a big park named Big Park. It was close to five o'clock when I returned and I was sitting on the front porch enjoying a Chatham Artillery Punch poured from a large frosty pitcher, when McAllister, haggard and worn from a full day of sitting at his desk, dropped himself into the chair next to me.

"I don't know how you do it, Grange," he said.

"Do what?"

"Write," he answered. "Especially something like a book." He shook his head slowly. "I get worn out writing on the back of a post card."

"You lack the primary attribute it takes to be an author," I continued. "Patience."

"Well, you're right about that. Speaking of writing," he continued. "Have you decided to write another book about all this?" He made an all-inclusive gesture.

"I would," I said, preparing to drop my personal little bombshell on McAllister's head.

"You would . . . but what?"

I was checking my written account that McAllister asked me to prepare, matching it with the three pages of the fax.

McAllister was growing impatient. "Do you know something I should know, Grange?"

I returned his concentrated stare and smiled before replying.

"I know you're two eggs short of a solved mystery."

* * *

CHAPTER THIRTEEN

"The Spaskio Egg and the Lily Egg." I had McAllister's undivided attention.

"What do you know about them?"

"Nothing for certain," I admitted. "Only some thoughts that I can't yet prove."

"Then think out loud," McAllister demanded.

"What do you know about a woman named Anna Manahan?" I asked.

"Apparently less than you know about Florence Martus," he answered somewhat bewildered, "Who is she?"

"Anna Manahan?"

"Yes, Anna Manahan."

"Better yet. Suppose I told you that there is a connection between Anna Manahan, although remote, and Florence Martus?"

"Who is Anna Manahan?" McAllister was losing his last thread of patience.

"Anna Manahan is the woman believed by many to have been the Grand Duchess Anastasia Nikolyayevna Romanov, the youngest daughter of the Czar Nicholas II and a survivor of the assassination of the Imperial Family."

"You mean like that old Ingrid Bergman movie?"

"That," I answered, "and another one just like it done about the same time with Lilli Palmer in the lead."

"Hollywood rubbish," McAllister scoffed.

"Listen to what history has to say," I suggested. Then see how you feel.

"The Bolsheviks said that the Czar had been shot on orders from the Ural Oblast Soviet, and the rest of the family evacuated to a safe place, but there were rumors that the entire family had been shot and killed, their bodies soaked in acid and burned in an abandoned mine outside of Ekaterinburg.

"The White Russians may have prompted the story of a coldblooded massacre to turn Russian peasants, who considered the Czar almost mythical, against Lenin. For that matter, even Lenin might have had reason to keep, at least, some of the Family alive to use as pawns in some international diplomatic game. After all, the Romanovs were closely related to the majority of ruling houses of Europe, including Kaiser Wilhelm of Germany with whom the White Russians were at war, and King George V of Britain, their ally."

It was time to consult my notes again, so I reached for the file that I had placed on the chair next to me. Finding what I wanted, I continued.

"In the early seventies, a couple of BBC television journalists uncovered a mass of information about this period of history that gathered and, for some strange reason, later suppressed by a White Russian faction. This 'file on the Czar' as the subsequent book was called, contained evidence that the Czarina and her daughters were taken to a special train to Perm, about a hundred miles from Ekaterinburg, shortly after the Czar was murdered. They were held for eight months under close guard in a squalid peasant hut in Perm from where Anastasia made several attempts to escape. There was even a doctor, Pavel Utkin, who swore an affidavit that he was called upon by Red Army soldiers to treat an assault victim in September of 1918, who identified herself by saying, and I quote, "I am the Emperor's daughter, Anastasia".

"Doctor Utkins's testimony is supported by statements by railway officials, local Soviet officials, Red Army soldiers, and the assistant head of White Military Control at Perm. In the summer of 1919, a man named Nicolai Sokolov smuggled these documents out of Russia, and for some unknown reason, they didn't notably surface again until the seventies when they were found in the library of the University of Harvard.

"It wasn't until 1991 that more information came to light when the Soviet Union began breaking up. Doctor William Maples, Director of the C.A. Pound Human Identification Laboratory of the University of Florida – Gainesville heard that, in 1979, the crushed skeletons of five females and four males had been discovered in a pit near Ekaterinburg. In 1992, working with Russian forensic experts, Doctor Maples announced that they had positively identified the bodies of the Czar and Czarina, their three daughters; Olga, Maria, and Tatiana, and the family doctor. The remaining three skeletons appeared to be those of three servants who were known to have been in the service of the Imperial Family at that time.

"Doctor Maples issued a statement to the effect that all the skeletons appeared to be too tall to be Anastasia nor were there any skeletal remains that could have represented Alexi."

"So the Florida doctor has disproved that the Czarina and her daughters survived," McAllister speculated.

"Ultimately, yes," I replied. "But remember that Perm was only a hundred miles from Ekaterinburg and, more importantly, Anastasia's remains were never identified.

"In the meantime, in 1920 a young woman tried to commit suicide in Berlin and, when the attempt failed, she was taken to the Dalldorf Insane Asylum for observations where she spent the next two years. She was totally withdrawn and consistently refused to answer questions, but never declared insane.

"Physically, this woman had weak lungs, a tendency toward pleurisy, and was chronically anemic. Above her right ear was a groove in her skull most likely made by a bullet creasing the bone, some of her teeth had been knocked out or loosened, most probably from beatings, and the arch and instep of one foot bore triangular scars as if pierced with a sharp instrument.

"In the two years she was at Dalldorf, she spoke fluent German but was occasionally heard muttering in Russian. Furthermore, she confided to some of the nurses who cared for her that she was, indeed, Anastasia. However, it was a former patient, Clara Peuthert, who, in 1922, told a White Russian officer that she had recognized a woman at Dalldorf to be Tatiana, Anastasia's older sister.

"Word of this identification reached a former police officer from Russian Poland by the name of Baron Arthur von Kleist who visited the mystery woman and gained her confidence. When she admitted to him that she was Anastasia, he secured her release, took her into his own home, and thrust her into the limelight by announcing to the world that she was Anastasia. Her reaction to von Kleist's revelation was to run away, and she spent the next five years in and out of hospitals."

"A nut case pretending to be a princess," McAllister observed, unimpressed.

"Possibly more than that," I said charitably. "She spent more than fifty years in court while people tried to prove her claim."

"Let me guess," McAllister interrupted again. "It was a claim that was never proved."

"You're right," I said, "but not for the reason you think."

He looked at me if to say I was being presumptuous by assuming I knew what he was thinking.

"Let me point out some pertinent facts," I said, undaunted by his nonverbal reproach. "The Czar's doctor, who presumably perished with the family, had a daughter, Tatiana Botkin, who was determined to expose the woman, now known as Anna Anderson, as an imposter. Instead, she immediately recognized her as Anastasia.

"The Grand Duke of Hessen — Anastasia's 'Uncle Ernie' — paid a secret visit to the Czar in 1916. Anna Anderson knew that and was able to describe events of the meeting in detail.

"The Czar's sister, Olga, who saw Anastasia only rarely, was convinced of her identity.

"Prince Sigismund of Prussia, a childhood companion, was in Central America when she first surfaced, so he sent her a list of questions only the real Anastasia could answer correctly. Anna answered every question accurately, often adding details the Prince had forgotten.

"In 1926, advised to go to Switzerland for medical reasons, Anna needed identity papers. The German Foreign Ministry issued a special identity card through the Berlin Aliens Office that, on the basis of police inquiries to date, the unknown woman was most certainly the Czar's daughter, Anastasia.

"The Dowager Empress Maria, in exile at the Danish Court, commissioned her brother Prince Vladimir of Denmark and Danish Ambassador Herluf Zahle to conduct inquiries. In spite of being obstructed and dissuaded, Zahle was convinced she was genuine. Grand Duke Andrei, the Czar's cousin and an experienced jurist, felt the same.

"Duke George of Lichtenberg took her into his castle in upper Bavaria and introduced her to everyone as his cousin and in 1928, Princess Xenia Georgievna, Anastasia's second cousin, took her to New York and introduced her to society and politicians alike as the Czar's daughter.

"The only uncompromising opposition to Anna Anderson's claim to be Anastasia came from Lord Mountbatten, her cousin. It was widely felt that he reacted out of some sense of guilt. King George V had actually quashed a British plan to save Nicholas through diplomatic means concerned that his position would be in jeopardy if he championed the Czar.

"Even the Hessen line of relatives, no longer concerned the claimant was seeking to inherit a non-existent fortune, changed their minds and supported the claim, but it was Anna herself who ended the over eight thousand pieces of court documentation and years of speculation. She had ceased to care. In 1977 she wrote a personal letter to a press agency formally declaring the case to be closed for good."

I had finished my short lecture just in time, McAllister was growing bored.

"So nobody really knows if this Anna Anderson, or Anna Manahan was really Anastasia?" he asked, not really caring.

"That's not the point." I tried to make him understand by changing the direction of the conversation.

"You had these eggs. . ." But before I could change the direction, McAllister interrupted me, smiling as if he had just invented banana pudding.

"Wait a minute, Grange; I see where you're going with this. But I was trying to think of what got me interested in what you were saying, oh yes, of course." McAllister resumed his serious look.

He had me confused.

"You mentioned that there was a connection between this lady, Anderson-Manahan-Anastasia, and Florence Martus!" He said accusingly.

"There is."

"Well?"

"I haven't completely figured it out yet."

"Great." McAllister was frustrated.

I was thinking.

"Give me a clue, Grange."

"May I finish my story first?"

McAllister did not answer me, but he also did not object. So I continued.

"Okay, you have these eggs, right?"

McAllister reluctantly nodded.

"Those eggs were appraised by an expert the other day. Were any of those eggs valued at a nice round figure I can work with?"

"Five of them were appraised at two hundred thousand apiece." McAllister's interest was barely surfacing. Probably because we were talking about something he understood more readily; treasure and money.

"And how much would they be worth if they were Imperial Eggs?"

"Imperial Eggs?"

"Anthony Wilson told us there were fifty-four Eggs. Forty-five known, two in photographs, and seven missing," I reminded him. "What if one of those two hundred thousand dollar eggs was an Imperial Egg. How much more would they be worth?"

"Just guessing?"

I nodded.

"Probably somewhere near a half a million."

"Good." I was secretly pleased that my idea had more merit than I had originally thought. "Now, suppose you could take your entire collection to someone who could positively identify them as belonging to the Imperial household?"

"Then they become so-called Imperial Eggs."

"Right!" I banged my hand on my stack of papers. "And who best to identify them as Imperial Eggs if only one member of the Imperial household is still alive?"

"Okay. . . Anastasia, the Czar's daughter." He conceded.

"Exactly."

"Now I'm lost." McAllister's enthusiasm dissipated quickly. He hated not knowing everything. "Where do the Spaskoie and Lily Eggs fit into all of this?" He looked as if in deep thought. "Where does Florence Martus fit in this?"

"Never mind ole' Florence right now. Let's back up again," I said patiently, something that I knew McAllister wasn't sharing. "Suppose you have a Faberge Egg collection and you want it to be worth more than it is. We already established that the best way to do that is to find someone with authority to confirm your suspicions. Someone in the family of the Czar, right?"

McAllister nodded.

"Everyone assumes that the Czar and his family are all dead, so Anthony Wilson's figure of fifty-four eggs has to stand, right?"

Another nod.

"Then someone comes along and says 'Wait a minute. I'm part of the Imperial Family. I can help you prove your claim!' Your fortune has now more than doubled except for one thing. This person can't prove that he or she was really a part of the Imperial Family and without them first proving that they are who they say they are, your claim is worthless."

"So, the best thing for me to do is to help that person establish their identity as a surviving Romanov so that they can authenticate my collection."

"Right." My turn to nod.

"If Anna Anderson-slash-Manahan is recognized, by law, to be the real Anastasia, and can then verify my collection, Wilson's number has to go up along with the value of my collection. Without the court's recognition, my collection consists of Faberge Eggs, but not Imperial Eggs." McAllister had a firm grasp of the significance of what I was saying, but he still had a combined expression of impatience and confusion.

"What?" I asked.

"I still don't see how that gets me my two missing eggs."

"Kaliniskov let it slip that there is a remaining associate in his plot," I explained. "In fact, he mentioned it twice. Suppose we find out who that associate might be by trying to locate the someone who might have a collection worth more if the collection contained Imperial Eggs?"

McAllister smiled while shaking his head.

"What!?, Bobby?"

"You know, for someone who was about to court the Grim Reaper whithout shitting his pants, you sure were attentive."

"Well, I didn't have much else to do while you were playing verbal chess with Kaliniskov." McAllister had me riled. "Besides, that's my job."

McAllister's eyes narrowed. "Why do I have the feeling that you already have someone in mind?"

I smiled knowingly. "Flipping through my information, I found about Anastasia, I found a name that surfaced more than once. This person was apparently very active in establishing that Anna was Anastasia and worked for years in a peripheral manner to obtain that goal. . ." McAllister cut me off.

"What about the 'Florence Martus' connection?" He asked, trying to 'jump-the-gun' again.

I ignored him and tried to continue.

"Anyway, Bobby." I had to back up a bit. "For years in a peripheral manner to obtain that goal. She..."

"She?"

"She," I continued as if I had not been twice interrupted, "petitioned Lord Mountbatten when he was alive, worked with the two BBC journalists, Summers and Mangold, on their research, and struck up a friendship with Princess Andrea of Greece, Queen Louise of Sweden, and Crown Princess Cecile, the Kaiser's daughter-in-law, for the sole purpose of pressuring them to recognize Anna as Anastasia. After that, it was a simple matter of finding out if she ever talked to Anna about Eggs."

McAllister was deep in thought, as if his eyes were reversed, staring back into his mind's thoughts, searching for the secrets of the universe.

I snapped him out of his reverie with my next statement.

"Bobby," no response. "This woman visited Savannah twice to see. . ."

"To see who?" That got his attention.

I smiled and continued. "To see some lady named Florence."

"Just how the hell do you know about all this, Grange?"

"I sent a fax to her husband."

"You did what?!"

"Anna married Doctor John Manahan, a former professor of history at the University of Virginia in 1967 in order to establish American citizenship. They lived together in Charlottesville, Virginia until Anna died on February 12, 1984."

"And her husband is still alive?" McAllister asked incredulously.

"He was almost thirty years younger than she," I answered. "I don't know for sure, but I think he married her more to protect her than for romantic reasons."

"And he remembered someone asking his wife about Faberge Eggs?" McAllister still hadn't lost his uncertainty. I think he was more interested in Miss Martus.

"Who better than a retired history professor?" I asked, grinning from ear to ear.

"And?" I loved to see McAllister sweat.

"I got an answer from him this morning," I said, drawing out the suspense as long as I dared. "It seems that, from 1968 to 1977, Anna received no less than ten inquiries, even more containing photographs, asking if she could identify certain items."

I removed a sheet of paper from my notes and slid it over to McAllister. It took him only a second to locate the name I had highlighted with a blue marker.

"Larkin!" He yelled at the top of his lungs. "Pack our bags! We're going back to Europe!"

* * *

CHAPTER FOURTEEN

It was raining so heavily, the low clouds hugged the landscape like a heavy wet blanket. It was useless to try to see the otherwise, beautiful landscape through the window of the speeding limousine. Larkin kept asking Mark if he was alright and fiddling with his sling, and McAllister, deep in thought again, had already made it known that he was not in the mood for small talk. The oppressive quiet made the drive seem even longer.

When we pulled into the cobbled driveway, the house looked the same as when we had last seen it, right down to the car in front of the garage. The only difference was that the top was up, the rain making puddles on the uneven canvass.

"Mister McAllister!" He appeared genuinely surprised. "How curious of you to be about the countryside. Especially on a day like today. Come in. Come in before you catch your death of cold."

"Thank you, Sir George." As we filed into the narrow hall, McAllister re-introduced us. "You remember my wife, Larkin and my friend, Granger Lawton. The fourth member of our party is Mark Schaeffer. Mark handles my security and protection."

Sir George Lancaster bowed to Larkin, shook my hand warmly, and studied Mark. "A bit unusual to employ a bodyguard with a busted wing, eh what?" He said lightly. "You must be very good." Mark didn't answer.

"Well, come on in," he repeated. "It will only take a minute to scare up a pot of tea to take the chill out."

"We're not here socially, Sir George," McAllister said, very business-like. "I think you know that."

For a brief moment, I thought Sir George was going to try to bluff it out. He held his neutral, almost trusting expression for a three count, and then folded like a becalmed sail.

"How long have you known?" he asked.

"Since yesterday," McAllister answered almost kindly. "Grange, uh, Mister Lawton, here, found a very interesting paper trail."

"Yes," he said knowingly. "Mother was not what you would call the most subtle of titled women. I always knew that if I were to fail, it would be because of the notoriety she created while she was still alive. Did you know that she died two days after Anastasia?"

McAllister shook his head.

"It broke her heart when she heard the news," he said sadly. "She considered Anastasia to be her last opportunity to prove she possessed the Imperial Eggs."

"What made her so certain the eggs she had were of the Imperial variety?" I asked.

"Quite simple, really," he said, speaking as if it were a matter of record. "Her father stole them from the private quarters of the Winter Palace."

We all looked at each other, somewhat surprised at the casual admission.

"My grandfather was Lord Cameron Hayd-Smith, part of a diplomatic corps that visited St. Petersburg in 1914 to discuss Russia's alliance with Great Britain," he explained. "I have never met the old man — he died in 1932 — but I read through some of his personal correspondence shortly after my mother died. Grandfather Cameron was always a bit of a rogue, it seems, a man who obtained title more for his colorful reputation and unorthodox personality than his ministerial bearing. As a lowest ranking member of His Majesty's political contingent, he was aghast at the ostentatious display of wealth and size of the Czar's home in what was then a besieged nation. Not necessarily a wealthy man himself; he was tempted beyond resistance and, finding himself alone on several different occasions in the corridors of the great mansion, simply helped himself to a few of the palace's treasures thinking no one would notice a few missing trinkets from among that almost garish display of wealth. Unfortunately, his prediction about pilfered ornaments proved true, and when the distinction between simple Faberge art and Imperial possessions became a matter of economic significance, he was never able to prove provenance.

"My mother began her quest out of a rather snobbish desire for social recognition, never alluding to how her father came into tenancy of the items she wished to authenticate."

"Larceny must skip a generation," McAllister remarked dryly.

Instead of taking offense, Lancaster turned to the thermostat – combination, released the panel door, and beckoned us to follow him into the cellar. Once in the windowless gallery, he walked to the far side and turned back a plastic switch plate set into the paneled wall. Beneath the plate was a handle which released a four foot by eight foot panel in the wall revealing another room at the back of the gallery. Simultaneous to the opening of the door, soft lighting came on in the hidden room. The gallery of special interest that Lancaster had once told us he wished to own was a hidden reality. On twenty-six pillars, each bathed in its own beam of directional lighting, stood a corresponding number of Faberge Eggs. The gallery had been so carefully laid out that it rivaled that of any museum display I had ever seen. When Larkin saw the Spaskoie Egg on a pillar, she choked back a reflexive sob that penetrated the senses of everyone present. Lancaster lowered his head, McAllister placed a hand on Larkin's, and I remained quiet.

In a choked voice filled with shame, Lancaster continued. "When I first met Lazarik Kaliniskov, he was posing as a Jewish art investment dealer. Somehow he was perceptive enough to recognize a touch of larceny in my soul and it took very little convincing on his part to recruit me as his partner. I was helpful in introducing him to various collectors whom he later relieved of their treasures by substitution. I never even knew he was Russian until I found out that the pieces were being shipped to the Soviet Union through a port very near here. For every two pieces that went out, I was allowed to keep one. He was only in it for the money, of course, whereas I felt my motives ran far deeper."

Lancaster turned to McAllister and, in the misted lighting; I thought I saw a hint of tears in his eyes. "Is it true you uncovered thirty-eight previously undiscovered eggs is Savannah, Georgia USA?" he asked.

"It's true." McAllister said. "But what do you know about Savannah, other than it was originally a British colony?"

"My mother heard some tale about a mysterious Russian man who sailed to Savannah, where he fell in love with a woman named Florence Martus. Of course, there were many versions of what happened there, most of it myths spread over the seven seas by sailors who had visited Savannah. But for some unknown reason, my mother was convinced that there was more to the story than a romantic fairy-tale; she was convinced that the 'Russian gentleman' brought looted Faberge treasure with him and hid it there somewhere. I don't know all the details that my mother either knew or suspected, but, it appears that my dear old mother hadn't gone completely mad."

"So it appears." McAllister said. "Did your mother visit the old lady, Martus, in Savannah?"

"Yes." Lancaster began. He scratched his head and continued. "Let's see. . . Twice I think. But when she returned, I overheard her saying to one of her friends that 'that old lady', Martus said that she was 'sworn into secrecy'. Just the recount of that story infuriated my poor old mum. She could not understand such a concept."

McAllister smiled at Lancaster's account of his mother's experience with Florence Martus. The old woman was considered by all to be somewhat of an enigma. McAllister ran his eyes over Lancaster's collection until he spotted the Lily Egg on the other side of the room. After making a mental note of its location, he looked back at Lancaster.

"Only twenty-seven are completed works," he said. "I plan to use the unfinished pieces to build a display on how the eggs were fashioned. Sort of a step-by-step visual history of the art."

Lancaster nodded his understanding. "Together with the seven eggs you already owned, your collection must be one of the finest in the world." It was clear that Lancaster was envious. "I can't even tell you how much I admire your position. It is beyond one's understanding."

"It is, indeed, Sir George," McAllister began, "it is certainly beyond my understanding that anyone would sacrifice the lives of over eighteen people to even acquire all the lost treasures of the world."

I am sure Lancaster was far removed from the distasteful act of actually killing all those people, and the "Dirty-Work" involved in his association with Kaliniskov, and he was unaware that their collective nefarious schemes resulted in the loss of as many lives, but he was just as guilty as if he had executed everyone himself. Lancaster was genuinely stunned.

"And I can't tell you how much it pains me to have to rescind my invitation for you to visit my gallery," McAllister responded, watching for a reaction.

Lancaster merely bowed his head. "I understand," he said.

"It was you who stole Antonio Tumbas' egg from his cottage in Cartres," McAllister stared rather than asked.

Lancaster nodded again.

"And I'm willing to bet that you had something to do with Luigi Paretti's clumsy attempt to defraud me."

Lancaster thought for a couple of seconds and decided to be truthful. "When I found out that Luigi was strapped for cash and on the verge of bankruptcy, I tried to recruit him into our little circle," Lancaster confirmed. "Instead, he became very independent. He told me he was capable of fooling the Russians, you, and anybody else. I don't know what his ultimate plan was, but whatever he had planned for anyone died with him in the accident. Lazarak and I were greatly relieved. Paretti could have ruined years of work."

"You should have been a little smarter, Sir George." McAllister sounded like a schoolmaster lecturing a delinquent student. "I don't have half the education and breeding that you were practically born with but, twice in my lifetime, I've proved that a little hard work and a lot of imagination can make dreams become reality. You mistakenly believed in short cuts instead of a greater vision." Lancaster seemed not to have been affected by McAllister's admonishment.

"Have you had the gems you found appraised?" asked Lancaster. "How much did you realize from that discovery?"

"Almost four-hundred million," McAllister replied frankly.

My jaw dropped. I knew it was more of a haul than my original Estimate. But I had no idea by how much.

Lancaster shook his head sadly. "I never dreamed. . ." he said, Unable to finish his thought.

"You allowed your dream to turn into a nightmare, Sir George."

Lancaster squared his shoulders and lifted his head to look McAllister in the eye. "So where do we go from here?" he asked with more fortitude than I believe he felt he really possessed.

"I'm taking my eggs." McAllister answered tonelessly, "the Spaskoie and the Lily."

Lancaster nodded. "And where does that leave me?" he asked, pointedly looking at Mark.

"You have nothing to fear from me personally, Sir George."

McAllister answered, noting Lancaster's obvious discomfort at Mark's presence. "In another place and time, I might have even admired your ambition, but now I have a family to protect and a civilized society to whom I might answer.

"We can't ignore the fact that you are indirectly responsible for more than eighteen deaths. Some of those were totally innocent of any direct involvement in your schemes. Some people will spend the rest of their lives suffering as a result of your actions."

"I never meant for anyone to get hurt." His head was again bowed.

"I sincerely believe that." McAllister replied, "but now is the time for you to face the consequences, whatever they may be.

"The Russians believe that Grange and I combined and conspired to murder four of their countrymen; three KGB agents and an In-tourist Guide. This morning I faxed a message to the Russian Consulate in Caracas, Venezuela detailing to Ambassador Bulganon your complicity with the late Major Kaliniskov. The reason I informed the Russians of these facts is to show them that the deaths of their citizens was a result of a counter-conspiracy that, if made public, would have embarrassed their government while at the same time prove that Grange and I not only acted in self-defense, but to their advantage."

McAllister's eyes met Lancaster's. "Sir George, I do not wish to spend the rest of my life looking over my shoulder and fearing Russian retaliation for a course of action not instituted by myself nor any of my friends.

"About three hours ago, a similar communication was delivered to Sergeant Abernathy of Scotland Yard implicating you in the deaths of Dorn Kublec and his wife and, for good measure; a copy was delivered to the Paris police naming you as an accomplice in the cold blooded murder of Sally Davis, Antonio Tumbas, and one of my security agents.

"The police of at least two countries will be here shortly, Sir George, so now I will take my property and leave."

"I could stop you, you know." Lancaster said it with little conviction.

"No, you couldn't," Mark spoke for the first time. The determination in his voice unmistakable.

"No," Lancaster reconsidered, "I don't suppose I could."

"You may not believe this, Sir George," McAllister said as he went to the pillar that held the Lily Egg, "but I wish you good luck, I think you're going to need it."

We left him standing at the door to his hidden gallery, a broken and dejected man. He said nothing as McAllister helped himself to the Lily Egg and Larkin picked up the Spaskoie Egg and we ascended the staircase to the ground level. Mark brought up the rear of our little procession, never taking his eyes off the despondent man who had raised tear filled eyes to once again, look at twenty-four of the remaining objects that had driven him down an irreversible path of deceit and despair.

We had just finished loading the eggs into protective cases and had just shut the trunk when two black sedans pulled into the drive. When they stopped next to us, Sergeant Abernathy and five uniformed officers got out of the vehicles. The sergeant walked up to McAllister.

"I thought I'd find you here," she said. "I only hope you haven't taken the law into your own hands."

McAllister shook his head sadly. "Just conducting a little unfinished business." He then half smiled. "I think you'll find Sir George in his basement gallery. I don't know how much cooperation he intends to give you, but I don't think he will be giving you much trouble."

"We received a call from the French authorities," Abernathy continued. "It seems that. . ."

Although muffled, the sound of the shot caused everyone to flinch. Mark, who had instinctively assumed a position between the house and the three of us, relaxed after it was quickly determined that none of us standing in the driveway was a target. Three of the uniforms sprinted to the door.

"Well, that makes nineteen," McAllister said barely audible.

Sergeant Abernathy turned a level gaze on McAllister.

"Is this your doing?"

* * * * *

"No," he said. "It was his idea. I guess when he realized just how many people were looking for him; he decided that this would be the best way to bring things to a close."

Sergeant Abernathy continued her gaze on McAllister, a silent gaze.

* * * * *

We were on the outskirts of London when McAllister spoke for the first time since leaving Sir George's estate in Exeter.

"Any more surprises?" he asked, knowing the answer but wanting to be reassured that it was over.

"Fresh out," I said, holding up empty palms.

"Larkin?" McAllister asked for the same reason.

She smiled and mimicked me, "Fresh out," also holding up empty palms.

McAllister and I both smiled at her innocent little performance.

"Well, I have just a couple of questions," McAllister pressed on at me. "You had some idea about him before you were able to prove anything. What tipped you?"

"Several things," I answered. "First, when Kaliniskov indicated he had a partner, I remembered that when Rastov was delivering his 'state of the situation' report to me, he failed to mention Sir George. He knew and mentioned every other stop we made on the way to St. Petersburg, including getting the door slammed in our faces at Theodore Faberge's house, but he never referred to our day long trip out to Exeter, Why? Because he probably wasn't told that fact by Kaliniskov because the major didn't want his subordinate to know he had a partner in an outside and conflicting enterprise.

Kaliniskov also said something about the British saying about good help being hard to find. That may not have anything to do with this, but it got me thinking in Sir George's kitchen having tea the first time we visited him, I was absently admiring his garden. Part of that garden was sunken window boxes filled with roses. The window boxes indicated a basement below the kitchen, but when we went down to the gallery, it not only didn't have windows, the room didn't extend far enough to reach under the kitchen. There had to be another, secret room, behind the front gallery.

"After that, while reading up on the Anastasia story, the same lady, Allison Lancaster, practically jumped off the page. It took only a three minute phone call to find out she was Sir George's mother and she was deceased. If she had owned Faberge Eggs, where were they? Sir George was an only child, so therefore, the proper choice to inherit. I don't know how many eggs the mother had, but it was obvious that Sir George didn't show any of them to us."

"What's going to happen now?" Larkin asked.

"Hopefully, the authorities will be able to sort out and return the authentic eggs to their rightful owners. The remaining ones will probably go to the British Museum. I guess the story is over." McAllister said.

"And the Russians?" She persisted.

"Embarrassed, but no longer vindictive," McAllister predicted. "They have a few bad apples in their already rotten barrel, but we saved them the trouble of an internal investigation. They will eventually start a similar program. I don't imagine that, in our lifetimes, we will ever know the true extent of their success with this one."

"What about you, Grange?" Larkin asked. "What will you do now?"

"I'm going home," I answered. "I've had a great and most exciting adventure, but. . ."

"Liar." McAllister cut me off. "I bet you had a wonderful time, huh?" Larkin and McAllister both smiled.

"Yeah, well." I agreed.

As if McAllister was reading my mind, he said, "Besides, Larkin, Grange has a grave to visit."

We were overcome by silence until we reached Heathrow Airport. Larkin and I were conspiring to keep a little secret from McAllister, at least until Larkin deemed the time appropriate to share the revelation with her husband. I guess she figured that it was time, because she retrieved a small package from her skirt pocket which was wrapped in ancient waxed paper, and began unfolding the contents. She again read the quill on parchment note then handed it over to me. She had previously shared the note with me while McAllister was pre-occupied with Sergeant Abernathy, so I re-read the scrawled message then nodded. Larkin motioned with her head toward McAllister and I passed it to him without comment.

McAllister looked at me with questioning eyes before he began casually inspecting the note in a cursory manner before giving Larkin and me a stern, suspicious look, then began reading and savoring the few words which comprised a single sentence.

Smugness, bewilderment and awe merged together to form an expression on McAllister's face transcending all comprehension; an expression I had never seen there before. As he read the parchment for the fourth or fifth time, his expression transformed into a smile bright enough to pale Las Vegas; as if he had just invented banana pudding.

"I was right, Grange," was all he said. . .

* * * * *

The note was somehow inadvertently scooped up by Larkin as she retrieved Antonio's Spaskoie Egg from Sir George's gallery. It was a simple quote written by Benjamin Franklin in 1735.

* * *

"Three may keep a secret,
If two of them are dead."

December 17, 1917.
Florence Martus
THE END?

* * *

EPILOGUE

McAllister sent me two eggs. One was religious in nature and could have been depicting the Sermon on the Mount with the central piece being a hill with hundreds of almost microscopic figures on it, all carved from a single chunk of solid gold. It was, by far, the heaviest piece of its kind I have ever held. The second was a small silver palace surrounded by scaled down acres of an estate complete with rolling hills of emerald grass, a silver brook, and tiny ruby horses grazing in the pasture. I'm sure it was some nobleman's country home, but I couldn't identify to whom it might have belonged. Number three was a yacht, most likely the Standart. It sailed on a sea of opal and when placed in natural sunlight, it looked as though the ocean were actually moving beneath the keel. I had a room, a little larger than a walk-in closet, added to the cabin where I could display the pieces, but very few of my friends knew much about Eastern European art, so it was primarily a personal study for my own enjoyment, one I regularly used when I wanted to be alone.

Along with the eggs came a cashier's check. The amount was staggering. An enclosed note said it represented a twenty-five percent share of the treasure. I had no idea how McAllister had arrived at such a figure or the percentage, nor did I care. It was far more than I expected. Since Payson is a rather small town and everyone would have known about the check by the end of the business day anyway, I boldly walked into the mobile-home sized branch of my bank, signed the check with a flourish, and asked for the full amount in tens and twenties. The astonished teller counted the number of zeros four times with fingers on both of her hands before she called the manager, a converted city-type who shook visibly when he came over to ask me if I knew what I was asking. After five minutes of allowing some of his self-important stuffing to fall out, I let him off the hook and told him to deposit the full amount to my account.

I guess it's pretty obvious that I wrote the book. It took me almost a year, a period of time that would have been greatly reduced had I not spent two hours at the cemetery three time a week. Every year on Sally's birthday, the Inn-In-The-Pines has an open, no charge, bar in her honor. But before you jump in your car and head for Payson next November sixteenth, let me advise you that it is a personal observance, almost reverently attended by her friends, and strangers are not encouraged to interfere.

Just last week, McAllister wrote me a letter, the first in almost three months. I read it in the easy chair next to my fireplace. . .

* * * * *

It began. . .

Dear Grange:

I'm finally getting the hang of this computer thing you sent me and the more I learn, the more I like. I especially enjoy the quality of letter I can turn out with this 'Word Perfect' software. Now, I never make a mistake. (That's a joke, Grange. Get it?)

Mark finally married that nurse from St Joe's who was his therapist, and just in time too. (Not what you're thinking). At long last I have managed to get Petri Sarzanov out of Russia and Mark and his new wife (Faith) formed an instant bond with the boy. They now live downtown Savannah in a beautifully restored townhouse which was built back in the 1700' s, and Petri is learning English at a remarkable rate and insists on being called by his American name; Pete Schaeffer.

The Russian government formally requested permission to send a group of students and their instructors to visit my Faberge gallery. Since this is obviously the olive branch I demanded from Ambassador Bulganon, I could hardly have refused. They will be arriving here on Tuesday of next week.

Your book is quite a hit here in Savannah and every time we go to the mall, the twins rush to the book store and point out to anyone who will listen, that their "Uncle Grange" is the man who is pictured on the dust cover. The book comes in third around here only slightly behind Forest Gump and the Summer Olympics. I can only hope that it is doing well in other parts of the country.

As always, Larkin sends her love. I guess you know by now that her father has been elected to the Senate in Venezuela's largest landslide victory in the country's history. He is already considered to be the most popular influential Senator of all time. If he had been a United States citizen, he could have been president by the end of the decade.

We are looking forward to your visit next Christmas, but please, this time, try not to spoil the kids with extravagant gifts. That's my job! Take care of yourself, Grange, and be sure to raise a glass for me on November sixteenth.

See ya' in Paradise!

Bobby

It was a typical McAllister letter. Six paragraphs that told me nothing I didn't already know. The difference this time was the post script, written in his own distinctive hand.

It said;

"Hey! Wait until you hear what I've got planned next. . ."

From somewhere deep within my soul, a long sigh escaped as I leaned back and closed my eyes and the single sheet of paper slipped from my fingertips.

*This story was completed on June 16, 1997. This final draft completed and re-typed on August 14, 1998.

– Bobby Ferguson